About the

Kate grew up in a small seaside town, where she spent her formative years being most strongly influenced by the unlikely combo of George Orwell, Victoria Wood and *Smash Hits*. She studied Writing and Publishing at university before spending over a decade working in film, mostly in New York, where she also dabbled in stand-up comedy. In 2011 she was part of the second Curtis Brown Creative novel-writing course; a short story anthology written by that group, *The Book of Unwritten Rules*, was published in 2016.

Kate currently lives in Brighton, a seaside lass once again. *Purple People* is her first novel.

With grateful thanks to Jane Bedwell-Mortishire, who helped make this book happen.

Purple People

Kate Bulpitt

unbound

This edition first published in 2020

Unbound
6th Floor Mutual House, 70 Conduit Street, London W1S 2GF
www.unbound.com

ISBN (eBook): 978-1-912618-72-9
ISBN (Paperback): 978-1-912618-73-6

Cover design by Mecob

Printed and bound in Great Britain by Clays Ltd, Elcograf S.p.A.

For Mum

Grandma and Grandad

And Lucy

Super Patrons

Nick Anderson
Julia Armfield
Selma Attride
Corinne Bailey
Alison Barlow
James Bates
Candice Baugh
Daisy Beaumont
Bridget Bell
Roger Bell
The Bells
Lisa Berry
Elle Bianco
Stewart Birch
Cecilia Blanche
Anna Boden-Jones
Georgina Bottomley
The Box Family
Harry Brignull
Gareth Buchaillard-
Davies
Andy Budd
Chris Bulpitt
Daphne Bulpitt
Graham Bulpitt
James Burt
Shannon Butler
Tom Castle
Melissa Chusid
Rosie Clarke

Gina Corrigan
Alis Cox
Laura and Bill Cox
Mel Crawford
Melissa Cunningham
Michael Daniels
Matt Davies
Melissa Davies
Andy Dennis
Becky Deo
Renny Deremer
Tallman
Beth Dodson
Eric Drass
Sarah Drinkwater
Alan Driver
James Ellis
Arusha Elworthy
Josh Emerson
Nicky Evans
Rebecca Ewbank
Lorna Farbowski
Paul Ferguson
Chloe Finlayson
Michele Foulger
Fox
Genevieve French
Franny Gant
Sara Gates
Katherine Gleason

Katie Gordon
Richard Gordon
Clemancy Gordon-
Martin
Veronica Gretton
Jamie Groves
Philippa Hall
Aegir Hallmundur
Kate hamer
Jenifer Hanen
James Hannah
Joanne Hardy
Kaija Hawkes
Val Head
Sarah Henderson
Gillian Hill
Abigail Hitchcock
Michael Hocken
Beck Holland
Roger Horlock
Chris How
Theresa Howes
Andy Hume
Danielle Huntrods
Curtis James
Paul Jaunzems
Cath Jones
Gareth Jones
Stephen Jones
H.C. Joseph

Himesh Kar
Jeremy Keith
Marja Kivisaari
Julia Koenig
Sharon Laine
Nathalie Laurent-Marke
Christian Lawrence
Mary Ann le Lean
Pete Leysinger
Paul Robert Lloyd
Dan Lockton
Judith Long
Emily Macaulay
Julie Malamute
Dan Marsh
Mish Maudsley
Alice Meadows
Erinna Mettler
Seren Morland
Nicky Muir
Alex Mullen
Chris Neale
Christopher Noessel
Michelle O'Loughlin

Chatrina O'Mara
Marion O'Sullivan
Benjamin Parry
Simone Pereira Hind
Dan Peters
Ruth Powell
Christina Prado
Carri Price
Rowena Price
Kate Rambridge
Leila Razavi
Annie Reid
Colin Carlos Robinson
Bruce Ross
Richard Rutter
Ivan Salcedo
Ben Sauer
Gillian Scanlan
Marrije Schaake
Anastasia Semenova
Ste Sharp
Mary & Michael Shaw-Yates
Rachel Shorer

Ryan Shrime
Emily Simpson
Laurie Sitzia
Mark Skinner
Jessica Spengler
Susannah Stewart
Annabelle Thorpe
C J Thorpe-Tracey
Christopher Tremayne
S Troeth
Sonja van Amelsfort
Michael van Digglen
Ellen Vries
Brigette Wellbelove
Lucy White
James Whittaker
Keeley Wilson
Joshua Winning
Lorna Woolfson
Frank Yeomans
Galabina Yordanova
Robb Young
ΒΣVΛП ƧTΣP'HΣПƧ

viii

Chapter One

Eve considered herself unshockable, but even she was surprised
when people began turning purple. She was also green with
envy, though would never have said so. What a scoop! It was
the story of a lifetime.

The night before it started Eve had been drinking. Not
excessively, just three (four?) whiskies with Adio at the
optimistically monikered bar, Happy Ending (their topics of
discussion, on a sliding scale of frivolity: the recently
resurrected homeland debate about capital punishment; just
where in this city recently single Adio and almost perpetually
single Eve might locate eligible men; and their favourite news
story of the day, which involved a cat, a burglar and an egg
whisk). So having clocked up only a few hours' sleep when she
heard the news, Eve was a little slow to react. Her response
was also dulled by the years she'd spent working in the world
of news reporting, which had equipped her with the perhaps
obvious but certain knowledge that few things you read or saw
were quite as they seemed.

'Eve, it's me,' came a rattled-sounding voice on the other
side of the Atlantic: her friend Womble, calling from the
homeland.

'Blimey, Womble,' Eve mumbled. 'It's five am. Where's the fire? Are you okay?' She was upright now, hunched towards the phone, but considered lying down again.

Womble sounded unusually unnerved. 'Ah, yes, sorry to call so early, I did wait as long as I could. There's something I think you should see.'

'The mind boggles,' said Eve, who couldn't begin to imagine what the cause of such an early alert might be. 'It better be good.'

'It's odd, really quite odd. No one knows what to make of it.'

Eve winced, and wondered if moving very slowly might outwit an imminent hangover from waking. Climbing cautiously out of bed, she noticed the glass of water and pair of painkilling tablets she'd put out for herself the night before; even while somewhat drunk, her sensible side could still get the better of her.

Eve stepped carefully through her dim, dawn-lit apartment towards the computer and logged into the Portal, entering her CIV code.

'Right,' said Womble. 'Type in purple and news.'

'Purple news?' Eve yawned. 'You've not been mushroom picking again, have you?'

Womble muttered a weary no, and directed her to photos that were seemingly causing the Portal to pootle very slowly indeed. Eve yawned, appreciating the delay. As the screen came into focus, she peered towards it, squinting at the pictures of a trio of shaken-looking men with a purplish pallor. Eve tilted her head, blinking, her brain trying to refocus this unlikely tint.

These were certainly arresting images. The most striking snap caught a man grinning demonically towards the camera, the front of his sweatshirt held high in clenched fists baring a chest the cloudy mauve of stormy seascapes. The strange, battered-looking tinge of his skin was as desolate as the grey street and the flat, industrial buildings around him. Nearby, two other men ran out of shot, skittering away from this mouldering ogre. Yet while only their heads and hands were showing, this pair were also peculiarly plum, if less bold in revealing it (in subsequent pictures they'd put up their hoods and stuffed mottled hands in pockets). They appeared to be stepping off a kerb, at speed, and that they were caught hovering mid-step, mid-air, added to the surrealness of the snap, as though they were superheroes – or supervillains? – who had not only changed colour but acquired the ability to fly. Their eyes flashed with terror, which seemed particularly incongruous; these looked like the now-so-prevalent type of lads whom you'd cross the street to avoid – the bullies, the hunters – and yet here, at the side of a road, they looked like wide-eyed, petrified prey.

Eve considered the men: the contrast of shamed and unashamed, and tried to zoom out, to calculate the truth, the bigger picture. She scrolled to the accompanying story.

Photos of three mysterious, ghostly men – who appear to have turned PURPLE – were released to newspapers across the country last night. The lavender lads apparently turned up at their local A&E, where SHOCKED staff called in the coppers, fearing a terrifying chemical accident. Nurse Holly Finlay, who treated one of the mauve men, said: "We were really scared there had been a biological leak or attack, or that they have a terrifying new virus which we could all catch. We don't know how many more people are affected, but our doctors are running tests and keeping the men QUARANTINED just in case. We're really hoping that whatever it is, it's not contagious." She added, "The men say they don't feel unwell, but of course it's not normal to look like that. There must be something wrong with them." A government spokesman said that the prime minister will make a statement later today, but revealed, "We can GUARANTEE that the good citizens of Britain have honestly no cause for alarm."

Eve figured her groggy whisky head indicated that she was (for the most part) awake, and not in the fog of a bizarre dream.

'Well,' she said slowly. 'That's different. April fool?'

'It's June.'

'Yes, it is.' She gave a small impressed nod towards the screen. 'It's certainly clever. They do look real. But they can't be. The photos are bound to be fake – a pot plant could tell you that you can't believe anything you see.'

'Do you see the government statement?' asked Womble, the tone in his voice approaching squeaky, adolescent octaves as he erred towards hysteria.

'Allegedly. The papers might have made it up.'

'But it's in all of them. And on the telly.'

Eve felt a mild spike of unease, but aiming for optimism said, 'Maybe it's a joke, then. Hallowe'en make-up or something. Too much blackcurrant cordial. The police'll be charging them with time-wasting in a minute, those'll be the further details.'

'Oh, I think it's real,' Womble retorted. 'The loonies have finally taken over the asylum.'

'Come on, don't be so daft!' Eve rubbed her eyes and moved into the kitchen to make some coffee. 'Where's the sensible guy we know and love? For a start, it must be biologically impossible. Can't you just ask one of the boys in the school science department to dispel the myth for you?'

'That's just it. I asked Bob and he said yes, it could be possible.'

Eve considered this, sceptically. 'Bunsen Burner Bob?'

'Yes—'

'The one who was in a Def Leppard tribute band and is a conspiracy theorist?' The smell of the coffee was making her feel more awake. 'Look, I'm sure it'll just turn out to be some stuff and nonsense. People will be talking about something else by the end of the week.'

'It's not a hoax. It's on the cover of all the papers. People are really freaked out.'

'Yeah well, people love a reason to get hysterical. And you know how much the papers love to put the wind up everyone. The *Daily Dispatch* probably got the photos first. You should worry about Poles, priests – and now purple people!'

'What is wrong with you today?'

'What's wrong with *you* today, Mr Four Horsemen of the Apocalypse? This is what I do all day, every day. Read news. Shocking news, wacky news, and a lot of blatantly untrue news. This will be some kids mucking about trying to cause a stir and impress their mates.'

'If that's true then why has the prime minister called a press conference?'

Eve sighed. 'Probably to tell everyone not to get so worked up and do something less boring instead. Maybe the ice caps have stopped melting and the polar bears are having a disco to celebrate. It could be anything.'

'Evie, I think dreadful things are happening. I get a very weird feeling about it.'

Eve paused, then said, 'Of course you do. You're Danish.'

Eve sat with her coffee, feeling very confused. In the newsroom she'd seen some dramatic things, and had known the energy that came from a situation where there were unknown elements keeping everyone on edge, anxious as to what might happen next. For some that was what drew them to the job, and these days Eve wondered, with increasing frequency, if she'd have lasted in the unpredictable, often heart-stopping world of hard news (though was this you'd-never-have-hacked-it tack simply another way of convincing herself it was fine that she hadn't continued to try?). She liked life in her present job, spending her days immersed in reasons to be cheerful. Still, she figured she'd been in the game long enough to gauge what a story was about. A political cover-up, PR spin, tall tales fabricated for fame and fortune, insignificant incidents talked up to fill sleepy day pages... But this was something else. It was unbelievably, implausibly ridiculous – and yet, unsettlingly sincere. If it were really nothing, why would all the papers run the story? Why even start to scare people before the facts were known – did they just want to make use of such a startling, striking picture? The photo could have come from anywhere, been an easily doctored shot. The only thing that gave the story any credibility was the government statement. They clearly seemed adamant that there was no cause for concern, which begged the questions, one, how could they be so sure, and two, if they were, why not properly elaborate and put people at ease?

Was this international news, Eve wondered; should she head into work? She switched on CNN. There was more on the furore about healthcare, and an emerging scandal involving a senator – no word of Blighty. So far, so good, she thought. But just as she was about to turn away, her eye caught the ticker running along the bottom of the screen. Some pertinent words slid out of the electronic wings and into view: 'More cases of 'Purple People' reported in the UK. Perplexed Brits await prime minister's statement.' Eve felt as though she'd slipped down a rabbit hole into an improbable Hollywood blockbuster, and half expected to see the news cameras shift to a sweatily concerned action hero on his way to save the day. She reached into the cupboard for a packet of Alka-Seltzer, and then sent Adio a message: 'Going into the office early. Curious things afoot. Think today is going to be an interesting one.'

Despite past stints working closer to the front lines, Eve's present role was rather more sedate. For her there was no Watergate-esque investigation, no intrepid reporting from conflicts or disasters (despite this unlikely fascination with the news since she was a young lass, she'd never fancied herself as a courageous correspondent – and just as well: as her dad had often joked, if she were sent to a war zone, she'd report from inside a broom cupboard). Her particular bureau had peculiar leanings – not for them tales of politics or pandemics, ecology or the economy, war or the celebrated soldiers of celebrity. *Say Fantastique!* specialised in stories of the extraordinary within the ordinary. Their tales were the tail end of the news, the incredible and incredulous, the warm and fuzzy 'And finally...' The *Say Fantastique!* archive could rival the feel-good factor of ABBA's back catalogue, with a hefty helping of tears, tenderness, heroics and hilarity, and an abundance of animal stories which would make Noah proud. While the headlines could leave you dismayed and despondent in a glass half empty kind of way, *Say Fantastique!* was a glass half full – with something fizzy, and perhaps an umbrella or one of those little flamingos – kind of place.

Eve leant back while she waited for her stirring, whirring computer. She glanced at the pin board which hung a little lopsidedly in front of her. In pride of place were an 'I heart NY' sticker (and boy, did she ever) bought the week she arrived in the city, a doodle of Pam Fox-Jones, she and Adio's fictional first lady of current affairs, and one of Eve's earliest bizarre news clippings, about a man who'd attempted to strangle his wife after she'd sucked a mint too loudly. To Eve this had seemed a brilliantly absurd and yet concise character study: years of unspoken, repressed tension, brought to a head by a lowly Polo. It reminded her of how often the briefest, daftest reports contained the most potent truths about human behaviour. People could underestimate that, she thought.

Also pinned to the board was Eve's signed photo of newsreader Annie Morris. Growing up, Eve had dearly wanted to be a newsreader. She had always been fascinated by the news – the relentlessness, the speed and the scale of these incredible, far-reaching stories, from life-changing, world-changing events to the personal tales of survival and celebration. She loved (and feared) the unpredictability of it, and the way these occurrences, whether explosive or emotional, united people. In a school careers essay she had earnestly stated: 'Being able to tell the news is one of the most important things there is. The news is really a never-ending story that everyone is part of, it is history happening around us.'

And if the news were a party then, in the young Eve's mind, the newsreader played hostess. Her childhood idols had been the elegant news ladies she saw on television. She had been transfixed by the glamour of their smoulderingly serious delivery, paired with subtle, smoky eyeshadow and drapey silk blouses. Clearly they were not only clever and successful, but bore all the attributes most fitting for such an authoritative role, appearing knowledgeable but unintimidating, commanding but reassuring, and able to inform the nation of calamities and catastrophes in a soothing, unalarming manner. They were the newsreading equivalent of mums putting plasters on scraped knees and giving you an ice lolly, yet wielded an added school-marmish sort of power. When things went askew – miserably soaring crime rates, riots, the fleeting, disastrous privatisation of the police force – they had presented everything in such a way that you could still doze soundly through the night.

Eve had wanted to be a newsreader more than she had wanted to be Wonder Woman, or her favourite telly detective, a no-nonsense broad who always solved the crime, while wearing fetching, bejewelled jumpers and managing to chase wrong 'uns even in her high-heeled boots. This desire brought with it a secret guilt, junior Eve having decided, should the moral dilemma arise, that she would choose becoming a successful news lass above things for the greater good; namely, tranquillity in her parents' marriage, or her brother's reformation to a less trouble-seeking soul. At a kindly neighbour's suggestion, she had approached her favourite national newsreader for advice, to no avail – though this later transpired to be due to her brother Simon's intervention, for he had got hold of the envelope (Eve's stamp had been licked with a wish and crossed fingers) and substituted the contents with the less impassioned lines of their mum's shopping list. Simon eventually confessed, thinking his trick hilarious; Eve had vowed never to forgive him. In recompense, for her twelfth birthday, their mum had arranged a visit to the local TV station, where Eve watched the news being recorded, and afterwards the presenters each gave her signed picture postcards of themselves (she had been struck by the fact that then regional news gal Annie had also kindly added 'Happy birthday, Eve!' across hers). Though even her memory of this was slightly tainted by a mortifying moment in the canteen. Whilst their mum was distracted by the sight of Annie and co – equally impressed by the abundance of local celebrities and the canteen's new 'frothy-coffee' maker – Simon had inked graffiti on their table (predictably embarrassing end-of-the-pier anatomies), only to be swiftly spotted and reprimanded by a passing weatherman. Eve had been utterly horrified, and dearly hoped Annie and the others hadn't noticed the incident.

Eve stared at the photo, at Annie's stripy shirt and shoulder-padded jacket, her easy, confident smile. Annie was a legend (*and* one of the first African–Caribbean women to deliver the news on British television), and while Eve might never have ascended to such great heights, she wondered, again, if she'd been too quick to steer away from that course. And why? Was it just, as she had told herself, giving the increasingly gloomy, fear-peddling realm of real news the slip for a more footloose, frivolous adventure? Or had seizing this Stateside chance simply masked her fear of failure?

It was Adio who had brought her to New York (she would later merrily refer to him as not only her boss and partner in crime, but also her fairy godmother), saving her from the assisting pool at a news corporation, where she fetched coffee, booked lunches, and typed emails signed with the disclaiming flourish 'Dictated but not read', all the while aspiring to a life that was more Kate Adie than Girl Friday. She'd been planning a change – this spell at the corporation had seemed like a chance to make some excellent contacts, but she hankered after more colour, and stimulation. She'd considered a return to the slightly terrifying world of the tabloids, where the pace was electrifying, and scandal crackled in the air, but knew the world where woeful celebrities and footballers' wives 'n' lives captured the front pages wasn't really the place for her. A more vigorous, less salacious publication seemed like a plan, though she had also pondered on a stint volunteering at an organisation abroad… And at that point Adio stepped in.

Having first bagged a cheap weekend in NYC, Adio had subsequently snagged a Big Apple boyfriend, and decided to make a transatlantic leap of faith, and give the city, and the boy, a more permanent shot. On the plane back from his initial getaway, while brimming with the smitten kitten-ness of holiday romance, Adio decided to put into action the business venture which he'd been percolating. *Say Fantastique!,* he figured, would go down a storm in New York, a city that was chock-full of the crazy and incredible, and in America, the land of perky positivity – what could be more perfect? (He was right, of course, and couldn't have known quite how timely a tonic it would be).

That was – Eve could barely believe it – more than a decade ago. The agency had not only become incredibly successful, supplying stories to newspapers and TV shows around the world, but a surprisingly popular cult hit too, with a rapidly expanding number of readers, including quite a number of notable folk. And Eve loved life as a Gotham gal. Everything about the city – the speed, the heat, the people, the possibilities – was intoxicating. Here, away from the life she had known, the expectations she had set for herself and those that had been set for her (never spoken, but implied: to seek success in the same way her brother sought failure), she could do as she pleased, be who she wanted. It provided her with a bubble, an escape from the disheartening state of the nation, politics, her past, with its hatful of mistakes and laments, and her family – her philandering father's disinterest, her mother's regret and her brother's lack of it. Here she could tune out, or tune in, what she liked. Just being here felt like a grand achievement.

'A penny for 'em,' said Adio, leaning over Eve's shoulder and hitting a button on her computer which brought their Portal page into view. He'd been quick off the mark that morning. As the newly updated page appeared before her, there was Pam Fox-Jones, with beehive askew and a puzzled expression on her lovingly inked, animated face. 'Purple WHAT?' quizzed her first speech bubble, while another declared, 'I need a sherry – make it a large one.'

'Oh, nothing... random nonsense.' When it came to her

family, Eve was sure she'd already bored Adio witless over the years, and when it came to querying her career, she didn't want to seem ungrateful. Besides, there were more pressing matters at hand.

'Wow, Pam looks great. I suppose *if* this did turn out to be something big – ' she pictured rolling dice and hoped the purpleness wouldn't transpire to be a freakish pandemic – 'her spin on it could be an opportunity for us at home.' More readers, she thought, an increase in advertising. A bridge between the silly and serious.

'Just what I was thinking,' said Adio, sitting down at his desk. 'Make a proper splash, get an empire-straddling, more tangible presence, and then if we did want to go back…'

'Speak for yourself!' Eve spluttered as a gulp of coffee went down the wrong way. She coughed. 'I'm in no rush.'

'Me neither, but…' Adio slid his chair towards the window, opening it and leaning out with a cigarette in hand, defying the building's rules, again. He raised a match and an eyebrow before continuing, 'Then if we did want to go back, we'd have already spread our tentacles, as it were.'

'Your tentacles already get us into enough trouble.'

Adio laughed and put his feet up on the windowsill, an elegant rebel. He would make a great model for an arty kids' action figure, Eve mused, accessorised with a highball tumbler and a paintbrush. He was so striking to look at, she always thought – graceful, but with an energy that fizzed through his body, out to the kinks of his dark hair, all angles and artful waves, like one of his drawings, and with cheekbones that rarely kept him out of mischief ('The bone structure of a Pharoah,' his Aunt Rashida would tease whenever she came to visit, a reference to their Egyptian heritage. 'You can imagine those chiselled in granite, can't you?').

Smoke wafted back into the room through the open window.

'I thought you were giving up.'

'I have given up. It's a notably strange day and this – *this* –' he held the cigarette aloft with a dramatic flourish – 'is not a cigarette. Oh no, this is a simple, antique de-stressing device, fulfilling its purpose before being caught in nicotine's enforced walk of shame towards oblivion. And that's another reason to spend time at home: you can smoke there. *If* you are a smoker, of course. Which actually I'm not.'

Adio leaned closer to the window and exhaled, the smoke moving sluggishly once caught in the balmy fug of the city's stifling summer air.

Smoking made Eve uneasy. Not just because she worried about Adio's health, or his setting off the building alarms and getting them into trouble for breach of their office lease. Smoking reminded Eve of home. Of her dad, mostly. And of the smell that still clung to you as you left pubs or clubs – lingering long past closing time, stubbornly claiming its frowsty place, and wheezing defiantly in the face of those who'd campaigned against its return to public places. A return which, with the recent rise in cigarette advertising, now seemed increasingly (and yes, surprisingly) permanent. Of course it was archaic that Blighty had regressed to being so fag-friendly. This was another side effect of the Repeal: the more you took away, the more folk appeared willing to give. The first infraction was the hardest, but then…

Adio was unusually still for a few minutes, then said, 'It's utterly illogical, isn't it, people turning purple. More illogical than usual. There are freaky, funny, accidental things which can occasionally seem dreadful at first glance and, maybe I'm wrong, but I suspect this won't be one of those.' He considered the ash accumulating at the end of his cigarette. 'It's something when the real news puts on its whirligig platform boots and comes over more bizarre than the bizarre news.'

Eve ignored her initial impulse, which was as much for her own benefit as anyone else's, to respond with chirpy optimism.

'Did you get any clues out of anyone at home?'

'Only that a couple of guys were attempting to uncover what some big government press conference was about and in the process of some very broad research, got those photos. No one knows more than that. Entirely random and unrelated to Number Ten? We don't know.'

Eve glanced up at the Polo clipping. A mint-related murder seemed quite mundane in comparison to whatever purple peculiarity might be afoot.

'Well, Womble's beside himself, and you've gone all sombre... I hope it is just some weird and one-off home-brewed fluke or something.' As she said this, Eve was wondering if she entirely believed it herself, already imagining the headlines.

'Whatever it is, it's an excuse for more whisky.' Adio winked at her, then flicked ash towards the heavy black ashtray he'd sweet-talked the barman at a fancy hotel into letting him take. 'What time do we need to tune into the press conference?'

'Eight o'clock.' Eve glanced at her watch. She was already tingling with prickly anticipation, desperate to find out exactly what was going on.

Chapter Two

The prime minister's speech had been extraordinary. The truth was stranger than any science fiction, seeming possibly insane and probably (surely?) illegal.

What was supposed to be a lunchtime press conference started late, leaving bowls of soup cooling and salad leaves wilting as the world waited with bated breath. News reporters chattered through the passing minutes, gamely and inanely attempting to guess what the big reveal might be, while workers gathered around TV sets holding unopened packets of supermarket sandwiches, too anxious to begin to eat, and mothers spoon-fed their little 'uns whilst wondering what kind of madness they'd borne them into. Television shots showed the cloudy, blustery weather in Blighty, which added to the tension, implying there was a definite storm brewing.

The Big Apple was still waking, but by now Eve and Adio had already spent a couple of hours monitoring the curiously coloured events in the homeland. Eve kept the photo of the purple men open in one corner of her computer screen, repeatedly glancing towards it, as though it might change when she wasn't looking. What did they know, she wondered; what must they be thinking?

Eve's friend Saffron had come by, bearing juice and vodka.

'Hello, trouble,' Adio greeted her, ushering Saffron in through the office door. As a hip-swinging burlesque dancer and drink-slinging bartender, this was quite early for her to be up, post-shift, and she was still wearing traces of last night's make-up. Saffron was feisty and perceptive, and had arrived in New York fifteen years ago, escaping the not-so-bright lights of a small city out West, intent on acquiring tattoos and a psychology degree. She had worked in a bar to pay for her studies, and two thirds of the way through her course realised she enjoyed studying the human condition far more via a shot measure than a text book, and ditched her academic career.

'Morning all.' Saffron saluted with one hand while clutching the clinking bag of drink in the other. She hugged Eve, and then called across to Joe, *Say Fantastique!*'s new third musketeer. 'Hello, Boy Wonder!' she said.

Joe muttered a shy 'hi', and continued zipping through clips posted to the Portal's video pages.

'This is crazy,' Saffron said. She set the refreshments on a table, declaring them to be emergency supplies, just in case. 'So, what do we know – any news on the news?'

'Nope,' said Eve, 'it remains a cliffhanger.'

'It's like a truly fabulous B movie,' Saffron said dryly. 'Triffids, body snatchers, purple people. Incredible. I can already feel a musical coming on.'

'Want to hear the best guesses?' Joe offered.

The girls nodded.

'Leak at nuclear plant,' said Joe, eyes focused on his computer screen. 'Radioactive waste, unidentified tropical virus, poisonous wild berries, alcohol poisoning, adverse reaction to medication, psychedelic drugs...'

Adio groaned, before adding to the list. 'Terrorist contamination of water supplies, terrorist contamination of meat supplies, terrorist contamination of beer supplies... and my favourite: alien invasion.'

'That would be amazing,' said Saffron. 'God, I'll be jealous if you guys get aliens before we do.'

'This is so loopy,' said Eve, glancing at the bottle of vodka and wondering about hair of the dog, 'If it does turn out to be aliens I almost won't be surprised.'

On television, the slick new prime minister, Theo Fletcher, emerged from behind the especially ominous-looking black door at 10 Downing Street. Appearing no less suave and assured than usual, he strode purposefully to the microphone, glancing calmly around in acknowledgement of the cameras, of which there were a substantially higher number than for the usual budget-cut and legislation announcements. As cameras flashed excitably around him, the prime minister moved forward, unblinking, smoothing down his sober, claret-coloured tie. Eve had noticed that you could gauge the severity of any impending announcement from the shade of his neckwear, from perky poppy to more worrisome wine.

'Today,' he began, 'there has been much speculation over the publication of some rather unusual photographs. There has also been considerable alarm, but I want to put your minds at rest. These pictures are not a hoax. Nor do they illustrate the results of any terrorist activity, chemical accident or unintentional contamination.'

At his use of the word unintentional, Eve's stomach lurched.

The prime minister paused. 'I had intended to prepare everyone for this obviously unexpected turn of events, and I apologise for the distress that may have been caused in learning about them in this upsetting, unorthodox way.' A flicker of annoyance crossed his face. 'I should add, too, that under the Anti-Incitative Distribution of Information Act, we will be taking action against those behind this irresponsible, and inflammatory, unveiling.

'The truth is, for many years we have seen a steep decline in decent behaviour and respect, and an increase in rudeness, harassment, and mindless, thoughtless violence. It has become so common and so widespread as to be often considered unremarkable. This is wholly unacceptable.' He looked around him. 'There are those who believe that they can ignore the rules that all good, honest people abide by; that there will be no consequences to their actions. Yobs who have been getting away with creating fear and anarchy. These people show utter disregard for others, and seek to hurt, to damage and to destroy. They destroy communities, and in too many cases, leave broken hearts and shattered lives. These people,' he stared directly into one camera, locked eyes with the world, 'are bruises on society.'

He again paused, then shook his head defiantly. 'Well, no more. When we asked for your faith in us, for your votes, we promised you that there would be an end to this behaviour. We warned those who sought disharmony and violence that there would be harsh penalties to pay. Perhaps too many years of ineffective solutions to an escalating problem belittled our stance, implied it to be an idle threat. It was not. As drastic as it may have seemed, the Repeal's curbing of much-abused technologies, including the Portal, and PortAble devices, has certainly made a difference to anti-social behaviour, to the way we all engage with one another – we've seen that. But it hasn't changed enough. We have considered many options. Harsher sentences. The discipline of national service. The deterrent of capital punishment. Even the extreme methods of chastisement employed in other cultures, which we rightly dismiss as too cruel. And then we created a more innovative solution. One that, finding you engaged in a criminal or anti-social act, quite literally makes its mark on you. That brands you as visibly bruised as our communities have been by your actions, and illustrates for all to see that you show no respect, that you seek to damage our society.'

Eve stared at the screen. Theo Fletcher seemed enraptured by his own words, becoming almost evangelical. He continued. 'This system will be one that provides constant observation and near-immediate results, and will exist alongside the traditional criminal justice system. Physically, this branding causes no ill effects, and will be reversible – but only given irrefutably improved behaviour.'

At this point the flashbulb frenzy seemed to increase, and the prime minister's speech was interrupted by an unsynchronised chorus of gasps, squeaks and a yelp. Unaffected, he continued: 'Whereas until now decent, law-abiding citizens have felt unsafe on the streets of this country's towns and cities, now it is those who seek malice who shall know no safety. We will find them and shame them, please be certain of that. As this young man can attest.'

The cameras widened to reveal the cause of the increasing flashes: beside Theo Fletcher stood a lad who was an eerie greyish-lavender hue. The colour change was mild but distinct, and made all the more pronounced beside the healthy freshness of the prime minister's complexion, and by the lad's own unfortunate attire: white sports shorts and a vest top in a garish shade of neon green. From these garments poked purple limbs – such strange, unnatural flesh – which looked mind-bogglingly bizarre.

To a stunned crowd, Theo Fletcher announced that this was Lee. He was, apparently, devilishly anti-social and unfit to be prowling the streets.

There was a wolf whistle from the one of the reporters.

In response, with a flash of rat-in-a-corner fury, Lee spat, 'I'll have you! What d'you think you're looking at?'

'You,' an anonymous voice retorted. 'You look ridiculous!'

In the corner of the screen, Eve noticed a woman reach into her pocket, presumably seeking that phantom limb, the PortAble phone, with which to snatch a snapshot. The hand appeared again, empty, her face registering neither recollection nor disappointment. Despite the time that had passed, people still forgot.

'Now, now, everyone.' The prime minister raised a hand, requesting calm. He turned to Lee. 'You would admit to being an ardent trouble-maker, would you not?'

Lee nodded nervously; he looked desperate to appear tough, but was clearly shaken and stirred and entirely unprepared for the situation in which he found himself. It also seemed that what might have once been cheeks reddening in embarrassment, or anger, today gave the illusion of Lee becoming an even deeper shade of damson, right before their eyes.

'You upset your family and neighbours, as well as complete strangers, in the town in which you live, with aggressive, often threatening behaviour, and after a violent outburst a few days ago in which you attacked an innocent man, *almost killing him*–' Theo looked solemnly towards the cameras before turning back to Lee – 'you subsequently found yourself... like this?'

'Yeah.'

'Just like that, overnight?'

Lee nodded again, his complexion becoming even paler, the purple a little more pronounced, as the blood drained from his face.

'And how did that make you feel?'

Lee was obviously loath to say it, and appeared to be

attempting to muster some bravado when the prime minister prompted him.

'Lee?'

'Scared. I didn't know what was happening to me. I thought I was dying.'

'Do you think you deserve this?'

Lee swayed uncertainly for a moment.

The prime minister took a piece of paper from his pocket and held it out for Lee to see. 'Well, do you?'

Lee looked down at his mauve hands before responding with a reluctantly mumbled, 'S'pose.'

The prime minister showed the piece of paper to the cameras – a photo showing a beaten, swollen, bandaged man's face. 'And did this man, who is still in intensive care – did he deserve this?'

Lee, now shaking, looked at his shoes. 'No,' he said.

'Look at him,' a journalist shouted. 'He's shaking! Would your victims shake, Lee? Would they beg you to leave them alone?'

Lee glanced at the prime minister, waiting to be rescued.

'Go ahead,' said Theo. 'You can answer.'

'Yeah,' Lee murmured.

'Speak up!' said the reporter.

'Yes,' Lee hissed.

'But did you stop?'

Lee shook his head, then, already anticipating the shout of 'louder', snapped, 'No.'

'If you hadn't attacked him,' said the prime minister, sadly, 'you wouldn't be here now. Purple.'

'Did it hurt, Lee, when you got, er...' The reporter searched for an appropriate word for the transformation. 'Purpled?'

'No. I don't know,' said Lee, before he was silenced by a glance from Theo Fletcher.

The prime minister turned back to the cameras. 'There will, of course, be some who say this infringes upon civil rights. To them I say: what about the rights of the good citizens of this country?' He again held up the photo. 'What about this man's rights? What of those who live their lives quietly, kindly, respectfully, responsibly? Who share care and concern for others and community spirit? Those who are valued members of society and seek only to create honourable lives for themselves, their families and neighbours, to love them and look after them? When those people are hurt, or worse, without provocation, for protecting their loved ones or their property, for helping others in need, trying to defuse a situation, or simply for standing up for public decency – where are those people's civil rights? To the troublemakers I say, if you attack the civil rights of those people, the honourable people, then you forfeit your own.

'I can assure you that the good citizens of this country have nothing to fear from this. I want you to be able to walk the streets without worry, and to feel safe in your own homes. I want you to live without harassment and violence around you in your daily lives. For those who challenge this safety' – a final pause – 'there will be nowhere to hide.'

The prime minister gazed intently at the crowd of journalists before him, waiting for their questions to begin.

'Prime minister, when were you going to inform people about this?'

'We were due to make a detailed announcement shortly, to present the facts before there was a chance for anyone to become unduly distressed. It was never our intention for the initiative to be presented in this way. As I've said, those responsible for the unauthorised disclosure will be held to account.'

'How many purple people are there?'

'There are ninety-seven affected individuals, to be exact. We've been monitoring them closely in a secure facility, though some will begin to be rehabilitated. Of course, now the scheme has become public, it will be used as an official part of our crime control methods, and numbers will increase.'

'How long have you been planning this scheme?'

'Obviously there have been many considerations, not to mention extensive scientific testing, so this has been something that we've spent a significant amount of time preparing.'

'Doesn't this have to be approved by law?'

'Given Clause Twelve of the 1989 Civil Disobedience Act, we are well within the law to instigate these emergency measures. However, we have drafted a "Purple Paper" which will be discussed in due course. After seeing the effectiveness of these measures, we have the utmost confidence it will be passed as a new more specific Act.'

'So the rest of your party supports the scheme?'

Theo Fletcher gave a satisfied smile. 'Absolutely, one hundred per cent. I think this initiative shows that we're not afraid to take drastic and decisive action for the benefit of this country. And I think this will begin to make people consider their actions more carefully.'

'Prime minister, isn't this convicting people before they've been given a fair trial?'

'Not at all. This alteration is put into effect while perpetrators are committing a criminal or anti-social act.'

'Prime minister, how exactly does this change occur? And when – during arrest?'

The prime minister smiled ever so slightly. 'No, there is no arrest. The act is witnessed and acted upon—'

'By who, the police?'

'By officers who monitor situations and act accordingly.'

'But you still haven't said how—'

23

'Or when!'

'And what offences will be punishable this way? Will you be releasing guidelines?'

The prime minister smoothed his tie again. 'At this time, I'm afraid for security purposes we have to keep operational aspects of the initiative guarded. We will be distributing essential information through leaflets to households, which will include a helpline number for those who have questions.'

'So what are people expected to do if they find they've turned purple?' The reporter tittered slightly at the ridiculousness of his own question.

'They should report to their nearest police station to be registered.'

'They have to turn themselves in?!' the questioner laughed incredulously. 'Does this system rely on that?'

'Not quite. They're hardly going to move about unnoticed, now are they?'

'They could just stay at home!'

The prime minister nodded. 'Indeed they could. Which would be a great help to us all, given that they're not safe on the streets.'

There was a brief moment of dumbfounded silence before the questions continued.

'If they turn themselves in, what happens next – they go to prison?'

'Their case will be considered, and they'll appear before a judge, who will determine the minimum timescale before they are "re-turned", and whether they also require a custodial sentence.'

'So they'll probably just remain at liberty causing trouble.' This reporter turned to the others around him, and with an indignant laugh, added, 'But we'll know to give them a wide berth.'

'Not at all. There will be a strict curfew between seven pm and seven am. And no more than one "turned" individual will be allowed in any public place at any one time.'

'They can't go round in groups then?'

'Certainly not,' said the prime minister.

'Whose idea was this, and do you expect it to be more successful than the failed privatisation of the police force?'

'The privatisation came into effect long before this government, as you know.' Theo Fletcher smiled. 'I expect this to be hugely successful. I think the people of this country can feel assured that this scheme is going to be a remarkable force for good.'

'But whose idea—'

'When will they—'

'And just how—'

The prime minister raised a hand to quieten the crowd. 'That will be all for now. Thank you for your time.'

Eve stared at the screen for a minute before turning to the others. 'Is this really happening?' she asked, gobsmacked.

'Wow,' Saffron whistled slowly.

Joe looked up from his computer. 'All the news pages are crashing.'

For once, Adio appeared speechless. 'Unbelievable,' he uttered, finally.

On the television even the newsreader, usually a typically unflappable beacon of calm, looked baffled.

'You can't imagine they're actually allowed to do this,' said Eve. 'Surely there are treaties and UN regulations against it.'

'He doesn't sound so interested in human or civil rights though, does he?' Adio was shaking his head in disbelief.

'But didn't he say it wasn't actually harmful?' Saffron chipped in. 'Maybe that's some sort of get-out clause. If you're not curbing someone's freedom and you're not causing them any harm. Hell, I'm not agreeing with it, but they had to have checked out the legal stuff. Otherwise they'd all be thrown in jail themselves. Or sent to the Tower, or whatever you kids do.'

'But you can't go around *dyeing* people,' Eve grimaced. 'They're not Easter eggs.' She picked distractedly at a biscuit. 'I'm amazed that it's actually physically possible. How on earth did they come up with it?' Perplexed, she added, 'Though actually, I do remember our science teacher at school telling us about a man who drank so much carrot juice that he turned orange. All those years of science lessons, and I think that's the only thing I remember.'

'It's crazy, for sure,' said Joe. 'But are they gonna make this look purple, too?' Forehead wrinkled in curiosity, he held up a brown arm. 'Seems unlikely. Which sounds like a rare plan for street crime to me.'

'You're right,' said Eve.

'Well, we need this,' Saffron said, as she unscrewed the lid on the vodka. She cocked her head to one side, and after a moment added, 'I know I really shouldn't say this – it's a very serious situation and all – but there's something kinda "Whoa, tiger!" about him, you know? I preferred him with the moustache, but still. I like to imagine underneath that sharp, debonair thing he's all silk sheets and fur rugs, that he'll tussle with the bad guy before pouring you a martini.'

Eve laughed. 'You,' she said, 'are what my gran would have called a caution.'

'There's something I wouldn't have guessed,' said Adio. 'Our own cocktail shaker-shaking, Judy Garland-belting Saffron hankering after a well-oiled spy type—'

'Like the Milk Tray guy,' said Eve, thinking of the fuzzy old chocolate advertisement that had recently resurfaced, featuring

26

a suave fellow who'll do whatever it takes to deliver the sweets his lady loves, and picturing Theo Fletcher skiing down a mountain (since the Repeal, nostalgic aspirations being used to flog confectionery, in addition to most other things you could care to mention, had become quite the phenomenon; looking backwards apparently made for brisk business).

'Hell, yes,' said Saffron, 'I love that smooth, posh thing.'

'You know, he's actually not that posh,' said Adio. 'He's from Wigan.'

Adio wandered over to the window and pulled out a cigarette packet. He appeared deep in thought.

'He's not giving much away about how they're doing it, is he?' said Eve. 'Kept dodging the questions…'

'I noticed that,' said Adio. 'It does seem weird – or, weirder than it is already. But then, I suppose he's hardly going to let all the cats out of the bag, especially when he's been caught on the hop.'

'Also,' said Eve, 'it was odd how Lee said he didn't know if it had hurt, when he was changed. How could he not know?'

'And Fletcher pretty quickly pulled the plug on him saying anything about that…'

Eve looked at her notes. 'Theo said, "You found yourself like this, overnight."'

They exchanged a glance. Adio didn't say anything, but stood by the window, slowly taking it all in. Eve turned to her computer screen, again looking at the shot of the purple men. What on earth happened to you, she wondered. What did you do, and how did you become like this? Beneath the news story, comments were being posted so quickly that they disappeared from view before they could be read, hidden beneath an ongoing avalanche of amazement and vitriol. Eve's eye caught some recurring words: serves them right… bastards…

madness. This sent her head spinning more dizzily than any hangover.

During the press conference they'd switched the office phones to answer-machine, and now Eve began to retrieve the messages. There was one from a journalist in the UK for whom she did some occasional freelance correspondent work, asking if Eve would gather some local opinions on the Purple developments, a similar request from a friend in India, and then a message from Eve's mum, sounding upset: 'Love, it's me. Can you call me as soon as you get this. It's your dad, he's – well, just call me.'

Her mother reeled off an unfamiliar number, which Eve dialled.

'ICU.'

Eve was confused. Had she called the wrong number?

'Hello?' said a woman who definitely wasn't Eve's mother, slightly brusquely.

'Oh, sorry – I was looking for my mum—'

The woman's voice softened. 'What's her name?'

'Linda Baxter.'

'Hold on just a moment and I'll get her for you.'

Eve heard some rustling and then something tapped against the receiver. One of her mother's earrings, she guessed.

'Eve?'

'Mum, whatever's going on, is Dad alright?'

Her mum sniffed. 'We're at the hospital – he's been in an accident.'

'An accident? What sort of accident?' Eve pictured a series of scenarios: a plug sparking in a faulty socket, a flame-riddled frying pan, a mangled car.

'A – well, we're not quite sure of all the details, but an incident, the police said. In a pub.'

'What did Dad say?'

'He hasn't said anything yet.'

'He is alive though?'

'Unconscious. But yes, alive.'

'Unconscious?'

'Mm-hmm.'

'When did the accident happen?'

'An hour – no, a couple of hours ago, maybe.' Linda sounded foggy, fatigued. 'The police said there was an altercation at the pub he was in,' Linda continued. 'Apparently some man punched him. That's what the witnesses said, anyway. He fell backwards and hit his head on the side of the bar, was knocked unconscious. So unlucky, the police said.'

An altercation in a pub. At lunchtime, Eve thought. Everyone else would have been watching, or waiting for, the press conference, but not her dad. The whole nation could be focused on one thing, suitably distracted, and he'd still find a pocket of trouble to get into.

'Eve? Are you there?'

Still absorbing it all, Eve's head bobbed in a slow nod. 'I'm here. What about the bloke from the pub, did they get him, has he been arrested?'

'They seem to know who he is.'

'A purple…' Eve muttered.

'A what?'

'Ah, nothing.'

'So we're here, waiting. The doctors aren't sure when he'll come round. His face is bruised – his lovely face. They think he might have a fractured jaw, and some damage to his back. They're running more tests on his head. But until he comes round they can't really be sure what the damage is.'

'But he will come round?'

Eve heard her mum's sharp intake of breath. 'They think so. They can't be sure. Apparently with head injuries...' She paused. 'It might be a good idea for you to come home... in case.'

Adio was now sitting up straight, staring at her intently. Eve glanced at the window. It might as well be closed, she thought. There was no air coming in, no breeze. The AC unit was no good for that either. Where was the fresh air?

'Will you come?'

'Yes. Of course,' said Eve. 'I'll look into flights.'

'Okay.' Her mum sighed wearily. 'We've had our ups and downs, and I know we've been apart for a long time now, but I'd never want anything to happen to him.'

'I know, Mum.'

'I can't believe it.'

In the background, Eve could hear a faint, 'Mum, can you give me some cash for the coffee machine?'

Turned away from the receiver, her mum called, 'Yes, I'll be there in a minute, I'm just saying goodbye to your sister.' Then to Eve, 'I'd best get back inside, see what's going on.'

'Simon's there?'

'Yes. Such a relief, that one of you is here.'

This wasn't an intentional slight, but smarted all the same. It made Eve feel guilty for not being with them, while simultaneously serving as a reminder of why she wasn't.

'Let me know when you're getting in.'

'Will do. 'Bye Mum.'

''Bye, love.'

Adio, Saffron and Joe hovered nearby, foreheads wrinkled in identikit concerned frowns. Adio could have drawn those on, Eve thought.

'You okay, doll?' said Adio.

'It's my dad. He's in hospital. Unconscious. Was in a fight, or something. I'm supposed to go home.'

'That sounds like a good idea,' he said.

'I'll look up flights,' said Joe, moving back to his computer.

Adio hugged Eve, rubbing her back. 'I'm sure he'll be fine. From everything you've said, he's always sounded exceptionally hardy.'

Eve, head rested on Adio's shoulder, mumbled in agreement.

'Here you go,' said Saffron, putting a vodka-infused orange juice on the desk beside her.

Eve sat down, slowly. She took a swig from the glass.

'Today is absurd,' she said. 'Maybe it's not real.'

Saffron squeezed her arm in a way that implied it was.

Naturally, Eve was scared for her dad. But also, more than that – and she hated herself for this, an awful, ungenerous reaction – she was angry. Angry that he would get himself into this type of situation – certainly not a first – and that once again she and her mother (and now, apparently, surprisingly, Simon) were scrabbling, worrying, hurtled into disarray. Eve knew that she should be selflessly worried, praying to some god or universe to make him well, that she shouldn't be thinking about herself, this was only about him, and that they'd never been through anything as life-in-the-balance as this. But after everything else, she was riled and resentful. However much time or distance she put between them, it seemed there would always be, eventually, a mammoth, drama-shaped magnet to draw her back in – for their mistakes, her dad's and Simon's, to rule their lives.

On the television, a news reporter stood at the end of Downing Street. 'I think this will go down in history as one of the most astonishing press conferences we'll ever witness,' he said, eyes blinking behind dark-rimmed spectacles. 'We've learnt that we are now living in a world where criminals are to be *dyed purple*. Incredible. It does make you wonder what on earth could happen next.'

'I'm going back to that,' said Eve, slowly.

Adio nodded.

Eve gazed at the screen. She knew she shouldn't think it, given the circumstances, but she felt a tiny thrill fizz through her at the prospect of being in Blighty, in the eye of this unpredicted storm – the mad, mysterious purpleness. It was quite a lure for the newshound in her, the girl who'd forever been transfixed by the unerring stream of world events, not just the comforting, funny side up.

Now Eve imagined Pam Fox-Jones, sherry in one hand, a sleuthing magnifying glass held up to one eye in the other, on the trail of the loopiest, most disquieting tale she'd ever encountered. Then Eve imagined *herself* on that trail – and she wondered: could this be, possibly, a purple path back to real news?

Chapter Three

The roads were already jammed with morning traffic as Eve returned to her apartment to pack. She tried to focus on something other than the purpleness by mentally filling her suitcase as she walked: homeland summers are greyer, and wetter, she reminded herself, picturing a rain mac, an umbrella, an assortment of jumpers. On the wide sidewalk, a group of young men strutted towards her, city peacocks with bare, tanned torsos, sweat-drenched t-shirts tied around their waists. They ribbed a skinny one about not yet being topless – 'Mikey, you hot over there?' – and as he pulled up his vest, about to slip it over his head, immediately Eve's thoughts shifted from toothbrushes and brollies to the photo of the purple men. In the office she'd stared at the snap, closer and closer until the Portal's pixels swam before her. She'd zoomed in on the stormy skin, wanted to reach in and touch it, to see if it could be real. Theo Fletcher is quite the magician, she mused, imagining the prime minister white-gloved and top-hatted, then, with a flourish, tapping a wand and tipping his hat to reveal... a little lilac bunny.

The lights at the pedestrian crossing had changed, and Eve re-routed herself to the shadier side of the street. The baking,

Big Apple heat would do that; make you zig zag back and forth, creating a longer, marginally cooler journey. She realised that with this detour, she was about to pass the office of dermatologist, and former fling, Dr Jake Spiretti. Things between them hadn't ended so well, but given his area of professional expertise, she figured today could be a good day to say hello.

Eve rang the bell and was buzzed into the building.

A bright-eyed, blemish-free receptionist looked up expectantly as Eve entered the waiting room.

'Hi, can I help you?'

'Hello. I don't have an appointment, but I'm a friend of Dr Spiretti's, and, well, I wouldn't usually stop by like this, but I wondered if he might be available for a quick word.'

The receptionist's eyes narrowed ever so slightly as if she was calculating whether Eve was actually a friend of the doctor's, which would determine what level of politeness was required.

'He's very busy.'

'Of course, I appreciate that.'

'And he's actually not here right now.'

'Ah,' said Eve, wondering how long she could wait. She glanced at the wall, at a poster identifying friendly versus not so friendly moles. She imagined the peachy skin in these pictures purpled.

'Perhaps you can make an appointment? Or speak outside of office hours?'

'I'm going to be away. I've got a flight this evening, so…'

The receptionist said nothing, but some seconds into the wall of silence, her gaze shifted just past Eve, with a sense of battle-lost disappointment.

'Hey, Samantha,' said Dr Jake Spiretti.

Eve turned.

'Oh! And hey there, Eve.'

'Hello, Jake.'

'This is a surprise.'

'I know. Sorry to drop in like this. It's been a while, but... I was just passing and I thought you might have some illuminating wisdom that few others would.'

'Intriguing,' said Jake, his chest puffing out a little. 'I guess that's medical and not dating advice? You know I'm engaged now, right?'

Ouch. Of course he was, thought Eve. Weren't they all.

Samantha's lips twitched, forming a mildly triumphant smile.

'I didn't,' said Eve. 'But congratulations! How exciting.' She hoped for his future spouse's sake that he'd developed a better grasp of the concept of fidelity.

'I've got a few minutes before the next one, right, Sam?'

Samantha nodded. Eve followed Jake through to his office.

'It's good to see you.' Jake sat on the edge of his desk, ran his tongue back and forth along his bottom lip; Eve remembered that at one time she had – briefly – found this quirk alluring. It had made her want to kiss him. Now she berated herself for such poor judgement.

'Mm, you too,' said Eve, wondering if she should cross her fingers behind her back. 'So, have you heard about this crazy new scheme in Blighty, of turning people purple?'

Jake smirked. 'Yeah, I saw it on the news this morning. It's nuts.'

'How would they do it?'

'Change a person's colour?'

'Yep.'

Jake shook his head, raised his hands in a 'who can say?' gesture. 'Hard to guess. There are plenty of possibilities...'

'There are?'

'Sure.'

'Such as?'

'Supplements.'

'Supplements? Like vitamins?'

'Sure.'

'Wouldn't you have to take a lot?'

'Probably. There was a guy who regularly took a silver-based preparation, and his skin turned blue.' Jake smiled. 'Remember that?'

Eve vaguely recalled having seen the man on television.

'I do, now you mention it. Sort of metallic-looking, wasn't he?'

Jake nodded. 'Poor guy. But medically fascinating. Remember that bar on 4th Street?'

Where they'd met. Jake had seemed charming, and single. Had made her laugh, and they'd ended up in a diner, talking until three am.

'Of course. Haven't been there for a long time. What else would cause the purpleness?'

'Make up.'

'Make up?' Eve looked doubtful. Jake was doing the lip-licking thing again.

'It could be a hoax. No real skin change, just some paint and imagination. People will believe anything you tell them.'

You would know, thought Eve.

'True. But if it isn't... how else could they do it?'

Leaning forward, Jake said, 'We should go for a drink sometime.'

'Well,' said Eve, sweetly, 'I would love to know more about the purpling, but no doubt your free time is filled with wedding preparations.'

Slowly, Jake straightened up. 'Look, there are plenty of ways a person's skin colour could be affected,' he said, casually. 'None would be instant. Quickest way to find out, just ask one of these purple guys what happened, right?'

His phone rang.

'So sorry, my next patient is here,' Jake said, standing, and shooting Eve one final charm-offensive smile. 'It's been good to see you. Thanks for stopping by.'

That was about as helpful as I should have expected, Eve thought, heading, back on track, towards her suitcase. Really she'd had no desire to see Jake Spiretti again, and it was certainly a shame he hadn't been more dermatologically insightful. But to be finding her way into this story… that was a better high than the finest whisky, or a charming stranger in a bar.

Later Adio arrived at Eve's apartment laden with Mexican food, and they spent the afternoon anxiously awaiting an update on Eve's dad, whose state remained unchanged, while watching the now delirious news outlets. Eve packed while Adio, between mouthfuls of tortilla chips, read aloud more reports of the purpleness, Eve gasping an occasional 'Really?' and crossing the room, half-folded garment in hand, to peer over his shoulder and read for herself.

Already the media was gorging itself on purpleness, conducting opinion polls, and speculating on both the way the colour change was occurring (claiming security reasons, so far the government remained tight-lipped about that) and how long the scheme would last. Every comment seemed glazed with disbelief, from the folk stopped on the street to the psychologists and opposition party MPs being wheeled onto rolling news coverage ('We could do a cool montage of people's amazed faces,' Joe had mused, noting just how many mouths were caught agape).

The shadow home secretary said, 'I'm dumbfounded. This is utterly preposterous.'

The representative for an association of criminal psychologists gazed offscreen for a few seconds before eventually saying, 'I think I can honestly say that myself and many of my colleagues are quite speechless.'

A grandmother interviewed in a park playground said, 'It's mind-boggling, really. Next we'll be seeing flying saucers.' (This was badly timed, as a frisbee flew across the screen just behind her).

And approaching her as she arrived home, reporters nabbed a quote from Theo Fletcher's mum, whom Eve considered impressively composed, given the circumstances.

'It's unprecedented, of course,' said Marianne Fletcher. 'But we have complete faith in Theo, and know that whatever he does, he does it with thought and consideration, and through honestly wanting the best for us all.'

As the Fletcher seniors' front door closed, the camera swerved joltingly to a journalist who quipped, 'If I'd started dyeing people, I don't think my mum would have taken it so well.'

It was too early, Eve thought, still too much of a shock, to try and make any real sense out if it. Blindsided opinion pieces babbled, most praising the prime minister for such brave, decisive action (his popularity was so immense that pundits frequently joked about what he would be able to get away with before his approval ratings dipped), while others were appalled, calling this an astonishing plot that felt like something out of a garish comic book, with Theo Fletcher the maniacal madman. There was a similar divide in the news reports themselves, scrambled together with the few available story-knitting facts. Despite this limited information, articles were padded with plenty of bluster and lots of distracting capitalised letters to reinforce the shock.

The PM was pretty much the only person NOT looking off-colour today, after his GOBSMACKING announcement that criminals are to be turned PURPLE. FED UP with soaring crime rates, the government hatched an ASTONISHING plan to keep the badly behaved in check, publicly SHAMING them as 'bruises on society', and giving them a matching SKIN OF SIN.

HUE DONE IT?

What he didn't reveal was how these undesirables are getting their DUBIOUS makeovers – but it sounds as though there could be TROUBLE ahead for anyone seen misbehaving near their local bobby. Forget being caught red-handed, now UNLUCKY lads and lasses who commit illegal or anti-social acts will be finding themselves MAUVE from head to toe…

Naturally, the newspapers were having a whale of a time finding ways to say purple: plum, heather, mauve, indigo, violet (it had reminded Eve of the song in *Joseph and the Amazing Technicolour Dreamcoat*, the one with all the colours, which they'd had to sing in junior school. She could never remember the full list of fantastic tints in that – or when to take a breath, for that matter – so she'd made the shades up as she went along, while trying to pause often enough that she didn't turn turquoise or cobalt or azure or sky or electric blue in the process). But *The Sun* had won with lavender. More precisely, they had shortened it, from the soothingly fragranced flower known to enhance sleep, invoking images of an oh-so-English country garden and box sets of soap given to elderly aunts at Christmas, to a derivative term coined with lickety split wit. Combine the derogatory 'chav' with a dose of purple colouring and some toilet humour, and what did you have? Lav.

Lee had become the first official Lav and his face was everywhere. All the papers had latched on to before and after shots, showing a young, surly, but pink Lee, alongside a shot of him from the press conference, now mottled and rattled. He was currently the only named Purpled person, and still quarantined at a secure facility with the others that the prime minister had mentioned, though the hunt was on for the three escapees who'd been snapped in the leaked picture. Unfortunately for them, it wasn't just the police who were on their trail, but every newspaper too. Those within the facility were due to be released imminently, but judging by photos of the place, it was already swarming with reporters, who were currently being kept at bay by a ring of uniformed police officers.

'A police doughnut,' said Adio, as he took a bite from a more edible one.

He and Eve watched a clip of a policewoman speaking to a journalist.

'It's quite a scene here,' said the reporter.

The policewoman raised her eyebrows, gave a curt nod.

'Were you aware of what was going on, of who was being held here?'

The policewoman looked at him, unflinching. 'I arrived today, I couldn't speculate on what was happening before then.'

'How will the inmates' security be maintained upon release?'

'*Their* security? I can imagine they'll get some attention, but I don't think their safety's at risk.'

'You don't think that the public might react quite strongly when they're back in their own communities?'

'In their current – ' the briefest of pauses – '*condition*, these individuals should pose a substantially lessened risk once they're back in their communities. Hopefully the public will appreciate that. Obviously, members of the public are also reminded that this initiative is now fully operational, and anyone can be affected, so *everyone* should show consideration and caution in their behaviour.'

'When you return to your usual patrols, will you be responsible for making culprits *Purple*?'

With what Eve had considered to be an exemplary poker face, the policewoman replied, 'I couldn't possibly comment.'

Eve gazed out of the window as the taxi pulled away. Across the road, a man with a dog exited the all-hours deli which she and Saffron sometimes ventured to late at night, giggling, already in their pajamas, but craving a slumber party fix of ice cream or potato chips. The dog stopped, squatting near the flowers bursting with almost surreal, technicolour brightness that filled rows of buckets outside the shop, reminding Eve of blooms as seen in a View-Master camera. The man lingered too, holding up a New York newspaper that had been tucked under his arm and scanning the headlines. It was still too early for it to have hit the presses, but Eve squinted, trying to catch an inky update, and any mention of the Purpleness.

The cab sped on, through streets swarming with high-spirited bodies spilling out of bars and into the clammy night air. They passed Eve's favourite seafood restaurant (the scene of one of her most memorably awful dates), and the first *Say Fantastique!* office, a fourth-floor walk-up in Chinatown which had framed paintings of dragons on every landing (she and Adio had spent many a sticky summer evening sitting on the fire escape there, watching the city below and pinching themselves that this was their new life). Then they crossed the bridge and were out onto the freeway, where billboards advertised action films and sci-fi shows, each of which had a premise that, however daft, seemed less preposterous than what she was about to go home to.

'So,' said the taxi driver, with an affable smile via the rear view mirror, 'you're English?'

Eve nodded, 'Yup. Been here a long time though.'

She looked at the ID badge displayed on the partition between them. His name was Earl, and he was smiling in the photo too.

'Hard to leave, right?' he said. 'A land of plenty. Plenty crazy, but good.'

'It's true,' said Eve.

'So you English got all these crazy people who're purple now, right? What d'you make of that?'

'I don't know.' Eve sighed. 'It seems unreal. I'm still getting my head around it. What do you think?'

Earl tutted. 'I'm not going to say judging a man by his colour could be a good thing. Seems backwards. Can't see how that'll help anybody, right?'

Eve murmured in agreement and looked out of the window. In truth, she wasn't yet sure how she felt about the Purpleness. It was, of course, insane – ludicrous, unbelievable and indefensible. But perhaps a crazier deterrent *was* called for, given the dreadful, intolerable things people seemed willing to do to one another, which often beggared belief. It wasn't just the foul play taking place behind closed doors, or large-scale atrocities planned by determined, detestable organisations. Since shocking tales of road rage and a tortured toddler led from a shopping centre to an unimaginable death, there seemed to be a level of violence that was almost banal, where inadvertently queue-jumping or looking at someone the wrong way could land you in casualty or worse.

Not long ago, a friend of Womble's had been ambling home from the pub when a couple of lads approached him with flying fists and no reason, leaving him lying in the street with a broken jaw. And the teenage nephew of one of Eve's schoolfriends had recently been stabbed after an accidental slight en route to a nightclub; instead of a merry evening peppered with lager and lasses, his night was deflated by a near-fatal punctured lung. Whenever she read of another hateful, mindless crime, Eve would wonder why people were like that, how the perpetrators of such acts became that way. To a lesser degree, she'd thought the same about her brother Simon, who seemed to have so little consideration for anyone or anything. No apparent empathy, no sense of responsibility, no concern for those he hurt.

But had things truly declined? Eve wondered. Or were they the same as ever, and she had just been too young to notice before? Was it the speed and volume of information to which everyone had access, with the Portal feeding an increasingly super-sized diet of news, that meant we could now know about everything that happens rather than a more digestible portion of it? Had we simply been cocooned before?

Or did the world seem more disturbed because that was how everyone was being programmed to feel? This was always Eve's next stop on this train of thought, and she guessed it would be pivotal in the popularity of the prime minister's new scheme. She loathed the sense of fear that had become such a popular currency and was relentlessly instilled in everyone, usually to peddle something, from dodgy foreign policies to antibacterial hand wash, and left you feeling under siege, constantly in danger from unseen enemies.

Even before her move across the pond, the persistent scaremongering had begun to dampen Eve's enthusiasm for a life in the news. Not long after her arrival in America, there had been a major terrorist attack. With the world on anxiety-pill-popping, terror-stopping high alert, every morning began with a reminder of that day's threat level, usually at the higher, hotter end of the spectrum, flagged in dangerously warm red or orange (Eve had thought they could jolly up the system with some appropriately coloured alarming icons – molten lava, sunburn, or the dwarf in the red coat from *Don't Look Now*). The increasing popularity of panic seemed at best unhelpful and at worst irresponsible. But how could you unravel the truth? She thought again of Theo Fletcher, of Lee the Lav, and how there was probably little you couldn't convince people of if they'd been successfully infected with enough unease.

And then, of course, there had been the Repeal, which seemed like a gateway drug to the Purpleness, when Eve thought of it now. Restricting access to some technologies, such as the relaunched Portal, where every move was tracked, and disposing of others, like the previously indispensable PortAble. The device had been held at least partially responsible for an escalation of inconsiderate behaviour, from the seeping, thoughtless cacophony of excess noise on trains and buses to invasive video-filming that ran the gamut from an irritation, and unsettling invasion of privacy ('You just never know when someone is recording you,' Eve's mum had said once, bewildered, having spotted a man surreptitiously filming from behind a rack of department store dressing gowns), to trophy tapings of a far more sinister kind.

When the Repeal was first announced, the outcry was extreme, with hundreds of thousands attending a Refuse to Repeal demonstration in London (organisers estimated attendance to have been two million; the police claimed half that). 'These things give us power, and you want to take our power away,' protesters exclaimed. Then prime minister Milton Hardy had proclaimed the PortAble's dark side: 'A contrary, ability-reducing enabler of narcissism and social withdrawal.' Adding, 'Didn't we manage perfectly well before?'

With the new regulations, nothing could be posted on the Portal anonymously, and all online activity could be traced to an individual civilian identifier called a CIV code. Critics claimed that it was an invasion of privacy, an infringement of human rights; supporters that it was for the greater good, *protecting* human rights by regulating what had become the Wild West, and that if you weren't doing anything dodgy then you had no cause for concern. In the physical world, they said, behave badly and the ISON cameras would catch you; why should life on the Portal be any different? Later, everyone had to admit that the Repeal had made life online more cordial, that it felt safer. Bullying and vitriol became a less easy fix when you had to expose yourself; weapons lost, power snatched from the nasty, the attention-seeking, the insecure. Initially dismissed as blustery legislation that was unlikely to be enforced, folk were soon unpleasantly surprised. Employers were encouraged to see casually insidious and unpleasant behaviour as toxic. Many companies introduced a declaration for staff to sign, and there were petitions and – ironically – public shaming for those that did not. At the point when prosecutions for Portal offences peaked, hundreds were losing their job every week; recruitment agencies rubbed their hands with glee.

That was, as the phrase went at *Say Fantastique!*, just the tip of the asparagus. The anti-social elements could perhaps have been overlooked. But what sealed the Repeal was the malicious bug that had infiltrated not one but two superpowers' nuclear systems and caused a simultaneous flushing of every automated toilet in Japan (naturally, for *Say Fantastique!* the flush-a-thon had been a winning story. Also, Eve remembered that, despite multiple technology experts asserting that the bug had been initiated from a PortAble, with many world leaders subsequently banning such devices, Womble's friend Bob maintained that this was a smokescreen related to the device manufacturers' not paying enough tax). In quite the photo opportunity, Milton Hardy had been pictured disposing of his;

there had been a lot of recycling to do. And while it had been controversial, you couldn't argue with the results.

So what was this, then, the Purpleness? A diabolical scheme built on a handy foundation of fear, or a necessarily extreme measure to protect the good folk, the decent and deserving? And would Eve despise herself for believing the latter?

The cab swerved to the kerb, pulling in sharply behind a shuttle bus from which spilled a pick 'n' mix of bags and passengers.

'Here we are,' said Earl, as a plastic crucifix swung from his rear view mirror. He got out of the cab and took Eve's suitcase from the boot while she gathered cash to pay him. As she took her case, he turned to her and said, 'Have a blessed trip.'

'Thanks,' said Eve, rolling into the airport terminal, thinking, I'm not sure blessed will be quite the word for it.

On the plane, Eve found herself thinking of a family holiday they'd taken when she was ten. Her father had booked for them to go on a package trip to Portugal, but for some reason – she couldn't quite remember now, but thought it was down to a problem with the travel agency – they'd instead ended up at a bed and breakfast on the Isle of Wight. Whether or not a troublesome travel agent, or some equally plausible excuse, had been the reason for their switch of locale, the trip had been during one of the brighter spells in her parents' marriage and, for a change, her father wasn't in the doghouse. Although she couldn't have articulated it until she was older, even then Eve had a grasp of the circular dynamic of their relationship: father does wrong by mother, mother is upset, father feels guilt (or irritation) and avoids facing both reminders of this disappointment and arguments at home by spending more time seeking solace elsewhere. Now, Eve wondered why her mum hadn't been firmer with him, refused to put up with his exploits; but Eve guessed it was something of a tightrope: she'd wanted him to stay and figured that challenging his behaviour would only push him further away.

The teenage Eve had fretted about whether her dad had ever really wanted to be with them, wondered if he'd been happy with their mum until she and Simon came along – if it was they who had caused the cracks in the marriage. She hadn't known that aside from being ridiculously in love with him, her mum had also felt the giddy thrill of winner's luck; Vince Baxter was handsome and charming, with the so-sure swagger of a rock star, and he had picked *her*. Linda, who was pretty and smart, but longed for the poise and confidence that some of the other girls possessed, hadn't expected to be swept off her feet by the kind of chap she usually only encountered in romance novels. In keeping with her parents' assumptions, she had expected to marry someone kind and dependable, reliable in providing all except excitement. She'd been courting such a fellow – a couple of years older than her, he was a man about town with good prospects – and she could picture their life together (although sometimes, in quiet moments, she'd feel a shortness of breath, and wonder if this was the thinning air of predictability).

In turn, Vince hadn't reckoned on the elegant, unattainable-seeming Linda who came from a nice part of town and whom he'd sometimes spot in a cafe near where he worked, nose in a book which she'd occasionally put down to gaze wistfully out of the window. Vince had a knack for attracting the gals who wanted something more, something else; but when he crossed paths with Linda at the pub, or down the dance hall, she was usually on the arm of a well-heeled sort of chap, all greased hair and shiny shoes, and she'd often seem to look right through Vince – which, naturally, made her all the more enticing (he wouldn't know until later that such apparent coolness was in fact poor eyesight). How proud he'd been when Linda accepted his proposal – that he, the wild card, had won her over the shiny-shoed sure thing! Her devotion was a high, and though he did love her, in his own way, was most intoxicated by the idea of snagging such an unlikely prize: a bird – and maybe a life? – so much fancier than he'd aspired to. Plus her reverence Teflon-coated his confidence, making him all the more alluring – and why should he deny himself? Linda knew how desirable he was, wouldn't have expected them to live the same life of monotony, monogamy, that everyone else signed up for. She found Vince's unpredictable-ness exciting, and unpredictability was the one thing he could guarantee to provide.

It was the night after their arrival on the Isle of Wight, and the family had gone out for dinner. It had been a warm evening, and they'd walked along the seafront enjoying the early evening sun, the laugh-filled chatter of other holiday-makers, and the tinny clatter of the amusement arcades, the beeps of the machines and cascading coins chiming with the chart hits that blared through cheap speakers. Her mum was wearing a white dress covered in little flowers, with spaghetti straps which tied at the shoulders, and silver sandals. Her dad sported a sky-blue shirt and a moustache. They strolled hand in hand, looking like something out of a glossy American TV show, glamorous, attractive – and not arguing – and Eve had felt like the girl who had it all. Even Simon wasn't behaving disastrously, though he did keep trying to kick seagulls, who were always too quick to fly away. Eve had breathed in the heady aroma of summer freedom: chips, suntan lotion, sea air and expectation, mingling with her dad's aftershave and her mum's perfume to create a scent so intoxicating Eve thought she might never again feel this content.

They ate at an Italian restaurant (a place that to the young Eve seemed so sophisticated, but which also served all-day fry-ups), where the waiter commented on how beautiful Linda looked. Vince looked peacock proud, whispering something in his wife's ear before leaning back and winking at her. Linda beamed and, catching Eve's eye, gave one of the most genuinely happy smiles Eve had witnessed from her mother (it still saddened her when she thought of it). Despite having already enjoyed Flake 99 Cones on the seafront that afternoon, they'd ordered ice cream for pudding. Simon had a monster amount of chocolate, nuts and whipped cream, their parents shared a banana split, while Eve had a knickerbocker glory all to herself, and as she held her extra long spoon above the towering bowl, she wondered if this was too good to be true.

Their parents had got talking to the family at the next table, who were also on holiday. The wife was pretty, blonde, wore shimmering blue eyeliner, and laughed at Eve's dad's jokes. The husband was stocky and would chime into what Vince was saying with a joke of his own before downing a long glug of beer. The four of them decided to move to the bar and share a couple more drinks, and gave the children some change to spend at the amusement arcade. Simon had badgered Eve to give him some of her coins, threatening her with a Chinese burn, but Eve had refused, and as they stood in a scowling stand off, she had very, very nearly stamped on his flip-flopped foot with her new mini-heeled party shoes. She could imagine how much that would have hurt. But then she'd pictured her newsreading heroines looking at her calmly and saying, don't let him get to you, don't let him spoil this evening that you've enjoyed so much. So instead she turned and walked into the maze of machines, ringing and whirling and clattering, taking herself and her money as far away from her brother as she could.

Eve won some coppers at the sliding games, and when one of the other kids came to tell her that it was time to go she still had twenty pence in her hand. Mum and dad will be impressed, she thought. But when they reached the bar, her father had a swollen eye and her mother's mascara was smudged from tears. Eve had clutched the twenty pence, thought of her parents' clasped hands, the wink and the smile, and her knickerbocker glory, and scorned herself for thinking such enchantment could last.

Simon had scowled at them. 'What happened?'

'Is he all right?' Eve asked her mum, quietly.

Linda sighed and nodded.

'Stupid people,' said Vince.

'They weren't stupid. Just drunk and... provoked.'

'Provoked? It wasn't my fault! We were being social. Friendly.'

Linda looked at him, saying nothing.

'What? I was only talking to his wife. He was all chatty-Cathy, complimenting you, and I didn't deck him one.'

'He didn't have his arm around me and he wasn't sniffing my neck.' Eve's mother sounded not angry but resigned.

'I wasn't sniffing her neck. I was asking her what her perfume was. It reminded me of yours.'

A flicker of crushed disappointment had crossed Linda's face.

'You think I deserved to be whacked for a bit of harmless fun? You were right there – you saw. We were just chatting. He must be mad.'

Linda turned away, towards the sea. Eve had tried to guess what she was thinking, whether she was considering stamping on his foot with one of her silver sandals. Instead she turned around, looked at his swollen eye and said, 'We should get back to the hotel and put some ice on that. And you two,' she told Eve and Simon, 'should get to bed soon.'

At the B&B, Vince checked his face in the dressing table mirror before again pressing the bag of ice that Linda had sheepishly requested from their landlady against the swelling. Simon, en route to fetch some toothpaste from their suitcase, stood next to him.

'Y'alright, Dad?'

Vince nodded. 'Yeah, thanks. Just irresistible, eh son?' he said, winking with his good eye.

Eve glanced across at her mum, who was reading – or pretending to. Eve had been watching, and hadn't seen her turn a page.

Eve leant back in her seat, eyes closed, still picturing them all in that room. She might be entirely wrong – and of course that wouldn't excuse her dad from blame for his current injuries – but she couldn't help but wonder if somehow history had now repeated itself. This thought was interrupted as the captain's voice announced that they would soon be landing, and with a ringing sound, the seatbelt sign blinked on. Oh, green and pleasant and now purple land, Eve thought, looking out of the window as the plane began its descent.

Chapter Four

Naturally, given the mere wink in time since the Purpleness began, back in Blighty everything appeared unchanged. Yet Eve was on high alert, eyes peeled for sightings of Purple people. It was an unsurprising but no less guilty truth that she really wanted to see a plum 'un, and, now she was here, felt expectantly a-flutter at the thought, it could happen *at any time*. She wondered what it would be like when she saw a Purple person. Would she want to hug them, to let them know that not everyone agreed with the witchhunt? Or would she be repelled, seeing dead eyes matching dull skin, someone as lacking in heart as Theo Fletcher claimed? The bruised or the bruisers? Or both?

She'd been hopeful as she ambled through the airport, but two raised hoods were red herrings, and an unlikely tinge, spotted in a distant queue – this is it, Eve thought, heart skipping – transpired to be the result of extensive tattoos. Be realistic, she told herself; if you were newly Purpled, it's unlikely that you'd be gadding festively on holiday, and even if you simply wanted to scarper, where in the world would they welcome anyone so inescapably singled out to be a troublemaker?

Other changes to the nation, meanwhile, were increasingly pronounced; the Repeal had resulted in an unexpected offshoot, commonly known as the Rollback, whereby, seemingly spontaneously, many things culturally and socially had begun to reverse. In a trivial, trifling way at first – old-fashioned foods such as gammon steaks with pineapple in the supermarket, and chains of high street stores re-adopting decades-dead branding – then later, a resurgence in letter-writing (away from prying eyes on the Portal), milk deliveries (which had increased by 6,000 per cent in the year following the Repeal), and other elements that you couldn't quite put your finger on, but inspired a flicker of déjà vu. As with the things which had been gradually forgotten as the world progressed – like letter-writing and milk deliveries – now some newer developments would slink back into the shadows when you weren't looking, as though they'd never been there at all. It was surprising how little resistance there was; apparently so much comfort to be found in what you knew, and could rely on ('As long as they stick to naff sweets and pay phones,' said Eve's friend Helena. 'If they crack out mother-in-law jokes, or the *Black and White Minstrel Show*, I'll start the revolution myself').

As Eve made her way through the wide airport corridors, she detected the faint smell of cigarette smoke, all the more noticeable now she was used to being away from it, bar Adio's sneaky puffing. Red, white and royal blue chairs clustered in sporadic rows beneath seemingly endless framed pictures boasting the best of British: the latest James Bond star – Eve could never remember his name – sat, fag in hand, alongside the newest, sleek Jaguar ('Still made in the UK'); the current captains of the English cricket and football teams sharing an Arkwright's beer; the modern, questionably efficient, solar-powered Teasmade; a shot of Live Aid; ice champs Torvill

53

and Dean getting Olympian gold after their Bolero; and a celebratory, cup-wielding snap from England winning the World Cup in 1966 alongside a picture of the trophy recently, finally, coming home. It was only as she exited customs, passing a bank of pay phones and catching a glimpse of the newspapers in a Quigley's kiosk, that betrayed any clue as to the nation's newly controversial hue. It was ridiculous, but Eve felt slightly disappointed. She'd expected the place to feel different, but of course it didn't yet, at all.

Eve was about to make a Quigley's pitstop when she spotted Womble and Helena. Womble was holding a small sign featuring a printed picture of Pam Fox-Jones with Eve's face super-imposed onto it. 'Welcome home!' it said, with 'Time for a sherry' scribbled just about legibly underneath. Eve laughed, trundling towards them with her luggage.

'Hi, wanderer,' said Womble, glad the sign had made Eve laugh (he muttered an 'I told you!' to Helena, who'd apparently admonished him, saying that the Pam picture might be too frivolous, under the circumstances).

'Hello, you,' said Helena.

'Aah, hello,' said Eve, giving them each a tight hug, before pulling back and looking at them expectantly. 'Is there any news?'

Helena shook her head. 'I'm so sorry, Evie,' she said. 'I spoke to your mum before we left and there's no change. But we'll take you straight over to the hospital.'

'Thanks, and thank you so much for meeting me.'

'Our pleasure,' said Helena.

'Yes, a trip to the airport is almost as good as a holiday itself,' said Womble.

'He's counting the hours 'til the school holidays.' Helena linked her arm with Eve's as they made their way towards the car park.

'Nearly there,' said Womble. 'I can't wait.'

'How are the young 'uns? About to pass their exams with flying colours, thanks to you?'

'Naturally. And now I shall tell them if they don't do well I'll have them turned Purple.'

'Oh, don't,' said Helena, with a note of irritation in her voice. 'It's not funny.'

Eve was about to tease Womble about changing his tune but, sensing tension, held back. Something to discuss later, she thought.

Helena pulled a parking ticket from her handbag. Eve could feel a rising anxiety with each step that they took towards the car and away from Quigley's. She needed a news fix.

'Can I just quickly grab some papers?'

'I knew it!' said Helena.

'Well, with everything that's going on…'

'Knock yourself out,' Helena said, before grimacing. 'God, sorry, wrong turn of phrase…'

'Ah, don't be silly,' said Eve, already quickening her step towards the newsagent's.

She stood by the piles of papers, and gave a quietly enraptured sigh. The Purpleness was splashed across every front page, of course it was. Eve surveyed the headlines, revelling in the scene, before scooping up two copies of every title and heading to the till.

The cashier glanced quizzically between Eve and the pulpy mountain.

'All of these?'

'Please.'

'You've got two here? Wait, of each?'

'That's right.'

'Huh.' The cashier paused then muttered, 'Mental.'

Bit harsh, thought Eve. 'Well, I just wanted to—' She noticed the cashier's finger prodding the sweatshirt-raising man's shoulder, as she pointed at the picture of the three Purple people.

'Ah. Yes. What do you think?'

The cashier stared at the photo, considering this. She tilted her head.

'Wonder what drugs they were on when they thought of it,' she said. 'But I suppose if that's what it takes.'

The cashier shrugged, then indicated to some chocolate bars lined up neatly on the counter.

'Chocolate?'

'No, just the papers, thanks.'

Eve loaded her haul into a shopping bag and strode, sated, back towards Womble and Helena.

Over the tanoy, there was a series of chimes, signalling an announcement.

'Gentlemen, if you're travelling today, why not pick up a set of Mills Brothers moustache-trimmers – on special offer at Kay Brand Chemists Duty Free. Yes, that's right – wherever you're going, impress with a moustache shaped by Mills Brothers, the only product with the silver seal. And for the ladies, take a look at Yardley's range of show-stopping neon cosmetics, which have just arrived in store – perfect for nights on the town. From Shanghai to Chicago, they're sure to get you noticed.'

Further chimes concluded the announcement just as Eve, Womble and Helena reached the exit.

'Too late to pick up those moustache trimmers now, then,' said Womble.

'Just as well,' said Helena, 'given that you don't have a moustache to trim.'

Womble grinned and rubbed his upper lip. 'Ah. I knew there was something missing.'

Helena pulled into a space in the hospital car park and switched off the engine. She and Womble then turned simultaneously to Eve, who was sitting in the back seat.

'How are you feeling?'

Eve took a deep breath. 'A bit sick.'

At the reception desk, Eve was directed to where Vince was being treated.

'Shall we come with you?' Helena asked.

'No, don't worry. Go and enjoy your weekend, I'll be okay on my own.'

Eve wandered through what felt like a dozen sets of swing doors before spotting her dad's ward ahead, at the end of a corridor. She stopped for a moment to let a woman on crutches move past.

'Sorry,' the woman said, inching slowly forward. 'Still getting my sea legs.'

Eve smiled and waited. Nearby, a phone rang, and a passing nurse quickened her pace to answer it.

'Hello? They never! In A&E? When did he come in – have you seen him? He's got police with him?' She gave a disappointed sigh. 'So we can't just go and have a look. Shame. You know Suba reckons they're putting something in kebabs? She says it's funny blokes being Purpled after getting in fights in the street, that they'll get a kebab on the way home, and that'll have something in it. Sounds mad, but who knows…'

Eve clocked this conversation. It made for an unlikely theory, as unlikely as anything could be these days, but she liked that someone had a notion about it at all. Plus a Purple person here in this very building… She made a mental note of that. Then, as the crutch-assisted woman nodded a thank you, Eve continued on to the reception desk at her dad's ward. With a dry throat, she introduced herself to the nurse.

'Hello there, Miss Baxter. Your mum and brother were here, but I saw them leave the ward a little while ago.'

'Really? They were expecting me—'

'They probably just went to get a cup of tea. There can be lots of tea breaks here, it's a lot of waiting around.' A sympathetic smile. She had a kind face; a fortuitous asset in this profession, Eve imagined. A silver name badge declared this to be Shona Attride.

'Shall I show you to your dad's room?'

Eve followed the nurse, a shiver of nerves tingling through her, numbing her hands and knees.

'Here we are.' Nurse Attride opened a door.

Eve walked into the room, and slowly towards her dad's bed. There was bruising on his face, and a medley of tubes poked out of him. She swallowed and, feeling unexpectedly light-headed, reached towards the side of the bed, pressing a hand against the mattress to steady herself. Doing so she inadvertently moved closer to Vince – closer than she was usually. Hugs between them were rare and awkward, but now she felt an odd urge to lean further forward, and – what? She couldn't easily embrace him, lying like that – maybe rest her head on his chest? She dismissed this notion, removing her hand from the side of the bed and tucking it in her pocket, before taking a step backwards and turning to the nurse.

'Do you have any idea when he might come out of this?'

Nurse Attride shook her head. 'It's hard to tell, I'm afraid.'

'Right.'

'You can talk to him. Sometimes it helps.'

Eve nodded, not sure what to say.

'I'll leave you.'

Eve stood quietly while the heart monitor bleeped, and another machine hissed. She looked down at her dad, who – incongruously – appeared quite peaceful. Having a nap while all this fuss occurred around him. If she was honest, Eve had partly expected – hoped – that he would be on the mend when she arrived, conscious, and lucidly chatting up nurses, asking if they could smuggle beer into his teacup. It would be true to form for him, to obliviously cause chaos and then charm his way out of it.

'Hi, Dad. It's Eve.'

There was a chair pulled up to one side of the bed. Eve sat down. She stared at the blanket that covered Vince; it was blue and bobbling, the way jumpers did. Minutes passed.

'We're all worried about you. Quite a scare you've given everyone. Mum's beside herself. I came back as quickly as I could. I thought you might be awake when I got here.'

Eve glanced around the room. There was a newly bought comb on the bedside table, resting on top of the cellophane packet it had come in. She looked at her dad's hair. Neat, tended to, despite the circumstances. Obviously her mother's doing.

'There was a couple on the plane,' Eve said, 'who'd just got engaged. It had been their first trip to New York, and he'd planned the proposal – was going to ask her on top of the Empire State Building. Which is sweet, I guess. But he was so overexcited that he'd asked her at the airport before they'd even left London. Imagine that. Being so eager to propose. Someone being so eager to propose to you.' Eve looked at the comb. She wondered if she would ever feel that; she seemed to get relationships all wrong.

What else should she talk about? Old memories, revarnished for the occasion? The weather?

'It's funny being home. You won't believe what's happening in the news. Theo Fletcher's starting dyeing people. Criminals. Which is bananas.'

Nurse Attride had re-entered the room. She stood at the end

of the bed, glancing at the monitors and making notes on a clipboard.

'As you can imagine, I'm already obsessing about it. I mean, people–' She paused. 'Turning purple. It's incredible. Can you really do that to humans? Should you? How on earth are they doing it?' Eve stretched, her body dull and itchy from the hours concertina'd on the plane. If the nurse hadn't been there, she'd have considered lying on the floor. 'You always said I'd make a rubbish war reporter. Which is probably true. But this I can do. I'm going to find out how they're Purpling people. You yourself say I'm like a dog with a bone…'

The nurse tucked away the clipboard, gave Eve a smile. Eve yawned, fidgeting in her seat.

'I'm babbling, sorry,' Eve told the nurse. 'Bit delirious. Not sure how helpful that will be with waking anyone up.'

'Don't you worry,' said Nurse Attride. She had taken a roll of sweets from her pocket and popped one in her mouth, before extending the packet to Eve.

'Mint imperial?'

'Oh. Thank you,' said Eve, noticing the retro design of the wrapper.

Nurse Attride looked as though she might say something else, but hesitated. Then added, 'Your mum said you were coming back from America.'

'Yes,' said Eve. 'Hence the babbling. Jet lag.'

'What do you do there?'

'News. Sort of,' said Eve.

'A newspaper?'

'A place called *Say Fantastique!* Fun news, mostly. But we're starting to do more reporting.'

'I've heard of it. My girlfriend reads it.'

'Ah!' Eve exclaimed, pleased.

'She's in A&E, and they definitely appreciate a bit of light relief...'

A phone began to ring.

'I'd better get that,' the nurse said, returning to the front desk.

To Vince, Eve said, 'The nurses seem very nice, so you might want to get your skates on, make the most of the attention.'

'Eve!'

Linda entered the room, with Simon behind her. Eve wasn't sure if her mother had overheard what she'd said.

'It's a relief to have you home, love.'

Linda looked as forlorn and fatigued as anyone would be after a sleepless night in a bedside chair. And the contrast of her typically elegant attire – today mostly emerald green, with a string of heavy glass beads clinking around her neck – only made her tiredness appear more pronounced.

'How are you doing, Mum?'

'Oh, so so.'

She and Eve hugged. From the corner of the room, still by the door, Simon gave a small nod in greeting. He was his usual scruffy self, though appeared less scrawny, less sallow. He actually looked healthy, as though he might be taking care of himself, which seemed hard to believe. More likely, Mum is taking care of him, Eve thought.

'Alright, sis?'

'Yep, you?'

There was a brief silence.

'Have there been any signs of anything? Even tiny movements?' Eve asked.

'I wish there had been, but not that any of us have seen.'

'Have the doctors got any idea of what will happen? Is there any kind of pattern to these... situations?'

'They've said we just have to wait and see. It could be days, weeks…' Linda whispered, as though Vince might hear.

'Well, here we all are,' she addressed Vince, smoothing the blanket around him. 'Eve's come back from New York to see you.'

'La di dah,' muttered Simon, almost inaudibly, but Eve could hear.

Really? Eve thought, even now? and gave him the withering look that she'd perfected years ago.

'Have you told your dad what you've been up to?'

'Yeah, Eve, tell Dad some funny animal stories. That will wake him up,' said Simon, with a pseudo-smile.

'Oh yes,' said Linda. 'Let's hear some of those.'

'Or some of your hilarious dating stories. Found a bloke yet?'

Linda patted Vince's hand, and said, 'Can you hear the chatter from these two? All of us together, it's just like old times, isn't it?'

The door opened and another nurse, wearing rather squeaky shoes, leant in.

'Sorry to interrupt. We just had a call from the police. They wanted to let you know that they've arrested the man who attacked Mr Baxter.'

'Thank God,' said Linda. 'I wonder what he'll have to say for himself.'

Quite, thought Eve, as she and Simon exchanged an unusually un-hostile glance.

Then, as the nurse was about to leave the room, she added, 'Oh, and because he's confessed, and they're definitely certain it's him, he's going to be turned Purple! Can you imagine?'

'Insanity,' said Linda.

Intriguing, thought Eve.

'What do you make of that, Vince?' Linda said. 'Who'd have thought of such a thing.'

Even under these circumstances her mother's fussing over Vince made Eve tetchy, and she slipped out of the room. Simon followed her.

'Going for a fag,' he said, slouching away.

Eve stood in the corridor, feeling tired and untethered. She moved to the ward's waiting area and sat on the floor, leaning against a chair with her legs stretched out. Remembering the newspapers, she pulled one from her bag, studying the front page, which featured a photo of Theo Fletcher and Lee, taken at the press conference. The headline read: 'NOWHERE TO HIDE'. The picture jogged something in her memory, a misplaced reminder her foggy, jet-lagged brain couldn't quite reach.

Eve sensed someone standing close by, and glanced up, worried that she was about to be declared a safety hazard, nestled on the floor. It was Nurse Attride.

'Should I move?' Eve asked.

'No, it's fine,' said the nurse.

'Is he okay?'

'Yes, no change.'

With a lingering glance towards Eve's newspaper, Nurse Attride hovered for a moment, then moved towards the reception desk. Eve watched as she tidied some scattered pens and a half-eaten tube of fruit pastilles, before leafing through a pile of paperwork. The phone bleeped, but had stopped again before the nurse could lift the receiver, the caller obviously having been grasped by something more pressing. Returning her attention to the newspaper, Eve's brain snapped back into action: she recalled the phone call about the Purpled man brought into A&E. Hadn't Nurse Attride said her girlfriend worked there?

With a tiny groan as she prised herself upright, Eve went

over to the front desk. Nurse Attride watched as she approached.

When Eve reached the desk, she placed the paper in front of her. Lowering her voice, she said, 'I think there was a Purple man brought here, into A&E?'

Holding Eve's gaze, Nurse Attride nodded slowly.

'I'm guessing you can't talk about it, but—'

'You want to find out how they're Purpling people.'

'Yes,' said Eve, surprised.

'I couldn't help overhearing… you were talking to your dad about it.'

'Oh, of course. As a medical professional, how do you think they could be doing it – actually changing people's colour, I mean?'

'I just don't know,' said Nurse Attride. 'I'd think it's probably ingested, or injected, but for colour like that, a strong change, all over, lasting a longer period of time, I would've thought it would need to be administered repeatedly, that there'd need to be a build-up to affect the skin cells. But that doesn't fit with people being Purpled overnight.'

'And your girlfriend works on the ward where the Purple man is?'

Another nod.

Eve was about to ask her next question when Nurse Attride said, 'All the things she sees and… she cried when she saw him. She said it felt cruel to inflict such a thing on anyone. A heartless punishment, she called it.'

What a tangled web it was, this Purpleness, thought Eve.

'I'm sure it's tricky, with patient confidentiality—'

'It's our job to protect patients,' the nurse said, 'but if you were trying to help, to find out what had happened to him, to all of them, maybe he would speak to you.' The nurse bit her lip. 'I don't know. Maybe this is a bad idea.' She was silent for a moment, looked down at the picture of Lee. 'Let me see. But I can't promise anything.'

'Of course. And thank you,' said Eve, adding, 'Was he brought here because of turning Purple? Was it having a side effect, or something?'

The nurse looked uneasy. 'Not quite.'

From her expression, Eve knew the truth was going to be loaded.

'Nurse Attride—'

The nurse turned to see a doctor approaching, blonde ponytail swinging as she walked. Her professional disposition would make her less prone to panic, but Eve saw the nurse's chest rise as she took a discreet, deep breath.

'Nurse, could I speak to you about Mrs Wu in bed twelve?'

'Ah, yes,' Nurse Attride gently exhaled.

With the doctor now within earshot, Eve said, 'Thanks so much for your advice. I'll wait to hear more.'

Nurse Attride gave a cautious nod, and walked away.

Eve had never been so keen to find herself in A&E.

Chapter Five

A plan was afoot. Mere hours after arriving in Blighty, Eve was due to meet a Purple person. She was cross-eyed with tiredness, and delirious with excitement. What would this lilac lad, Luke, have to say about the Purpleness, and, specifically, how he'd become this polemical shade of plum? Eve could barely contain herself.

In the meantime she had sat in her dad's room, flipping, transfixed, through the day's papers, searching for clues. With the scheme no longer a secret, a small number of the first 'batch' of Purpled people – the ones who'd been held at the secure facility that Sweatshirt and pals had escaped from – had been returned home, though none had yet agreed to be interviewed. With such all-round tight-lippery, tips as to the Turning were not to be found, but there were stories from some unlikely angles regarding the offending flesh.

In one article a dermatologist claimed indigo skin would require specialist moisturiser, but a disclaimer in exceedingly small print noted that he had not yet met, let alone examined, a Purple person, and in what appeared to be a first in anticipating a new commercial demographic, one of the recommended creams was from the doctor's own skincare brand. Meanwhile, presumably guessing that they wouldn't receive an objective hearing, with the truly Purpled people approached by the *Daily Dispatch* declining to be interviewed, the paper had 'plummed up' a model and sent him out onto the streets to be photographed. The result was a series of pictures of a clean-shaven chap in ripped Levi's (showing a keen attention to detail, even his knees were damson), pouting as those nearby scowled at him; in one photo, a woman swung her handbag towards him, and in another a teenage girl gazed flirtatiously in his direction, the lilac effect no match for his Elvis lips and cheekbones.

At the end of Nurse Attride's shift, Eve had followed her to the ladies' bathrooms, where they'd gone into neighbouring cubicles, and undressed; as agreed, Eve passed her own frock under the partition, and in return appeared the nurse's uniform, complete with mint imperials in the pocket. Once changed, they reconvened by the sinks.

'Lucky it fits,' said Eve.

Nurse Attride nodded, nervously smoothing the fabric of the dress she was now wearing. 'This isn't the kind of thing I do,' she said. 'Kelly's the daring one.'

'Tell me about it,' said Eve. 'I hate the idea of getting into trouble for anything. I think I'm allergic even to the thought of it.'

Nurse Attride let out a slow, meditative breath. 'But here we are. So. Just follow the signs to A&E, and Kelly will be waiting by the coffee machine. She'll be there in –' Nurse Attride checked the time – 'six minutes. It's a bit of a maze, but hopefully you'll find it easily.'

There was a creak as the main door to the bathrooms opened and a woman clasping a bunch of roses entered. She hovered, unsure what to do with the flowers, eventually resting them on the counter behind a sink before disappearing into a cubicle.

Nurse Attride busied herself with washing her hands, and Eve mopped her own clammy mitts with a paper towel. They exchanged a glance in the mirror, then Eve made her way out into the corridor. Exhilarated, but terrified.

Attempting to appear confident in where she was going, Eve tried to remember the route the nurse had advised. This would have been a great time to have a PortAble, she thought – to seem distracted by that while most other people she passed would have been engrossed in their own. Whatever you do, she told herself, do not make eye contact with anyone; inviting interaction was bound to blow her cover.

As instructed, Eve was about to take a right turn at the sexual health poster, which in block capitals declared 'BETTER SAFE THAN SORRY'. She was wondering about the message it sent to imminent parents en route to the neighbouring maternity ward when she felt a hand on her arm.

'Excuse me, nurse,' said an elderly gentleman. 'I'm looking for my wife, she's on the Sanderson Ward. How do I get there?'

Eve turned, feeling hot, and faint. What would the penalty be for impersonating a member of medical staff? With alarm, she wondered if she would be Purpled.

'The Sanderson Ward?' Eve had no idea where it was. She needed to stall for time. 'I'm so sorry, I—'

'There you are, Dad!' A woman rushed up behind the elderly man. 'We had a nightmare in the car park. Those ticket machines, they drive you mad.' Acknowledging Eve with a smile, she added, 'I hope he wasn't holding you up, nurse,' and to her dad, said, 'Now I think we need to go this way…'

Eve nodded and, before they could ask anything else, hurried away.

Approaching A&E, she could see a tall nurse beside a coffee machine. Five foot ten, with dark, wavy hair, Nurse Attride had said, and a wristwatch that has a bright red strap. This seemed to be her – but she was deeply engrossed in conversation with a police officer, the two of them subdued. Eve loitered, attempting to cover her fish-out-of-water nervousness by studying a whiteboard covered in wipe-clean notes, and dearly hoping no one spoke to her. Eventually the tall nurse looked over, and Eve touched the top button of her uniform, the signal she'd been told to give. The tall nurse excused herself and walked towards Eve.

'Nurse Murray?'

'Call me Kelly. You must be Eve.'

'Thank you for this, I do appreciate it.'

'I'm afraid there's not much to thank me for,' said Kelly. 'Luke passed away ten minutes ago.'

Eve was aghast.

'If he hadn't been turned bloody Purple…'

'Are you saying he actually died from being Purpled? It was a side effect?'

'You could say that.' Kelly shook her head and sighed, clearly angry. 'If I smoked, I'd have a bloody cigarette about now. We spend our days trying to save people's lives…'

'Of course…'

'And this is just… so unnecessary. So preventable.'

'I suppose it is. They didn't need to do something so barmy.'

Fixing Eve with an unwavering stare, Kelly said, 'Luke was so distraught about being *turned Purple*' – at these words, she grimaced – 'that he wanted to kill himself. I thought he was pulling through, but with what was in his system…'

'How awful… that he felt so desperate,' said Eve. 'And his poor family.'

Kelly nodded. 'It beggars belief, it really does. I'd better get back. Sorry there wasn't more we could do. I would have liked to help him. I hope you're still going to try.'

'Of course. Perhaps…' Eve retrieved the business card she'd

intended to give Luke, featuring the biroed addition of Womble and Helena's telephone number. 'They may not want to, but if his family feel like talking, maybe you could give them this.'

Kelly looked at the card, adorned with the squiggle of Pam Fox-Jones's hand-drawn face and a picture of a koala holding a phone. Nothing says intrepid news reporter quite like a koala, thought Eve.

'Sure.' Kelly raised her eyebrows, put the card in her pocket, and walked away.

Eve stood, dejected. She felt tired, sad – and guilty that she should claim disappointment at not meeting poor, Purple Luke. Rueful, too, about feeling such fascination for the Purpleness, given this devastating consequence. Yet she remained determined to find out more.

For now, though, she thought, best get back to Dad. And Nurse Attride, with her uniform. About to retrace her steps, Eve noticed that the policeman whom Kelly had been talking to was now getting himself a coffee; he watched as brown liquid squirted in fits and starts into a tin mug. I could certainly use some caffeine, she thought, sidling up to the machine. Standing behind the officer, she said, 'Such terrible news.'

The officer turned, sniffing suspiciously at the contents of the cup in his hand. He had a grey-flecked bushy moustache which, Eve noted, would make him a prime candidate for a Mills Brothers trimmer.

'Poor lad,' Eve continued. 'Imagine feeling so devastated about being Purpled...'

'That's one way of looking at it,' said the officer. He peered towards the machine. 'Do you know where the sugar is with this thing?'

'I think there should be a button...'

'Oh, right.'

'What's the other way?'

'Eh?'

'Of looking at it. The young man being Purpled.'

'Look. I know it's your job to try and patch everyone up, regardless. You don't judge. But I don't suppose you were working here when the boy came in who'd had his ear near bitten off by that Luke?'

'I wasn't—'

'Or when he bit another bloke's nose? That was messy. He needed a lot of stitches.'

Eve pulled a face, feeling queasy, before remembering she was supposed to be a nurse and wouldn't be squeamish.

'Or the people he's attacked with, variously – ' at this, the police officer began a finger count to underscore the weapon tally – 'his fists, a baseball bat, a cricket bat, a concrete bird bath, and – ingenious this – a piece of skirting board, with nails in?' The officer took a sip of his coffee. 'That's a lot of sugar,' he said, approvingly. 'So, while it is sad that he topped himself, and I do appreciate that we shouldn't speak ill of the dead, quite honestly, he won't be missed. Many, many people will now avoid a battering from him. So I'm sorry to say, I don't find the news that terrible.'

Eve wondered if she looked as cross-eyed and conflicted as she felt.

'What would you do,' she asked, sincerely, 'to try and stop the anti-social behaviour? Why do you think people like Luke behave the way they do?'

'There,' said the officer, 'is the million-dollar question. For a lot of them, when I'm seeing them for the fiftieth time, I think: here we go again, all going through the motions. Should we just lock 'em up, and throw away the key? But that's a canny thing with this Purpling, isn't it?'

'What's that?'

'Don't even have to pay to keep them locked up! They have to isolate themselves. Curfew. Pretty much house arrest. That'll save a few quid. Genius.'

He raised his cup in a farewell gesture, and Eve watched as he made his exit through a revolving door; spinning slowly, it sent the officer outside into the sunshine, and, as incoming deliveries, spun out a hobbling man and a small child with a saucepan on his head. Turning away, a weary, bleary Eve made her way back to the other side of the hospital before any passing accidents or emergencies could detain her.

Eve had dozed off on the way to Womble and Helena's, once again dressed in her own frock, nestled on the back seat with the bag of newspapers beside her, her head lolling and rolling with the car's movements. She had been told by the on-duty nurse that she should get some rest, assured that they would call if there was any change to her dad's condition. Simon had already gone home, but Eve had left Linda asleep beside Vince's bed, one hand resting on his blue blanket.

They pulled up outside Womble and Helena's home, in a small town not far from the big one where Eve had grown up. As Helena turned her key in the lock, barking began indoors.

'Hi, Mr Bailey,' she said, as a shiny Golden Retriever bounded to the door. A scruffy terrier continued to yap. 'And hello, Sven.' Helena scratched the terrier's ears and he stopped barking, now licking her hand instead. 'Come on in,' she said to Eve.

'Wait 'til you see what we've resurrected in your honour,' said Womble.

'Though it's only there temporarily,' Helena told him.

'Yes, my love.'

Womble steered Eve through to the kitchen. There, she

noticed some familiar faces peering towards her. Womble's favourite band, straight-faced Swedes, The Svengalis, framed, and hanging a little wonkily on the wall.

'Wow,' she said, stepping towards them. 'That takes me back...'

'Doesn't it?' said Helena.

'My boys,' said Womble, wistfully.

Eve gazed at the poster, raising a hand to her mouth, covering a yawn.

'You must be exhausted after your flight, and the hospital,' said Helena. 'Why don't you go and get ready for bed. I'll bet you've barely eaten, have you?'

'I had a weird thing from the hospital café.'

'I'll bring you up a sandwich, but we can chat tomorrow. And in case you wake up early, and are in the mood for something fluffier than all those hysterical newspapers, there's a stack of magazines for you in the spare room,' said Helena.

'Send yourself to sleep with pictures of skirts and eyeshadows,' said Womble. 'I do it all the time.'

As she lay in bed, Eve sighed appreciatively, stretching, luxuriating at finally being fully horizontal. Her flight seemed so long ago, New York so far away. She thought of Luke, laid stiffly in a morgue somewhere, and her dad, knocked out, in his hospital bed. When would he start to recover – if he recovered? The news was a great distraction from that worry, but what could she do to investigate the Purpleness while sitting at his side, waiting? What could Luke have told her, if they'd had a chance to speak? It was far-fetched (though given what had already happened, little could now be that fantastical), but following the police officer's impression of Luke as a less sensitive soul, was it possible that perhaps he hadn't killed himself – was there a more sinister possibility? It was something to consider. Maybe Womble's friend, science teacher Bunsen Burner Bob, would have some ideas. I must prepare a list of questions, she thought, but nodded off before she could think of any, the duvet rising and falling gently as she quietly snored.

The neon numbers of the clock radio declared it to be 6:04. Eve had tried to get back to sleep, but it was no use. She yawned. Ordinarily she would joke about being able to reach hibernation levels of shut-eye, which reminded her of a popular *Say Fantastique!* story about a girl in Blackpool called Susan who'd slept for two months, waking for only a couple of hours every few days. The newspapers had called her a variety of things: Sleeping Beauty, Snoozy Susie, and Eve's favourite, captioning a photo, 'Susan: Well Rested'.

Picking up the pile of magazines that Helena had put out for her, Eve padded downstairs. The dogs heard and followed her, tails wagging as she let them into the garden. While the kettle boiled for tea, Eve rang the hospital.

'ICU.'

'Morning, this is Eve Baxter, I just wanted to see how my dad is.'

'Hello, Miss Baxter. There's no change, I'm afraid. Your mum is still with him.'

'Ah, okay.' It had been nearly two days now. Was this a bad sign?

'I think there was a message for you.'

'From my mum?'

'No, a man called. Nurse Attride took the details…' There was a rustling of paper as this nurse searched for the message. 'I'm so sorry, I can't find it, but I'll ask her to call when she comes on shift, if that's okay?'

'Great, thanks. Do you know what time she'll be there?'

'She's due on at eight.'

Surely the only person the message could be from was a relative of sadly (or perhaps not so sadly) lost lavender lad, Luke?

Eve looked at the kitchen clock; there would be a couple of hours to wait before she found out.

The kettle reached its crescendo, steam rising towards The Svengalis, as though the band were, not inappropriately, shrouded in dry ice.

Poking from behind the poster, Eve noticed an old photo of herself with Womble and Helena; it tipped into view at an angle, a blob of Blu-Tack holding it in place. The three of them were beaming, drinks in hand. They looked so young, Eve thought. The tinsel surrounding them showed it was taken close to Christmas. It might even have been the party where they'd first encountered Magnus (oh, Magnus... Though these days, she tried not to think about him too much).

Eve had met Womble, and later Helena, at university. Back then Womble was known predominantly for his preoccupation with tidying and recycling (hence the nickname) and his passion for The Svengalis. He was one of the typical music-obsessed boys found at college – the kind who headed straight to the nearest record emporium when their grant cheque came through, and got excited about bands that no one else had heard of appearing at the student union. The type whose method of breaking the ice, throughout freshers' week, was to invite everyone back to their room in halls, and get the assembled chatting, beers in hands, accompanied by the soundtrack of their host's pet LP. Womble had adorned the wall of their student kitchen with a Svengalis poster, and the band would gaze down with their haphazard Scandinavian cool, watching as F Block's students ate toast and kebabs late into the night and in the morning stole someone else's cornflakes.

Womble looked as though he himself could have been a Svengali. Half-Danish, lanky and fair-haired, with a healthy, get up and glow complexion. Eve always found him good-natured and fun to be around, with a serious side that presented itself at the most appropriate moments; he had a canny knack of being there at the right time with the right words of wisdom. They'd bonded in halls in the first year, and subsequently shared a house with Helena and Womble's friend Doug.

Eve and Helena had met during their second term. While sitting in the college canteen one lunchtime, quietly reading, Eve had been approached by a pair of charmless, over-friendly lads who interpreted polite disinclination to chat as a sporting challenge. Minutes ticked by in which she failed to get shot of them. Then she noticed a girl at a neighbouring table rising up and stalking over; this was Helena. Eve had been awed by this girl's striking, nonchalant elegance, which was part bohemian, part glam rock: a stripy, woolly dress, huge tartan scarf, plus clumpy boots and a halo of an afro. Both the latter added to her height – though she was a couple of inches shorter than Eve, her stature felt far greater.

As Helena reached the table, the lads turned towards her, assuming they had a new target for their cockiness.

'Alright, dar—'

Helena had stood unassumingly, first acknowledging Eve with a small nod, then turning to briefly consider the boys with a look which was at once disapproving and disinterested. The boys visibly wilted, shoulders slumping into their plastic bucket seats.

Returning her attention to Eve, Helena had said, 'There you are,' adding, in a tone that declared she knew the answer, 'I'm not interrupting anything, am I?'

Eve shook her head.

To the boys, Helena said politely, 'Don't let us keep you.'

With punctured bravado and not enough wit to respond, they sloped off.

'Thanks,' said Eve. 'That was impressive. So withering. Do you have magical powers?'

'If you'd grown up with my mother, you'd also have perfected deadly disapproval,' Helena said, with a laugh.

'Can I get you an appreciative drink?'

'Sure. Fancy something stronger than a Kia-Ora?' said Helena, as they redirected themselves to the student union bar.

They were a complementary match, each eminently sensible, in their own ways: Eve the daydreaming optimist, Helena cheerfully pragmatic. As they sipped their final drinks on a night out, Eve would abracadabra a scribbled schedule of last buses and trains, while Helena would have squirrelled away cash for an emergency cab, remembering the times they'd run for an infrequent night bus, or stood waiting for one, eating soggy chips in the rain.

When Eve and Womble decided to find a house-share, she invited Helena to join them. The unexpected development of a simmering sexual tension between Womble and Helena provided many hours of discussion and entertainment, like the teasing will-they, won't-they relationship in a television show. So when Eve suspected her own lurking attraction to Doug, it didn't seem sensible to indulge it – with the already present lustings, added to all their newly acquired junk and economy boxes of teabags, there just wasn't room in the house for any more romantic drama. Her regrets in both current affairs and romantic ones were still to come.

*

Sitting with a mug of tea and a plate of jam-smothered toast, Sven and Mr Bailey at her feet awaiting any crumbs that might fall their way, Eve reached towards the pile of magazines. The cover of one featured a blonde, bland model with frosted pink lips and offered 'New Ways to Keep Fit – Tips From Those Who Know', 'Fashion Update: Stripe Yourself Slim', 'Art Attack – Unleash Your Creative Self', and her favourite, 'Gloss Eyed: Creme Shadows that Stay Put'. Eve didn't think this looked like Helena's kind of thing at all, then noticed that it was a complimentary copy sent to the veterinary surgery where she worked. Eve turned to the next one. 'Ms Anarchy – What Our Favourite Rebels Are Doing Now', 'Same Old Style? – How to Push Your Fashion Boundaries', 'Did Your Nan Tan? Bronzing Through the Decades', and 'Thinking Woman's Crumpet? We Meet Theo Fletcher'. Eve immediately turned the page.

It's been almost two years since Theo Fletcher moved into Number Ten, and unlike many of his predecessors, the PM's popularity is consistently rising. There's no end in sight for this honeymoon period, either. Polls show that if there were an election tomorrow, he'd lead his party to victory with 40 per cent of the vote – and even those who support opposition parties would swing for him! But it's not just at the ballot box that he's winning. It seems when it comes to Britain's broads, Theodore William Fletcher can do no wrong. So we were thrilled to get an audience with the prime minister, aka Britain's most eligible bachelor.

Fletcher grew up in Wigan, the youngest of three siblings (his older brother, Edmund, is an engineer, like their father; his sister, Isabelle, is a lawyer), all of whom received scholarships to the grammar school where their mother taught English. Theo was popular, and combined being outgoing and sporty with his academic pursuits: he played football and chess, learnt the powers of persuasion in the school debating team, and claims he had his eye on Downing Street from a young age.

'My parents were very politically engaged,' he told us, 'and would often say that you had to be involved in what was going on around you, that not having an opinion was simply not an option. You can imagine how thrilled they were when I was made captain of the debating society! Though I was just as pleased because I really liked a girl on the team and it gave me an excuse to walk her home – under the guise of society business, of course!'

After studying economics and history at university, during which time he took a gap year – that turned into two – as a volunteer at a disaster relief agency, he joined a humanitarian aid organisation based in Frankfurt. Having proved himself as an analyst there ('probably not the part of my life you're most keen to talk to me about,' he rightly observes!), he returned home to immerse himself in the thick of UK politics. 'I had to go and experience other things before throwing my hat into the ring,' he says. 'It was important to me that I learned something other than this, that I reminded myself why politics is important – or should be important – to us all.'

His popularity was cemented further six months ago when his friendship with 11-year-old Londoner, Jermaine, whose father was killed on his way to work in an unprovoked attack, was revealed (this had been kept private and was only made public following a leak by a parent of another pupil at Jermaine's school). They bonded at a fundraising event for families who'd lost loved ones to crime, and Theo has subsequently been spending time with the youngster, attending his school football matches, and frequently visiting him and his mum, Jacky. In a rare comment about their friendship, Theo said, 'No one can replace Jermaine's dad, and that's not something I'm in any way trying to do. But we've both lost someone we love, and aside from being rewarding and a lot of fun, spending time with Jermaine and Jacky has been as much of a support to me as I hope I've been – and will continue to be – to them.'

Single since his fiancée, Laura, was killed nine years ago – one of six victims in a horrific car crash caused when vandals threw a concrete bollard from a bridge above a motorway – he's been quoted as saying *he strives to do well in Laura's honour, and that he's not looking for romance while in office, instead being 'dedicated to one commitment: serving the people of this country'. With increased funding of both the NHS and a partly re-nationalised railway (those of you who commute will no doubt agree that rail travel satisfaction is at an all-time high), he's certainly keeping his election promises, and says next on his agenda is tackling crime and anti-social behaviour. 'I really believe that gaining some control of that will have a huge impact on the quality of people's lives; it just can't be underestimated,' he says. 'I'm not afraid of taking a big, seemingly insurmountable problem, and wrestling with it – and I always plan to win.'*

Want to know what else he told us? Of course you do…

MW: *Prime Minister, thank you so much for talking to us.*

TF: *My pleasure. My sister would have had words with me if I hadn't!*

MW: *You've already been in office for two years now. How has it been for you?*

TF: *Incredible. It's like climbing a mountain – you've a huge, pretty daunting, task ahead, but the sense of achievement when you make progress, when you can look out and see how far you've come, is beyond description. You breathe in the mountain air, and think: anything is possible. I can do this – or rather,* we *can do this.*

MW: *You've already got some major achievements to your name in that time. Which are you the most proud of, and what do you hope will be your next great accomplishment?*

TW: *Obviously there are things which I think everyone is pretty thrilled about – our support for the National Health Service, and public transport, and untangling the disgraceful privatisation of both those services. But on a personal level, I think providing an accessible childcare network is something that is going to be a massive help to a* lot of families, and make something which was a large financial burden, and a hindrance to many mothers being able to return to work, easier and more bearable. I think my late fiancée, Laura, is smiling down on me somewhere for that. As to next steps: education, and crime control.

MW: Do you think the way in which you lost Laura will affect your approach to crime?

TF: Of course I've thought a lot about this, and I have to say I don't think it will. What it does give me is a complete understanding of what victims of crime go through, and also a desire to have an entirely robust justice system. But then – and this has been said by many people, many times – it's just as important to tackle the issues which lead to crime as much as the crimes themselves.

MW: It's often said that your approach is the polar opposite of your predecessor, the late Milton Hardy. What would you say about that?

TF: Milton was a great man, and a great statesman. We were of such different generations – he was older than my father – that of course we would have incredibly different approaches and outlooks. He definitely brought warmth and a more traditional, even comforting, style with his leadership. With such a successful career in education, so many years spent encouraging young people and showing them the way, being part of communities, he really understood what people want from those in power – from life – and he led this country in a wise, humane way. Some might say he could be old-fashioned, but I think at that time, with various problems this country faced—

MW: Do you mean, for example, the privatised police force, which he inherited?

TF: Absolutely. That, and other issues, along with the incredible speed at which technology was changing – or attempting to change – the way we live, he handled very deftly, always making decisions in the way he thought would benefit the people of this country. If you look at some of those decisions – the restriction of certain technologies, including many computer games, and opting to reinstate Commerce-Free Sundays – you can see how, in comparison to developments in some other countries, we've reclaimed aspects of our society and communities that might otherwise have been lost.

MW: You're frequently credited with – like Milton – being one of a dwindling number of politicians whom people consider to be really genuine, and in whom they're happy to put their faith. Why do you think that is?

TF: Ah, well… It's hugely flattering if people feel that way, of course. I'm here to serve the people of this country, and if anyone puts their faith in me to do that, and believes I'm doing it with the best intentions, then hopefully I'm doing something right. My main motivation is people knowing they can count on me to work hard for them – relentlessly so – and make decisions which I feel will benefit us as a society.

MW: You're also a bit of a – dare we say it – heartthrob, often getting the sort of reaction usually reserved for film stars. What do you make of that?

TF: [laughs, and also – calm yourselves, ladies – blushes] My friends rib me for it, of course. Mary, my housekeeper, thinks it's hilarious, especially when she's picking up the socks I leave all over the house, or sees me trying to cook. Good job I went into politics, by the way – I'd make an awful chef. But really, hopefully that means I'm likeable, and maybe that my passion – which it genuinely is – for doing the best I can in this position of immense responsibility, comes through.

MW: Can we ask how Jermaine is doing?

TF: I'm afraid I don't think it's fair to discuss him. He deserves to be able to maintain his privacy, not to be thrust into the spotlight because of me. Sorry.

MW: Finally, we hear there's been the pitter patter of tiny feet at Number Ten – namely, a new puppy! How's he getting on?

TF: Oh, he's a rascal! He's a rather adorable but mischievous Jack Russell called Archie. The good news is that aside from being a glorious companion, he's helping me keep fit. With the amount of takeaways I eat working at home so many nights, it's good to get out and have a walk!

MW: You walk him yourself?!

TF: Not all the time, but as often as I can. I'm trying to be a good dad!

Ladies, you read it here first! And with that, we left the prime minister to return to more important matters safe in the knowledge that we're in very good hands.

'Morning,' said Womble, appearing on the stairs. 'How are you feeling?'

'As though my brain has turned to custard.'

'Well, there has been a lot going on. Coffee?'

'Lovely,' Eve nodded.

Womble switched on the radio, just catching the end of a news bulletin and the protestations of an MP who seemed keen to encourage a debate about capital punishment, an enthusiasm which many felt was inflated by his shares in a pharmaceutical company which produced the compound used for lethal injections. Eve shuddered at the thought.

As the bulletin moved on to the weather, Womble said of the MP, 'He's wily.'

'Aren't they all,' said Eve.

Womble made a wordless noise in agreement as he poured beans into a coffee chute. He was about to speak, but looked towards the hallway before announcing, in a loud whisper, 'I agree with Theo Fletcher though. With the Purple Scheme. I have to say, after my initial—'

'Hysteria?' Eve smiled.

'*Concern*... I don't think it's all bad. It could be just the spur that some people need. Things can't go on like this, for sure. I'm sick of seeing how some of the kids at school turn out – they just throw their lives away. Sometimes I look at them and think, this is the best we can do? This is the best *they* can do? And it's not only the really bad ones who are more surly and disruptive than they need to be. They need some discipline, some fear. A kick in the pants. I feel quite strongly about it—'

'I'm noticing that.'

'And I'd like to be able to discuss it without being shot down every time,' Womble sighed. 'It's a bit... contentious here. Hel is not a fan, as you can tell. It's been causing a bit of tension. After that press conference, I said, good, someone's giving people a kick up the pants, and Hel went beserk.' Womble mimed an angry face and hands raised like claws.

'You look like a werewolf.'

Womble's posture returned to normal as he sighed again and retrieved an almost empty bottle of milk from the fridge. 'You didn't hear the milkman, did you?'

'I don't think so.'

'Anyway... What was weird was the way the kids at school were talking about it. Something so incredible couldn't help but catch their imagination, and I guessed they'd all be against it, but what was amazing was that they weren't.'

'Kids form their opinions from their parents a lot of the time, though...'

'They do, but so often they not only get demonised – all young people are out of control, blah blah – but they're the ones who are intimidated, or attacked, and some of them were saying, it could help me. If all bad people are going to be turned Purple, and if I'm not Purple, maybe I'll be given the benefit of the doubt. And if there's this new form of protection on the streets, then I'll be safe.'

'They mostly agreed with it?'

'Not mostly, no. But for something that had only just happened, I was surprised – pleased – that some of them agreed with it. Most of them thought it was just like something out of the *Captain's Law* comics. The Juniors will be playing Purple People in the playground before you know it.'

'I don't know what to make of it all,' said Eve. 'I'll think, this is outrageous, you can't do that to a person. And then I'll think, but maybe if that's what it takes... I just don't know. It's incredible, and fascinating. But also confusing.'

'Most people are confused about it.'

'And we should be careful, don't you think? You do seem quite determined already, when we barely know anything about it...'

'I think, look, it's a plan, it might work. Let's give it a chance. Hel thinks it's terrible. She says, we need a fairer society, for everyone to have opportunities.' Womble shook his head, tutted as he poured a dribble of milk into his coffee. 'But I don't think it's all down to that. And even if it was, you can't solve that problem right now, just like that.' He snapped his fingers.

'What problem?' said Helena, wandering into the kitchen in her dressing gown.

'Ah, we're almost out of milk,' said Womble, holding up the glass bottle.

'Oh. I think the milkman's just been,' said Helena, yawning as she headed towards the front door.

'To be continued,' Womble whispered.

Helena returned to the kitchen, milk in hand. 'Make me a coffee, would you?' she asked, leaning over to kiss Womble good morning.

'Of course, my love.'

'Morning, Evie.' Helena leant over and gave Eve a hug. 'Sleep alright?'

Eve nodded, then leant her head wearily on Helena's shoulder.

'No news?'

'Nope. He's still the same.'

'What time do you need to be back at the hospital?'

'As soon as, really.'

'I can drop you on my way to work.'

'Thank you. By the way, how's the new vet getting on?'

'Rory? Seems nice. Quiet. I don't know, I think he—' Helena shrugged. 'I can't tell if he's still settling in, getting the lay of the land, or generally a bit... buttoned up. Honestly, he's a bit too straight. Trying too hard, you know? He could loosen up a bit. I think it'd do him good.'

'He just got divorced,' said Womble.

'Yeah. Sounded tricksy,' said Helena.

'She got custody of the dog,' said Womble.

'He must miss it,' said Helena. 'He was offering to dog-sit for someone the other day.'

'Maybe he's trying to restore some order to his life,' said Eve, 'work being a good distraction. And it's always tricky when you start a new job, he might just want to prove himself.'

'Absolutely. I get it. I just want him to relax. Still, he's good at his job, and the old dears love him. Plus we've been so busy, it's a relief to have an extra vet on board. This whole push to get more abandoned pets re-homed is great—'

'Climate change,' said Womble. 'Don't have a child, get a dog!'

'But we were busy as it was, and that just tipped things over the edge.'

'I read in one of those magazines that Theo Fletcher's got a dog,' said Eve.

'Yep, and now everyone wants a pooch like the one at Number Ten. Very predictable.'

'Lemmings!' said Womble.

'Yes, dear,' said Helena, taking the coffee he'd just made her. 'Though I think you and Bob should invite him out with you one night. He doesn't seem to know many people round here, so he'd probably appreciate it.'

'Anything for you, my love,' he said, prodding a slowly disintegrating Weetabix with a spoon.

'That reminds me,' said Eve. 'Do you think Bob would be up for a chat about the biological possibilities for turning a person purple?'

'Oh, he would love that,' said Womble.

The phone rang.

Helena answered, mouthing, 'It's for you,' and passing the receiver to Eve.

'Eve, hello, this is Shona Attride.'

'Ah, hi,' said Eve.

There was a brief silence to acknowledge the previous day's adventures which couldn't be discussed. Then Nurse Attride said, 'I have a message that was left for you.' There was a pause. 'From a guy called Jason. He wanted to talk to you about his brother, Luke.'

The message was about Purple Luke! Obviously Nurse Attride was having to be cautious as to what she said, but there was no one to overhear Eve.

'Crikey,' she said. 'Kelly had a chance to speak to him?'

'Your message was passed on, yes.'

'That's amazing. Will you thank her? Did he leave a number, or is he going to call me?'

'I've got a number for you.'

'Brilliant,' said Eve, grabbing a pen. Would Jason know anything about how Luke came to be Turned? Eve dearly hoped so.

'I really appreciate this,' she said.

She hung up the phone, and found Womble and Helena both staring at her, expectantly.

'All being well, I might have an illuminating interview on the horizon,' said Eve.

'And you're meeting the police,' said Womble.

'Oh, yes.' Eve felt instinctively queasy at the thought of yet another Baxter encounter with the law. But also sensed the opportunity for wheedling some Purple intel from them. How hard could it be, she thought. They've all been taken by surprise with the scheme, they're on the back foot...

As far as Eve was concerned, where there was a will, there was definitely a way.

Chapter Six

They were due to be meeting in a park close to the hospital. Eve had suggested a café, but Jason insisted the park would be better. 'My friend might come with me,' he'd said. It had crossed Eve's mind that meeting two people associated with a Purpled person in a park could be dicey. But that was making the sort of assumptions that the scheme encouraged, and besides, she wanted to find out more about Luke (as a precaution, she'd told Helena her plans; 'Poor love,' Helena had said. 'Honestly, the Purpleness is just vile').

Eve sat on a bench with a cup of tea, looking over the questions scribbled in her notebook.

When did Luke become Purple?

Was he aware of how he turned Purple? (oral i.e. supplements, or injection… ?)

What were the events leading up to him becoming Purple?

Was he with anyone else who was turned Purple?

How long did the transformation take?

Did he experience any physical side effects?

Eve tapped her pen against the wooden seat, took a sip of tea and then almost spat it out. Like the startling fall in a dream which wakes and disorientates you, she felt her internal organs drop. There appeared to be a real-life Purple person walking towards her. Was she hallucinating?

She tried not to stare, but it really was the strangest thing. His skin was a blueish-mauve, which reminded her of the hydrangeas in her grandparents' garden. His lilac-ed arms and neck poked from a grey t-shirt, against which his skin looked all the more sombre. His fair hair was so short that his violet scalp was visible underneath. That and his blonde eyebrows made him look like a negative of himself. It was startling. Seeing photos couldn't quite prepare you for the real thing – it was like catching sight of a yeti, or Nessie. It appeared so unnatural that Eve wondered if Dr Jake Spiretti had been right, that this was an elaborate ruse, pulled off with the industrious use of stage make up. And yet, when your eyes had adjusted to the unexpectedness, it did look more simply like skin that was entirely bruised. Thus Theo Fletcher's branding of such hue-mans as 'bruises on society' was damningly apt. Eve was transfixed.

She was so distracted that she hadn't noticed Hydrangea's companion, who was a more traditional shade of beige.

'Eve?' said the beige man, as they approached.

Was she imagining this? Eve was certain she'd woken this morning, already been to the hospital and seen her dad before coming here. But perhaps it was all a dream?

Eve nodded, rising slowly. 'That's me.'

'Jason,' said Beige.

'Jason!' said Eve. 'So good to meet you. Thank you for coming.'

'And this is Finn,' said Jason, putting a hand on Hydrangea's shoulder.

'Finn,' said Eve. 'Hello.' She extended a hand to shake his and watched, in what felt like slow motion, her pale, peachy palm clasp his plum one. The bruised effect was disconcerting; Eve wondered if it pained the Purpled person to touch them. She watched; Finn didn't flinch.

'I told Finn you want to find out how people are being Turned,' said Jason. 'That's why he's here.'

'Great, thank you,' said Eve, 'both of you. Shall we sit down?'

Jason and Finn sat side by side. Eve sat down sideways on the bench, to Jason's right, and turned to face them both. 'What happened to you?' she asked Finn. 'How did they do this?'

Much to her surprise, he said, 'I've no idea.'

'You don't know?'

'Nope.'

'Do they sedate you while they do it?'

'No.'

'Does it happen at a police station?'

'No.'

'Were you arrested before it happened?'

'No.'

This was like Twenty Questions.

'Did you see it happen?'

'Yes. Well, no. I just saw my skin start to go like this.'

'But did you see what happened to make it turn?'

'No.'

Eve glanced down at her list of queries.

'What happened in the lead up to your skin changing?'

'I went out, was at the pub, came home, went to bed, woke up in the night, and there were patches of me going this colour. Really weird.'

'When was that?'

'Friday.'

'And you started to change colour on Friday night?'

'Yeah. Well, Saturday morning.'

'Did something happen at the pub? A fight? Any incidents? Something that might be considered criminal, or anti-social?'

Finn looked uncomfortable.

'Well...'

'Look,' said Eve gently. 'I'm not here to judge, I'm just keen to work out how this has happened to you.'

'Right. Well. I'm not usually... I'm not one for—'

'What Finn's trying to say is that he's not like my brother, he doesn't get into trouble with the law.'

Finn looked sheepish, may have blushed, but it was hard to tell under his mauveness. 'And my family would... Anyway. I'm not proud of this. I did it as a dare, really... but I stole a box of money.'

'A box of money?'

'Those charity things they have in shops, next to tills. There was one in the pub, and I took it.'

'Did anyone see you? Were there any police officers there?'

'I don't think so. I mean, I'd had a lot of beer by then, you know, it being Friday night. If someone had seen me, they would've said something, right? Told me to put it back? Told the people behind the bar?'

'You'd think so. After that, did you have another drink, that someone could have put something in? Did you feel anyone bump into you, or – this sounds mad, I know – inject anything into you, maybe?'

'Well, like I say, I don't remember that much, but I don't remember anything weird, either. I'd have felt it if I was injected. There could have been something in my drink, I don't know.'

'But you did have another drink after you took the collection box?'

'I think so.'

'Anything else that you can remember, however small it might seem? Any encounters with anyone after you took the box, on the way home?'

'No, sorry. I mean, I've been thinking about it, but I just don't know. I walked home, didn't meet anyone or talk to anyone or anything.'

'And there weren't any other incidents before the pub? Earlier that day, or on Thursday, or earlier in the week?'

'No. I was just at work, nothing special.'

'It's so peculiar,' said Eve.

'I know, I don't get it. It's like a weird trick,' said Finn.

'If you like,' said Eve, 'I could take the collection box back for you.'

This wasn't an entirely altruistic suggestion; she did wonder if the managers of the pub from which it had been taken might let her take a look at the ISON footage from that night.

'Great,' said Finn, with a look of relief.

'What about Luke?' Eve asked Jason.

'He was in that place, whatever it was, with the guys who were in the papers.'

'The first photos, the man in the sweatshirt, and the other two?'

'Yep.'

'Was he... was he his usual colour when he went there?'

'Yep. He was on remand. Which wasn't a big deal for him. He was inside, you know, a lot. Then he tells Mum they've moved him, said he isn't allowed visitors.'

'Did you know where he was?'

'He said the name of some place. But it wasn't local. We didn't know where it was. And when he said we couldn't see him—' Jason shrugged. 'He'd been in a few jails, so we didn't think it was a big deal. I thought he didn't want Mum spending money to get there, that was why he said not to come.'

'How long was he there for?'

'A month, might've been longer. We stopped hearing from him. Which wasn't that strange, he'd do that sometimes when

93

he was inside. Then Friday he turns up, delivered by police van, at Mum's. And he's Purple.'

'Did he say what had happened?'

'He said some stuff. He said what had happened in that place. There were a lot of them.'

'Purpled people?'

'Yep. All the blokes there. And after they'd been made Purple, they weren't allowed to speak to anyone outside.'

'No communication at all? Letters?'

'No.'

'How did he become Purple?'

'He didn't know.'

'Really? So he arrived and he was his usual colour, and then at some point at that facility, he became Purple?'

'Yep.'

'Did any of the others there know what had happened?'

'No. He said they ran tests on them.'

'What sort of tests?'

'Physical tests, doctors checking them, he wasn't sure what for.'

'Maybe for side effects,' said Eve, jotting this down in her notebook.

'They made them do a lot of counselling,' said Jason. 'Made them watch videos of victims of crime talking, and their families, you know, saying how it had felt, to have whatever thing happened to them happen to them. They told them they were scum.'

'They used that word?'

Jason considered this. 'Might not have, that was probably just how Luke told it. They told them they were wicked and deserved to be punished. Oh, and… I didn't get this bit, I thought maybe they were trying to help, but there were no mirrors there.'

'So they couldn't see what they looked like?'

'No. Well, they could see it when they looked at themselves, you know, their arms and legs and body, but they couldn't look in a mirror. Luke couldn't see his face.'

'But they would see each others?'

'Yeah. Strange.'

'And what effect did all of it have on Luke?'

'I think he was angry. Frustrated. I mean you would be, wouldn't you? You've turned a funny colour...' Addressing Finn, Jason said, 'No offence, mate,' before continuing, 'You don't know what's happened to you, or what it means, you're locked up with a load of people who have also been made that colour, and you can't talk to anyone you know. I think it sort of... messed with his head. He was always a hard nut, you know – I was scared of him, I'll be honest – I saw what he did to people, but he never laid a finger on me, or Mum. He was just like a powder keg all the time, some small thing and bang, he was off. But when he got back, he seemed... I thought maybe they'd drugged him.'

'Sedated him?'

'Yep.'

'And, if you don't mind talking about it, what happened before he was taken to hospital?'

'So. He'd been pretty strange all day. Which you would be, you know, sent home a funny colour, that no one's seen before. You're going to feel weird, aren't you? You can't escape it. Anyone you see can see it. He just sort of sat about. On the sofa. Drank...'

'What did he drink?'

'Beer. Maybe vodka? He talked to Mum a bit. She was hysterical, you know? "How did this happen to you? What did they do?" And he just didn't know. Then really late – I was in bed, Mum was in bed, we thought Luke was in bed – there was a loud smash. I thought, here we go, he's kicking off, which would be typical for him, really, like before. Definitely before. Usually if he was kicking off about something though, he'd find someone to take it out on. He was locked in the bathroom. I thought I'd stay out of the way, really. But I could hear Mum banging on the door, saying let me in, let me in – frantic. He wouldn't reply. So she called the ambulance. They were thrilled to get our address... They came though, kicked the door in, and he was unconscious, on the floor. He'd taken a load of pills.'

'Do you think... ?'

'He topped himself?' Jason was quiet for a moment. 'You would never think he would top himself. Never.'

'So it could have been accidental, the drinking, taking some pills, and if he'd already been sedated... ?'

'Do you know what's strange, though,' said Jason. 'The crash we heard – he'd hit his head so hard against the mirror that it was smashed.'

'Another accident?'

'Or that...'

'Go ahead,' said Finn. 'Say it.'

'That seeing himself in the mirror...'

The three of them sat silently for a while.

'How are you feeling?' Eve asked Finn.

Finn shrugged.

'You're brave to be out.'

'Mm. My uncle's a police commissioner, he'll get me changed back. Soon. I didn't hurt anyone.'

'Your uncle's a police commissioner? And you *can* get changed back?'

'I hope so.'

'But still you spoke to me?'

'Luke wouldn't have got Turned back,' said Jason. 'I wanted Finn to talk to you for him.'

At this point a group of young men around the same age as Eve's companions wandered into the park. They stared at Finn as they passed, heads turning in unison like a mob of meerkats. Eve kept her expression neutral, but felt her heartbeat pick up pace; with swagger, plus an exchange of glances and smirk-inducing whispered remarks, this seemed to be the sort of assembly that'd look for trouble, and would a Purple person be more, or less, of a target? Finn may have been thinking the same thing; his feet bobbed up and down in a nervous twitch.

To Eve's surprise, the meerkats gave nods – of approval? – in Finn's direction, and ambled on. She watched as Finn kicked his previously agitated feet in front of him, legs spread, and leant back, now a picture of casual confidence.

Addressing Jason, Eve said, 'I'm curious – and I say this as someone whose brother has been in trouble with the police his whole life – why do you think Luke behaved as he did? Before the Purpling. When he would attack people.'

'I've no idea. He'd get so wound up. But he seemed to enjoy it. You'd watch him, and he'd get a rush from it...'

Eve wanted to ask more – about where they grew up, their home life, the rest of their family... but she didn't want to be insensitive, given the circumstances. With her own family background, she knew as well as anyone that sometimes there wasn't a well-lit explanation behind any bad behaviour (and if there was an explanation, was that enough of an excuse?).

Jason's words echoed Eve's assessment of herself and Simon. 'You look at him and me, we grew up the same, but... I couldn't do what he did. To hurt someone, to physically hurt them... No, I couldn't do it.'

During the earliest of Simon's skirmishes with the law, when the police came round Eve would be sent to her room, kept out of the way. But as their visits became more frequent, shielding her seemed an increasingly pointless pretence. After a couple of years, Linda knew how two or three of them liked their tea and that one officer, a stoutish guy, was allergic to wheat, so could never eat the digestives. And there was always something new with the charges. Simon dabbled, fairly unsuccessfully, in all sorts of things, but if there were an E for effort on his criminal record, it would have been awarded for theft, and getting into fights. 'Apparently we're never going to get any peace, are we?' Linda had once said to him, exasperated, during one visit from Anti-Wheat and a less intolerant colleague. The police visits had gone from being met by tears and disappointment to bitterness-tinged defeat. 'I just don't know where he gets it from,' Linda would say, seemingly perpetually surprised at his behaviour, implying that she would only expect such rotten wood when criminality had already grown in the family tree.

One time Simon had been growing marijuana in the seldom-used garden shed. He'd improvised the requisite light with a pair of old desk lamps, one of which subsequently overheated and caught fire when the family was out. A next-door neighbour spotted smoke escaping under the shed door and managed to tackle the infant blaze, but his wife had already called the fire brigade who, upon surveying the scene, subsequently alerted the police.

Eve had watched as her parents stood beside the blackened shed, with Simon and a couple of bemused officers.

'Get your coat, son, and let's go down to the station for a chat, shall we?' said one.

'You're arresting him for that?' Vince had asked, looking incredulously from the officer to the charred, wilted weeds lined up pathetically across the shed floor. 'He was hardly going to get anywhere with those, was he? He'd have better luck hawking glue-sticks.'

Eve hadn't been sure if their dad was more disappointed by Simon's relentlessly illegal activities or by the distinct haplessness of this particular endeavour.

Usually he was one for goading, for starting the fire (whether literal or metaphorical) and then walking away, and his rap sheet was repetitive when it came to criminal mischief. But a disregard for the law and a rarely seen sense of empathy could make for worse misdemeanours. After one incident that had landed an acquaintance of Simon's in hospital (verdict: misadventure), Linda had said, 'Never thinks of anyone else. Like father, like son,' before excusing herself to get her coat.

As far as Eve could remember, it had been her only utterance of its kind.

At the hospital, Vince's condition remained unchanged. Linda sat reading the biography of an actor who'd been most successful many moons ago, debonair and twinkly-eyed in monochrome, always getting laughs – and the girl. Simon flicked half-heartedly through the papers' sports pages, attempting occasional dad-oriented comments which would fall flat after a few words, his doubtful attempt at engaging Vince floundering like a hooked fish hanging in the air (Simon had suggested to Vince that they go fishing once – his friend Duncan had gone frequently with his dad, packing rods and sandwiches – to which Vince had murmured inconclusively).

Eve had wanted to work, to percolate on the meeting with Jason and Finn – her first encounter with *an actual Purple person* – and to search what they'd said for clues. Or at the very least, bury herself in the day's newspapers, which she'd stocked up on at the hospital kiosk. But she found herself unable to concentrate, too anxious from the bleeps and hisses of the machines, her Mum's enforced calm, and Simon's itchy irritation. It was stifling.

Simon had excused himself for yet another cigarette when the police arrived. Two officers knocked on the door, behind the glass, one of them holding up a hand in an introductory gesture. They hovered outside in the hallway.

Linda squeezed Vince's hand again. 'We'll be right back,' she told him, answered by a bleep and hiss.

Eve and her mother stepped outside. The female officer introduced herself as PC Elworthy; the male looked familiar to Eve, but she couldn't quite place him. He looked too young to have been to their house, back in the day.

'Mrs Baxter,' the male officer said, shaking her hand. 'I'm sorry to hear about your husband.'

'Ex-husband, really,' said Linda, 'but thank you, Frankie.' She turned to Eve. 'Doesn't Frankie look smart?'

Eve nodded, still nonplussed.

Back to Frankie, Linda continued, 'Following in your dad's footsteps?'

The officer smiled. 'That's right. He's in the force again now, too.'

'Is he? So who's in charge of The Fox?'

'Debs. She and her husband are running it.'

'Frankie!' At last Eve twigged. 'I didn't recognise you.'

'Don't worry, it's been a good few years.' To PC Elworthy, Frankie said, 'Eve used to babysit me and my sister.'

'Right.' PC Elworthy nodded, then, opening her notebook, said, 'Shall we sit down?'

They settled on some plastic seats in the unit's reception area; chairs lined the walls, and they took a corner quartet, their meeting forming a V, with PC Elworthy being careful not to bump her knees into Linda's.

Linda nervously clasped her hands together.

'So, what can you tell us?'

'The man we've identified as having perpetrated the attack on your husband is now in custody and has admitted the assault.'

'He's confessed?' Eve asked.

'He has, yes. And we have eye-witnesses to corroborate his statement.'

'What happened?'

'It was an unprovoked assault. Your father was at the bar, the assailant approached him, subsequently striking him in such a way that your father fell backwards, hitting his head on a table. It was obviously very unfortunate that he fell as he did – nine times out of ten he shouldn't have come away from that with more than a black eye.'

'Why did he hit him?'

'Why do some people do anything? Pointless violence. The barman said the assailant was complaining about how long he was having to wait to be served, and your dad told him to—' PC Elworthy consulted her notebook – '*Pipe down* were the exact words, so the barman said. With some idiots that's all it takes. Just another thug with eager fists, I'm afraid.'

'So you've charged him?'

'Correct,' said PC Elworthy, looking up as Simon returned and, seeing this gathering in the corner, walked warily towards them.

'The officers are filling us in on the man who hit your father,' Linda said.

'Right,' said Simon. He sat down next to Eve, and perched on the edge of his seat, fidgeting.

'The message we were given said something about him being Turned Purple...' said Eve. 'Is that really true?'

Her plastic chair squeaked as PC Elworthy shifted uncomfortably.

'That is correct, yes. Under recent guidelines an offence like this would incur such a penalty.'

'When will it happen? And how?'

'He will be treated later on today,' said PC Elworthy. 'We're not able to give any further details as to what that entails.'

'Will he be kept in custody?' Linda asked.

'No, he'll be released later tomorrow and bailed until his court hearing.'

'And he'll be Purple?'

'By the time he wakes up tomorrow morning, yes.'

'Gosh,' said Linda.

'Who'll do the Turning?' Eve asked.

'I can't comment on that,' said PC Elworthy, pursing her lips.

'Purple,' Linda said. 'It's astonishing.'

'What if it doesn't work?' said Eve.

'It's early days, but so far we're finding the scheme effective,' PC Elworthy said.

'No, I mean, what if he doesn't Turn Purple? What if it doesn't work on him? I mean, how are you—'

PC Elworthy said, 'Experience thus far assures us it will. So he'll get what's coming to him, don't you worry.'

'Not like the old days, eh?' said Frankie, trying to lighten the conversation.

PC Elworthy put her hat on, signalling their departure. 'We'll be in touch if there are any further developments.'

Eve watched them stride down the corridor. Police one, reporter nil, she thought. Then, applying her *Say Fantastique!*

cute animal filter, pictured a perplexed squirrel: this was going to be a hard nut to crack.

The Shifty Fox peered down, one paw in the air as he moved stealthily forward, lit by the moonlight. The pub sign remained the same: a suitably shifty fox with sinister Hound of the Baskervilles leanings; rusty red against a navy sky which made black silhouettes of the unfortunate fowl behind him.

It was rare that Eve truly craved alcohol, but by lunchtime she needed a distractingly stiff drink.

Debbie was behind the bar when Eve walked in. Eve's nose immediately twitched at the whiff of smoke in the air (there was one good thing about being in the hospital, she thought, before immediately chastising herself). When she was younger, babysitting for Debbie and Frankie, Eve had found it fascinating, spending time in a pub before she was old enough to drink there. The tunes from the jukebox and the clattering of coins in the fruit machine had seemed like decadent sounds from another world which Eve couldn't wait to be part of. They mingled in the air with cigarette smoke and the hopeful aromas of aftershave and hairspray, as guys winked across the bar at girls who batted their eyelashes from beneath the flick of Lady Di fringes.

Glancing around now, Eve saw that everything looked almost identical to how it had decades ago – the whirling pattern of the wine-coloured (and no doubt wine-doused) carpet; the flashing lights of the fruit machine; the fuzzily focused and now faded photographs hanging on the walls, a gallery of hair dos and fashion don'ts from across the decades. Even the songs playing seemed to be the same. Eve was confused. She was sure she'd been back here since she moved to New York, and it hadn't been like this.

'Hiya, Eve,' Debbie said. 'We've not seen you in a while.'

'I know,' Eve replied, 'And am I going mad, or is everything in here new – but old?'

Debs laughed. 'The wonders of the Rollback… Dad had kept a load of stuff in the garage, and one of his mates found the games machine and convinced him to bring it in. So of course then it snowballed…' She shrugged. 'What can I say? People love it. Except Mum, that is. She wasn't best pleased. "Brian, so now we will live in a timewarp?"'

Photos on the wall near the till showed Debs and Frankie's family over the years; the lessening volume of their mum's hair, their dad in uniform, then out, then in again, and two young children – presumably Debs's kids – beaming over the side of a paddling pool in the garden.

'How are they, your mum and dad?'

'Great, thanks. Just celebrated their thirtieth wedding anniversary.'

Debs plucked a nearby picture frame from the wall and laid it on the bar next to Eve. Each with a champagne glass raised to the camera and a cocktail parasol tucked behind one ear, the couple smiled for the camera. It was becoming odd to look at natural skin colours, Eve thought, noting the naturalness of Ming and Brian's Asian and European complexions, and realising she was constantly on the lookout for lavender folk.

'Anyway,' said Debs. 'How are you? It's a bit of a Baxter reunion you being here too. Simon's been in quite a lot, with your dad a few times.'

Eve felt a pang – of what, jealousy? Jealous of those two?

'How is your dad? I heard what happened.'

'He still hasn't come round…'

'I'm sorry. He'll be back on form before you know it, I'm sure. Now, what can I get you?'

'A gin and tonic, please.'

Eve felt someone tap her shoulder, so lightly she almost didn't notice. Beside her, also all grown up, was Duncan (it was like that recently resurrected TV show, *This is Your Life*, in here this evening, she thought, featuring a personal parade of blasts from the past). He gave her a warm, unwavering smile.

'The usual, please, Deb, and I'll get whatever Eve's having.' Duncan reached into a pocket for his wallet.

'Duncan!' Simon's childhood partner in crime; or rather, all but crime. Duncan was the sensible one, and – oddly, to Eve – they'd been inseparable.

'Hello, stranger.'

Debbie and Duncan exchanged some friendly banter as she poured the drinks; she handed him his change, which he discreetly dropped into the tip jar.

'Blimey, it's been years,' said Eve.

'Certainly has. What brings you here?' Duncan asked.

'I was at the hospital and Frankie was there, which made me think of this place, and so… I thought I'd come by, have a quiet one.'

'I heard about your dad. I'm really sorry. Any news?'

'Not yet.'

'You okay?' Duncan's forehead creased with concern.

Eve poured the little bottle of tonic into her gin, watching the lime slice bob about. 'Sort of… I—' She was about to comment on how it was less her dad's condition than her feelings about it which were worrying her. She gave a shrug. 'Anyway.' She glanced behind him. 'What are you up to?'

'Lunchtime pint. Change of scenery, quick flick through the paper, you know. Not that there's much worth reading these days…'

'*Au contraire!*' said Eve. 'I think the Purpleness is fascinating.'

Duncan's head tipped diplomatically from side to side. 'It's remarkable, that's for sure.' He squinted. 'I've been trying to avoid getting roped into conversations about it, but you'll be well versed, won't you. What do you make of it? You for or against?'

'I'm not sure… The guy who punched my dad is getting Purpled – maybe that's a good thing. But overall, I don't know.' This despite her conversation with Jason. Luke had been so violent, caused such damage to others – hadn't he deserved to be singled out? But then light-fingered Finn… Eve looked at Duncan. 'You?'

Duncan was mid-sip. He put down his glass. 'Fletcher's right in that everyone should be able to feel safe. But I don't think it's a kind way to treat people, whatever they've done. There's going to be a protest against it, so the papers say.'

'Really? I'd like to go to that.'

'Yeah, I was thinking about it. Do you want to… ?' He indicated towards a table, and they sat down.

'Simon said you're living in New York?'

'You two still gad about together?' Eve was surprised.

'I know he's away a lot, but when he's here, yeah.'

'Oh.'

'You should come along next time me and Si meet up.'

'Ah… from the encounters I've had with him since I got here, I don't think that's a good idea. I don't see things improving between us.'

'He's not all bad.'

'He's just been pretending all these years?' Eve briefly covered her face with her hands. 'I'm so sorry. I don't know what it is with them, they just have this ridiculous effect on me. Always have. I shouldn't be such a wench, I know – especially right now, I must sound dreadful – but he and my dad just drive me nuts.'

'I know how things used to be,' said Duncan. 'Can't say I

was surprised when I heard you'd upped sticks. That's some distance you've got yourself there, but life is short, right?'

Eve half-nodded, looking down at the lime slice.

At the hospital earlier, she had realised she'd forgotten how proud she used to feel of her dad. How he'd turned heads. But then, she knew what was coming. The shame. Pride before a fall, every time. And now, did she think that if – *if* – he died, he'd just go, oblivious to everything he'd done, getting away without acknowledging or apologising for any of it? That anything Eve might want to say – if she could let herself dwell on it long enough to find the words, to condense so many years of bitterness and disappointment into a deliverable nugget – would go forever unsaid? Did she want him to say sorry? Or, even if he had the chance, would it be too late? Was she crazy to crave an apology as much as his recovery?

Duncan touched her arm. 'You okay?'

'Sorry,' said Eve. 'My brain keeps wandering.'

'Understandable,' said Duncan. 'So, are you New York's answer to Diane Forbes yet?'

Diane was one of the newsreaders from their childhood.

'Becoming ever older and not presently reading the news? I certainly am.' Eve gave a wry smile. 'I seem to have become a little distracted from that path.'

'Really? I'm surprised.'

'I think I'm a bit surprised too.'

He was looking at her, curious. His eyes were a greyish blue (not that she tended to notice the shade of people's peepers), and this observation brought a random fact learned at *Say Fantastique!* unexpectedly to mind: that the song 'Smoke Gets in Your Eyes' is surprisingly popular at cremations. The nonsense your brain is filled with, she thought, taking an over-eager sip of gin and accidentally tipping some down herself.

Eve was mortified, but Duncan laughed, and ducked over to the bar to grab some serviettes.

'I remember when your dolls used to present current affairs programmes!'

Eve groaned, attempting to hide behind a gin-tinged napkin.

'That's quite enough about me,' she said. 'What are you up to these days?'

'Carpentry,' Duncan said, adding, with a straight face, 'Just like Jesus.'

Eve laughed, then noticed his toned arm muscles, and had to remind herself not to stare.

'That must be satisfying.'

'To build a thing from scratch, yeah. Gives you a sense of achievement. And it's a… meditative sort of process, I suppose.'

Eve nodded, thought of she and Adio, plugged into the Portal, glugging vodka, and of Duncan in his workshop, carving beautiful, lasting creations; of Womble, teaching, and of Helena at the surgery with ailing animals. No frivolous occupations for them.

'I've bought an old house which needs a lot of work. There's a big garden – I'm trying to sort that out. So that's a project, keeping me out of mischief.'

'Of course you'd be out and about in the garden. You were in that kids' wildlife group – you were always gadding about with them.'

'Ah yes, being the green-fingered little anorak that I was. Not much change there. I'm a green-fingered big anorak now! You can't beat being outdoors, part of the actual world. Puts things in perspective. They should make everyone spend more time outside.' Duncan grinned. 'Seeing as they're so keen on forcing things on people now.'

'True,' said Eve. 'And how's your dad?'

'Good, thanks.'

'Still fishing?'

'Still fishing,' Duncan smiled. 'How's your mum doing?' he said. 'She must be beside herself.'

'Yeah. You can imagine. It's…' Eve let out a slow breath.

'They were sweet together,' said Duncan.

'Are you *quite* sure about that?' Eve reached across and gently put a palm to Duncan's forehead, as though checking his temperature.

'They could be good fun.'

'Very diplomatic.'

'It was never dull.'

'Correct,' said Eve, about to comment further when a policeman approached the table. It was Frankie.

'Hi again,' he said. 'I was told I might find you here. Your dad's come round.'

'He has? Is he okay?'

'Seems to be in good working order. He recognises everyone.'

'Wow,' said Eve. She put her hands on the table to steady herself. It was a little wet from the gin. Her dad was okay. Which was incredible. Yet was it terrible that she slightly dreaded seeing them all?

'I'm going back to the hospital,' said Frankie. 'I can give you a lift.'

'Yes, thank you.'

'I just need a quick word with Debs – see you outside.'

Frankie headed towards the bar.

'What fantastic news,' said Duncan, standing to give her a hug goodbye.

'Yep,' said Eve, now momentarily distracted by how strong Duncan was; that had been an unexpectedly medicinal embrace.

'It's been great to see you,' said Duncan.

'You too.'

'Give your dad my best.'

'Will do.'

Eve waved a goodbye in Debs's direction and headed outside.

'I've never been in a police car before,' said Eve, who couldn't help thinking of how many times Simon had been delivered home in one.

'Congratulations,' said Frankie, amused. 'You're a model citizen.'

'Thank you, officer.'

'It's good news about the bloke who hit your dad.'

'Absolutely.'

'He's a right piece of work, I can tell you. It was a pleasure to see him tucked away in the cells.'

'He'll be getting Purpled sometime around now...' said Eve.

Frankie nodded.

'I can't imagine.'

'I know. It's pretty weird.'

As innocuously as she could muster, Eve continued, 'It'd be odd to see that being done to you.'

Frankie glanced at her. 'I suppose, if that's what happens.'

'Is it?'

Frankie slowed down as they reached a red traffic light. 'I can't talk about that.'

'Rats,' said Eve.

They waited, watching the light.

'It's such a puzzle. It would be strange to have a top secret operation, where some people don't know how they're Turned but some do.'

'Eve,' said Frankie, 'if you're trying to pull a sly one on me here...'

'Can you tell me if those Purpled after a crime see how it happens to them?'

'No.'

'No you can't tell me, or no they don't know?'

The light turned to green. Frankie gave a faint smile as he pulled away, impressed by her determination.

'Take your pick.'

'They can't know.'

Frankie said nothing.

'Do you know how they're Turned?'

Again, Frankie was quiet.

'I know this is a crazy question, but are *you* doing any of the Turning?'

'Eve!'

'Sorry! It's just so – *mesmerising*, the whole thing. I want to know more.'

They passed a man walking a whippet, who gave Frankie a wave; Frankie raised his hand to wave back.

'Who's that?' asked Eve.

'A bloke who used to work at the station.'

'Nice dog.'

'Yeah. He used to have a greyhound, not sure what happened to that.'

'Maybe it shrank,' said Eve, and Frankie laughed.

They pulled into the hospital car park. Frankie turned off the engine.

'Eve, you know if I talked about any of this, I would be in major trouble?'

'I can imagine.'

'I really can't say anything about it. Even if I wanted to, I can't.'

'Okay.' Eve paused. 'Do you want to?'

'*Eve!*'

'That's a yes!'

'You're incorrigible! It's a no. It has to be, you know that.' Frankie took a breath. 'I also think – it might be best not to go around asking people about it. Those in the know are really secretive, keeping everything under wraps. After the way everyone found out, the top brass are being really jumpy, so my guess is they'd over-react to any sort of investigating.'

'I'm not investigating. I'm just curious. Thought I'd be cheeky and ask, on the off-chance you could say anything.'

'Well, I'm sorry, but no go.'

'I understand.'

'It was good to see you though. Glad your dad's on the mend.'

'Thanks so much for letting me know.' Eve moved to open the door. 'And for the lift.'

'You're welcome.'

Eve walked back into the hospital, picturing the little squirrel banging its head against a tree.

Chapter Seven

When Eve arrived, Vince was sitting up in bed, with Linda beaming beside him.

'Dad,' said Eve, 'you're back in the land of the living.'

'Hi, love,' said Vince, as Eve leaned over to kiss him.

'Aren't we lucky?' said Linda. 'No lasting damage.'

'You've got the all clear?'

'Yeah, they seem to think so. They're doing scans and whatnot. It takes more than this – ' he tilted his head back and forth – 'to keep me out for the count.'

'We were so worried,' said Linda. 'Such a frightening thing to happen. We really thought we might lose you.' She put her hand on Vince's arm.

'No such luck,' said Vince, as he looked up and winked at her. To Eve he said, 'And here you are, back from the Big Apple. That's what it takes to get you home, eh?'

Eve murmured a non-specific response.

'What happens now? How long are they keeping you in for?'

'A little while so they can keep an eye on him,' said Linda. 'Then he'll be able to go home.'

There was a moment's quiet as Eve's parents exchanged

smiles and fond, tactile touches. For once Eve wished that Simon was there to interrupt the proceedings with an inappropriate remark.

'Mum's told you that they got the guy who hit you?'

'So I heard.'

Eve was about to ask if he'd also heard what would happen to him – of course, Vince had missed the whole Purple saga – when a nurse entered the room.

'Mr Baxter, how are you feeling?'

'Alright, love, thanks,' then with a chuckle that turned into a raspy cough, he added, 'I'd feel a whole lot better if you could sneak me in a beer and a fag.'

The nurse smiled. 'I don't think the doctor would approve of that, would she?'

'Can't blame a bloke for trying, eh?' said Vince, with another wheeze. He squeezed Linda's hand. 'You being here the whole time, it's really something.'

'Anything for you, you know that,' said Linda.

'I'll go and get us some tea,' said Eve, already feeling the need for more gin.

Twenty-four hours later, Eve was waiting at a bus stop. A sticker for an enterprising taxi company had been bunged onto the framed timetable introducing an element of public transport roulette to anyone wanting to catch the number 93 on a weekday evening, which reminded Eve of the days when folk would simply order a car service from their PortAble. That night she was going to the recording of a televised debate; she looked at her watch, calculating how much time she'd have to get ready before going out.

Vince had been given the all-clear and was due to be discharged the following day; he'd be going to stay at Linda's while he recuperated. Even an end-of-the-pier psychic could accurately predict what would happen next; the way her parents were behaving, Eve wouldn't be surprised if they were officially re-entangled before she'd escaped back to New York. But for now, of course, there was still the Purpleness, ripe for unravelling.

The information she'd gleaned from Jason was enlightening in some ways. It seemed most likely that Luke had been part of the Purple trials, hidden away while the government figured out whether the science of the scheme would work. Less illuminating was the mystery surrounding the method of transformation. Eve hadn't anticipated no one knowing how it had happened to them, instead assuming they simply weren't allowed to say anything. And strangely, there was no comment in the newspapers as to how people were being Turned. Eve was certain that other reporters were investigating – surely? – but it seemed that the best chance for jimmying any kind of useful information into the proceedings would be a pretty substantial leak from someone in the know. Presumably this meant slippery-lipped police or senior government officials. Eve remained determined regarding the overall task, but doubted her ability to rustle up either of those. Her first attempt, to sweetly procure details from Frankie, had failed, and if she was going to have an intel-rustling shot with any officer of the realm, it would have been him. She'd read him bedtime stories, for goodness' sake (his favourite had been one about a daredevil turnip).

Eve had just visited the pub where Finn seemed likely to have been Purpled. The landlords had gone for mid-century décor: crimson velour banquettes, starburst clocks and ads featuring Brylcreemed lads and polished, nip-waisted ladies. This was matched by the music including tunes by a band that her dad had used to like – and the sensory overload of timewarpiness, added to the increasingly brain-fizzing puzzlement of the Purpleness, quickly threatened to make her feel quite woozy. But she had returned the collection box, and the appreciative pub owners had let her take a look at the ISON footage from that night. Eve watched a recorded Finn pinch the box and tipsily hide it, not at all convincingly, under his shirt. She saw him go outside to his friends, return to the bar to retrieve the remainder of his just-bought round, then loiter outside again, laughing and larking about. Eve didn't see anyone approach him, or bump into him. She couldn't even see anyone paying Finn any particular attention, and the owners said they hadn't seen anything out of the ordinary. She scrolled back and forth through the footage, thoroughly perplexed, until the landlady loudly cleared her throat, asking Eve if she wanted a drink. Eve had politely declined, handing back the ISON monitor, and with parting words of gratitude, made her way towards the door.

The bus arrived, and as she took a seat, Eve glanced at the headline on one passenger's paper: 'Lav Thug Killed my Hamster'.

Five days in, with few new developments and little information, most papers were coasting as best they could, continuing to fill pages with strident opinion pieces heavily peppered with public reactions: '"What they need is a war to go to," said Cliff Barr, 76'; '"I fear this isn't a very Christian approach," said vicar Ewan Dunn, 47'; '"Oh, is that really happening?" said Nellie Hughes, 92.'

The papers were also padding out minor sightings of Purple people. Eve's favourite of these: a milkman in Stockport almost crashed his float when he passed someone who'd been Turned; he was fine, but there was plenty of spilt milk. (That, Eve had selected for *Say Fantastique!* – certainly a good 'un for deftly bridging the daffy and topical, and seasoned with a typically British quirkiness which would sell well overseas.)

All this, as so far there were few Purple folk to be found. Most of those from the original facility were yet to be released (Luke seemed to be one of the few who had), and any newly Turned lads and lasses appeared to be keeping a very low profile, certainly not participating in interviews where they were likely to be vilified. Which meant the focus had remained on poor, Purple Lee.

Journalist friends of Eve's had told her of the already ferocious competition to get an interview with Lee, but he'd remained in custody after his appearance with the prime minister and it was looking unlikely that he'd be granted bail. Not that the reporters were deterred. Allegedly more than one newspaper had offered to provide Lee with top legal representation in return for access to him and rights to his dismal story. In the meantime, Lee's father had already been splashed across one front page, pictured standing beside their garden gate – before the family had to be relocated – with the caption 'Lav Dad Begs: Don't be Like Lee'.

Father of shamed thug Lee Bowen, the first criminal revealed to have been turned PURPLE, has urged people to take his son's plum predicament as a warning. 'If you don't behave, YOU could be next,' Cal Bowen said. 'Everyone probably thinks it won't happen to them, but never in a million years did Lee think he'd end up like this.

Since the press conference on Friday, when the prime minister revealed that the violent violet lad had nearly beaten an innocent man to death, Lee's family has been under ATTACK. 'We had so many BRICKS through the windows that we've got no windows left,' he said. 'We've had to board them up, and the letterbox. You wouldn't believe what people were putting through that. For what they're doing, they should be turned Purple too.'

When asked what he thought of Lee's behaviour, Cal said, 'He's *been in trouble for a long time, and we didn't know what to do about it. Me and his stepmum have done our best, his mum and his stepdad have done their best, but he was OUT OF CONTROL. He's been joyriding. He gets into fights. He hit an 80-year-old neighbour, who ended up in hospital, for not letting him push to the front of the queue in the fish and chip shop. Basically, he's a right little s***. We wanted his younger brothers and sisters to be able to look up to him, but now we're just worried they'll turn out like him and be Lavs too.'*

Some people might be surprised to know what Cal thinks of the mauve measures. 'Lee couldn't go on behaving like he was, this is going to be a lesson for him. He deserved to be Turned, definitely. I only hope other people will THINK TWICE before they do something stupid and turn out like Lee – everyone hates him, he's LOCKED UP, miserable – and Purple.'

Newspaper on her lap, Eve looked at the photo of Cal Bowen, haggard and haunted. Could he have done anything differently, raised his son to be an angel, not a jackal? Had outside influences made Lee this way? Or had a genetic blip left him borne on course for this most dubious of honours: Lav number one, unlucky for some?

She turned the page. This paper had certainly taken a definitive stance on the Purpleness. Inside was a rogues' gallery called Lav Line Up where photos would now be published daily of all those newly Turned, along with details of what they'd been caught doing.

Stuart Ashworth, 19, and Sam Taylor, 22, Dartmouth: led a DRUNKEN FIGHT outside a Chicken Fried Chicken fast food restaurant, which left two people in hospital.

Rob Rallin, 34, Enfield: seen threatening another man with a MACHETE.

Darren Mortimer, 46, Manchester: noted in an altercation outside a pub, during which he SLASHED a man with a broken beer bottle.

L.J. James, 17, Newport: observed fleeing a stolen car which he'd driven dangerously, CRASHING into a Belisha beacon and nearly hitting a pedestrian, and his dog. Found to be FIVE TIMES over the legal alcohol limit.

Leanne Murphy, 24, Reading: made violent THREATS against a neighbour, and claimed she would STRANGLE Percy, the neighbour's CAT, despite already being cautioned following six months of verbally abusive behaviour.

These individuals thought they could behave abominally and get away with it. Not any more! It's our promise to the great British public that we will name and shame ALL Purple people – call our LAV LINE to report one!

Blimey, thought Eve, what a witchhunt. With her stop approaching, she rang the bell, calling a thank you to the driver as she hopped off. She was looking forward to the debate, if with some trepidation. Given their utterly opposing views on the Purpleness, attending with Womble *and* Helena felt foolhardy, but they'd both insisted on coming. To – hopefully – ease the tension, and put them on their best behaviour, Eve had suggested that they invite Rory, the new vet. Helena had thought that an unusual social invitation, but Rory had seemed keen. 'I guess it's a night out,' Helena had said. Poor Rory, thought Eve. He couldn't have realised that this enthusiasm, if it transpired to be pro–Purpleness, could be a descending bucket in the well of Helena's estimation.

When Eve got to Womble and Helena's, Helena was already fuming. She'd had tickets to a gig by experimental rockers

Eat Your Greens, but the show had been cancelled after an announcement that the band's bassist had been Turned.

'Seriously,' she said, 'you just couldn't make this stuff up.'

'Oh dear,' said Womble. 'What did he do?'

'What did he do?' Helena retorted. 'I don't know. I don't care. This whole thing is moronic. It's as though... I don't know, evil aliens arrive and start destroying the planet, and we're all just saying, oh, look how cute their ears are.'

Womble, who had been looking through the Lav Line Up, said, 'Now, do any of them seem like decent people?'

Eve peered at the machete-wielding, face-slashing, cat-threatening mini mob, and couldn't say they did; sullen faces, defenseless crimes.

'You don't know their stories,' said Helena, peering into a cupboard.

'I don't need to! They sound awful, the lot of them. And everyone knows the difference between right and wrong. Plenty of people who've had a rotten time in life *don't* go around taking it out on other people.'

'True,' Helena agreed, 'but then put them through the courts in the normal way, and lock them up.'

'What if this is a better way?'

'It's *not* a better way. How can you not see how offensive it is?' Helena said, placing a mug in the KitchenKlene dish-washing unit before slamming the door shut.

So far, the Purpleness seemed to have cast a definite cloud over this household.

Womble said nothing, but shook his head, despondently, his nose wrinkling, either from a further glance at the Lavs' gallery, or the floral aroma just released into the air (KitchenKlene had produced a range of truly silent kitchen appliances – 'Retro Styling, Futuristic Ability' – which would announce the end of a cycle by emitting the scent of peach blossom, tea rose, or white musk, depending on your preference, though after a number of complaints a more manly aroma, 'Alpine Fresh', was about to be added to the range).

With a glance at the clock, Womble stood up, saying, 'We need to leave in twenty minutes.'

Crikey moly, thought Eve. Guy Fawkes would have marvelled at the mass of explosives ready to go off tonight.

The atmosphere in the car was artificially calm. Eve sat in the front seat, next to Helena. Womble was in the back, tapping his foot to a song playing on the radio; Helena pursed her lips, saying nothing.

'There he is,' Helena said, as Rory came into view.

Rory was standing bolt upright, waiting next to a recently manufactured red telephone box. These were mostly the same as the old ones, though the doors on the new models felt flimsier, lacking the grand heft of their predecessors. Rory was using one of the box's glass panes as a mirror, smoothing his already tidy hair.

'Oh, by the way,' said Eve, 'Can we not mention to anyone this evening that I'm looking into the Purpling? You never know who's going to be at these things, and Frankie made it sound as though gabbing about it might not be wise.'

Helena turned to Eve. 'I'm very much admiring your work,' she said, with a smile. 'You are becoming quite the sleuth.'

They pulled in next to the telephone box.

'Hiya,' said Helena, as Womble scooted over so Rory could climb in next to him. A sartorial match for Helena's description of his personality, Rory was dressed smartly, in a pressed short-sleeved shirt and cotton trousers. He was also wearing deck shoes.

'Evening,' said Rory.

Helena introduced him to Eve.

'Nice to meet you,' she said.

'Likewise,' said Rory, before adding enthusiastically, 'This is fun.'

'Hmm,' said Helena, glancing in her wing mirror as she rejoined the stream of evening traffic.

'Helena said you got the tickets through work?' said Rory.

'Yup, that's right,' said Eve.

'Thanks for letting me join you. I must say, I like *Say Fantastique!* – it's been quite–' Rory seemed to pause mid-sentence. It felt like being part of a satellite link-up on television, with a brief, stilted time lag even though he was right there. Was he having a very low-key seizure, Eve wondered. She glanced at Helena and Womble, neither of whom appeared concerned.

'Heartening,' Rory eventually continued. 'Especially lately. That lady who saw Elvis Presley in a fried egg. That was–'

Another pause. Eve waited.

'Hilarious. A fried egg!'

'To be honest,' said Womble, 'I thought she was yolking.'

Rory laughed, but there were groans from the front seat.

'Sorry,' said Womble, chuckling at the awfulness of his joke.

Eve noticed Helena's mouth twitch into another smile. Maybe this evening won't be so dramatic after all, Eve thought, picturing a Catherine wheel spinning decreasingly slowly before falling dully to the ground.

A temporary television studio had been set up at a grand town hall, and there were already protesters outside – some with placards featuring Theo Fletcher, his face painted Purple – who chanted: 'Purple people. No no no. Theo Fletcher. Go go go.' Jostling for space beside them were campaigners with brightly coloured banners asking: 'Who do you want to protect? US or THEM?'

Security was robust, and each audience member had to show their CIV pass before being admitted. As their bags were checked, Helena glanced towards Eve, relaying her disapproval, and that was before they'd reached the metal detector.

They were being herded through the entrance hall when Eve saw Helena, who was close in front of her, falter, startled, and heard Womble utter an exclamation in Danish.

'What the—' said Helena.

Eve followed her gaze to a man with mauve skin. He was middle-aged, stout, with a glimpse of purple belly poking from beneath his shirt. His balding head was a shiny lilac. He was flanked by a police officer, for protection or detention it was hard to say.

Helena, shaking her head at the injustice of it all, smiled in solidarity as they passed.

'He might have murdered someone for all you know,' Womble muttered, close to Helena's ear.

Rory, meanwhile, peered at the man – taking in his head, his hands, his belly – apparently too astonished to react.

Eve knew how that felt. As they reached the entrance to the studio, she glanced back to see the crowd's reactions to the Purple man. There were wide eyes and slack jaws, looks of disgust, and of sympathy. One man, standing almost nose to nose with him, loudly declared, 'You're a disgrace.' Another clapped a hand on his shoulder and said, 'Look after yourself, mate.' Eve felt a hand on her own arm as an usher politely requested that she move along.

They took their seats in the studio, mid-way back, behind a row of eager students, whose excitable chatter was punctuated by laughter and hoots of agreement.

'Remember the days?' Eve said to Womble and Helena, but both were quiet. Too soon, she thought, remembering how far her jaw had dropped when she first saw Finn. In addition to their own thoughts, they were possibly – probably – stewing over one another's reactions to the sight of the Purple man. They'd taken seats on either side of Eve, which she wasn't sure was a good sign.

The guest panel for the debate made their entrance. Eve swayed like a faulty pendulum, trying to establish the best view, or any view, around the willowy lad in front of her. The calm and capable host, Desmond Goodacre, looked out at the audience.

'Welcome to this special edition of *Question Time*. Tonight we'll be discussing one of the most controversial initiatives of recent times. Not since the privatisation of the police force has a scheme caused such a strong reaction. But unlike that development, which was predominantly unpopular, responses to the Purple Scheme are proving to be starkly divided, so we're looking forward to a lively debate.'

Desmond smiled and glanced around him, continuing, 'I'd like to welcome our panel, who tonight are Gwen Thomas, the home secretary; Rupert Barron-Clency, the shadow justice minister; leading criminal lawyer Immy Birch; *Daily Dispatch* columnist Ella Breally; broadcaster, author and comedian Ed Fitzpatrick; and finally, someone who's been campaigning against the Purpleness with a coalition of organisations, including human rights charity Humane, and the very newly formed Parents of Purple People, or PoPP, entrepreneur Magnus Jones.'

Magnus. Eve leaned forward, peeking around the tall student, her heart-rate a-gallop. She suspected her eyes might have momentarily sprung out of her head like in an old cartoon.

Helena needled Eve's ribs with her elbow.

'Magnus!' she mouthed, incredulous.

Womble whispered in Eve's ear. 'That's your Magnus, isn't it?'

Her Magnus. Oh, how she'd wished.

'That's him,' Eve nodded, still facing forwards, eyes on the panel, finding she couldn't look away.

'He's done alright for himself, getting on a programme like this. We'll have to look him up later, see what he's been doing.'

Eve already knew that, though she didn't say so. It was funny, seeing Magnus now, right in front of her, after years of looking for him – in bars, on the street, even, ridiculously, and now, ironically, in the audience on TV shows – wondering when he would turn up. Once she had thought she'd spotted him in a New York deli wearing his 'Bells Not Bombs' t-shirt, but having spent a moment tucked behind the tinned vegetables, steadying herself, when she finally moved to get a better look he had gone. Given his attire, she had considered whether the sighting was just a figment of her imagination.

'Right then,' said Desmond. 'Let's get started. Our first question is from Leila Ali.'

A young woman wearing a patterned scarf looked evenly towards the panel.

'How effective do you think the Purple measures will be in combating crime?'

'Gwen, this was your party's initiative, so let's start with you.'

With a lilting Welsh accent, Gwen began, 'Naturally, I think it's a groundbreaking plan for significantly reducing crime. We're already beginning to see, just as we'd anticipated, a drop in crime on the streets. Which just goes to show what an effective deterrent this is, and how we can achieve swift, impressive results in making this country's streets safer. We've also been very pleased to have received such positive feedback from the public, most of whom seem jolly happy that at last some genuinely dynamic leadership has been taken on this issue.'

There was a response of both claps and jeers from the audience.

Rupert Barron-Clency, the shadow justice minister, stepped in. 'I must take issue with Gwen claiming a drop in street crime. There's no conceivable way that this could be judged accurately at such an early stage, and it's very important not to be making exaggerated claims,' Rupert grumbled (his spotty tie and matching pocket square were jaunty even if his comments were less so). 'There are probably fewer people on the streets because everyone – and not just those likely to commit criminal acts – is too terrified to venture out, in case they're turned Purple! The streets aren't safer, they're *more* fearful. What we need is a better conviction rate and less lenient custodial sentences to keep criminals off the streets. And *on* the streets we need more ISON cameras, which have had tremendously impressive long-term results for tackling crime, and more visible police officers. This Purple Scheme is just silly, and makes us look ridiculous. Our country must be a joke to the rest of the world.'

'It was your government's cost-cutting that reduced the number of police on patrol though, wasn't it?' said Magnus.

'It's a fair point, Magnus, but we'll come to you in a moment,' said Desmond. To Rupert he said, 'So you're not in agreement with your colleague, Hugo Clarence?'

There were some laughs from the audience.

'Yes, I'm surprised at your response, Rupert,' said Gwen. 'Some may not have seen this as an obvious move from us. But given that your party not only instigated the disastrous privatisation of the police force, which then hardly became a beacon of satisfactory justice – and by the by gave the UK our worst conviction rates for thirty years – but is also renowned for having little interest in the man on the street… well, I find it amazing that you'd criticise this scheme.'

'Thank you, Gwen, you have had your say,' said Desmond. 'And to clarify, Hugo Clarence was quoted as saying' – he looked down at his notes – "I wish we'd thought of it. Good idea. Dye all the feckless buggers."'

There was a ripple of laughter from the audience.

'I think he might have been taken out of context,' said Rupert.

'Really?' said the host, unimpressed. 'Well then, Immy Birch, moving on to you.'

Immy's poker-straight hair swung as she shot a disdainful glance towards the politicians. 'We certainly are making a spectacle of ourselves,' she said. 'It seems hard to tell whether we look daring or stupid. And it does contradict everything our justice system is supposed to represent: the right to a fair trial… innocent until proven guilty. So whether or not it's effective, I think we have to ask ourselves, at what cost do we continue with these measures? What type of justice does this provide, and is it setting a very dangerous precedent? I believe in our pre-Purple system, and I think that while it's not faultless, it is at least democratic.'

'Sensible woman,' said Helena, quietly.

'She would say that, she'll be out of a job!' whispered Womble, in retaliation.

'Thanks, Immy,' said Desmond. 'Ella?'

Columnist Ella Breally smiled at the audience, looking to Eve like the journalistic equivalent of a cartoon villainess. 'I'm astonished to say that I wholeheartedly agree with Gwen, and the prime minister. This is an excellent way of making our streets safer for those who deserve to feel safe, and for shaming those who shouldn't be able to prowl around causing trouble.

Frankly, if you're a degenerate who's not fit to participate in society, I'd rather you were marked as such, rather than, *if* you actually get caught, getting let off on some technicality or given community service, a pat on the head and a bag of cough drops, and then being free to cause more harm.'

There was a smattering of applause from the audience. Eve could see one lady in the front row nodding passionately, while beside her another woman shook her head in despair.

'I think you're rather undermining the justice system,' said Immy Birch. 'And with these measures, if you're not given a custodial sentence, you'll still be on the streets—'

'But you'll be noticeably Purple,' Ella interrupted with a short huff. 'Which will give decent people a warning to stay away from you, as Theo Fletcher says, *if* you dare show your face in civilised society.'

'I'm mortified to find myself saying this,' said popular comedian Ed Fitzpatrick, who was wearing a shirt covered in small zebras. 'Maybe it's my age – I'm not the spritely socialist I once was – but I'm actually somewhat in agreement with Ella. I'm not sure that this is *exactly* the way to go – dyeing people seems pretty far-fetched – but I think a lot of people are tip-toeing around, trying to be politically correct, but let's say it: crime and anti-social behaviour have got out of control, and what, over the last twenty years, has worked in trying to stem that? Apparently nothing. The Repeal might have had a very minor effect, but you can still get stabbed for looking at someone the wrong way, or nicking someone's parking spot, and as unacceptable and outlandish as the Purple Scheme may be, the crimes taking place on our streets are equally so. This may not be the best solution, but it's a start, and I'm glad we're managing to take decisive, if drastic, action.'

Continuing their whispered dispute, Womble said, 'So true! I always did like him. His sitcom is very good.'

'You asked if it had been written by chimps,' said Helena.

One of the students turned around, fixing them with a youthful frown.

Eve was doing her best to disguise her palpitations at the sight of Magnus. It was now his turn to speak.

'I know this does all feel like an absurd dream sequence in a strange film – or maybe *The Ed Fitzpatrick Show*.' There was laughter from the audience before Magnus turned to Ed and said, 'Which I do really like, by the way – just ask my missus!'

Eve bit her lip. Magnus looked just the same, a keen energy fizzing from his PoPP t-shirt as he leant forward, engaged, as ever, putting his elbows on the desk in front of him and emphasising his points with animated gestures.

'And it seems ludicrous that we're discussing this, that it's actually real,' Magnus continued, running a hand through his hair, leaving a clump poking out to one side. 'The Purple Scheme would be laughable if it weren't so criminally insane. It isn't effective for combating crime, it's a crime in itself. Of course people want to feel safer. Of course we all want to feel that we have a justice system that works, and at the moment it doesn't always, despite the efforts of many good, hard-working people. Sure, in the short term the Purple madness might get some people off the streets, but at what cost? Is that going to help someone with bad behaviour change their ways? When and how do they stop being Purple, and if you take an angry, disaffected person and Turn them, won't branding them that way make them angrier and more likely to reoffend? In the long run, this could actually create more crime. Instead of dyeing people, we should be talking about how to prevent crime and anti-social behaviour. Through education, through having ready employment for people, through having decent role models for young people as they grow up, setting standards. It's not exciting, it's not like living in a sci-fi film, and there are no snappy results, but I think that's the responsible, decent way for us to lead by example. The behaviour we see around us may not be acceptable, but, regardless of whether it's effective or not, neither is this solution.'

There was a round of applause from the audience. Eve really wished she had a large glass of wine.

'The voice of reason,' said Helena. 'He always was a smart guy.' She caught Eve's eye and mouthed, 'You okay?'

Eve gave an uncertain nod.

'Namby pamby nonsense!' said Ella. 'Mollycoddling them is just as much a part of the problem.'

'Ella, I think the causes are closer to the hysteria-inducing door of your workplace,' said Magnus.

'What about its value as a deterrent?' Desmond asked.

'We used to hang people as a deterrent. In other countries you can have your hands chopped off, or be stoned to death. Do those work as deterrents? And if they do, does that justify such ugly penalties?'

'Hang on, though,' said Ed Fitzpatrick. 'Can we just do a quick show of hands – are we allowed to do that, Des?'

'I don't see why not.'

'Right then,' Ed addressed the audience. 'If you would be significantly less likely to behave badly in public for fear of being Turned Purple, raise your hand now.'

The panel watched as the majority of audience members, Womble included, raised a hand. Helena, cheeks sucked in, quietly shook her head, arms firmly at her sides. Eve, who'd never behaved badly in public, and fearing Helena's wrath, abstained. Rory glanced around, seemingly in wonderment at the human coral of raised arms.

'Though isn't it possible,' said Immy Birch, 'that here we

have a well-behaved, socially-engaged audience who weren't likely to offend even before this scheme?'

A microphone was placed in front of one young woman who had raised her hand. 'I'm already watching what I do, and I'm not usually in trouble,' she said.

'I'd be careful,' said Womble.

'In contrast to your wild, spontaneous ways?' said Helena.

'Anyone else like to comment?' Desmond asked.

One of the students said, 'I think most people know it'd be unlikely to happen to them, especially if they don't take part in fights or things like that, but the Purple thing seems so mysterious that you just don't know... It seems like you might as well be really, really well behaved, just in case, 'cause you really don't know what might happen.'

A couple of people nearby nodded in agreement.

'Thank you,' said Desmond. 'Now, another question, from Zachary Naylor.'

Zachary had short, sandy hair and wore a t-shirt with a logo that suggested he was a marathon runner. He cleared his throat.

'For those who don't agree with the scheme, what alternative measures would they suggest for controlling what has seemed, quite honestly, to be an increasingly uncontrollable situation?'

'Rupert, let's start with you,' said Desmond.

'Tougher sentencing, for a start,' said Rupert. 'If you've committed a crime, there should be a heavy penalty for that. Plus increasingly harsh sentences for repeat offenders.'

'May I?' asked Magnus, and Desmond nodded.

'But at what cost, Rupert? I know your party's floated the idea of life imprisonment for persistent offenders – and in fact, so had Theo Fletcher, a while ago – but even purely from an economic point of view, that's just not viable.'

'When it comes to public well-being, we're not going to put a price limit on that,' said Rupert. 'We've also considered reinstating National Service, which, if anything, would provide some real discipline. There are too many people in this country who could do with a large dose of that.'

'Hear, hear,' said a lady wearing a pair of bright-green-framed glasses. 'People need discipline, and purpose, we all do.'

'Hang the bastards!' someone shouted, and with a stern look into the audience, Desmond responded, 'We will not be having any of that.' Then, more genially, he indicated to an older gent in military uniform and said, 'The gentleman in the third row...'

'That's all very well, Mr Barron-Clency, but your government made critical and might I say devastating cuts to the armed forces. Are you saying we should top up the numbers with a batch of undisciplined yobs who will most likely be wholly unsuitable to serve? And that we should put aside valuable, not to mention extremely limited, resources to train them?'

'I think if other countries have an excellent national service programme, I don't see why we can't.'

'Moving on...' said Desmond. 'Immy?'

'I don't think we need an alternative to the pre-Purple justice system. It has served us for a long time, and is fair and democratic. This is the template used by most of the developed world, and we should – and can – put our faith in it. Magnus is correct, too, when he says we need to consider ways to *prevent* crime and anti-social behaviour. Those are the solutions.'

'And Magnus? Any final points on this from you?'

'I really do believe progress will be made when we focus on education, and employment. Also, as a parent, while I don't think you can lay the blame for all bad behaviour at a parent's door—'

'Look at Lee the Lav!' someone in the audience shouted.

'Now, now,' chided Desmond, again looking into the crowd.

There were more whispers from Helena and Womble.

'That Lee's really been getting it in the neck, hasn't he,' she said.

'So did the guy he beat up,' he said.

'It does seem as though Lee may have been from a violent home,' said Magnus, 'which would give any of us a disadvantaged hand in life. But what I was going to say was, while parents can't take all the blame, in our families, and communities, and society as a whole, we do have a responsibility to guide our kids, and both teach them, and show them, respect. That was something Milton Hardy worked quite hard for, and it's an approach I think – ' he gave a small, self-deprecating shrug – 'is really important.'

There was a rousing round of applause.

'Can I just say something?' said Ed Fitzpatrick.

'Go ahead,' said Desmond.

'I'm a parent myself, and I agree with what Magnus has just said, but we can only live in some kind of respectful utopia if everyone adopts the same values, shows consideration and respect. And really, when is that going to happen? I'd love if there was a happy, squishy, natural mung-bean solution. But in the meantime, I think maybe we should give the Purpleness a chance. Especially considering that given the half-baked responses we've just heard, no one seems to have any particularly inspiring alternatives.'

There was more enthusiastic clapping from the audience.

Ed Fitzpatrick gave an impish grin and tipped his head in bowing appreciation.

'Now,' said Desmond, 'our next question is from Helena Arthur.'

Womble turned to Helena, bewildered. Ignoring him, she gave Eve a gratified smile before standing up.

'In Britain we like to consider ourselves a progressive nation. Doesn't this scheme take us back to the unenlightened days of branding, and also encourage a newly manufactured form of racism?'

Magnus peered into the audience, a look of surprised recognition on his face. Helena wiggled her fingers at him in a very small wave.

Eve aligned herself with the tall student, hoping she was hidden behind him. What would Magnus think if he saw her?

Gwen was first to respond. 'Unlike branding, this is pain-free and fully reversible,' she said.

'What about the psychological damage?' Magnus asked.

'What about the psychological damage to the victims of crime?' Gwen countered. 'This is simply marking people for what they are – troublemakers, and simultaneously being able to warn members of the public, who have the right to know. As to racism… that's preposterous, this is nothing of the sort.'

'Branding was barbaric. This is as physically harmful as dyeing your hair, am I right, Gwen?' Ella asked.

'Absolutely,' she replied.

There were a few groans from the audience, and one from Helena.

'And racism?' Desmond asked.

'It's not racism,' Ella snorted. 'That's ridiculous. Racism is the result of ignorance, this is just a signifier of behaviour. Calling a spade a spade.'

Throughout the audience were people wincing at her choice of words. Ella seemed oblivious.

'Dear God,' said Helena.

Ed the comedian had been scribbling notes, which he looked up from, thoughtfully.

'Firstly,' he said, 'I think there is a comparison to be made here with branding, both are obviously physically marking someone, singling them out. But as much as people have laughed at Gwen and Ella, the reason we would consider branding, or some other punishment from the dark ages, so barbaric is because of the pain of it, and also that it's then a lifelong stigma. This is something that isn't physically going to hurt you, and can be reversed, that you can earn your way out of. As I've said, I don't think it's the best plan, but it does have some merit. And racism… I really hadn't thought about it like that before. Obviously judging someone by how they look is wrong, we all know that, and this is creating a situation where you're expected, actually encouraged to do that. But unlike other prejudices, this – if we're to believe the system works – is marking you accurately. It's making this the exception to the rule of not judging a book by its cover.'

'That was a very important question, Helena,' said Magnus, with a smile. 'And yes, Purpling does do both those things. Following on from what Ed just said, in terms of racism it's basically setting the example that you can judge someone by their colour, and it's potentially very damaging to the increasing tolerance we've achieved in our society. Also, you can be Turned for a number of things, so are we to judge someone who's committed a violent assault in the same way as someone who's, say, a shoplifter? And if someone's involved in an altercation, what are their circumstances, were they defending themselves, were they provoked? All of these things we would hear in a trial, but of course in these cases you're condemned before you've been tried, and we're being told to judge without knowing the facts.'

Stooping slightly to whisper to Eve, Helena said, 'I love Magnus. He always was brilliant, wasn't he?'

Eve nodded, wondering if anyone would notice if she

fainted and tumbled out of her chair (and with any luck, down the stairs and towards the bar).

To one side of the audience, a woman took the microphone and said, 'Do you want to be prime minister? I'd vote for you!' She giggled, and some other members of the crowd laughed too.

'An admirer!' Desmond said to Magnus, with a chuckle.

Gwen Thomas looked as though she was about to speak.

'Did you want to add something?' Desmond asked.

'I was going to say, in response to Magnus's comment, the circumstances are witnessed and taken into account in any situation where someone is committing a Turn-able offence.'

'And decided by... who?' Magnus said, expectantly. 'Are there secret police watching us?' He looked to the audience and shrugged. 'We don't know, do we?'

There was much clapping from the audience.

Eve's internal quivers were briefly stilled by this question, despite the fact that it was from Magnus. She watched the panel's reactions, most particularly that of Gwen Thomas, who she guessed was the only one likely to know the secrets of the Purpling. Gwen had pursed her lips and looked down, giving nothing away.

Now she cleared her throat. 'It's been said many times before, mainly by the prime minister, but it can't be stressed enough that elements of the initiative are extremely sensitive and for security reasons must remain confidential.'

There was a smattering of jeers from the audience.

'Did anyone else want to comment on this?' Desmond asked.

A woman in a striped jumper stood up. 'I'm sorry, but if you're committing a crime or being anti-social, you deserve to be Turned, and you deserve to be judged.'

This was followed by a round of claps.

'Exactly,' Womble mouthed, silently.

'I think we've time for one more question,' said Desmond, 'which comes from Celeste Owusu.'

'This is a way of identifying people who participate in *visible* crimes and anti-social behaviour. But what about other crimes, like domestic violence, which is devastating, and affects *a lot* of people, and white-collar crime, like tax evasion and fraud? Which may not be public, but are just as immoral.'

'That's correct,' said Immy. 'If we look at those affected and the crimes they've subsequently been charged with, and at the crimes listed in the documentation that's been made publicly available, the scheme only targets street crime or offences that are committed in public. Which does limit its reach.'

'Another reason to knock it on the head,' whispered Helena.

Eve expected Womble to respond, but he said nothing.

'We are considering potentially expanding on that,' said Gwen, keenly, 'but this scheme seemed most effective for tackling street crime, which is the area of criminal behaviour shown to be the public's biggest concern by a considerable measure.'

'Which shows,' said Magnus, 'that targeting certain demographic groups is of more concern to the government than others. If you're out of sight, you're out of mind. So if you aren't paying due corporation tax, don't worry!'

'Better a more forceful way of cracking down on loutish behaviour than not cracking down on anything at all,' said Gwen.

'Ed, let's finish with you,' said Desmond.

'The lady is absolutely right with her question, but baby steps... Look, I've already said it this evening, but I think we should give the Purpleness a fair chance. It might be a bit bonkers, but we're a bonkers nation, right? It's crazy, but it's imaginative, and at the moment it seems to be doing some good, even if as a deterrent alone, from what some of the young people in the audience have said this evening. So let's see what happens. *Vive le violet*, right?!'

There were some laughs and repeated calls of '*Vive le violet!*' from the audience. Ed grinned.

'And on that note,' said Desmond, 'thank you to everyone here in the studio, and to all those of you at home for watching. Good night.'

'Incredible,' said Helena. 'Really astounding. Though Magnus was fantastic, Eve. Should we try and say hello?'

Eve licked her lips, her mouth dry. 'I'm not sure we'll get to go backstage,' she said. 'We don't have passes.'

Helena leaned towards her, gently prodding Eve just below her collarbone.

'Are you quite sure about that? Don't you want to see Magnus?'

'He probably won't remember me.'

'Eve! He obviously remembered me, so he'll certainly remember you. Come on, let's go.'

Chipping in, Womble said, 'You know you'll regret it if you don't.'

'Exactly,' said Helena.

Eve wanted to say, I'm glad to be something you two agree on. Instead she said, 'Do you think there's a bar?'

'Backstage there will be!' said Helena, linking her arm through Eve's, and leading her towards the exit.

Approaching an usher, Helena said, 'We're supposed to meet our friend Magnus, who was on the panel – how do we find him?'

Here's a situation assisted by the lack of PortAbles, thought Eve.

'You know him?'

'Exactly.' Helena gave a trustworthy smile.

'Can I take your name?'

'Helena Arthur.'

The usher raised a walkie talkie. 'I've got Helena here, a friend of Magnus Jones. Is it okay to send her through?'

The handset emitted a crackle, then, 'Hold on.'

This has the potential to be horrifying, thought Eve.

Another crackle. 'Roger that. Go ahead. Just note any CIV passes, please.'

Having checked their passes and jotted down their names, the usher said, 'Follow signs to the studio lounge. You'll be met there.'

'Thank you,' said Helena sweetly.

She took Eve's hand as they followed photocopied arrows deeper into the building.

'Clammy,' said Helena. 'You okay? I know this is a big deal.'

'Actually, I could do with some air,' said Eve, who'd noticed a fire exit at the end of a dusty corridor. 'I won't be long. I'll come and find you.'

This needs a coat of paint, Eve thought, as she ducked down the corridor, passing faded, peeling posters for long-gone committee meetings and community projects. The bar on the fire exit door was stiff and creaky, but after a good shove she managed to get it open. Then, so that she wouldn't get locked out, she placed her bag on the floor as a makeshift door wedge. Next to her, a window was open, paint flaking from the frame. Eve peered in: an office filled with cheap furniture and stacks of files which had overloaded the shelves and were now manoeuvring across the office, piling up on one side against a wall.

Eve sighed, leaning back against the bricks between the fire exit and the window. There was a coolness to the evening air, and she stood looking at the trees nearby, zen and still under the inky canopy of the night sky. How strange, she thought, that after all this time Magnus and I are in the same building.

Magnus loomed large in Eve's life, casting a disproportionately long shadow, given how soon things had ended (or to be more accurate, never truly started). She hadn't actually seen or spoken to him for over a decade, since a while before she'd moved to New York, but to her he represented a spiked handful of things. Mainly regret. Not cute or timid or viewed through a Vaseline lens lamenting, this was a hulking beast of drooling, dribbling, teeth-gnashing, foot-stomping, stomach-churning, heart-breaking wretchedness. She knew, too, that it wasn't just *him*, but the beacon he'd become, which made her feel woeful. A missed opportunity, the first failure in an impressive series that was her apparently doomed love life. When relations with the latest in a (short) string of unsuitable beaus bit the dust, she would quietly berate herself that it had been a slippery downward spiral since Magnus.

She knew very well that she had inflated the importance of their minor courtship out of sensible proportion – was aware that had she met and married some other, magnificent lad, Magnus would now barely cross her mind, just as she was sure she had not crossed his in these subsequent years. But, that she had rarely met anyone she thought so remarkable, so brilliant, so easy to be around, and – the clincher – who had somehow effortlessly made her feel like the girl she secretly hoped she could be... that was still hard to reconcile herself to. As was the fact that, although it was light years ago, water under the bridge, immaterial to anyone but her, and something utterly unchangeable even if it were true, she believed with absolute certainty that he was someone who was supposed to have been significant in her life. Maybe they would only have been together for five minutes (surely he would have bored of her?), but she was convinced – exceptionally so – that there was a journey she was supposed to have taken with him, and she'd missed it. And while there was nothing to be done, Eve often wondered who she might have been if she'd quelled her fears, or simply told him how she felt. She imagined in a parallel universe there was an Eve who had shared a better part of her life with Magnus and was quite different to this one, the woman she was now. The other Eve had succeeded where this one had failed, had created a fork in her life that her twin had yet to find, and this Eve desperately wanted to know what the other one was like. Who might she have been had she got it right, however briefly, with Magnus?

If there were gods of destiny plotting people's lives, putting opportunities in their paths, then they had tutted and sighed as Eve trotted past their signals, repeatedly mistaking green for amber and moving on to her (seemingly still to be fully revealed) plan B. She imagined them to be playing elaborate games of chess, or dealing with an all-encompassing version of air traffic control. Were there different departments – would folk bleep off the relationship radar and onto the careers chart? Was it like playing a computer game with wilful and often stupid pawns – would the kindly controllers punish you with a less spectacular fate if you kept missing the chances they were setting up, creating more work for them, or take pity as a door swung shut, making sure there was a new one to greet you? Would they shout and cheer as targets met their goals ('crack out the bubbly, Moira, those two have unwittingly won wedded bliss, two kids and a cottage in Wiltshire!') or groan like football fans whose favourite team just lost a goal ('Snakes alive! What is wrong with her? You give people a perfectly simple task... We're gonna need more beer, Gerry').

Eve had certainly learned her lesson. She had liked Magnus so much. If only she'd told him so – along with the important disclaimer that she was inexperienced in love and terrified of getting hurt. But her young, silly self had misinterpreted that vulnerability and apprehension as disinterest, convincing

141

herself that she wasn't so sure she really liked him after all. And so, after what was sure to have been for him an awkward smooch, Eve had closed the door and never clapped eyes on him again.

Given that historically, in the time they had known one another, their lives had continually crossed, and often in unexpected ways – the gods of destiny getting to lark inventively about – Eve had convinced herself that one day her chance would come back around. But not long after she'd moved to New York she heard Magnus was married with a baby, then two, rather putting the tin lid on that notion. At which point, following Eve's rueful wails, Helena had sent her what had been a perfect letter: 'Where would you rather be: there, hot-footing it round the Big Apple, living the life fantastic, or here, washing Magnus's pants?'

Occasionally Eve had thought about contacting him – a cheery blast from the past – but really, what would be the point? He had a successful, settled, life, and what was there to say? It would seem wholly inappropriate to try to clear the air now, however much she wanted to – for him it could only be a needless interruption. Whatever words she wished she had said should have tripped off her tongue years ago, or be forever left unspoken.

And now, here he was. Successful, charming, a family man. And Eve? Professionally: fluffily indeterminate. Romantically: a failure, apparently set to be perennially single.

In the wake of the Magnus affair (or rather, lack thereof), Eve had promised herself to never again see things she should have said or done illuminated in the rear view mirror. This seemed to have had the effect of sometimes sending her too far to the other extreme. However much she tried to keep her expectations low, apparently her manifest terror at again messing up and missing out meant that she now did too much, attempting, albeit breezily, to leave little unsaid or undone. But as she threw one last verbal or written hand grenade at any limping fling, she'd comfort herself with the knowledge that she wasn't going to look back and wonder, what if? There would be no more mistakes of Magnus proportions. And yet, as another dalliance quietly imploded, she'd think, here I go again... I've been getting it wrong since Magnus.

Not long ago she'd found herself contacting another ex of sorts, in a short, inoffensive message asking after some *Say Fantastique!* story-related information she thought he might have. It was an unnecessary enquiry – she could easily have found the details elsewhere – and she'd flinched as the Portal's mail service had chimed, accepting its delivery from her screen to his. A swift and amiable response included the news that he had recently got married *to an amazing woman*, and Eve had cried, those letters clouding in her vision (she did wonder why he'd worded it so – the twist of a knife). Not because she had wanted to marry him – really, she rarely thought of him – but it seemed all the men she'd felt most ardently about had now eagerly settled down, and none of them with her. She wanted to be someone's amazing woman, but instead felt like the also-ran, the girl who no one wanted.

And yet again, she had thought back to being on the doorstep with Magnus, and told herself: you are a failure.

Eve blinked, distracted, as beside her a light came on in the office with the open window. She heard footsteps, then a door shoved firmly shut.

A female voice huffed, 'It's Watt. I got the message. What does he mean, he might have lost it? Before or after a Turning?'

Eve's mouth gaped; what was this?

'As he'll be well aware, that is completely unacceptable. The kind of error that could jeopardise the entire scheme. Tell him he needs to find it – no ifs or buts – and report to me first thing tomorrow morning. Plus he's suspended from duty – effective immediately.'

Eve heard a phone receiver slam down, followed by more footsteps, and a heavy clunk as the door closed. She peeked through the handbag-enabled gap in the fire exit and at the end of the corridor saw a police officer stride past. Was this Watt?

Hands pressed against the cool wall, Eve waited for her heart rate to slow from quickstep to waltz. What on earth was all that about – what had been lost, and who had lost it? She took her notebook from her bag, writing the conversation down, wanting to be able to make sense of it. This felt significant, though akin to finding one blurry piece of a jigsaw with no other parts of the puzzle to help her see the bigger picture.

You won't find any more pieces by standing out here, she told herself, the fire door slamming behind her as she headed back inside.

Chapter Eight

A man in wellington boots smiled down at Eve, trowel in hand. He had white hair, a bushy moustache, and a lot of vegetables. 'Dig for Britain!' the poster merrily advised. 'Get an Allotment'. Eve had taken a right turn at the top of the hallway, following in Watt's footsteps, and now found herself in a strange crescent-shaped corridor which looked out onto a courtyard. She glanced around, but couldn't see anyone. The doors to the nearby row of offices were all closed. Eve stood quietly, listening. Nothing.

'Eve!'

She turned to see Helena rushing towards her.

'There you are! I came to find you. Are you okay? Did you get lost?'

'Did you see a police officer? Woman? Shortish?' Eve asked.

'No,' said Helena. 'Why?'

'I just...' What did Eve think she would do if she found Watt? Say, hello, senior-sounding police officer. I just surreptitiously overheard your conversation, and wondered if you'd be so kind as to let slip the very much classified way in which you're turning people Purple. But if she could at least see her, try and work out who she was...

'I thought she might be able to help with something,' said Eve.

'Is this a diversion from seeing Magnus?'

'Have you seen him?'

'No, not yet. The backstage usher started being very particular about checking our CIV passes on some database.'

'I guess there are government ministers there, so they're going to be extra careful.'

'They'd already checked them!' said Helena, irked. 'Anyway, I thought with all that we should probably go in together, so wanted to find you.'

'Thanks,' said Eve, linking arms with her as they retraced their steps, returning to the trail of arrows.

'You alright?'

Eve nodded. 'You? I've not seen you two like this before.'

'I'm so angry.'

'A lot of people agree with it.'

'That doesn't make it right.'

'I know, and – sorry, that wasn't what I meant, that it does, it's just... there seem to be a lot of usually intelligent, sensible people who think maybe it can work.'

'But it's so wrong. Judging people by a colour.' Helena threw up her hands. 'Frankly I'm astonished that anyone could support that. That my own husband could believe in something that's so fundamentally awful. And damaging.'

'Just to be devil's advocate though... what if it works?'

'It's still wrong.'

'But—'

'It's wrong. If they carry on doing this, it's saying, it's a perfectly acceptable thing to judge someone by their colour. Hell, it's encouraging it. We're colour-coding people so you can just look at them and make a snap decision. There has to be another way.'

146

'Maybe Womble's just thinking of it from a different angle, after being with the kids at school, wanting them to be discouraged from getting into trouble.'

'Of course he's seeing it differently. *He's* never going to be judged at face value, just walking in the door somewhere, before he's even opened his mouth.'

Eve wasn't sure what to say.

'You agree with it?' Helena asked.

'No. I don't know. I don't – but then I think of people not being able to get away with things, like the guy who hit my dad, and I wonder if maybe it could work.'

'Because you'll be able to look at someone and know whether they're dangerous or not, whether you should trust them or not.'

'I suppose so.'

'How can that be right? How?'

'It's not right, it's—'

'It's Theo Fletcher with some insane, offensive claptrap that he's dressing up as two wrongs making a right.'

'I know. I do know that, but then I'll think, if it makes people change their behaviour…' Eve's justification trailed off. 'I can see how frustrating it is for you, but Womble's got good intentions. He'd never mean to upset you.'

'I know, but siding with this scheme seems ignorant. Having the luxury of being able to look at it and be oblivious. I'm really trying not to let this whole insanity get to me, but – it feels impossible.'

'There's an Anti-Purple Scheme rally on Saturday. Do you want to go?'

'I'd love to, I really would. I think that might make me feel quite a bit better, actually. But I'm working and I can't get out of that now.'

'Can't Rory cover for you? You could ask him.'

'He's in too. If I didn't have surgeries booked I'd try and take the day off.'

'Speaking of Rory,' said Eve, 'I don't want to be mean, but what's with the time delay thing? Surely that's tricky when he's giving a diagnosis… Mrs Smith, I'm afraid to tell you that your dog…' Eve held her breath, pursed her lips.

Helena tried not to laugh. 'I think it's just a nervous tic.'

Eve continued to say nothing.

'You're terrible!' said Helena.

When they re-encountered Womble and Rory, the boys were deep in conversation with a backstage usher.

'Everything alright?' asked Helena.

'Yep, just chatting,' said Womble, looking a little guilty.

'Shall we go in?'

'Just so you know,' said Womble, 'apparently Magnus has left.'

'Bugger,' said Helena.

'And so has Ed Fitzpatrick,' Womble added, disappointed.

'Is Gwen Thomas still there?' asked Eve.

'No, she's gone,' said the usher.

'Blimey,' said Eve. 'Does it get that awkward afterwards?'

'The wine delivery didn't arrive,' said the usher, 'which may have something to do with their departures.'

A thought occurred to Eve.

'I don't suppose Inspector Watt is here?' she asked.

'Who?' said the usher.

'She's a police officer.'

'No. Haven't had any police in here.'

'Oh.'

'So, it's orange juice with Ella Breally?' said Helena. 'I think it's time we went home.'

The last of the protesters were rolling up a banner as Helena drove past. Eve watched as they diligently packed everything away, obviously old hands at activist pursuits.

'What a shame we didn't get to see Magnus,' said Helena. She reached over and gave Eve's arm a squeeze.

'He seems very...' Rory paused.

Eve pursed her lips, and tried not to catch Helena's eye.

'Involved,' said Rory, finally, 'in the Purpleness. How do you know him?'

'We met at university,' said Helena. 'And I have to say, he seems exactly the same now as he was back then.'

Helena began to tell the story, and while it partly made Eve feel like poking herself in both eyes, she figured it was at least a distraction from Womble and Helena's plum contention. Plus, there was no escape: the Magnus chapters had already begun replaying in her head.

They'd met at a pub near their university, at a fundraising bash in the December of their final year. A tinny yellow-gold plastic 'Merry Christmas' hung across the bar, while the walls were decked with concertina'd paper bells and snowflakes, and worn-looking tinsel with kinks from where it had spent repeated years stuffed in a box in the cellar. Eve had tugged Helena's sleeve and indicated towards a lad stood by the jukebox, a palm pressed against the window of its audio delights, considering his options whilst swigging from a bottle of German beer. His dirty-blond fringe would occasionally swing forward, obscuring his view until he swept it back using the hand in which he held the bottle, the other remaining fixed to the jukebox.

'That's him,' Eve said. She had seen this guy posting flyers for the fundraiser around the student union and he was the reason she had impressed upon Helena that they come.

'Hm,' said Helena, noncommittally, biting on a crisp. Given the unlikely suspects Eve seemed to latch onto, and not always to be easily dissuaded from, even Helena was learning to hedge her bets.

Greg, it would transpire, had grown up not far from Eve, a fact which was about all they had in common. Though it would take her a while to realise this, and in the meantime she cultivated a crush, based on little more than looks, and lacking in lively conversation, or any other form of engagement, for that matter.

Not so with Greg's friend Magnus, who was unassuming and perceptive, with a sharp sense of humour and a sweet sense of mischief. Eve had been hovering near the jukebox when Magnus appeared. Tallish, with short, scruffy brown hair, and wearing a 'Bells Not Bombs' t-shirt in reference to a military campaign the government had started the previous Christmas.

'Are you choosing the playlist for the entire night?' Magnus had teased Greg, approaching him with a bottle of beer.

Greg mumbled and again moved his fringe out of his eyes.

'I thought you might need one of these.'

'Thanks, man,' said Greg, finally removing his hand from the jukebox, downing the remainder of his present drink, and turning to accept the new one.

A jangling tune began to play.

'Oh, I love this,' said Eve, technically to Doug and Helena, but hoping Greg would overhear.

Apparently *not* hearing her, but turning to the jukebox with a frown, Greg said, 'What? I didn't pick this.'

'What did you pick? Something festive – a bit of Kit Barbary?' Magnus grinned, referring to a crooner from some years back who'd had a string of yuletide hits.

Greg had groaned.

Eve took this comment and shoehorned an opportune moment into it.

'If I'd known Kit was on the cards, I'd have worn my Christmas jumper!' she said.

Helena, turning briefly from the Snowball Doug had bought her (she'd considered it sceptically as Doug had handed them over: 'Two for one!' he'd said. 'I thought you girls might like them'), wore a rare look of surprise at Eve's diving in without any wing-girl assistance.

'A Christmas jumper!' said Magnus. 'Excellent. What's on it?'

'A disco robin and some fetching sprigs of holly,' said Eve, 'though possibly it'd be a bit small these days – I don't think I've worn it since I was twelve.'

'A disco robin?' Magnus asked, twisting slightly and lifting an arm in the direction of a decorative reindeer as he moved into a disco-dancing finger-pointy stance.

'Yup!' Eve smiled. 'And do you, or your friend,' she turned to Greg, 'have any Christmas jumpers hidden away in the cupboard?'

Greg had looked across to a gaggle of giggling girls who'd just arrived.

'Do you have a Christmas jumper, Greg?' Magnus nudged.

There was a pause and then…

'No.'

At this Helena, her back to their conversation but all ears, repeated the look she'd given the unexpected Snowball.

Still waters, thought Eve.

Leaning forward, Magnus confided, 'I had one. My aunt knitted it. A lovingly made, one of a kind number featuring Action Man's head – ' he indicated towards his chest, outlining a large oval – 'wearing a scarf and a woolly hat – with snowmen on.'

'No!'

'Oh yes. It was a work of art.'

'Your friends must have been... envious?'

'I think so. I'm Magnus, by the way, and this is Greg.'

Greg nodded, his fringe swooping.

'I'm Eve, and this is – ' Eve swivelled round to her friends – 'Helena, and Doug.'

Swivelling back, Eve asked, 'And what do you two do?'

'Ah, well now...' said Magnus. 'When not carefully considering the jukebox options, Greg is a smart, alluring soul who studies English lit with a side order of philosophy. He was in the habit of cycling everywhere, but a few days ago had a particularly riotous night out and has yet to remember where he left his bike.'

'Thanks,' said Greg, looking embarrassed.

'Also, he has a pet spider plant.'

'My sister gave that to me, so I have to try not to kill it,' said Greg, with a smile (a nice smile, Eve thought; it had been worth the wait). He was about to say something else when there was a high-pitched squeal, apparently emanating from a microphone.

'Hi everyone, thanks for coming,' said a chap on the raised platform in one corner of the room that constituted a stage. 'I'm Adrian, I run the student union, so some of you will have seen me around. I wanted to do a quick introduction, and thank you, to the bloke amongst us who's made all this possible. He's been so dedicated to these events for the last few years – well, they were his idea – and I don't know how we'll find someone so ace to fill his shoes next year. He's a—'

'Genius!' someone shouted.

'A prince amongst men!' called someone else.

Adrian laughed. 'Exactly. Actually, for a genius – studying physics, no less – who seems to know a ridiculous amount of things, he does a really princely job of not making anyone else feel stupid.'

'He must be good, Ade, not making *you* feel stupid,' a member of the crowd teased. 'Aren't you doing P.E.?'

There were some laughs and Adrian said, '*Sports therapy!* Anyway,' he continued, 'as well as these parties, he's been doing an excellent job of monkeying around lighting gigs at the student union. I'm definitely going to miss having him here next year. Now, where are you Magnus?'

Greg patted Magnus on the back as he made his way across the room.

Taking the microphone from Adrian, Magnus said, 'Thanks Ade, that was quite the introduction.' With a smile he added, 'If you see my eyes watering, it's just that I'm… allergic to tinsel. It's been really heartening doing these events, and seeing how enthusiastic everyone's been, I've been a bit bowled over by that. Now, I know there are loads of things to be worrying about in the world – can you go to that bloke from your Thursday lecture's party *and* finish your essay on time? Is there any bread in the cupboard that hasn't got mould on it?' Magnus grinned. 'But you know, if those are our problems, then we're lucky, and if we've got time to hop down the pub and have a beer or two with our friends, why not do that for a good cause? We've done this for the last couple of years, donating to a different local organisation, and this evening the cause is the county hospital's sadly underfunded A&E unit. Some of the staff have joined us this evening – hands up those of you… don't they look lovely? And now you know who to go to if you have a funny turn this evening.' Magnus laughed as a piece of lime was pinged towards him. 'Fair enough,' he said, running a hand through his already mussed hair, leaving one clump standing on end like an antenna. 'Oh, and actually that's a good reminder – Gloria the charming landlady here has asked me to mention that there's going to be an open mic night here from January. So if you fancy yourself as a budding songsmith or comedian, you know where to come. You'll be relieved to know I won't be entering and flinging any more terrible jokes at an unsuspecting audience! On that note, I'll pipe down and let you get back to the task at hand. Thanks everyone for coming tonight – it really is great to see so many of you here. Now, please drink and be merry!'

There were some whistles and a round of applause.

Eve tried to clap without spilling any of her half-empty Snowball; Helena whistled, loudly. Magnus made his way back towards Greg, slowly, as people kept stopping him to chat or to congratulate him on a successful evening. Eve noticed an enviably handsome guy called Rick, or rather, Slick Rick, known around campus for, one, having done some modelling (he'd allegedly auditioned for a big jeans brand's TV ad, but while the facts surrounding that were hazy, it was undisputed that he had appeared in the poster for a range of pork pies), and two – not unrelated – having a different girl in tow every week. Just now he scowled as the lass he'd been chatting to (or up) turned to catch Magnus's attention.

Back in Eve's circle, Doug leant across to Greg. 'Have you been taking the post-war British literature class? I think I've seen you at the Monday lectures.'

'Yeah, that's right,' said Greg. 'There's a way to start the week.'

Eve gave Helena a glance which said: that turned out nicely! Now they had an in with the attractive, if not so chatty, Greg.

The next morning, she commented to Helena, 'That Greg's an enigma, isn't he?'

'Not the word I'd use,' Helena had replied.

And that had been the start of it.

Water splashed onto Bob's Iron Maiden t-shirt as he rinsed out test tubes while humming an old heavy metal song. It seemed incongruous to be able to do such a thing as melodically as he was, Eve thought. She was perched on a stool in the first row of benches, the only time she could claim to have been at the front of the class in science. In her school years she'd sat at the back, daydreaming or doodling on her notebook. Bob wiped his hands on a cloth, then returned to his desk.

'So, Womble says you're working on the mysteries of the Purpleness,' Bob said. He tapped his fingertips on the table. You could tell he was a drummer. Aside from the tribute-tastic turn, he and Womble had played in a band together for a while.

'I'd like to understand how they're doing it. I'm intrigued to know what the possibilities are.'

'Mm, wouldn't we all,' Bob agreed. 'And I'm pleased you asked, because I've been thinking a lot about that. I've studied quite a few interviews with Purple people, and I can't find any clues. That may be because all output is being strictly controlled. The government are definitely being more cagey than usual with what information they release.'

'Especially since the Landell Responsible Reporting legislation was passed,' said Eve. 'They've been saying less rather than more for a while now, certainly since before the Purpleness started.'

Bob nodded sagely. 'So, basically, there's very little to go on. But, a scientific sort could deduce some facts. An environmental infection seems unlikely, as specific individuals are targeted, rather than groups of people. And if there was something in the air, then other people might get accidentally Turned, and we've heard in many cases there were other people around who weren't affected. Unless they were and

155

were given an antidote and we just don't know about it. But for now, let's assume the Turning agent isn't airborne. There doesn't appear to be any direct physical contact with anyone – at least, not consistently – during which they could have been injected. And none have, as far as I'm aware, reported feeling anything that could have been an injection or its obvious side effects, such as broken skin or swelling at the point of entry, which you have to imagine there would be some cases of, given blood types, and allergies. It's possible that the Turned people have consumed some fluids or food which could have been doctored. I'm not sure about that.'

From the corridor, there came a loud crash. Bob glanced in the direction of the noise, eyebrows gently raised.

'Just a second,' he said, moving from his desk towards the door. He leaned out into the corridor.

'Drew.'

'Sir.' This from someone Eve couldn't see.

'Everything alright?'

'As ever, sir.'

'Great. I figured as much. Setting fire to bins, for example, has less impact after school when there's no one here to see them.'

'Right, sir. Like a tree falling in the woods. Nobody hears it scream.'

Drew came into view; he would have been a quintessential shaggy-haired teenager, shirt half-untucked, tie askew, had it not been for his hair being dyed bright blue. Behind him appeared another dishevelled boy.

'Mo.'

'Sir.'

'Are you alright? Were you two fighting? Is that what I heard?'

'I think they call it horsing around, sir,' said Drew.

'Mo, anything you'd like to add to that?'

'No, sir.'

'Off you go, then,' said Bob, watching them meander away.

He closed the door, returned to his seat. 'Sorry about that. Now, where were we?'

'Well,' said Eve. 'We'd reached, if it's not airborne or injected, but might be ingested – what could it be?'

'Just the question!' With a glint in his eye, Bob reached for a bag, from which he pulled a stapled set of papers. 'I do have a theory,' he said.

Eve tried not to smile.

'Recently, a pharmaceutical company was about to launch a new tanning product. A new treatment that, with only one application, would tan you for an elongated amount of time – months, at least.'

'Crikey,' said Eve, thinking of the lithe, gilded girls who had been an epitome of beauty for as long as she could remember – athletic limbs stemming from bikinis on LP covers and in perfume ads, representing the elegantly exotic, glossily and gloriously implying life's a beach (here was another type of tinted person that the papers loved to describe: bronzed beauty, sun-kissed stunner, golden goddess). Though those perfect pictures neglected the risks: skin cancer, a leathery hide later in life (like aging tennis stars, and idle souls who'd accumulated years on yachts and cruises), and, more recently, the orange glow of those cheaply emulating the look.

'That'd be bound to be a money-spinner. What happened to it?'

'It got withdrawn not long before it was due to be launched,' said Bob. 'You'd think it would be for health or safety reasons, or because they needed to do more testing or something. But there were no risks or complaints filed with the drug administration, it just vanished without trace.'

'Maybe they hushed up the bad press?'

'Perhaps. But usually, the failure of a massive new product would at least result in some big executive being fired, or the downturn in projected sales harming share prices. But I looked into that. This was going to be their most major product launch for over a decade, and not only is there not a ripple of negativity, their share prices have gone *up*.'

'They could've created a better product?'

'But if you've invested so much money in this one and it's all set to go, and there could be negative rumblings if you pull it for no good reason, wouldn't you launch it, and worry about more new products later? That way you're going to be a market leader, and one seen to be constantly upping your game. Basically, the tanning market is like male baldness.' He ran his hand through his own thick hair. 'So providing there wasn't a safety or recall issue, they'd have to have been in line to make a fortune.'

It was an interesting story, though Eve noticed they seemed to have veered rather off topic.

'But what does this have to do with the Purpleness?' she asked.

'I think Crayne, the pharmaceutical company, sold the patent to the government.'

'For tanning?'

'For colouring people. Orange, purple, it's all the same.'

Eve's mouth gaped in a silent gasp as she grasped what he was saying.

'I see... Wait, though... How was the tanning thing supposed to work? Usually it's a cream or a spray or a pill, all things that you'd have to use knowingly, right?'

'An excellent question. And that's the beauty of it: this was to be a new, specially created system.'

Eve waited expectantly for Bob to reveal all. He was quiet.

'What system?' she asked.

'To have such a long-lasting effect, logic would dictate that it must be something taken internally, so not a spray or a lotion. But I'm not sure, yet.'

'You don't know what the actual product is?'

'It changes people's pigment in a revolutionary way!'

'But you don't know how. It could be an injection, or a digestible liquid – a drink, maybe? – which wouldn't fit with the Purple Turning scenario.'

'Exactly. It's a conundrum.'

'If they'd run trials,' Eve said, 'would those results have been published anywhere?'

'Not that we'd have access to, until it was made available for public consumption.'

'So there's no way of finding out how it works?'

Bob began tapping his index finger on the desk. 'I haven't been able to yet. But I have a hunch about it. I'm pretty sure this is what they're doing.'

'When was it supposed to go on sale?'

'Three months ago.'

'Do you have any documents about it?'

Bob handed Eve the stapled papers. She turned over the first couple of pages, which were copies of articles from a scientific journal – an announcement of the product being in the works, and another about its surprising withdrawal from anticipated release – eventually coming to the triumphant promotional statement.

Crayne Industries Launch Revolutionary Tanning Tool

Crayne Industries CEO Sherry Berger is thrilled to announce that the company's ground-breaking tanning product InTan will soon be publicly available.

'*This is a revolutionary system, which is truly going to change the way the world tans,' Sherry Berger declared. 'While we've been aware for many years that traditional suntanning is very damaging to the skin, safe alternatives have been messy and provided short-lived effects. But now you can look beautifully bronzed easily, and for prolonged periods of time. All with one easy application of InTan. We couldn't be more excited, and we know the world is going to feel the same way.'*

She also unveiled that renowned model Carla De Lora has a new role, as product spokeswoman. 'I just love InTan – it's fabulous!' Carla said. 'Now I can have the perfect tan, all the time. I can't wait for everyone to be able to share in this secret!'

Full details will be issued upon InTan's launch on 12 April, when it will become available exclusively at Bell & Styles department store and branches of Gilded Tub Beauty Spa.

The countdown to extraordinary, long-lasting tanning has begun!

Eve glanced up from the page.

'Tell me again what makes you think that this is connected to the Purple Scheme,' she said.

Looking over from some beakers he'd been stacking, Bob said, 'Intuition. It seems ridiculously coincidental that a very profitable product which dyes people for extended periods of time should become unavailable to the public, seemingly without hurting the company's reputation or share price, shortly before a national campaign for dyeing people starts. It would've taken *years* for the government to develop and test such a thing – certainly longer than Fletcher's been in power.'

'Who else have you talked to about this?'

With an air of beleaguered acceptance, Bob said, 'Let's just say that not everyone is open to considering the more hidden possibilities, so I thought I'd hold off on mentioning this one, just 'til I have more to back it up.'

'Right,' said Eve. 'Can we keep this between us for now, then? And we'll swap any more information we can find?'

Bob perked up considerably. 'Of course! People may dismiss my ideas, but I know when I'm on to something. They just don't realise that it can take a fair bit of digging to get to the evidence. If these things were easy to prove everyone would know about them already.'

'There is a chance, though, that other people might be aware of this too, and reach the conclusion you have, isn't there?'

'Possibly,' said Bob, 'but Crayne are covering their tracks.'

'They are? How?'

'Crayne is apparently in talks with another corporation, discussing a possible merger. They've put other product launches on hold too.'

Now you tell me, thought Eve.

'So it could be that they're just waiting to see what happens before they launch InTan and the other things?'

'Nope,' said Bob. 'I mean, it could be. But I don't think so. I'm pretty sure it's more than that – it's too much of a coincidence, isn't it?'

'Indeed,' said Eve, not sure she believed his theory after all, but figuring it was the best lead – the only lead – she had so far.

'Oh,' said Eve, 'I overheard something which… well, it does and it doesn't give a clue.' She pulled out her notebook, reading the lines she'd scribbled after hearing Watts's phone call. '*What does he mean, he thinks he's lost it? Before or after a Turning? That kind of error could jeopardise the whole scheme. Tell him he needs to find it – no ifs or buts – and report to me tomorrow morning.*'

'Crumbs,' said Bob.

'I know. I should add that I shouldn't have heard that, so…'

'I will repeat nothing,' said Bob, with a lip-zipping gesture. 'Now then. Let's find Womble and go for a pint.'

Eve picked up her bag and followed him out of the lab.

En route to the pub, Womble cleared his throat. 'I hope neither of you mind, but I invited Rory along to join us.'

'You two bonded at the debate, did you?' said Eve.

'I think so,' said Womble. 'We had a good chat, and… Well, it was interesting talking to him about the Purpleness. And Hels wants me to help him settle in, so that's what I'm trying to do.'

There was some shouting a little further down the road; Bob squinted into the distance.

'Drew Fisher,' he said. 'What's he up to now, I wonder.'

'He's a loose cannon, that one,' said Womble. 'So you two had a constructive chat, did you?'

'We did, right, comrade?' said Bob.

'Yes,' said Eve, and to Womble: 'Thank you for the investigative matchmaking.' Then, looking up, she added, 'Oh, look, chaps.'

Ahead stood Rory, holding a packet of cigarettes. He was framed by another red telephone box, in which a man appeared to be having a very boring conversation, his head bobbing up and down like a nodding dog.

Womble called to Rory, who looked surprised, and stuffed the cigarette packet in his pocket as they approached.

'Having a sneaky fag, hey?' said Womble.

Rory looked panicked, then dejected. 'Since I…' he began. There was a pause. Bob appeared momentarily concerned, but Eve now anticipated the delay. 'It's a bad habit, since I got divorced. I want to give up, but…'

'Me too,' said Bob, 'I'm trying to stop. I'd rather the tobacco companies weren't making a profit from me. Capitalist cretins.'

Eve and Womble exchanged a smile.

'And who's this?' said Eve, crouching down to pat a pug whose lead Rory was holding.

'This is Brewster,' said Rory. 'I'm looking after him for a couple of days.'

'He's adorable,' said Eve.

'I really want to…'

They all waited patiently.

'Get another dog,' said Rory, staring sadly at Brewster, who sat panting, bug-eyed.

'Onwards to the pub?' said Womble.

The four of them sat down at a table.

'So, how was your day at the surgery?' Eve asked Rory.

'Ah, good, thanks,' he replied. 'I operated on a sheepdog. And a gerbil.'

'A gerbil?'

'Yes. Actually, I think you'll like this story,' said Rory, with warming confidence. 'It wouldn't move away from the fridge, and the owners couldn't work out why. It turned out…'

Eve, Bob and Womble leaned forward.

'It had swallowed a magnet! A fridge magnet! And so it couldn't move away from the fridge.' Rory mimed his neck jerking to one side, as though magnetised.

Eve laughed. 'Poor thing,' she said, 'though that is an amazing story.'

'It's dreadful,' said Bob.

'Is the gerbil okay now?' Eve asked.

'It is. The operation was successful. The magnet is removed.'

'I have to ask,' said Eve. 'Do you think they'd do an interview for *Say Fantastique!*? Because that's what my partner Adio would describe as right up our gangplank.'

Rory laughed. 'I'm sure they would. I can ask them.'

'That'd be great, thank you.'

'The debate was interesting, didn't you think?' said Womble.

'Yes,' said Rory. 'Though it was a lot of big opinions in a small space! Food for thought, as they say.'

'What do you make of it, then?' Bob asked. 'The Purpleness, that is.'

Eve was curious to know this; Rory had seemed borderline dumbstruck by much of what had happened at the debate, which had obscured his stance. And she was keen, as ever, to know how people felt about it, especially as she was still seeking a definitive opinion of her own.

'I try not to talk about it,' said Rory. 'It seems to be such a...' Another pause. 'Hot potato.'

'You agree with it, though, don't you?' said Womble, eager to be around someone on-side for a change.

'I do, yes. I think. It's controversial, but...'

Eve, Bob and Womble sipped their drinks, waiting.

'Maybe it can work?'

'Tell us what *you* make of it,' Womble said to Bob.

'I'm wary of it. It's a shady government scheme to control us, using fear.'

Rory looked aghast. (Eve guessed he probably didn't come into contact with many conspiracy theorists). 'You'd rather the criminals control the streets?'

'They don't control the streets. That's just what Fletcher – and possibly the criminals – would like everyone to believe.'

'The thing is—' Womble began.

Time for a break, thought Eve, who was, unexpectedly, approaching Purple overload. She stood up. 'Anyone for some crisps?'

A pint glass appeared on the bar, brought to rest on a newspaper Eve was flicking through, its contents sloshing overboard, dampening the headlines.

'Alright, sis.'

Eve looked up to see Simon – and Duncan – standing beside her. She contemplated the pint glass, and the soggy newsprint; Simon's mildly mocking 'gotcha' smile implied he was still well aware of his ability to rile her.

'Hello,' said Duncan, giving Eve a hug. 'It's good to see you again.'

'You, too,' said Eve, feeling briefly flustered by another close encounter with his biceps.

A young woman behind the bar brought over the last glass of Eve's order, and Eve handed her a twenty-pound note.

'Want a hand with those?' asked Duncan.

'Sure,' said Eve, less sure about Simon crossing paths with her companions.

'Gents,' she said, assigning the new round of drinks. 'This is Duncan... and Simon, my brother.'

There were nods and hellos before Eve gathered with the new arrivals at one end of the table. Simon and Duncan sat on small stools, the boys' jagged, crunched legs a row of right angles.

'How's Dad?' Eve asked.

Simon opened a bag of pork scratchings, and tipped a few into his mouth.

Munching, he said, 'Rine. Mum larking rafter him.'

Eve looked at Simon as he ate more scratchings, mouth open, the crackling jumbling around like the contents of a washing machine in a vegetarian's nightmare.

'And... how are you?' she said, such familiar words suddenly feeling chalky and unusual when directed at Simon, politeness between them being an uncommon language.

'Me?' Simon said, suspicious.

'Yes, you.'

'Fine,' he said. He prodded a finger into his mouth, poking

165

about to retrieve a stray pork morsel, before wincing; Eve suspected that Duncan had kicked him under the table. 'You? Still here, then?' Simon said slowly, as though he'd been asked to speak in Mandarin.

Womble caught Eve's eye, giving her a questioning thumbs up sign. She responded with a smile and a nod.

To Simon she said, 'Still here, yep.'

Duncan smiled, looking between them, proudly, like a sports coach who'd insisted that two warring teammates would find they were actually very alike, if only they'd just try and get along.

'Where are you working at the moment?' said Eve.

'I'm not,' said Simon, waggling a hand in front of his face as a bee flew past.

'Ah,' said Eve.

The bee had alighted on the sterile flora of the flocked wallpaper; Simon lifted a beer mat, about to swat it.

Duncan deftly slipped the mat from Simon's fingers.

'Si!' he said. 'Leave the poor bee alone and drink your pint. Honestly! What's it ever done to you?'

Simon mumbled sheepishly.

'In all these years, you'd think some of my conservationist ways might have rubbed off on you…'

They both laughed.

Simon prodded Duncan with his elbow, nodding towards an attractive, unassuming young woman standing at the bar.

Duncan shook his head.

'Mate… we're having a drink with your sister!'

'Don't mind me. I don't want to cramp you boys' style.'

Eve could have anticipated her brother's response to this – 'That'd be a first' – but as Simon opened his mouth to speak, Duncan silenced him with a good-behaviour-inducing parental stare.

Simon looked again at the woman. 'She looks nice. I could tell her you're a tree-hugger, that you lived in the forest, they love all that.'

Duncan rolled his eyes.

'I've only got your best interests at heart,' said Simon.

'For which I'm eternally grateful,' said Duncan.

Eve said, 'You lived in a forest?'

'Yes,' said Duncan, wryly. 'Did you hear about The Battle of Horton Forest?'

Eve said, 'I did not.'

'The council had agreed for part of it to be felled because some property people were offering to pay shedloads to build a big holiday park there. A "conservation retreat and spa" they called it. Conservation! What a nerve. So there was a big, drawn-out protest. I spent four days living in a tree.'

'Blimey,' said Eve. 'And what happened?'

'The police were pretty rough with the protesters, broke one guy's arm. But the project got shelved. Debatable as to why. The councillor in charge, who just happened to be friends with the property developer, got fired. All in all, the powers that be didn't come out of it very well.'

Eve was about to comment on how unquestioning she'd always been of authority; so uneventfully well-behaved, toeing the line – but then figured it might sound like a slight against Simon.

'Bloody plods,' Simon said.

Duncan murmured inconclusively.

'I'm going to go to the Anti-Purple Scheme march tomorrow,' he said. 'Either of you want to come?'

'Nah, not my thing,' said Simon. 'Besides, I've already got plans. I'm gonna be busy recovering from a hangover.'

'Absolutely, I was planning on going,' said Eve, considering it an optimum opportunity for research. 'There are supposed to be some Purpled people going, aren't there?'

'You wanna gawp at them?' said Simon.

'I want to talk to them,' said Eve.

'What, about whether they've seen Jesus in a slice of toast or something?'

'Ah, you *do* pay attention to what I do,' said Eve.

'See, he's as endearing as a bear cub,' said Duncan, playfully ruffling Simon's hair. Peering towards Simon's face, Duncan told Eve, 'There's *definitely* movement which might commonly be considered a smile.'

Hiding this, Simon puckered his lips and stood up. 'Want another drink?' he said, barely waiting for an answer before moving towards the bar.

Duncan smiled at Eve, unflustered by any twitchy Baxter behaviour.

'So,' he said, 'the march should be interesting.'

Shouldn't it just, thought Eve, who was also wondering how she could hatch a plan to investigate InTan.

Chapter Nine

Eve looked out of the train window. She was going to the Anti-Purple Scheme rally – on her own, after Duncan had failed to show up. She'd called him multiple times, only to hear repeat performances of his answer machine greeting, which she now knew off by heart: 'You've reached Duncan. Who knows what I'm doing, but leave a nice message, and I'll probably get back to you.' It seemed out of character for him to be unreliable, but then what did she know? He was Simon's friend, after all. Eve almost thought of calling Simon to see if he knew where Duncan was – possibly they were hung over somewhere, together – but no doubt her brother would get much mirthful satisfaction from her having been stood up. Hell, knowing him he probably instigated it, she thought.

A newspaper on the seat beside her boasted 'The Anti-Purple Scheme Rally: All You Need to Know'. Eve flipped through the pages until she found a double-paged map of the march's route, its borders filled with facts about the day's events and the organisations involved.

Today's rally has been organised by leading human rights charity Humane. For more than thirty years, staff at Humane have been battling to protect and support people around the world who are oppressed, imprisoned or tortured, particularly those held by brutal political regimes and persecuted for their beliefs. But when George McPhillips founded the organisation, he didn't envision having to take action regarding events here in the UK. 'I'm appalled,' he said. 'We should be leading the way with human rights, not taking a match to the sense of fairness and justice we've achieved.'

Humane went swiftly into action with campaigns against the initiative, and George is hoping that large numbers – thousands, if not tens of thousands – will attend today's rally to show solidarity for, as he puts it 'an end to this atrocious scheme, which is a crime against humanity'.

The march commences at 12 noon, departing from Victoria Embankment. It will proceed to Hyde Park, with the rally taking place there from 2.30pm. Rally highlights include talks from a number of high-profile speakers, including writer Flo Mackintosh, renowned human rights lawyer Steph Alexandrou, justice campaigner Billy Cox, and entrepreneur Magnus Jones.

Magnus again! Eve tried to ignore the bubbling sense of failure that accompanied any mention of him, especially today, with Duncan's non-appearance, and read on.

There will be musical performances from outspoken singer-songwriter Iggy Interception, along with popular ska bands Township and The Furys. George McPhillips said, 'Obviously there's a serious point to the event, but hopefully in addition to being seen and counted in the fight against the Purple Scheme, people are going to really enjoy themselves. It's always a terrific, uplifting thing to feel the solidarity of the crowd around you – and with the great bands who've agreed to play and everything else that'll be taking place, we should have quite a festival vibe going on too. People really should come and join us!'

Underneath was a schedule for the afternoon's events. Eve carefully tore the pages out to keep with her for reference. As she folded them she saw what was on the following page: an interview with Magnus. There was an accompanying photo of him sitting on the edge of a desk in his studio, casually dressed in a Humane t-shirt, jeans and Doc Martens, the wall behind covered in framed posters for various tours and campaigns he'd worked on, and though there was a warmth and approachability to his expression, even here, in smudgy black and white, to Eve his unnerving, unwavering gaze seemed to say, *I see you, Eve Baxter*, in a way she wasn't sure anyone else had. A highlighted quote from him declared: 'If you want something, you should be willing to fight for it – don't wait for someone else to fight for you.'

Eve sighed and continued to crease the pages into a flat, neat rectangle, knowing that even as she now folded Magnus out of sight, these sheets would end up being tucked away somewhere, further reminders that she wouldn't throw away. After the near-miss at the debate, she wondered if she would see him at the rally, and would she want to, given the choice? Had seeing Helena reminded him of her? What would he make of her achievements, so far from the aspirations she'd confided in him all those years ago, if he even remembered her at all? Given where they both were in their lives, he the nation's campaigning sweetheart, she a world-class purveyor of pet stories, Eve wasn't sure what she would have to say for herself, if their paths crossed. Her knees tingled and she felt a bit breathless at the prospect. She attempted to distract herself, looking out of the window at the fields of sleeping sheep, and washing lines draped with sheets and waving shirts.

The Embankment was bustling with protesters, and a more diverse crowd than Eve had expected. Young, old: from parents with pushchairs to poncho'd pensioners, and an assortment of banner-waving, placard-holding, these-boots-are-made-for-walking-wearing, cheery, chanting folk in between. Eve joined the edge of the march, watching the people around her: a middle-aged collective in sun-hats and sensible shoes with rolled up broadsheets poking from their backpacks; a couple with two small children, both looking perplexed – a son in a stroller and a daughter on dad's shoulders, gazing out across the crowd; a band of students dressed as barristers, wrapped in safety-pinned black-sheet gowns and wearing wigs fashioned from loo roll tubes and cotton wool. Eve took out her camera so she could snap the merriest contingents for *Say Fantastique!* Just wait until Adio sees these, she thought.

There were the banner-wielding posses, pledging home-made, hand-painted allegiance: Pets Against Purpleness had brought their dogs and, from what Eve could see, a ferret with them, while D-I-S-C-O Says N-O wore flares and mauve fancy-dress wigs, and were accompanied by a boom-box, currently blasting the appropriately titled tune 'Don't Leave Me This Way'. Some marchers, bleary-eyed and clutching coffee cups, didn't seem too keen on the latter, and either hurried or slowed their pace so as to move away from the music. Charities and trade organisations, meanwhile, marched with mass-produced placards in neon colours. One group, representing a student union, were chanting 'Purp-le, purp-le, no, no, no, Fletch-er, Fletch-er, go, go go', and not far from Eve half a dozen friends, probably about her own age, kept piping up with a song to the tune of an old pop record: 'They're only human, let's give them all a break. Don't turn them purple, it's a big mistake.' A couple of the warblers laughed and pulled faces at their inability to hit the high notes.

A woman next to Eve, probably a bit older than her, and seemingly with her boyfriend and another couple, said to Eve, 'Good turnout, isn't it?'

'Definitely. You've come far?'

'Yeah – got a coach down from Leeds early this morning. I'll be needing an early night tonight!'

Further over, Eve spotted a small crowd of lads who looked, if she were going to commit the judgemental sin of assigning them to a stereotype, like the sort who would usually have been found partaking in some Saturday football hooliganism or a right-wing rally, in bovver boots and bomber jackets, despite the heat. One was shouting so loudly that with his now-red face and bald head he looked like a body topped with a beetroot.

A little further ahead a policeman managed to just about curtail the contents of a pot of purple paint that a Pro-Purpleness protester was about to throw towards the crowd. A few marchers were lightly splattered, but when they saw how the scuffle had left most of the paint on the policeman and the protester they laughed it off. One flecked marcher twisted around, continuing to walk, but now backwards so he could shake his fist at the protester and repeat the 'No, no, no' chant at him. The protester squirmed in the policeman's clutches, but was frogmarched away.

'Why would you care about people who don't care about you?' a grandfatherly man called from the sidelines, looking on sadly as the procession continued past. There was something that made Eve want to stop and talk to him, but she was now surrounded by people and being swept along.

'Theo Fletcher, Terminator!' shouted another Pro-Purple protester, before adding gleefully, 'Keep on Turning!'

Eve and the coach trip couple shared an astonished look, and they walked on.

By the time they reached Hyde Park, it was already packed with thousands of mingling marchers. Many people were covered in purple face paint, and some had added flowers or peace symbols to their cheeks – Eve later spotted a number of stalls offering such a service, like the kind usually found at festivals and carnivals, where children would come away with beaming faces decorated as tigers or butterflies. She also spotted a fair few 'Lee' masks, like the cardboard cut-out ones of pop stars and royals that were stocked by party shops. Each wearing one of the masks, some teenage boys in shorts and t-shirts posed for a photo, their arms raised in combative gestures which reminded Eve of karate. Generally the mood of the rally was jolly, but this photo opportunity seemed a tad disturbing. How was Lee already a fancy-dress character? Did the Purpleness signify something for kids to parody, or, worse, admire?

'Lads,' Eve found herself saying, approaching the teenagers with her camera. 'Mind if I take a picture?'

A couple of the boys had pushed up the masks so they were on top of their heads, but pulled them back into place.

'Yeah, go for it!'

As the camera clicked, the boys shifted their positions, mirthful splutters coming from behind their masks as they egged one another into various elaborate poses. In one they adopted a uniform strong-man stance, their mostly weedy biceps not quite bulging.

'Thanks,' Eve smiled. 'Much obliged. And can I ask, what do you make of all this?'

'It's a laugh, isn't it,' said one.

'Not really,' said another. 'You wouldn't wanna be Purple, right?'

'I would!' said a third.

'Nah, you wouldn't.'

'It'd be cool.'

'Cool? You wouldn't be able to leave your house.'

'Yeah, but everyone would think you were hard.'

'Your mum wouldn't – you'd be in big trouble.'

174

They all laughed.

'What made you come here today?'

'Dunno. To see what it was like.'

'To see real Purple people!'

'And have you?'

'Yeah. They look so weird. Like aliens.'

'You were scared of them.'

'No, I wasn't. I felt sorry for them.'

'You want to be one!'

'You *are* gonna be one!'

More laughter.

'Well,' Eve lifted her camera and said, 'thanks for the picture.'

The boys grinned and continued to lark about.

Glancing around for other potential photos, Eve saw an actual Purple person, the first she'd encountered at the rally. Although this was the third Turned soul that she'd seen, Eve's breath still caught in her throat at the strangeness of his appearance. He was a pinky-blue hue, which at first could appear to be a trick of the light, until anyone of the natural palette of peach, beige or brown came into view.

The man was at a hot dog stand, which seemed somehow incongruous, reaching into his pocket for money to hand to the stall-holder. A woman in the queue, probably about Eve's parents' age, gave the Purple man a warm smile, before paying on his behalf. The man nodded in thanks before taking the hot dog, the stall-holder's arm and the mauve-tinted one meeting under a serviette-wrapped bun. Momentarily remembering the camera in her hand, Eve jolted out of her slack-jawed reverie and sneaked a couple of snaps. As she again lowered the lens, she noticed others around her staring too, bug-eyed at the close proximity of this strange skin. Ignoring them, or giving an admirable impression of doing so, the man joined a nearby friend who, arms folded, shot a terse look at anyone whose

175

glance lingered on his mate for more than the briefest of moments. Then they wandered into the crowd.

Eve looked down at her camera, recalling the pictures she'd taken. A close-up captured the hot dog, something of a tanned limb itself, a dividing line between the stall-holder's pinkish, slightly sunburnt flesh and the compelling wounded indigo (their composition formed a stunted cross of sorts, and Eve imagined it as the country's flag, illustrating an astonishing state of the nation). She had surprised herself; it was a lucky shot, and a good one.

Here in the park, there seemed to be plenty of Purple people, which contravened the restrictions put in place for them, specifically that no more than one Turned person could be seen in public at any time, and Eve wondered how the organisers were getting around that. They were being interviewed by camera crews, questioned by human rights campaigners wearing fluorescent tabards bearing the Humane logo, and approached by fellow marchers, who would ask them how they were and give them a firm handshake in solidarity. Eve watched one man embrace a Purpled guy that he'd just spoken to, squinting as she saw the latter – surely not? – lift a wallet from his supporter's pocket. She glanced around to see if anyone else had noticed, but apparently they hadn't. Before she could walk over to tell him, the man went to reach into his pocket and realised. Eve watched his face register surprise, disbelief and then – what? Indignation, anger, disillusionment? He turned to find the Purpled man in the crowd, but of course he was already gone. The wallet-less man walked away, shaking his head.

Nearby, Eve noticed a Purple person talking to one of the Humane representatives. They were standing near a bench. Eve walked over, reaching into her bag to find her sandwiches, and feeling a dejected pang as she did so – this was a lunch made for Duncan and her. She sat down, cheese and pickle sarnie in hand, and tuned into their conversation.

'You don't wanna know, mate.'

'Well,' said the rep, 'whatever it was that caused you to be Turned, we're here to talk to you. We want to know how you are, how people who've gone through what you're going through are getting on.'

'How people who've gone through what I'm going through?' the Purple man laughed, nastily.

As though surveying the crowd, Eve stole a glance his way. He was wiry, with close-cropped hair, a narrow chin, and beady, flinty eyes. With the pointiness of his features and the triangularness of his head, he reminded Eve of the kind of Stone Age hammer that was pulled up during archaeological digs; he was the sort of person you'd instinctively shy away from on the street, whether or not he was Purple.

'Seeing as you're so interested,' sneered Stone Age, 'I was with a couple of mates, and we gave some bloke a few kicks. When I say a few, he ended up in hospital. Black eyes, broken bones, internal injuries. He hadn't really done anything, we were just bored and fancied giving him a kicking. Would you still like to hear how I'm *getting on?*'

'If you'd like to talk,' said the rep, 'I'm here to listen. We want all Turned people to know they have support.'

Eve had noted the rep's body language was steady and professional. He stood straight, making respectful eye contact, and when he spoke he sounded firm, neither rattled nor sympathetic. But Eve wondered if this was one instance where he thought a person being Turned was actually a good thing.

'Really? Here's what I think of your support.' With some gargled phlegm-mustering, Stone Age spat on the ground. 'Pathetic. All the softies here, all caring and sharing when really they're pleased as you like, being able to spot the thugs, like colouring by numbers. What a joke.'

Stone Age appeared in Eve's peripheral vision, stomping away.

'And yet you're here,' the rep murmured, under his breath.

Eve looked round and saw him completing a form attached to a clipboard.

'He seemed like a nice boy,' said Eve, having already checked that Stone Age was well out of earshot.

'It definitely takes all sorts,' the rep replied. He glanced at a colleague to the other side of Eve, who was busy talking to a younger Purple person, then walked off, into the crowd.

Taking a bite of another sandwich, Eve listened in to the second rep's exchange.

'What time of day was this?' she asked intently, pen poised ready to note the response.

'Evening, but not late. I dunno – say seven?'

The rep appeared to check a box on her form. 'Were there many other people around?'

The Purple youth gave her an incredulous look. 'I'm not stupid. I wouldn't have been taking it if there was, would I?'

'Sorry,' the rep said, before adding, as though this lad was less au fait with criminal behaviour than she was, 'You'd be surprised. People get away with all sorts in broad daylight.'

The boy looked neither surprised nor interested.

'So, you didn't notice anyone in the vicinity? No police officers?'

The lad shook his head. 'Nah.'

'And as you left, with the bike?'

'I cycled away pretty fast, and I didn't see no cops.'

'No one who might have been a plain clothes officer, perhaps?'

The boy shrugged.

'So, just to confirm, you didn't see anyone around you?'

'No cops, no.'

The rep smiled patiently. 'Anyone at all?'

'A few geezers outside a pub, but it was some doors down, not right where I was. Maybe someone walking a dog, a bloke using a pay phone. But none near me, none looking at me.'

The rep nodded, jotting everything down. 'And then at what point did the colour change occur?'

'I watched telly, went to bed, got up the next morning.' He held up his hands. 'And this.'

'How did it make you feel?'

The incredulous look again. 'Yeah, brilliant, charmed.'

'Had you heard about the Purple Scheme before this happened to you?'

'Yeah, course.'

'It didn't deter you?'

'I wouldn't have done it if I thought this was gonna happen to me, course not. But I didn't see no one who was gonna catch me, so who was gonna make me like this? No one I could see.'

'How have people treated you since the change?'

'They give me looks. They watch me. I ain't murdered no one. Ain't hurt no one. A bike, right? It's nothing. I'm being judged for nothing. This is wrong, real wrong.'

The rep nodded again. 'Absolutely. Well, we're fighting to get this changed. And we're providing legal advice, and counselling, if you'd like either of those. Any other comments you'd like to make?'

'I'm no angel, right, but I ain't hurt no one, and this don't help me. Sometimes you do things you shouldn't do, but... sometimes what else are you gonna do? Nothing's gonna improve for me now, right?'

The rep looked at him earnestly. 'It can, really. You can turn

179

things around,' she said. 'We've got counsellors here if you'd like to talk to someone? Or get legal assistance?'

'I dunno about that...'

She handed him a card. 'Take this. We really want to help, so please do call if there's anything we can do.'

The lad looked at the card and gave a cautious nod.

As he departed, the rep said, 'Best of luck.'

Eve approached the rep.

'Hi,' she said with a smile. 'Great work you're doing here.'

'Thank you. And thank you for coming today. It's really heartening to see so many people united against this.'

'Absolutely. I was curious about a couple of things. How is it that the police aren't doing anything about there being so many Turned people here? I thought there wasn't supposed to be more than one in any public place.'

'You're right about that, but we got a special dispensation for this event.'

'Really?'

'Mm. George McPhillips can be very persuasive! Actually, they weren't allowed to take part in the march itself, but they're allowed to be here until three pm. And you'll have noticed all the extra police officers keeping an eye on things. Along with an assignment of parole officers, they're also going to be escorting them from here so there's no rowdiness – ' the rep rolled her eyes – 'when they leave.'

'Oh, right,' said Eve. 'It was good that you were able to get that dispensation, then. It must be the only exception so far, isn't it?'

'It is, yes. The police weren't at all happy about it. Hopefully the scheme won't last long enough for there to need to be many more.'

Eve murmured in agreement. 'Also, it seems strange that no

one knows how the Turning is happening. Is Humane looking into that?'

'We're trying. It's very frustrating. The government won't release any information, and we're trying to investigate, but our priorities are the welfare of Turned people, and campaigning to overturn the scheme, so... All we can do is ask Turned people what they remember, which so far isn't very much at all.'

So much for useful research, Eve thought, swallowing the last bite of her sandwich.

Taking occasional pictures, Eve weaved through the crowd. A couple of the speakers had already said their piece, and Iggy Interceptor was completing his set; on one of the screens broadcasting the onstage action, he'd just announced his last song, so Eve made her way forwards, delving into her pocket for the newspaper's schedule, which she was fairly sure had listed Magnus as up next.

Over by a tree, near to a family having a picnic, a small group of Purple people appeared to be loitering, a gathering of abnormal, stained cells. There were five or six of them, though a couple more (was that Stone Age?) joined the sidelines as Eve was passing. Most were smoking, and they looked tense – as you would, no doubt, if you were subjected to relentless gawping (however well-meaning that might have been today), and now, together, could see your tarnished self reflected in the faces of other marked souls. But still... were they up to something, or simply seizing the rare opportunity to be around others going through the same ordeal? A quick survey of the area showed a lack of police, or Humane reps, as far as Eve could see, and no one else appeared to have noticed the gathering, though perhaps, as per the general public's pre-

Purple, pre-empowered days, anyone who had noted the assembly was pretending not to. Naturally they were here to give any Turned folk the benefit of the doubt, but they had form, didn't they? Maybe people assumed that nothing would, or could, happen here. Even if the plum flock had the opportunity, why do anything to create more trouble for themselves, or to harm those who were here to support them?

Eve glanced over, and one of the Purple men noticed, glaring at her with narrowed eyes which implied she'd do best to look away. Eve felt something in her stomach lurch, and not the cheese sandwiches. Unsettled, but telling herself that for them, surely this was a day's respite from the usual damnation, she moved on.

'And now,' George McPhillips announced, 'I'm very pleased to welcome someone who's been a long-time Humane collaborator, and become an incredible champion of the Anti-Purple cause – just wait 'til you see what he's got up his sleeve! It's the tremendous, exemplary Magnus Jones.'

There was a cheer from the stage area, and Eve hurriedly walked towards it. Spotting the bright tabard of a Humane rep slightly ahead of her, she caught up with him, tapping him on the shoulder.

'Excuse me,' she said.

The rep glanced back at her – he seemed distracted, possibly intent on getting towards the stage too.

'It's probably nothing,' Eve said, attempting to make a snap decision on how best to present this, 'and I wouldn't want to be a snitch, but there's a group of Turned guys over there,' she waved her arm towards the tree, 'and I don't know… will they get into trouble – more trouble – if they're caught together? What with the regulations and all?'

The rep wrinkled his nose, then glanced briefly towards the stage. 'I'm sure they'll be fine,' he said. 'We wanted this to be a day where they could share their experiences, get a bit of moral support, so if they're getting that, then great. I wouldn't worry. They'll be having to leave soon, anyway. Might as well let them enjoy their last moments with like...'

He'd walked into an awkward cul-de-sac of a comment. Like-minded, tinted, troubled?

He shrugged. 'Let 'em have their last moments of solidarity for the day.'

Eve nodded, not sure if he was being unduly lax, or she was being unduly fretful.

They reached the considerable crescent of people surrounding the stage. Magnus had taken the microphone and was encouraging the crowd to give George a round of applause.

'George McPhillips, everyone,' he said. 'What an amazing gent. He's made such a colossal difference to the lives of so many people, has so many incredible achievements under his belt. And the latest of those is getting us all here today. How brilliant it is to see such a massive turn-out. Not that it's for me to say – but someone needs to say it – you should all feel really proud of yourselves for standing up and being counted, for fighting the good fight for justice – ' there was a cheer from the crowd – 'which really does make an immeasurable difference.' Magnus smiled. 'Can I just ask you: Purple People?'

There was a ripple of laughter from the crowd, who chanted 'No, no, no!'

'And the ridiculous Purple initiative?'

'Go, go, go!'

Very savvy of him not to mention Theo Fletcher, Eve thought.

'Now, I'm here to read statements from some people affected by this frankly ludicrous scheme, to speak on behalf of those who are still too traumatised by what's happened to them to go out, to be able to be here with us today. I'm also joined by some special guests who'd like to share their stories with you directly, and as today is about their stories, I'm going to start as I mean to go on. Ladies and gents, please welcome Davey.'

Magnus turned, stretching an arm out towards one side of the stage. As he did so, something seemed to catch his eye. He kept his composure, shaking the hand of Purpled person Davey, and leaning forward to extend this into a man-hug – confusing Davey, who'd appeared nervous enough about the handshake. But from her side of the crowd, Eve could see Magnus using this embrace to indicate to George, behind Davey's back, that something was wrong. She saw George look out, beyond the crowd. Eve followed his gaze to see a trio of Purple people attacking a policeman, and other small bands of Turned men beginning to throw punches at other officers. One man had an aerosol can which he sprayed in a policeman's face, coating him with purple paint. The officer screamed, covering his eyes. Hearing the commotion, members of the crowd rushed back to try and break up the fights, but were kicked or punched, and in one case, warded off with a knife.

'Okay everyone, we seem to be experiencing some trouble,' said Magnus, 'but please stay calm, and *don't* panic. Can we get some stewards to support the crowd…'

George was indicating to those in tabards to stand between the audience and the clusters of fighting. Dozens of additional police officers were emptying out of nearby vans and arriving from other parts of the park, some in riot gear, rushing towards the disturbance.

'Please don't try to intervene,' Magnus continued. 'The cavalry's arrived, and hopefully this unfortunate outburst will be controlled very shortly.'

There was a muffled shout of 'You should pay for what you've done to us!' as the offenders were surrounded, outnumbered and strong-armed into submission. A pair of officers ran past the edge of the crowd where Eve was standing, and she heard one of them spit, 'See what you get with this namby-pamby nonsense...'

By now a number of attendees were heading out of the park, away from the trouble. Small children were crying, being hurriedly rolled away in their pushchairs. Other attendees, not able to see what was going on, frowned and stood their ground, unsure whether they should stay or go. Seeing them leave, Magnus shook his head and, moving his mouth away from the microphone, swore. Davey, still on stage and frozen in place, looked dismayed.

'Please, don't let this be what today is about,' Magnus urged the depleting crowd. 'Stupid actions by a misguided few should not spoil what we've achieved today – what *you've* achieved today.'

There were some cheers from the audience, but one voice shouted: 'What if they don't deserve it? What if we should leave them to be Turned after all?'

'Honestly, we can't think like that. There's a much bigger picture here, much more at stake. *Remember why you came here today*. We have to stick together. Right, Davey?'

Davey nodded, and took a nervous, hunched step forward, scanning the crowd for signs of hostility.

Calling out to the audience, Magnus said, 'And you need to listen, everyone, please!' He put a hand on Davey's shoulder. 'Now, why do you think it's important that we stand united?'

'Because you can't... you shouldn't define someone by their worst action, the most stupid thing they've done. Because then how do they get past that? How do they have the will to be better, to improve themselves, if everyone's expecting the worst from them?' Davey's voice trembled.

'What happened to you?'

'I was an idiot, of course I was. Got in a fight outside a club, then turned out like this.' He looked sheepish. 'I thought that was a funny come-down off the pills.'

There was some laughter from the audience.

'Now I've lost my job, I was going into the army and they don't want me any more. I might have ruined my life for a pointless brawl. But you know that's half an hour out of my Saturday night. I'm not a loser. I had a job, I worked hard, I look after my nan and my mum. This,' he held up his Purpled hands, 'is not who I am. But now it might as well be.'

'Thanks, Davey,' said Magnus, looking him in the eye and giving an appreciative nod. 'Everyone remember why they're here?' There was a rousing cheer. 'Good. Now, we're going to make an impromptu change to the schedule with some lovable troublemakers who're going to knock your socks off – in a good way...'

Magnus swivelled as a black-clad quartet of guys and girls marched purposefully onstage. This was The Furys. Their singer snatched the microphone from Magnus and announced, 'This fighting is bollocks! We came here united, and that's the way we're gonna stay, right? Now I wanna hear you SING!' With a crash of drums and a squawk of guitar, they launched into their first song.

Eve could see Magnus had ducked out from the wings, and now stood with George facing a couple of Humane reps, their angrily shaking heads and rapidly gesticulating hands implying they were fuming and frustrated. Eve had considered going over. After all this time, to keep being so close, and yet not... But it hardly seemed like an opportune moment to introduce herself.

With the stage behind her, Eve made her way through the crowd. The remaining Purple people were being escorted away, glum, plum faces amid appeals for compassion: 'Most of us are here for a peaceful protest...' 'Can't you see we're not all like that...' 'I haven't done anything wrong...' To the last comment, one policeman said, 'Now if that was true you'd be the same colour as me.'

A woman approached the policeman. 'Aren't they allowed to stay a bit longer?'

'Not after what just happened.'

'But it seems unfair—'

'Rules are rules,' said the officer. 'And if this lot realised that, there'd never be any trouble, would there?'

The woman watched them go. 'We're right behind you,' she said, 'whatever it takes!'

Moving out of the park, Eve turned down a side-street which led to a small coffee shop she knew of which, being in a less stumble-upon-able location, she hoped wouldn't be too busy. Upon reaching what she believed to be the place, she stood outside for a moment, confused; the once common-or-garden café was now the Jitterbug Tea Rooms, with big band tunes playing on an old gramophone. Surprised, she went inside.

Eve noticed a few placards leant up against the wall behind the cafe's coat stand. She guessed that half of the patrons had been at the rally: clad in t-shirts, parkas and trainers, they chatted with the enthused passion and cheer that came from taking an active stand for something, believing you could make a change, and being surrounded by a sea of similarly minded others as you did so. The remaining customers were accompanied by more leisurely shopping bags, occasionally staring, intrigued, at the marchers in their midst. A German-sounding man, who was sharing a generous slice of Victoria sponge with his wife, put down his fork and cleared his throat before addressing a group at another table.

'Excuse me,' he said, 'the protest – what is it for?'

Two boys, sixth formers, Eve would guess, leant forward with lanky enthusiasm. 'It's against the Purple People initiative,' said one.

'Yeah,' said the other. 'It's completely mad, and any sensible people don't like it, so we're here to get the government to take notice—'

''Cause if they see all the people here today they'll have to think again.'

'I see,' said the German man, nodding. 'That would be a democratic conclusion, would it not?'

'It has to happen,' said one of the boys.

'It *will* happen,' said the other.

'It is good that you march,' the German man responded politely, clearly less convinced of the outcome, before returning to his Victoria sponge.

Eve reached the counter.

'I'll have the Blitz Tea,' she said. 'That's just an ordinary tea, right?'

'Yes, English Breakfast,' said the waitress.

'Right,' said Eve. 'And a scone, please.'

Behind her, a man ordered a fancy coffee.

'We don't do those,' the waitress said, apologetically. 'We only serve refreshments that would have been served during the war.'

The man winced, as though in deep, unfathomable pain.

'I swear this country is becoming more and more like a theme park,' said the man, addressing the air.

Eve smiled at him and looked around the room for a seat. There was a spare stool at a counter by the window, though beside it were a couple of precariously propped banners which she didn't want to knock over. Then she spotted a chair at a table where there was a woman sitting alone; she was looking down, reading a newspaper. Taking her tray, Eve headed over.

'Do you mind if I sit here?'

The woman looked up. Eve nearly dropped her tray.

'Go ahead.' The woman pulled her cup and a pair of sunglasses towards her, making room on the table. She then looked at her watch, a calculating flicker crossing her face before she turned back to the paper. She was quickly engrossed, and tucked her hand under her chin as she read.

Eve took a seat. She swallowed, trying to act normally, before taking out her notebook, setting her pen beside it as she took a look at the group of sixth formers, an attempt at appearing distracted.

The woman looked at Eve and gave a quick smile. Eve tried to assess whether she was open to engaging with anyone – Eve would guess not, that she must get stopped all the time. But then a family walked past, the father with a child on his shoulders, the mother wheeling a pushchair in which another child sat. All of their faces were painted Purple. One of the children turned and, seeing the woman, waved at her; the woman waved back. Eve couldn't help herself.

'Have you been on the march?'

The woman nodded. 'Yes,' she said. 'Marches are often quite heartening, I'd say. Democracy in action.'

That voice! So familiar, and comforting.

'You?'

'I was there, only just left to… have a bit of a break. Were you there when the trouble started?'

'No, what happened?'

'Some groups of Purple people attacked the police.'

'Was anyone hurt?'

'I'm not sure. One of the policemen had paint sprayed in his eyes, so he can't be in good shape.'

'That's awful. George and the Humane team must be so upset.'

'They didn't look too happy.'

The woman let her newspaper rest on the table. 'What do you think of it all?' she asked.

'I'm still figuring that out.'

The woman's expression changed; she appeared pleasantly surprised at this answer. Acknowledging Eve's notebook, she said, 'You're a journalist?'

Eve wasn't sure if that made her want to laugh or cry.

'I work for a news agency… well, we're not so grand, more frolicky news, really. We supply cheery stuff, funny commentary on things, to newspapers and TV shows.'

The woman appeared to be considering this.

'We've been running it from New York. It's called *Say Fantastique!*'

'I knew you were going to say that!' the woman said. 'I love what you do there. And I love Pam Fox-Jones. My friends call me Pam!' She laughed.

Eve was truly gobsmacked. She'd been about to take a sip of tea and nearly dropped her cup. Do not cry, she told herself.

'That's more amazing than you know,' she said. 'You must get people saying this all the time, and it's probably quite tedious, but I am such a fan of yours. Honestly, this is the biggest treat to meet you. Well, again, sort of, but that was years ago. When I tell Adio that I bumped into you today and that you love Pam, he won't believe it.' Eve took a breath. 'Oh, and I'm Eve, by the way.'

The woman extended her hand. 'Annie,' she said. 'Lovely to meet you.'

Annie Morris! It was just as well Duncan had stood her up and Magnus had been in the thick of Humane things or this would never have happened. Eve wasn't sure how to contain her excitement. She took a bite of scone.

'Pam's brilliant. The cameramen are always teasing me that I've got a bottle of sherry under my desk, cheeky sods,' Annie said. With impeccable timing she added, 'When actually it's a flask of gin.'

Eve was having trouble swallowing her mouthful of scone. 'Pam was Adio's idea. He drew her as a doodle for my birthday card one year. When I was growing up I always wanted to be a newsreader, so he thought that would be a hoot. Then we used her for the site, and now she's got a life of her own.'

'And she's got a purple beehive,' said Annie, approvingly.

'Well, we're trying to tackle more topical things…'

'I noticed. Very astute. You have a different perspective to everywhere else. You should make the most of it.'

'The perspective of a hedgehog on a skateboard, or a hang-gliding dog?'

Annie laughed. 'Not that – there *is* that – but you have a distinctive appeal. Plus you're independent, and you really can't underestimate how much people value that. Given that the news corporations are sometimes felt to be biased…'

Diplomatic, Eve thought.

'These days,' Annie said, 'small can be especially mighty.'

'Here's hoping…'

'Did you just say we'd met before?'

'I came to visit the News South studio years ago. My mum arranged it for my birthday. I came with her and my brother. You gave me a signed postcard – I've still got it.'

Why on earth would you say that, Eve berated herself. What an idiot.

'Really?' Annie looked touched. 'That's lovely to hear. I hope you had a good day, and that it was interesting.' In what

Eve guessed was a reference to *Say Fantastique!*, Annie added, 'Though perhaps we seemed quite sombre.'

Eve wanted to say, sombre was exactly what I wanted, but didn't trust herself to utter anything sensible.

Annie considered Eve for a brief moment, before looking across at a table of welly-wearing placard-wavers, gathering themselves and their banners together, ready to head back outside.

'The rally was still going?'

'It was when I left. The Furys had just gone on and were livening things up, so...' She's going to leave, Eve thought, thinking of all the things she wanted to ask her, including questions about the Purple Scheme. I shouldn't have mentioned the postcard – that'd make anyone want to run away into a riot rather than be subjected to such fawning nonsense.

Annie was folding her newspaper, but paused, and looked at Eve.

'You had a question?' she said.

'Yes.' Eve was curious. 'How did you... ?'

'Years of interviews,' said Annie. 'Makes it easy to pick up on when someone has something they want to say.'

This was not only one of Eve's newsreading heroines, but an incredibly experienced journalist who'd spent decades working at one of the country's biggest news organisations. Could – should – Eve ask Annie the one question she most wanted to put to her?

Leaning forward, Annie said, 'Trust your instincts, Eve.'

Pushing her plate to one side, Eve took a breath.

'No one is saying anything about how the transformations are happening,' she said, 'and I'm very curious about that.'

Annie sat back. She nodded. 'Go on.'

'It seems improbable that there aren't people looking into it.'

Annie tilted her head. Another nod.

'But I want to look into it. I want to find out. Mostly because it's fascinating – isn't it?' This said with rhetorical wonder.

'It is incredible, yes.'

'But also because...' How not to sound like a moron? 'I know I've been caught up in silly news, that I must seem frivolous. But I spent most of my life transfixed by proper news. I just sort of... got waylaid. But this story. It sounds barmy, but it's mine. This scheme is ridiculous, and sort of comical, in an awful way, but also earth-shattering. And I want to crack it.'

Eve expected Annie to be reaching for her jacket, but did she instead detect an intrigued glint in her eyes?

'You'll be aware,' said Annie, 'that it's all been very need-to-know. My impression is that very few people have the full scoop on how it's being implemented, certainly not any journalists.'

At this, Eve thought of a recent photograph she'd seen of Annie at a dinner with Theo Fletcher, and the friendly relationship they supposedly had.

'And I don't know any officials who've talked about it,' Annie continued, 'even off the record.'

'It's so strange that publicly no one seems to be asking about it.'

'Well,' Annie said, 'I suppose people are distracted by the bigger picture. If you're for the scheme you're not interested in how people are being Turned, you're just glad that they are. If you're against, it's not how it's happening that concerns you so much as that it's happening at all.'

'I know. Obviously it makes it so much more effective, that it's so secret. That they can create more fear that way. A mysterious bogeyman who can get you at any time, you don't know where or when, or how, only that he's all around you. For the good, that gives them strength, a sense of protection, and justice. For the bad, it's supposed to keep them on edge, let them know that they can be caught at any time, that they can't get away with anything.'

'Hats off to them,' said Annie. 'It's very clever. And means the government will want to do everything it can to maintain that secrecy. Particularly after the way the scheme was revealed. I'd imagine they'll take an extremely dim view of anyone getting close enough to let the cat out of the bag.'

'Do you think they'd Turn them Purple?' Eve joked.

'I actually wouldn't be surprised,' said Annie.

'Really?' Eve faltered. 'So you think it could be dangerous?'

'Undoubtedly.'

'An inadvisable investigation, then?'

'I wouldn't necessarily say that,' said Annie, with a conspiratorial smile.

Chapter Ten

It was highly likely that, had there not been any trouble at the rally, it would barely have been reported at all. But, gleeful at this gift of violet violence, the papers were ablaze.

Seven police officers were injured yesterday when Purple THUGS attacked them at a rally AGAINST the Purple Scheme. Hundreds of people attended the event, including some families with TOTS who were left TERRIFIED when violence broke out. The HOOLIGANS claimed to be protesting at the force's involvement in Turning delinquents, even though the government has yet to confirm that it's bobbies on the beat who are behind it. Officer Jim Woodbeam is still in hospital after purple PAINT was sprayed in his eyes. Fellow cop Nic Django said, 'Doctors are doing everything they can to save his sight. What he's going through you wouldn't wish on anyone. The animals who did this to him deserve much worse than being Turned Purple.'

ZANY musician Iggy Interceptor, who performed at the rally and is known for supporting controversial causes, was overheard to say, 'It's TYPICAL that a bunch of trouble-makers have to RUIN the day. I didn't come here today to support that kind of behaviour. It's a disgrace, man.'

Courageous PM Theo Fletcher was horrified at the reports, and said, 'It's a real shame that a day that was showing support for those who've been Turned ended in such tragedy. While I appreciate those decent non-Purple people who attended the rally did so with democratic intentions, I think, unfortunately, this illustrates that we are right to segregate some members of our society, who simply cannot be trusted to behave peacefully or with respect. It also shows that sadly it was an error on our part to lift the restriction on the number of Turned people allowed in public places for this event; that was a one-off relaxation of the rules, which will not be repeated. My thoughts are with those who were hurt in the line of duty, and I wish them all a speedy and full recovery.

We asked for YOUR SAY, and here are some of your thoughts:

'I'm a retired police officer, and I'd like to thank my colleagues for putting themselves in the line of fire to protect others. Their dedication is an inspiration to us all.' Barbara, 63.

'I don't know why anyone's surprised. Wot were they thinking, having a rally for them in the first place? Barmy!' Gordon, 51.

'It's disgusting, throwing people's goodwill back in their faces. They deserve to be Purple AND rot in jail.' Fleur, 27.

'Maybe they can be given an extra dose, so they're more Purple than the others?' Alan, 49.

On top of that, the number of Purple people had increased significantly, even in the nation's smaller towns and villages, and each day mauve mugshots filled an ever expanding number of column inches. On the TV vox pop clips Eve had watched that morning, a man in a navy anorak had said, 'They're spreading like fungus. Scum!' whilst a psychologist in a patterned blouse said, 'It's really very dangerous to be demonising people this way.'

Some of those initially held in custody were now back in their homes, some hiding behind boarded-up windows which had already been sprayed with growling graffiti declaring 'A Lav Lives Here'. There were stories of people who would begin to Turn while they were out and about, or at work. One man was at the till in a supermarket when the change commenced, causing the cashier to faint; another was on a bus when his Purple patches began to appear, only realising when the old lady beside him let out a piercing shriek. Speaking to reporters later, the driver said: 'It's bloody dangerous having people turning Purple willy nilly, all over the place. I nearly had a heart attack.'

But even with the rising number of lilac lads and lasses, there was no respite for original Lav, Lee, whose stepdad had now been Turned too. 'Like Father, Like Son', ran the headline, alongside Baz Collyer's photo.

Looks like the apple doesn't fall far from the tree when it comes to Lee Bowen. His stepdad, Baz, must have been setting him a thuggish example – having just been Turned for not one, but TWO violent offences. At first Baz claimed he'd been unfairly made a Lav after defending Lee's name by HEADBUTTING a man making comments about his wayward stepson. But that wasn't the crime for which he got Purple punishment. In fact, after leaving the shop where the headbutting incident occurred, he was seen PUNCHING Lee's mum, Vicky. 'I'm relieved Baz is with the police now,' said Vicky. 'I've been really SCARED of him for a long time – and I'm not the only one he's been using as a punch bag.'

In the Lav Line Up were half a dozen perpetrators (or, as the papers now preferred, 'purpetrators') of stabbings, one of which had proved fatal; numerous men and a teenage girl who had been involved in pub brawls; a woman who – this was particularly unpleasant – had thrown acid in the face of an alleged love rival; and a man who, for kicks, had stolen a disabled man's mobility scooter and dumped it by a bus stop a mile away.

The dogs bounded into the room, ahead of Helena, who'd taken them out for a walk.

'Any word?' she asked Eve, referring to no-show Duncan.

'Nope.'

'Huh.'

'There'll be a perfectly rational explanation,' said Womble.

'Glad to hear you still appreciate the word rational,' said Helena.

At this, Womble looked towards the Svengalis poster and raised his eyebrows, as though theirs too might rise in solidarity.

'Well,' said Eve, both wondering aloud and hoping to defuse this exchange, 'not being psychic, I'd be intrigued to know what that explanation is, though I'm guessing it involves beer and Simon…'

Given these assumptions, she was neither worried nor too interested. But, never one for unsolved mysteries, she felt a twinge every time the phone rang, so it didn't help that Womble and Helena had received a handful of silent phone calls. Having not been home for any of these instances, Womble teased Helena that she might be imagining them – 'Perhaps it's shy aliens trying to make contact.' To which Helena retorted, 'I think you've been spending too much time with Bob.'

Eve pushed the pile of newspapers out of the way. As usual, there had been no new clues today. But based on Bob's InTan theory, in her notebook Eve had made a list of potential avenues for investigation:

Crayne Industries

Bell & Styles
The Gilded Tub Spa
Carla De Lora

Quite an enigma, Carla had recently separated from her Swiss millionaire husband, heir to a watch-manufacturing fortune, after a scandal involving his dealing with dodgy diamonds being smuggled through human mules. This was a story where revelations stacked up like a pile of pancakes, and the tabloids reported the split in headlines that surprised no one, such as 'Carla's Hubby's no Diamond Geezer', and 'Stop the Clock! Carla Calls Time on Marriage'. Now allegedly cloistered away, quietly recovering from the break-up, Carla hadn't been seen in public for months. Unfortunate timing, Eve thought – no pun intended – for if only there were some way to speak to her, Carla was one person guaranteed to know InTan's secret.

The press office at Crayne Industries had been as forthcoming as Eve had anticipated, despite her posing as someone she hoped would be unlikely to arouse suspicion.

'Hi, this is Sarah, calling from Carla De Lora's office. I'm her new assistant, and I'm just pulling together details of her endorsements so we have an overview of her upcoming commitments, when she... you know, is ready to dive back into her schedule.'

'Sure, okay,' said the press officer, giving Eve a glimmer of hope.

'You're the office for InTan, am I right?'

'That's correct.'

'Great! So, I can't see any pending appearances or shoots, and wanted to check there's nothing I should be aware of?'

'There isn't, no. Did Carla not tell you that the product's no longer scheduled for release?'

'No! Oh my goodness, I'm so sorry. Carla's… well, she's on holiday at the moment, and I'm just catching up on everything in her absence, ready for when she gets back. That's such a shame! She looked incredible in the photos. I had my fingers crossed I might get to try it. Did you?'

'No, but then personally, I'm not one for tanning. Everyone else here was pretty excited about it, though.'

'I'll bet. What with it lasting so long. What is it, a pill?'

'I…' The press officer paused, and there was muffled talking as she covered the receiver. 'I'm sorry. For commercial reasons, that's confidential, so we would only be able to talk about the product with Carla herself.'

'Gosh! Right, of course. I'll have to ask Carla to spill the beans, then! And actually, speaking of spillages, I've… um… managed to tip coffee over a couple of the pages of her InTan agreement. Might someone be able to send over another copy, do you think?'

'You'd have to ask the legal department. Though honestly, if I were you, I'd ask Carla's lawyer, or agent. Our legal team would only send it on to them, anyway.'

'Great, that's so helpful, thank you,' said Eve.

Or rather, she thought, absolutely no help at all.

Next she tried both Bell & Styles and the Gilded Tub Beauty Spa, posing first as a beauty journalist, and then as a keen customer prepared to pay any price to become so exclusively golden, to no avail.

Eve sighed, underlining Carla's name on her list. How, she wondered, am I going to track down Carla De Lora? She didn't know anyone Carla worked with, and if she was off the grid somewhere it would be even trickier to engineer getting to talk to her.

Hoping she could find some mention of InTan – evidence of its existence was proving to be highly elusive on the Portal – Eve waded through a slew of articles featuring Carla. She found beauty tips, fashion tips, and an infinite number of mentions on party pages, before stumbling across what seemed to be a particularly fortuitous photo: Carla in a new anti-Purple Scheme portrait, swathed in mauve lighting, remaining typically elegant, the most luminous of Lavs, taken by Magnus. Did she dare approach him to ask for help?

Following both Annie and Frankie's cautions, inviting anyone else to partake in her (admittedly low-fi) investigation meant potentially luring them into a murky, governmental spider's web. And if they were caught, what would be the consequences? What punishment would be handed to those who tried, or succeeded, to unveil the scheme's secrets? Also, what if Magnus, in turn, were to enlist Humane's help? Eve presumed they were already researching the path to Purpledom, and while their clout, and manpower, could only be beneficial to uncovering the truth, with a tight grip on her spade *she* wanted to be the one to undig it.

There was another, worse, consideration, too: making a fool of herself in front of Magnus, again. If he even remembered her and responded to any message she sent, he could think the InTan notion was the most laughable thing he'd ever heard. What she might hope for (enjoying each other's company, maybe hitting upon what had happened, or not, back in the day), and what would actually transpire (who knew what nit-witted embarrassment she could unleash upon herself), might be poles apart. How would she feel then? Was Magnus the answer? Or might there be another way?

Eve doodled an approximation of Pam, with a speech bubble asking 'How?' Maybe Adio could do something with the

InTan idea, she thought. Plant the seed in an unexpectedly tanned Pam.

Keen for a distraction, she called the *Say Fantastique!* office, regaling Adio with recent events.

'Annie Morris a Pam fan!' he said. 'There's something to celebrate.'

'Purple Pam *is* ludicrously popular. Have you seen the tidal wave of messages about her whooshing into the Portal? People are loving her mauve specs and beehive.' Eve could hear Adio puffing on a cigarette. 'You really do need to give up,' she said.

'I know, doll. But moving on... How's your dad settling in?'

'He's good, pretty much back on form. He's supposed to be taking it easy, which at the moment translates as my mum looking after him, and them cooing over each other. I'm leaving them to it, possibly more than I should be.'

'They need a chaperone?'

'They need something, that's for sure.'

'In other news,' said Adio, 'have you seen the response your report on the rally has had, mon fleur?'

'I know. It's heartening. Also, tell me what you make of this,' said Eve, relaying Bob's InTan theory.

'I had a fling with a guy who worked at Crayne,' said Adio.

'Did you?'

'Indeed. You remember – François. French. A scientist. Gorgeous.'

'Oh yes! You followed him to that conference in Boston.'

'I didn't follow him! That's an outrageous insinuation, missy. He invited me.'

'Is he still at Crayne?'

'Nice change of tack. I don't know. But I can find out.'

'What I was thinking,' said Eve, 'is that I might just go there, say I've got an interview – about something fluffy, obviously, so as not to arouse suspicion – and see what I can find out. If I had a name of someone to ask for, that would be a huge help. Otherwise I'll just pick one at random off their page on the Portal.'

'Though if you're looking at them on the Portal, that'll be tracked.'

'I know. But surely, even if InTan is a part of all this, it'd be a really long shot for anyone to have figured that out. Most people wouldn't have a reason to have heard of it. Even the folk who were sent the press release all those months ago are unlikely to be preoccupied with a beauty product that got shelved. So I doubt the powers that be are going to expect anyone to have linked the Purple Scheme to Crayne. If there is a link.'

There was a pause and the sound of a match being struck as Adio re-lit his cigarette. 'The InTan thing could have legs,' he said.

At that moment the office smoke detector went off.

'Bugger,' said Adio. 'Gotta go. Be good, doll.'

'I could say the same to you—' said Eve, as the line went dead.

She pictured a variety of packages – tubes, tablets, sprays and syringes – each featuring a large black question mark. Eve's Pam sketch needled her: *How?*

François had proven to be as golden as InTan allegedly was. He no longer worked at Crayne, but had given Adio the names of three former colleagues who Eve could try talking to.

'You were cautious, weren't you?' Eve had asked.

'Mostly,' said Adio. 'Look, I trust him. I asked if he knew anything about InTan, and he said no. But he thinks these people might. Two work in the research lab, and one is in a product planning department.' With what sounded like a smoke exhalation, he added, 'And as a bonus, François is in New York next week.'

'So you're taking him for an appreciative drink?'

Adio laughed. 'It'd be rude not to.'

Armed with the names of these potentially wise musketeers, Eve was now at the end of a four-hour train journey to Cardiff, the location of Crayne's sleek headquarters. Outside the station, she shielded her eyes against the bright sunlight as she searched for a taxi rank.

Eve approached the first cab in the queue.

'Hello,' she said, 'I'm going to the Crayne Industries offices.'

'Hop in, love,' said the taxi driver.

About to follow his instructions, Eve squinted through the window at him.

'Did you know—'

'Ah, here we go,' said the cabbie. 'I suppose you're not going to get in now.'

'No, no. I'm getting in,' said Eve, swinging the door shut behind her.

The taxi pulled away.

'You seem to be turning Purple,' said Eve.

'I am *not* Turning Purple,' said the cabbie, emphatically. 'I am *un*-Turning Purple.'

'Oh,' said Eve, a hundred questions starting to fizz through her mind. But the cabbie didn't require any prompts, and continued to talk.

'I did nothing wrong, I'll have you know. Went to the pub, as I always do on a Monday night. Had a nice time with my mates, thank you very much. Outside, there's a couple of lads pestering this girl, I told them to leave her alone, and they start on me. Both of them! Cheeky sods. My mates come outside, give them what for, they scarper. I have another drink, courtesy of the landlord, go home, wake up—'

'And you're Purple,' said Eve.

'Exactly. The nerve of it. I went to the police station and gave them what for. I am a law-abiding citizen! I was protecting a member of the public – which is your job, I told them. Well. Off they went, to check with some person higher up the food chain, no doubt. Oh, we're so sorry, Mr Rees, we'll rectify this mistake, Mr Rees. So now, I am being Re-Turned to my God-given colour, thank you very much.'

'That's incredible,' said Eve.

'It's disgraceful, is what it is,' said the cabbie.

'Do you mind if I ask you some questions?'

'Knock yourself out.'

'Do you know how you Turned Purple?'

'No idea.'

'But you saw a police officer nearby?'

'If there was one, they should've been helping that poor lass, being harassed by those thugs.'

'So you didn't see any police?'

'Not so as I noticed, no.'

'Did you feel anyone touch you, or could someone have put something in your drink?'

'Of course I felt someone touch me.'

'You did?'

'The thugs who were attacking me!'

'Of course. Anyone else?'

'How many people do you want me to be accosted by?'

'None!' said Eve, sweetly. 'How did they Re-Turn you?'

'Don't know. Don't care frankly. As long as I'm back to normal. Though I've a good mind to take them to court for loss of earnings. Don't leave the house until you're fully recovered, they said. Well. I've already lost half a day's work dealing with the results of their incompetence. I'm not missing the rest of my shift because it takes who knows how long to get back to normal.'

'But you didn't see how they administered the antidote?'

'No.'

'You were sedated?'

The cabbie paused. 'No. I don't think so, love. I was talking to them and next thing I know I was coming to – in a cell! To add insult to injury. Apparently I fainted. Never fainted before in my life. It'll be the shock, I suppose.'

'How long do you think it was between when you fainted and when you came to?'

'Ah. I don't know. Not long. They wanted me to wait while I began to go back to normal, but I said not a chance, I'm going back to work. And here I am. Earning a crust, like the hard-working, law-abiding citizen I am.'

'You got Turned last night, you went to the police station this morning, somehow they administered an antidote during the time between you fainting and coming to, and now this afternoon you're back at work – does that sound accurate?'

'It does. It's going down though, to be fair,' he said. 'Only a few more patches, aren't there?' The cabbie glanced at himself in the rear view mirror. 'That side of my cheek. A bit on my neck. And some on my arms. Look a bit like birthmarks, don't they?'

'Yes,' said Eve, thinking of the marbled colouring of dappled ponies.

'Anyhow,' said the cabbie. 'What brings you to Cardiff?'

Eve considered telling him the real reason she was there, but thought better of it. Err on the side of caution, she told herself.

'Work meetings, you know, quite boring,' she said.

'Hard to top my story, eh?'

'Absolutely.'

'Here we are,' the cabbie said, pulling up outside Crayne Industries.

'Thank you,' said Eve, as she climbed out of the cab. 'I hope you have an uneventful rest of your day.'

'So do I,' said the cabbie, chuckling as he drove away.

The offices were part of a futuristic development on the outskirts of the city, a green and grey utopia at the end of a long driveway, far enough from the road that you could barely hear the traffic. Instead visitors were greeted by the trickling lilt of a fountain adorned by an arresting quartet of bronze cranes. They took centre stage in a smart slate pond, from either side of which ran a moat-like stream, encircling the vast modern building. Crayne HQ was a tall, sprawling block of marbled concrete and tinted glass, which glinted in the sun, reflecting the surrounding trees and passing birds back at you in a way that implied, it seemed to Eve, that very little penetrated this fortress – though perhaps this suspicion was a result of her own conspiracy-minded motives. She was sure, however, that in a line-up of Edens, you would identify this as having been conjured by a pharmaceutical company: neat, clipped, clinical. The grass was a saturated, almost emerald hue, trimmed uniformly short, like an army regulation haircut. And where were the people to populate such a haven? Inside, tinkering with test tubes and press releases, mulling over mergers?

Still, let's give this a whirl, thought Eve, as she moseyed over one of the wide footbridges that crossed the stream, wondering whether she'd make it past the next hurdle: that most contemporary portcullis, the corporate reception foyer.

Eve looked up, deliberately doe-eyed, as she entered the high-ceilinged lobby, which managed to feel simultaneously airy and claustrophobic. Soft chairs on strangely-angled stick legs were scattered along the far walls, leaving the not unsubstantial walk from the silently sliding main doors to the polished bank of reception desks dauntingly clear. Eve had worn low heels, which clicked as she stepped carefully across the shiny floor; she wondered if everything had been purposefully designed to elicit maximum intimidation.

She smiled as she approached a receptionist.

'Hello,' she beamed. 'What a beautiful building, isn't it? Gosh, you're lucky. At our gaff you're dicing with death every day just with the ratty carpets, which are curled up all over the place like an elderly sandwich.'

The receptionist was wearing a smart, well-fitting suit. He smiled politely.

'And how can I help you today?'

'Well,' said Eve, 'I have a meeting with… Ooh, hold on, let me just check.' She reached into her bag, and pulled out a slip of paper. 'Let's see. My colleague arranged it, and what do we have… Ah, so, I'm due to be meeting Molly Applebaum.'

The receptionist tapped into a computer.

'She's on holiday.'

'On holiday? Cripes,' said Eve. 'Are you sure?'

'That's the information I have.'

'Is today… it is the fourteenth?'

'It is.'

'I see. Okay. So, I was also due to see – ' Eve glanced at the piece of paper again – 'Igor Bagrov.'

More tapping.

'He's working from another site today.'

'You're kidding!' said Eve, beginning to look upset. 'I've spent four hours on a train to come here today, especially for these meetings. So Molly and Igor are definitely not here?'

'They're not here.'

'I just don't understand it. Let's hope third time lucky,' she said, 'or I might cry.'

'You have another name?'

'Yes. Mina Patel.'

Tap tap tap.

'She's here.'

'Hallelujah!' said Eve. 'Well, that's a relief.'

'I'll let her know you're here,' said the receptionist. 'What's your name?'

'Eve.'

'Eve—?'

Now, thought Eve, do I give a false surname, on the off-chance that we hit the jackpot and they come looking for me? Or give my real name, assuming this is the sort of place likely to check CIV passes?

'Fox,' said Eve, thinking of The Shifty Fox.

'Eve Fox,' said the receptionist. 'That's snappy.'

'Takes no time at all to sign a cheque!' said Eve.

The receptionist raised his eyebrows, and the phone receiver.

'Hi there, I have Eve Fox here for her appointment with you.' The eyebrows went up a notch. 'The meeting was arranged by her colleague, she says.' Leaning towards Eve, he said, 'Ms Patel has no record of the meeting.'

'No!' said Eve, 'Oh no, no, no. This is a disaster. Honestly, all this time setting these meetings up, and now a day out of the office to be here. And then to not get the interviews. My boss is going to flatten me.' Eve started taking deep breaths, as though she might hyperventilate.

'Interviews?' the receptionist asked. 'Which company are you from?'

'I write for the Potion Pages in the *Daily Dispatch*. Which I know some people find morally questionable,' said Eve, adding, 'the paper, that is, not the Potion Pages, which are, I like to think, rather good. But what can I say... my mum is proud. Anyway... Mina should have received Portal post about the 'Behind the Scenes' series we're doing.'

The receptionist relayed this, then shook his head: no dice.

'Oh dear,' Eve said. 'I know we must seem hideously disorganised, but usually everything is arranged with military precision. I'm sure you can imagine. You know how fond the *Dispatch* is of the military! But my colleague... I shouldn't say this.' Eve tipped her head forward, as though sharing a confidence. 'He's been completely out of sorts since Whisky's diagnosis.'

'Whisky?'

'Yes. His dog.'

'I see.'

'It's bad enough that we've made a shambles of organising this – I'm so sorry, by the way, this must feel like such a waste of time for you.'

The receptionist shook his head, his mouth opening like a goldfish.

'And to not get the interviews is bad enough, but he's going to be in so much trouble.' Eve gasped, as though a thought had just occurred to her. 'If he gets sacked...' Eve paused, before whispering, 'And I'm sure you can imagine how brutal the *Dispatch* can be... Well, I dread to think of how he's going to pay Whisky's vet's bill. It's a very expensive condition.'

Eve had hoped for a last-minute reprieve, but the receptionist said nothing. 'Well, gosh, I'm babbling on, and none of this is for you to have to deal with. I'm so sorry to have wasted your time. And please apologise to Ms Patel for the confusion.'

She turned to leave, walking slowly as she re-folded the piece of paper and placed it in her bag. Then pivoted round, clicking back across the stone floor to where the receptionist was just hanging up his phone.

'I don't suppose I could use the bathrooms? Before I head back to the railway station?' she said.

The receptionist hesitated, then said, 'Of course. If I can just see your CIV pass.'

Rats, thought Eve. Rumbled.

She fished in her bag, and produced an ID card.

'This says Eve Baxter... I thought you said your name is Eve Fox.'

'It is!' Eve made a swooning face. 'I have now been married for three weeks, three days and – ' she glanced at her watch – 'forty-six minutes! But my new CIV pass hasn't come through yet. Goodness knows what's taking them so long. Maybe they're busy making everyone purple passes or something mad... who knows.'

The receptionist blinked, by now truly bamboozled.

'Please go through,' he said. 'The bathrooms are on the right.'

About to be buzzed into the main Crayne hive, Eve was frantically wondering what she should do with her new-found access to the building. So she wasn't paying too much attention to the young woman who came through the door, seemingly making a beeline for her.

'Eve Fox?' the woman asked.

'That's right,' said Eve, apprehensively. Was she about to be escorted to the ladies'?

'I'm Mina, you were supposed to be interviewing me? Anthony suggested I should say hello, given the journey you've had to get here.'

All the way from New York, thought Eve. She looked behind her, and the receptionist smiled. Anthony, you are a legend, she thought. If only he knew how grateful she was.

'Shall we make the most of the sunshine?' said Mina.

Eve followed her outside.

To one side of the building, out of sight when you first arrived, was an area dotted with wooden picnic benches, which appeared to have been arranged according to a very specific mathematical equation. Despite her traditionally line-toeing nature, Eve felt an urge to nudge them all by a few inches when no one was looking. Though she suspected that here, someone was always looking; what she'd assumed to be a ray of sunlight through the trees was, she noticed, the reflection of an ISON camera attached to a sturdy branch. Careful to behave as though she hadn't seen it, Eve took a seat with her back to the camera, though guessed there would be plenty of others, keeping a watchful eye.

As Mina rested her elbows on the table, a gold charm bracelet slid down her wrist.

'I had no idea about the interview, sorry,' she said.

'Our fault completely,' said Eve. 'We're just doing a sort of day in the life for different people in the beauty industry. Who are the folk behind your favourite lipstick, or perfume, or tanning product.'

'The thing is,' said Mina, 'that we do have to get approval for any conversations we have with the press, so there's not much I can say, really.'

'Oh. Well, this is more about the personalities than the company,' said Eve, 'painting a picture of the people who help bring products to life.'

'I can't talk about anything that happens at Crayne without permission,' said Mina. 'That sounds boring, I know, but I'm sure you're used to having strict policies if you're at the *Daily Dispatch*.'

212

Perhaps I'm paranoid, thought Eve, but did Mina's inflection in this statement – was that a querying *if?* – imply that she didn't entirely believe Eve's story?

'Maybe we could do a telephone interview?' Mina suggested.

'How about having a chat now, so it has some "in person" colour, but I'll hold fire on using anything until you've got approval?' Eve asked, adding, with a smile, 'What's the worst that could happen?'

'I could lose my job,' said Mina. Maintaining eye contact she continued, 'Like your friend with the dog. Whisky, wasn't it?'

There had been a pause after the word friend.

'Yes, that's right,' said Eve, thoroughly confused.

What the hell was going on? If she didn't think Eve was from the *Daily Dispatch* (I guess consider that as some kind of compliment, she thought), who did Mina imagine Eve worked for, and why had she agreed to come down and meet her? Why suggest a phone conversation? And as to the significance of the word *friend…*

It was a gamble, but then wasn't everything at the moment? 'My colleague had a friend who worked here, François. Do you know him?'

With no hint of surprise in her reaction, Mina said, 'I do.'

'I don't suppose you've spoken to him recently?'

'I have,' said Mina. 'In fact, I just heard from him today.'

'Did he happen to say anything about going to New York?'

'He did, yes. Mentioned that he has a friend there who he'd like to help.'

It was Eve's turn to hold eye contact.

'I definitely wouldn't want to get anyone into trouble,' she said, 'so perhaps we should hold fire on the interview for now. If we get permission to do it later though, there are a few products I'd love to talk about.'

'Okay,' said Mina.

'Including the most incredible-looking tanning product. The press release said it was revolutionary! But it's not going to be released.'

'No. That was a surprise, but...' Mina shrugged, seemingly disinterested in InTan's fate.

'I was so curious about it. I don't suppose you know how it works?'

'I'm afraid that would be confidential company information,' said Mina. 'I wish I could help, I really do, but I can't answer that. Did you have any other questions?'

This felt like a genuine invitation; Eve's instinct was that Mina did want to help.

'If you have time...'

'Yes, I have a few more minutes.'

Eve studied the charm bracelet, from which dangled a tiny Eiffel Tower, a heart and a dainty filigree key. She was certain Mina was willing to tell her something, Eve just had to ask the right question.

'The strangest thing happened on my way here,' she said. 'My taxi driver from the station had been Turned Purple.'

'Oh no,' said Mina. 'That must have been traumatic.'

For her, or for him? Eve wasn't sure.

Thinking of what Bob had said, Eve continued, 'And it made me think of that tanning product. It's funny, isn't it. Desirable for us to change one colour, but not another. Yet in a way, they're the same thing.'

'Yes,' said Mina. 'I suppose that's true.'

There was a few seconds' delay before Mina's mouth opened in a subtle jaw-drop, her forehead wrinkling as she considered this.

'Are you... ?' Mina paused. 'Are you saying... ?'

Show your hand and pray it doesn't backfire, Eve thought.

'Perhaps they're linked, yes.'

214

'But that would be—'

'Unlikely, you'd think,' said Eve, 'and faintly preposterous, even. But possible. Especially given that InTan was withdrawn. Because there wasn't anything wrong with it, was there?'

Rather abruptly, Mina stood up.

'I should be getting back,' she said.

'Of course,' said Eve. 'I appreciate your time.'

Approaching the main entrance, they shook hands, Mina carefully considering Eve.

'If you think of anything else,' said Eve.

Mina nodded, silently, before they parted ways.

As Eve turned and crossed a footbridge, the crane's bronzed beaks open in a silent goodbye, she caught a subtle movement in a wispy-leafed tree; an ISON camera swivelling slowly, following her departure. Eve felt the hot fizz of electricity shoot up her spine. Apprehension, fear – and the thrill of being on the right path, with no idea what would happen next.

It occurred to Eve that she had made a rookie mistake in imagining Crayne's staff would know that InTan was linked to the Purpling, if indeed it was. Of course, thinking about it now, it was likely that very few people would have been informed, given how secretive the scheme was. The less folk who knew, the less chance there would be for anyone to blab, especially inquisitive lasses like Eve.

So she was no further ahead, though could have put herself in a sticky spot. If Mina told anyone that Eve had been seeking to connect InTan to the Purpleness, who knew what the consequences would be?

And yet… It seemed odd that having suspected there had been more to Eve's visit than she'd declared, Mina was still willing to meet her. Perhaps she wanted to be aware of any untoward approaches to the company, to show due diligence and let her bosses know. Or perhaps François had vouched for Eve and Adio, implied that Mina should assist them, if she could.

Eve felt a restlessness ebbing through her, flowing up and down her limbs, seeking an escape; it made her fingers twitch. Supposing InTan *was* entwined with the Purpling. If you were a chemist, who'd created a distinctive commercial product which had a – some might say – vacuous, superficial intent, would you not feel disturbed that it had been coopted for more dangerous political use? Or might you feel vindicated that such an ingenious biological device was being employed more profoundly, getting the recognition it deserved? Perhaps you wouldn't care either way. Hadn't history shown that people could turn a blind eye to many things while they weren't directly affected? The Purpleness felt like that. For all Eve's own indecision, she found folks' willingness to go along with things, the groundswell of acceptance for questionable schemes like the privatisation of the police force, the Repeal, the Purpleness – despite the apparent downsides, the potential losses to them – to be remarkable. And it left you wondering: what can be taken from you before you cry out, or rebel?

Back at Womble and Helena's, Eve had been sharing the day's developments with Adio when his cigarette had set off the office fire alarm, yet again.

So when the phone began to ring, Eve groaned as she picked up the receiver.

'See, what did I tell you? Next you'll be burning the place down, and then we'll be in real trouble.'

There was silence.

'Oh, you again,' said Eve. 'Speak up, we can't hear you.'

'Eve, it's Duncan.'

'Oh. Hello stranger.'

'I'm so sorry for disappearing on you on Saturday. And for not calling before now,' Duncan said, sounding weary.

'You missed quite a day,' said Eve, 'but I figured you and Simon had a big night out and you were still recovering.'

Duncan was briefly silent. 'You could say that,' he said, eventually. 'I know this will sound stupid, especially after I let you down, but might you be able to come over?'

'Now? I was just doing some work.'

'Please?' There was the faintest whine to Duncan's voice.

Honestly, Eve just wanted to crack on. Despite the tangled-wool state of her brain, she sensed she was on the cusp of *something*. But her stomach rumbled. She could just stop for dinner.

'I suppose we could meet near here. Or at The Fox?'

Duncan exhaled slowly, and said, 'I can't go out. I need to meet here. I'm really sorry. There's a good reason, I promise.'

'You sound as though you're being held hostage or something,' said Eve, thinking of a *Say Fantastique!* story about a man who briefly kept a travel agent captive after being sold a holiday to Land's End instead of Lanzarote. 'You've not got a saucepan stuck on your head, or superglued yourself to the sofa, have you?'

Duncan gave a small but despondent laugh. 'Not quite. I can't tell you how grateful I'd be to see you.'

Eve sighed. 'This is all very mysterious. But okay.'

'Thank you,' said Duncan, sounding rather emotional. Steady on, Eve thought. This is a bit of a strong reaction to missing a day out after downing a few too many shandies.

Feeling awkward, she said, 'I'm on my way.'

Even for a girl with a vivid imagination, Eve was having trouble working out what could have happened to Duncan during the last couple of days. And why not just tell her whatever it was over the phone? She didn't know what to think, but if he was spending time with Simon, trouble wouldn't be far behind.

Further down the carriage there was a noisy altercation afoot. A group of people with suitcases obscured Eve's view, but the row appeared to have erupted between a young woman with two small children – a toddler, and a baby in a pram – and an older lady.

'You judging me?' the young woman said.

'No.'

'Then what was that look for?

'I didn't give you a look.'

'Liar. I saw you.'

'I didn't give you a look. But I was going to ask if you'd mind moving your shopping so I could sit down.'

'That's what the look was about. Fine, I'll move them.'

'Don't worry, I'll sit somewhere else.'

'Yeah, that's right, run away.'

'Excuse me?'

'You judge me, then you run away. I'd've moved the bags, you didn't need to judge me. Who do you think you are? No respect. You may judge me, but God will judge *you*.'

The older woman began to move away.

'That's right, keep moving. Thinking you're so high and mighty. The world doesn't need people like you, judging. Why don't you just go home and kill yourself.'

The older woman turned round, open-mouthed. 'What did you say?'

'I said you should just go home and kill yourself.'

The train began to slow as it reached a station, and the mother stood, now ignoring the older woman and gathering her shopping. A couple of other people moved towards the doors, not looking in the direction of the mother, Eve noted. One man had a cigarette in hand, ready to light up once he'd alighted from the train. If I smoked, I'd need one too, Eve thought. She felt a collective sigh of relief throughout the carriage as the doors closed and they pulled away again. Eve glanced towards the platform, at the man now putting his cigarette to his lips, and the mother, striding along as though nothing had happened. As she looked, Eve ensured her face was set in a blank, unreadable expression, lest the mother catch her eye. The elder of the children glanced up at his mother, fixing his attention on her as she stared straight ahead. He took small, quick steps to try and keep up with the pace of the pram. Eve worried about him tripping or falling behind, though she knew those were of course only the most immediate concerns for him. What else must he have seen, what on earth would the future hold for him and his sibling? As they slid out of sight, Eve mentally crossed her fingers and sent a silent wish into the ether for them.

A girl who was sitting with her boyfriend leaned towards the altercation woman.

'Are you alright?'

The woman gave a small, grateful smile, but her hands, laid on top of the bag on her lap, were trembling.

'Her poor children,' the girl continued. 'You can't imagine how they'll turn out, hearing their mum talk to people like that.'

'And claiming to be religious!' said someone else. 'Any God she believes in must be preparing to strike her down with lightning...'

'Appalling behaviour,' one man said. 'And if that's how she is with people she doesn't know...'

'At least it's being stamped out now,' said someone else. 'She'll get Turned at some point, behaving like that.'

'Yes,' laughed a man about Eve's age. 'God may not judge you, but Theo Fletcher will.'

There were some chuckles from other passengers. Eve felt a flutter of relief that the young woman could now be punished for the nastiness they'd just witnessed, that it was her, not them, who should feel fearful. Maybe the prime minister was doing something for the greater good after all.

Unpleasant as the disturbance on the train had been, it had at least served as a diversion from trying to solve the riddle of what had happened to Duncan. But as he opened his front door, standing well back, out of sight to any passing neighbours, it became obvious. Eve tried to cover her shock, but such an attempt was a tall order.

Duncan was – subtly but most certainly – Purple.

Chapter Eleven

Eve stepped inside and followed Duncan into the darkened house. All the curtains were closed.

'I'm so sorry,' he said. 'I woke up that morning to this, and I... couldn't believe it. I didn't know what to do, let alone how to ring and explain myself. I should've called and just made something up, but I was in shock. I couldn't think straight.'

Eve took him in: he was almost entirely covered – wearing a sweatshirt despite the warm day, the sleeves pulled down over his hands, jeans, and even socks, he was obviously not able to bear to see any part of himself, of his now tinted skin. She looked at him sympathetically, at the sadness and embarrassment in his blue eyes, seemingly bluer now, next to the mauve, she thought, ridiculously.

'Oh, Duncan,' she murmured, reaching up to touch his cheek. Duncan closed his eyes, scrunching his face up around them.

'I can't believe it,' he said. 'I haven't spoken to anyone, haven't left the house. Obviously. I think I'm supposed to turn myself in,' he gave a bark of a hard laugh, 'but I can't imagine stepping outside the door again.'

Eve put her arms around him, rubbing one hand across

his back, like comforting a baby, thinking of the purple skin beneath. He stood limply, silently. In the street there was the energetic bounce of a football being kicked about by a group of kids, and then a triumphant cry of 'Goal!' Duncan flinched at the sound of the world outside. Trapped.

Eve pulled slowly away, looking up at him and noting the darkness of his eyelashes against the mauve.

'At least you've got good colouring for it,' she said with a smile. 'Imagine what a disaster it would be if you were ginger.'

What she supposed was a laugh from Duncan became gargled.

'I'm sorry I dragged you here,' he said. 'I thought I was going to go mad if I didn't see someone. That I'd just be found here in a few years' time, having starved to death.'

'Oh, no—'

'Fletcher would be pleased though, wouldn't he? A Lav suitably shamed into not leaving the house, or ever wanting to be seen again.'

'What actually happened?' Eve asked, leaning back a little but with a hand holding each of his arms, like one Lego figurine reaching forward to grip another. 'Do you want to talk about it? I can make us a cup of tea and you can tell me.'

Duncan's mouth twisted. 'The milk's gone off.'

'Hasn't the milkman—'

'I put a note out. I didn't want to have to go outside.' Duncan stared at her, pained. 'Even just the doorstep. I know how stupid that sounds.'

'Right,' said Eve. 'I'll go to the shop. Then when I get back you can tell me what happened.'

Duncan nodded, his eyes bright, and watery. 'Sorry,' he said, 'I'm not usually this pathetic.'

'Women love a sensitive man, didn't you know?'

'But probably not a Purple one,' said Duncan.

222

Eve's mouth was set in a small 'O' of disbelief as she wandered towards the shop, at one point almost getting herself run over as she crossed the road. She'd looked, but not really *looked*, seeing only Duncan's mauve face swirling in front of her.

Duncan. Purple. Of course, it should have occurred to her. What other reason would anyone have for not being able to leave the house these days? But, despite being Simon's closest ally, he'd always seemed to be a good soul, a rule-abider, and she was surprised that he'd done something worthy of being Turned. Reasons to be Purpled did seem to run quite a gamut, though, so it could be something fairly harmless... or maybe it was a mistake, like the Cardiff cabbie. What Duncan had (or hadn't) done was one question, along with to whom, and how. And what could she do to help him? It was dreadful to see him so distraught, more so as she believed that he must (surely?) be innocent. If a supposedly savage character like Luke had been so affected by being Turned, what chance did a sensitive soul like Duncan have? What about all the others who were Turned, she wondered, did they feel so distressed (those in the Lav Line Up appeared defiant, more than anything), and if they were guilty of behaviour worthy of being Purpled, did they deserve to feel such anguish? What if Duncan was guilty too?

Eve had reached the shopping precinct. Most of the shops were shut now. She made her way past the butchers, the grocers, the Post Office, and Radio Rentals. She paused outside the latter, drawn in by the still flickering displays in the window, including one for the newest addition to KitchenKlene's silent range – a vacuum cleaner. It featured a cute computerised face on the front, which would smile and display the exclamation 'Hungry!' when in use, and when ready to be emptied would raise its pixelated eyes upwards, flashing 'I'm full!' On a TV set, a looping commercial showed the machine in use, endlessly hoovering up dirt from a carpet which would go from grubby beige to cleanly cream. She watched it switch, again and again; a suitably mindless distraction from considering Duncan's predicament. At least some messes can be easily cleared up, Eve thought, as she turned and walked towards the grocery store.

For once, Eve avoided the rack of newspapers, all with Purple faces peering from their front pages. Taking a basket, she tried to concentrate on the things she should buy: a goodly stock of tinned things suitable for someone who isn't planning on going outside any time soon, and fresh fruit and veg to counteract that fact; juice, long-life juice; milk, long-life milk; cereal and… Eve stared at a box of Corn Flakes, one corner emblazoned with an invitation to 'Win a Super River Adventure!' The sight of its nutritional claims set a vitamin-packed train of thought rattling through her head, and she wanted to turn and ask someone, 'What sort of supplements do you think a Purple person might need? Vitamin D? Iron?' She leaned forward, her bowed forehead touching the crest of the Corn Flakes' cockerel, and sighed.

One grey day during the summer holidays, when Eve was twelve – it was probably not long after the TV studio visit – Linda had been running a pottery course at school, and had left Eve in the boys' care, having clearly decided she would be fine with her brother if sensible Duncan was also on hand (Eve wasn't sure where Vince was; this must have been during one of his absent phases – not that he was reliable during the spells when he was technically at home).

'We've got my boring sister to look after,' said Simon, as Duncan came through the door.

'Hiya, Eve,' said Duncan.

'Hi,' said Eve, looking up from a book.

'I don't know why you didn't go to that potting thing with Mum,' said Simon.

'I'm always going to those things with her. And I wanted to read my book.'

'So our style is cramped for the day, big time,' said Simon.

'When do you ever have style?' Eve asked. 'The only thing you have is a knack for trouble, everyone knows that.'

'I'm just going to leave you here,' said Simon.

'Mum will be so cross if you do.'

'What do I care? She's always cross about something.'

'Well, if you actually ever behaved—'

'What did you want to do today?' Duncan asked them. 'I thought we could go to the swimming pool. Or down to the river?'

'Yeah, let's go to the river,' said Simon.

'Eve?'

'Sure. Mum made us some sandwiches, we can take those.'

'Let's take the football, we can have a bit of a kick about,' said Simon.

They fetched their jackets.

'I'll have a pack of those,' said Simon, pointing to a packet of cigarettes behind the counter.

'Will you now?' the shopkeeper said. 'And how old are you?'

'Sixteen.'

'No, you're not,' said Eve.

'Shut up,' said Simon.

'You shouldn't smoke. Mum says it's bad for you, everyone says it's bad for you.'

'What does Mum know about anything?'

'That's a sensible sister you've got there,' said the shopkeeper.

'She ruins everything,' said Simon, before storming out of the shop.

'I don't like him, but I don't want him to die of tobacco poisoning,' said Eve, thinking of the video they'd been shown at school, about the dangers of nicotine.

'Let's pay for these,' said Duncan, putting some bags of crisps on the counter.

'And I think your friend had some chocolate that he forgot to pay for...' said the shopkeeper, indicating towards a circular security mirror on the wall, reflecting a view of the aisles.

'I said I'd pay for it,' said Duncan, counting out the remaining coins from his pocket.

When they got outside, Simon was still in a temper, staring sulkily across the road towards The Shifty Fox.

'They won't sell you any,' said Duncan.

'I know that,' said Simon.

'Shall we go?' said Duncan. 'How about a bit of ball practice on the way?' He took the football from Simon and began to bounce it along the pavement.

Simon thawed a little and kicked the ball. Eve trailed behind, nose in her book, trying not to walk into any lamp-posts.

Eve had been lying beside the river, wriggling away from a patch of dry, itchy grass, when the older boys appeared. There were three of them, from the year above Simon, striding along. Two of them held long sticks, which they occasionally prodded at things in the water. Their eyes narrowed when they caught sight of Simon and Duncan, and as they approached Eve felt a small shudder of foreboding. Pretending this was due to a wasp, she swatted her arm.

'What are you doing here, Baxter?' one of them said.

'What does it look like?'

'And you've got your little friend with you?' This referred to Duncan; they hadn't seen Eve.

Simon looked at Duncan, who was as tall as he was. 'Nothing small about him, from what I can see,' he said.

'Can't he speak for himself?'

Simon stepped forward. 'Funny, I thought you were talking to me.'

'Leave it, Si,' said Duncan.

'Yeah, leave it,' the boy mocked. 'After all, you don't want to get into a fight or anything, do you?'

'Bugger off, why don't you,' said Simon.

'Too scared to fight?'

'Nope. Just not sure you're worth the hassle.'

'What about your friend?'

'Just leave him.'

'It's alright, I can look after myself,' said Duncan, warily.

The older boy smirked. He came forward and raised an arm, as if preparing to punch Duncan, who ducked. The older boy missed. Like lightning, Simon responded with a swift smack that sent the boy stumbling backwards, shocked, his nose bleeding.

'I'll get you,' he said, as the trio backed away.

'I doubt it,' said Simon, ambling nonchalantly back towards the river.

'You alright?' said Duncan.

Simon nodded and shook his smarting hand; he and Duncan shared a relieved laugh. After the older boys were out of earshot, Simon glanced towards Eve.

'Don't tell Mum.'

'I won't,' she said.

'You better not. And what are you smiling at?'

'Nothing,' said Eve, who couldn't possibly tell him that she was impressed.

'Are you laughing at me?'

Eve rolled her eyes. 'No.'

'I think that's some sisterly pride,' said Duncan.

'Maybe,' said Eve. 'Don't tell Mum.'

Duncan laughed, and after a nudge from him, even Simon managed a smile.

But oh, how the mood could change. Later, after they'd eaten their sandwiches, and Simon and Duncan had sat, chatting nonsense, then played about with the football, the boys had waded into the river.

Eve had reached the penultimate chapter in her book.

'How deep is it?' she asked, looking over.

'Come in and see.'

'No thanks.'

'Too busy being boring, as usual.'

'I'm reading.'

'Exactly.'

'Speaking of boring, don't you ever get bored of being mean?'

'Don't you ever get bored of being annoying? Like in the shop earlier. You're embarrassing.'

'*I'm* embarrassing?'

And then, face clouding over, Simon sploshed towards Eve, reaching across, grabbing her hands and pulling her in.

'What are you doing?' Eve spluttered. She tried to resist, to stay upright, but tipped forward into the murky water.

'Simon!' Duncan shouted.

Eve was face down in the river, splashing with flapping arms. Though there was a quick current, it wasn't too deep, and she managed to manoeuvre herself up, kneeling with her head and shoulders poking out of the water. She was too shocked and breathless to stand.

Duncan arrived beside her, and leant over, arm outstretched, to help her up.

'Are you alright?'

Eve nodded.

'The water's cold. Better get out, and dry.'

Eve clambered onto the bank, Duncan behind her. He passed her his jacket.

'Put this on. You might want to take your wet top off – there's a tree over there you can change behind, we won't look.'

Eve scurried away. As she did so, she heard Duncan say to Simon, 'What was that about?'

'She was being annoying.'

'But Si... that was out of order. Could've been dangerous. If this was a different river... And you must have frightened her.'

'I was just playing. She can take care of herself.'

'No need to scare her though, is there? I know you two wind each other up but...'

'Yeah, well... sorry.'

'Don't say it to me, Si, tell Eve.'

'She won't care.'

Behind the tree, where they couldn't see, a shivering Eve had cried, hot tears mingling with running drips of cold river water.

'Are you alright?'

Eve lifted her head, blinking, embarrassed.

'We've got a stool if you want to sit down. Do you need water? Or some sugar? There are some sweets behind the counter.'

'I must have come over a bit faint, sorry.'

'I thought so. Either that or you were reading the small print,' the shop assistant smiled.

'I'll just pay for everything, and then go and get some air.'

'Right you are,' said the shop assistant, lifting Eve's basket.

At the till, Eve glanced up to see if they still had the security mirrors in here. They didn't – though of course, there were ISON cameras.

'Those are heavy, sure you'll be alright?'

'Yes, thank you.'

Eve went outside. She needed to get back to Duncan, who would be wondering where she was. But she still felt light-headed, so took a seat on a bench outside. Eve glanced across at The Shifty Fox, considered going in for a quick, steadying drink. Instead she reached into her pocket for a packet of mints.

On the side of a nearby bus shelter was a tobacco advert featuring an attractive couple exchanging flirtatious glances, each holding a cigarette. Along the top it read: 'Let the good times roll'. An elderly lady with a blue rinse tucked under a hairnet, and a string bag bulging with vegetables, sat down in the shelter, obscuring the smoking couple. Eve thought of Adio, setting off the fire alarm, and of home – New York home. What was she doing here, really? Aside from seeing her dad – and hadn't that been mostly out of a sense of duty? – what did she expect to achieve? Trying to solve a ridiculous riddle, a head-scratcher that had so far proved uninteresting or unravel-able to reporters who were smarter and more experienced than her. Would she manage to help Duncan, or Jason, by following an improbable trail involving a tanning product?

Outside one of the shops was a pay phone. Eve gathered up the groceries and walked towards it. She dialled the *Say Fantastique!* number, and Adio answered.

'Hi, it's me again.'

'Hello, you. What's happening?'

'I don't know… weirdness.'

'Weirdness other than your mum and dad being re-entangled and people being turned Purple?'

'Mm.'

'Do you want to come home?'

'Yes. But no. I can't, yet.' Eve wanted to cry. She wanted to help Duncan. She wanted to keep scratching away at this until she'd unearthed the secrets of the Purpleness. But somehow, here, surrounded by her family and her failures, any achievement felt almost impossible. Why did these homeland mountains feel so much more difficult to climb?

'I miss you,' she said.

'I miss you too, doll.'

'I miss normal life, I think. Remind me why I'm here?'

'Now your dad's on the mend, to report on the Purpleness and potentially crack the uncrackable story behind it, transforming both our humble, hilarity-fuelled company and the fate of the nation.'

'Small ambitions, then.'

The phone beeped, hungry for more coins.

'I have to go,' said Eve. 'Thanks for the sanity – or insanity – check.'

'Can I do anything?'

'No, I—'

There were more beeps and the line went silent.

'Just wanted to hear you,' she said.

Eve picked up the shopping and headed back to Duncan's.

The kettle whistled as they finished unpacking the groceries. Eve poured hot water into two cups, removing the lid of the newly acquired milk. She handed a mug to Duncan, who let out a contented sigh.

They returned to the living room and sat on the sofa. Eve turned to one side, legs tucked under her, facing Duncan.

'So,' she said, 'tell me what happened.'

Duncan swallowed, hesitating.

'I was on my way home from the pub—'

'Were you on your own?'

'No, with some people, some friends—'

'Anyone I know?'

Duncan paused, fished a speck of something out of his mug. 'No, I don't think so.'

'Sorry, I'll stop interrupting. Go on.'

'We'd only left the pub a few minutes before, weren't far away, and some other blokes were approaching, not anyone I knew, and one of the guys I was with made a remark to one of them. I didn't even hear what he said – something stupid, derogatory, to deliberately wind him up. Which then became one of those "what did you say?", "you heard", posturing things. The other couple of guys I was with, there were four of us, were saying, come on, let's get home, but one of the other blokes took a punch at my friend. I stepped between them to try and stop it, and then another of the blokes from the other group punched me, and it just escalated. Stupid. A scrap in the street. I'd been trying to calm everything down, but then you go to defend yourself and…' He stared into his mug, eventually taking a gulp of tea. 'Someone shouted out of a window that they'd called the police, and we pretty much stopped, I suppose thinking you couldn't be too careful these days.' He gave a wry laugh. 'And we went home. No one looked badly bashed, apart from a couple of scrapes and bruises. I'd only had a few pints so wasn't drunk. Got in, had some toast, watched a bit of telly, went to bed. I woke up the next morning to come and meet you – went to brush my teeth, looked in the mirror, noticed the – ' he cleared his throat – 'subtle change to my appearance, threw up, have spent the last two days wondering what the hell happened, and here we are.'

'Bugger,' said Eve.

Duncan's nose twitched. He let out a sigh.

'I just...' He paused. 'I don't look for trouble. I don't get into trouble. I mean, I'll climb up a tree to protect a forest, but that's trying to look after something, isn't it? And you know, I suppose I was trying to look after my friends.'

Eve thought of the questions the Humane rep had been asking the Purple lad at the demo.

'Did the police arrive after the person shouted out of the window?'

'No.'

'Did you see any police around before then?'

'No, not that I noticed. But in the middle of the scrap, I can't say I was paying attention.'

'Was there anyone else around?'

'I don't know. A couple of people had left the pub before us, they were further up the road. A bloke came out of the fish and chip shop – his dog was barking outside – and I think there were other people in there. A woman walked past us–' Duncan looked embarrassed – 'and one of the guys said something to her, drunkenly... not meaning any harm, but being an idiot. So there was her. I don't remember anyone else.'

'That's quite a memory, I'd say.'

'I dunno.' Duncan, sleeves pulled over his hands, brushed at something on his chest.

Eve looked at him, at his mauveness. Flummoxed, she resorted to her usual questions, hoping eventually a clue would peek through, like a whiskery mouse from a crack in the skirting board.

'So no one bumped into you or, I don't know, you weren't drinking anything that could have been spiked?'

'I was drinking in the pub, but after that, no. And I had quite a few blokes bumping into me when the fight was in full swing, so…'

'When you realised what had happened, did you see any marks on your skin, anything that could have been a cut, or an injection mark or something?'

'I didn't look. I couldn't bear to see it, the…' Duncan's volume seemed to have been turned off as he mouthed the word. 'Purple.'

'Of course.' Eve rubbed her forehead, gently, trying not to betray the extent of her frustration. 'I just don't understand how it happens. You said the group you got into the fight with were people one of your lot knew?'

Duncan nodded.

'What about the others you were with? Are any of them Purple?'

'I don't know. I couldn't bring myself to ask them. I thought if I did, I'd have to say why I was asking, and I wouldn't be able to lie. I didn't want them to know.'

'But they might be Purple too. Wouldn't that make you feel – awful as it is – a bit better? Not so alone in dealing with it?'

Duncan's face contorted. 'I don't want to be like this. I'm not…' He shook his head. 'This isn't who I am.'

Eve believed him but, regardless of the circumstances, he had been in a fight. Just like the kid at the rally had been stealing a bike. This system didn't recognise degrees of misbehaviour, or context. Although, when it went wrong with the cabbie he'd been Re-Turned, so surely it was possible?

'Maybe if you go to the police and explain… You must be able to appeal.'

'I don't know.' Duncan put his hand across his face, rubbing his temples. 'I'm not sure why I thought it'd be a good idea to drag you into this, sorry,' he said. 'I shouldn't have told you. I just wanted to explain. And I thought if I told you over the phone, you wouldn't come.'

'I would've come. Of course I would.'

'I'm sorry I missed the march.'

Eve gave him a supportive glance which said, as if there's anything to apologise for.

'I would've fitted right in.'

'Don't say that.'

'It's true.'

Duncan glanced down at his fingertips, which were peeping out from beneath his sweatshirt sleeves. He closed his eyes again.

Eve took a sip of tea, watching him across the rim of her mug.

'I'm going to stay for a while, if that's okay, so whatever else you want to say, you can take your time. I'm here.' She rested the side of her head against the back of the sofa.

'Why stay?' Duncan asked.

'Why not?'

There was silence, the only noise the kids playing outside.

'This may not be the time to ask,' said Eve, thinking, though, that it might be a distraction, 'but – why were you friends with Simon?'

'He's not all bad you know.'

Eve looked unconvinced.

'I liked him. He was bolshie, confident,' Duncan said. 'Fearless, really. I wanted to be like that. Some of the things he'd do, even just the way he'd talk back to people, I couldn't believe he got away with it.'

'Tell me about it.'

Duncan shrugged. 'We got on. We backed each other up. He was always alright with me.'

'He was, wasn't he?' said Eve, not having thought about it before.

'I probably felt a bit more rebellious, invincible around him. And maybe I was his foil, or something. The teachers thought he couldn't get into too much trouble with me tagging along, that I was a calming influence.'

'Yep – my mum thought you were good for him. I was thinking earlier about that day we went down to the river, when I'd got him into trouble in the newsagent's.'

'About what happened when he came out of the shop?'

'Yes, he was still in a grump about the cigarettes. I know I was an annoying goody-two-shoes, but that's what little sisters are for.'

'It wasn't that.'

'Really? What, then?'

'He didn't tell you this?'

'Tell me what?'

'He saw your dad and some woman, quite cosy, going into the pub across the road.'

All these years later and Eve still felt stabbing pains at stories such as this. She swallowed. 'But why didn't he say something? When did he tell you?'

'That night. I don't know why he didn't say anything to you. I suppose, what would have been the point? Though you might have realised why he was so angry that day.'

'He was always angry.'

'He really flew off the handle though, didn't he?'

'I was used to it. I always felt that he didn't care about anyone. Not just didn't care but… his behaviour was so awful sometimes. Unfathomable. We were in the garden one day… Mum and Dad were lying on a blanket, Simon and I were playing – or I was playing, and Simon was mucking about, and there was an egg which had fallen out of a bird's nest, and he stamped on it, really hard. Mum looked over and told him not to do that, that it was horrible, and he did it again, harder, grinning. I remember looking at him and thinking, I'm sure they brought the wrong child home from the hospital. For years I hoped there had been a terrible mistake, and my real brother would be returned to us. That we'd be in all the papers as this crazy swapped-at-birth story.'

'What did your dad do?'

'I don't remember. Probably nothing.' Eve sighed. 'I used to worry that it was having me and Simon that made my dad the way he was, but then secretly I started to blame Simon, that my dad was so embarrassed to have a son like him that he didn't want to be with us.'

'Did you ever say that to him?'

'Once or twice, when I was really angry. I know how awful that is.'

'He was sensitive about it, more than he probably let on to you.'

'About our mum and dad?'

'Yes.'

Eve winced. 'I know I shouldn't have said it, that was terrible. I used to be such a mouthy, know-it-all little sister. And I did used to wind him up. I just didn't want to let him get away with being dreadful all the time. If he was going to be horrible to me I wanted to try and stand up to him.'

'I remember you being very tolerant of it all. You used to sit with a book, or in front of the telly, completely zoned out from whatever tantrum Simon was having, or if your mum and dad were having a row. One time they were in the kitchen fighting about something, really shouting – it must have been something Simon had done if I was party to it – and you walked in, picked up an orange and started peeling it, as if nothing was happening.'

'At the time I think I was testing myself, how much I could ignore it. I'd think – ' Eve blushed – 'what would Annie do? And try to rise above it.'

'Annie? Oh, *Annie*.' Duncan smiled. 'Annie Morris, of course.'

'Yes. She always had something much more calamitous on her plate.'

Outside there were shouts from the young footballers before a car alarm went off.

'More tea?' said Eve.

'Yes, please.' He reached over to put a hand on her arm, emitting a sudden moan at the sight of his fingertips before hiding them beneath his sleeves again.

'For a while there I forgot about this,' he said. 'I haven't got changed, haven't had a shower… I can't bear to look.'

'It's okay, that's perfectly understandable. It's a…' Eve struggled for a suitable word. 'It's an impossible thing to try and get your head around. But let me help.'

Eve went upstairs and began to run a bath, searching amongst the few, blue masculine products for something foamy which might create some body-obscuring bubbles. She found some at the back of the bathroom cabinet – lavender, ironically, in a dusty bottle with a purple lid – and poured it under the tap (wondering, had this belonged to an ex?). Then she had what she considered a fairly ingenious idea, and returning downstairs, dug around in her handbag for the eye mask that she'd been given on her flight.

'Right,' she said, 'There's a bath running, and before you get in, you can put this on.'

They went up to the bathroom. Duncan stood apprehensively in front of her. 'How will I see?'

'I thought you didn't want to see.'

'What if I fall over?'

'That's why you're having a bath, not a shower.'

'But I—'

'Trust me.'

With sleeves still covering his hands, Duncan took the mask from Eve. 'What's that smell? It reminds me of—'

'Oh, I found it at the back of the cupboard. It's quite girlie, I know – must have belonged to a former lady of the house,' said Eve, thinking that, at this particular moment, failed relationships were a better connotation than the word 'lavender'.

'So I put this on, get undressed, and climb carefully into the bath.'

'Exactly.'

'I don't want you to see me.'

'I won't.' Eve left the room, pushing the door to behind her. Then she stood there, on the landing, listening to the muted splashes, trying to imagine Duncan – the whole of him – and his bruised skin.

Chapter Twelve

Eve stayed the night at Duncan's, worried about leaving him on his own feeling so distraught. They'd sat talking, and not talking, until late, eventually falling asleep on the sofa midway through a ridiculous film on television that featured werewolves running amok in a small town. Duncan must have woken in the night, for the following morning Eve found them covered in a blanket, soft but ticklish wool. It was a blue, green and orange tartan, and she ran her finger along one of the orange lines until it stretched beyond where she could lazily reach. She gazed up at the ceiling, at the pale, papery lampshade, the new-looking grey carpet, and the chic, chunky coffee table which Duncan had made from reclaimed wood. Rough but beautiful, sanded but smoothly lumpy blocks of timber. She'd learnt last night that Duncan had built much of the furniture in the house. Solid, dependable, graceful, and in most cases made from rescued wood. Saved, nurtured, given another chance.

Eve turned carefully and looked towards Duncan, who was deep in sleep. He appeared peaceful, his skin paler, a little pinker, making it more lilac than greyish mauve. Not wanting to disturb him, she laid her head back down, now resting just under his shoulder. He stirred, instinctively crooking his arm around her. Eve bit her lip, wondering if she'd be able to get up without waking him.

She could hear a radio playing next door, and tuned her ear to the sound, trying to identify the song that was playing. It sounded like an oldie, optimistically melodic, with jangling harmonies. Which reminded her of dancing around the kitchen with her mum one time, to 'He's So Fine', an old record by The Chiffons. Her mum had twirled, long hair swinging, and they'd laughed, while Eve's dad sat at the table, sufficiently distracted from the sports pages of the paper to smile at them, winking at her mum, and then Simon.

It was strange, Eve thought, that she had so many snapshots like this – happy times, which seemed so idyllic – when actually she'd spent much of her childhood worrying about her parents' relationship, the tumultuousness, sensing her father's one foot out of the door, and her mother's trying to keep his wandering eye focused at home. The sunny moments had seemed significantly dwarfed by the cloudy ones. It was interesting too, she pondered, that in this particular flashback, Simon seemed so agreeable. She had few memories like that, what with the stockpile of mortifying recollections filed, featuring him as the villain of the piece.

Duncan twitched, and turned onto his side, now facing Eve. She stared at his skin, so close, and so incongruous; so alien, next to his dark, unaffected eyebrows, eyelashes, and morning stubble. She thought of the murky water that they'd clean paintbrushes in at school, the bottom halves of washing-up liquid bottles filled with water that would turn milky and grey by the end of class. Or the fake bruises she and her friend Sophie would create using a palette of cream eyeshadows. They'd swirl the green and mauve with a slick of red lipstick, then wave apparently hurt arms in front of their mums, who would look appalled and worried until the girls giggled and admitted the ruse. She glanced at his lips, which were a deeper, rosier purple than his skin. Eve was staring at them as he woke; she and Duncan both blinked at their unplanned proximity.

'Morning,' said Duncan.

'Hi,' said Eve. She liked the closeness.

He was about to smile, then caught sight of his hand resting beside her. He let out a low groan and pulled his arm away from her, tugging sleeves back over his hands, which he folded in front of his face. At that moment the phone rang. Neither of them moved. The answer machine kicked in.

'Who knows what I'm doing,' said a cheerful, recorded Duncan, 'but leave a nice message, and I'll probably get back to you.'

There was a pause. 'Dunc, you there? It's Simon. You didn't call me back the other night. You alright? Got a bit hairy, didn't it? That lot, honestly, on the lookout for trouble. Bit lively, eh? Sorry 'bout that, mate. But ring me, yeah? Let's have a pint. Without the excitement, this time... probably. Right. Bye.'

Eve, sitting upright, looked from the phone to Duncan, who closed his eyes, now with something else to try and wish away. The room was still, silent except for the sound of Dusty Springfield singing next door. Eve noted that her heart was galloping, beating so much faster than the music.

'Simon?'

Duncan could look her directly in the eye, but had no words. He turned away.

'Simon was the one who got into the fight? Who you tried to help? Who made this happen to you?' She was presenting these as questions, which was pointless, she knew. 'Oh, Duncan.'

'I was with Simon,' he conceded. 'He couldn't have known—'

'So Simon started the fight?'

'Eve, this isn't going to help…'

'Did he start the fight?' she asked quietly.

Duncan sighed and nodded.

'Simon. Unbelievable. But believable. Ruining things, all the time.'

'He doesn't mean to…'

Eve looked at Duncan, faintly puzzled. 'You always support him.'

'He's my friend.'

'I know… But that seems like a much better deal for him than you. He makes a pretty lousy effort to avoid trouble. And somehow it's always someone else who suffers the consequences.'

Duncan said nothing.

'Why didn't you call him the morning after this happened? He might have been Purple, too.'

'I knew he wasn't.'

'How?'

Duncan looked away.

Eve leant back against the sofa. 'Because if he was, he'd have called you.'

She put a hand on his arm, giving a gentle squeeze. 'I'm so, so sorry this has happened to you. I'm going to make it right, I promise.'

'I don't think I can live like this.'

Eve thought of Luke, the Lav from the hospital.

'Don't say that,' she said. 'We're going to look after you. We're going to fix this.'

'I just want to be on my own,' Duncan said, wrapping himself tightly in the blanket.

'I'm not sure that's a good idea…'

'Please.'

'I don't want to leave you.'

'I just need some time. It's hard to see you – ' his voice became a whisper – 'and see what I'm not any more.'

'Duncan…' Eve reached towards him, but he recoiled. 'What can I do?'

'Just leave me. Please. Go.'

Eve stood, feeling wretched, wanting desperately not to leave him.

'I'm coming back. Soon. So don't go getting comfortable on your own.'

Eve tried to hug him, but he gave a small shake of his head.

The paintwork on Duncan's front door was immaculate; even if you peered really closely, you could barely see the slim stripes from the brushwork. Proud but unassuming quality, a fine attention to detail, all transmitted in sage-green gloss. Having pulled the door shut behind her, Eve stood on the step, questioning her agreement to leave. She could stand here, waiting, until he was ready for company again. Eve thought of Luke, and of Kelly or Nurse Attride having to tell any of Duncan's friends that something similarly dreadful had happened to him. Surely Duncan wouldn't feel that desperate. But Eve really had no idea; after twenty-something years, the two drinks she'd had at the pub with him the other day gave her exceedingly limited insight. She considered him up the tree in Horton Forest, fighting for its survival, and imagined he could find that strength for himself. But wasn't it often easier to go into sure and blinkered battle for an external cause than it was to assume that same belief for oneself? Eve laid a finger lightly on the doorbell, but didn't push. Though doubtful, instinct told her he'd be okay, for now, that if he really wanted her to go, there were more practical things she could do than standing here, limply fretful.

Another door. More admirable paintwork; this time the number plaque Linda had crafted during the Easter holidays one year, which was only slightly weatherbeaten, despite its age, still greeting visitors in all its hand-painted floral glory.

Eve knocked again, louder this time. Simon came to the door. His skin was as peachy as hers.

'Alright, sis,' he said, stepping back to let her in. 'To what do I owe the pleasure?'

'I see you're looking well,' Eve said, bitterly.

Simon was nonplussed. 'Thanks,' he said, perplexed. 'Good to know I can have a couple of big nights out and not suffer too much, eh.'

'Oh, yes. Good to know you're not the one suffering after one of your nights out.'

Simon looked cautiously concerned about what she might be implying, and followed her through to the lounge.

Eve glanced around. 'Where's Mum?'

'Out back with Dad.'

Looking into the kitchen, through the window Eve could see their parents sitting on garden chairs, Vince dozing, Linda reading. There must have been something buzzing close to Vince as, with her magazine, Linda swatted it away.

Simon leant against the wall. Now he appeared faintly bored, long desensitised to hysterical tongue-lashings from the females in his family. Eve looked at him, slouching, disinterested, and wondered if there was any point in even trying to get him to see the error of his ways. So much wasted breath; she imagined those heated words airborne, floating up

245

to fill a hot air balloon, and lifting her far, far away. Then she thought again of Duncan. Poor, purple Duncan.

'Look,' said Eve, 'I'm here about Duncan.'

Still slouching, Simon didn't even look at her as she addressed him, instead pulling at a thread on his t-shirt. Eve thought of Duncan's sweatshirt sleeves, how he couldn't even bear to look at his own hands.

She began again, more venomously this time. 'Duncan is Purple. Because of the fight outside the pub the other day. Because of you. He is Purple, and you're to blame. But never mind, because you're okay.'

'What?'

'You heard me. Duncan is Purple. It's your fault.'

'He can't be.'

'He is, I've seen him with my own eyes.'

Eve couldn't remember Simon being speechless due to anything other than sulkiness or insolence. He appeared genuinely shocked.

'Anything you'd like to say?'

'I didn't know. I didn't see anything... If I'd known I wouldn't have—'

'Wouldn't have what? Let Duncan bear the brunt for something borne of your stupidity? And recklessness? How, *how* do you get through life caring so little for anyone around you? I just don't understand. It boggles my mind, it really does.'

'Is he alright?'

'Oh Simon, *please*! He's *Purple*! He's terrified, and miserable, completely beside himself. He hasn't spoken to anyone, let alone left his house. How do you think he feels, you moron? How do you think he feels for suffering for something that you got him into?'

Simon looked down.

'I'm telling you, this is it. Enough. You are going to put

this right. You're going to explain that it's your fault Duncan's been Turned. For once you're going to behave like a responsible, truthful, human being.'

Simon said nothing.

'I'm not kidding, Simon. All these years – all the worrying, and fretting, Mum wondering what would happen to you—'

'She wasn't bothered. She knew I'd be alright.'

'God alive, Simon, what goes on in that head of yours?' Eve asked, incredulously. 'She never stopped worrying about you, wondering what disaster was around the corner, what the police would roll up to tell her next, preparing for the worst. You never take responsibility for anything. Leave destruction in your wake and just amble off, completely unconcerned about anyone else. I know that for some reason—'

Vince had wandered into the kitchen, and called over to them.

'Alright, you two,' he said with a nod.

'Alright, Dad,' said Simon.

'How are you feeling?' asked Eve, as calmly as she could through clenched teeth.

'Not too bad,' said Vince, wincing a little and rubbing his back. 'Look who's here, love,' he called towards the garden.

Linda came indoors and into the lounge. 'Hello! This is a nice surprise,' she said, giving Eve a kiss. 'Fancy a cup of tea?'

'Yeah,' said Simon.

Eve narrowed her eyes at him and stalked into the kitchen behind her mum. Simon followed them and sat down.

'Simon wanted to talk to you about Duncan.'

'What's the point of talking to them about it? Let's just go and see him, see how he is.'

'You do know that it's only by some random stroke of luck that it's not you that's Purple, right? And that if you were, your easy, breezy life of leisure and hours at the pub would be somewhat curtailed? That you would be named and shamed and endlessly judged.'

'I already am.'

Eve hadn't expected that, but said, 'Really? I wonder why.'

Linda placed their teas on the table. Eve's mug was covered in stars and had 'No 1 Son!' emblazoned across it in cartoon writing.

Vince took a sip of tea, calm but bewildered. 'What's going on here?'

'Who on earth is Purple?' asked Linda.

'Tell them,' said Eve.

Simon rubbed at a non-existent mark on the table. He sat quietly for a moment, avoiding their gaze, before clearing his throat.

'I was out on Friday night with Duncan and some of the lads. We got into a fight after, really by accident—'

'Oh, Simon...' said Linda.

'Was it by accident?' Eve prodded.

'I might have made a comment, bit of banter, you know, with some blokes we ran into on the way home. One of them went to start something with me, Dunc stepped in, it all got a bit... busy. Apparently Dunc is Purple now.'

'Duncan was involved in the fight?' their dad asked.

'Yes.'

'But?' Eve interjected.

'But only 'cause he was trying to stop them starting something with me. He got dragged into it a bit.'

'What about the others? Are they Purple?'

Simon shrugged.

'Sounds like you had a lucky escape, Si. Not good for Duncan though. None of you should be fighting. Look what happened to me. It could've been a lot worse. One of you could've been hurt, you could've hurt one of them. It does

248

happen, you know that. You carry on that way and you'll be bottled. Or Purple. And I won't be able to say I feel sorry for you.'

'You really do need to be careful,' said Linda.

Vince took another sip of tea. 'Got any biscuits, love?' he asked Linda.

'Is that it?' Eve asked, incredulous. 'Am I the only one that thinks this is at all serious? One of his friends is Purple because of him.'

'Sounds like Duncan was fighting too,' said Vince.

'Trying to stop the fighting,' said Eve. 'Simon should turn himself in.'

'What good is that going to do?'

'He's guilty. He'll be taking responsibility for that.'

'How does that help anyone?'

'Well, it'll be showing solidarity with Duncan, who's less guilty than Simon is.'

'So we'll have two Purple people?' said Vince. 'Two for the price of one?'

'Maybe. Or maybe if he explains, the police will let him swap with Simon.'

'You want your brother to be Purple?'

'He's guilty! Would you have liked the guy who punched you in the pub to have got away with it? You were pleased when he was Turned, weren't you?'

'This is different.'

'How?'

Their dad turned to Simon. 'Was anyone hurt?'

'No.'

'No? You mean you don't know,' said Eve.

'And it sounds as though they were the ones who started the fight?'

Simon nodded.

'He provoked them!' said Eve.

Linda handed Vince a packet of Banjos.

Unwrapping one, Vince said, 'I do love a wafer.'

Eve looked around the table, the three of them saying nothing. She could feel herself getting redder, and wanted to cry in frustration. My father gets punched in the jaw and reels mum back in, my brother gets into a fight and his friend is the one who turns Purple, Eve thought. Leopards. Unchanging spots.

'Well, brilliant,' she said. 'Let's just carry on the family game of no one ever owning up to anything, or taking any responsibility, shall we? I don't know why I thought this would be any different. For the record, Dad, you're useless. Always too wrapped up in yourself and your quest to be some kind of Lothario. Couldn't have given two hoots about mum, or me, or Simon, so is it any wonder how he turned out.'

'Eve!' said Linda.

'You.' She turned to her brother. 'If there's the slightest shred of decency in you Simon, you'll do something to help Duncan, who's apparently shown more loyalty to you than you deserve.' She looked to Linda. 'And mum... Honestly, why do you put up with all this?'

'Look, love,' said Linda, 'I know things weren't always easy, and that you don't agree with some of the choices your dad and I have made, but... well, we're happy. And Simon is your brother, and you just need to accept the way he is.'

'What about Duncan?' Eve asked, looking from her mum to Simon. 'Should he be happy? Should he accept the way he is?'

Simon said, 'Dunno what makes you think you can just swan back and start—'

'Start what, telling the truth? Letting a near-death experience in the family shock us into gaining some

4444444444444

perspective, showing a bit of sense, seeing the bigger picture? Not carrying on behaving idiotically – hurtfully – all the time?'

''Cause you're so perfect.'

'Hardly. But at least I'm not living my life like this…' Eve flung her arms out, gesturing towards the three of them, and knocked her mug onto the floor. It smashed loudly on the kitchen tiles, dribbles of liquid running into the cracks. The bubbly writing was broken into pieces, its sentiment shattered.

'I'll leave you to clear that up,' she told Simon, 'which would be a first, wouldn't it?'

Eve headed for the door.

Chapter Thirteen

The walls at The Happy Hen were a striking shade of custard, seeming to will the place into perpetual sunshine. With a piece of toast, Eve mopped up the even yellower remains of a fried egg and pushed her plate to one side. She stared ahead, out of the window.

There had been both encouraging and discouraging developments. After Eve's departure, Simon had visited Duncan, who now appeared to be in somewhat better spirits, aided not only by his friend's arrival, but by the multiple cans of beer Simon had brought with him. Duncan assured Eve that Simon was going to stay and keep him company, that they were going to eat pizza and watch films. He gave a tipsy burp as he told her this (in the background, she heard Simon exclaiming, 'Bloody anchovies!'). Eve figured that given Duncan's heathered state, they wouldn't be venturing out, so even with Simon's influence, there had to be a limited amount more trouble they could clamber into.

Eve paid her bill. She decided to make a detour.

The long, residential road curved around one side of town, the terraced houses interrupted occasionally by a convenience shop or a specialist store that either couldn't afford high street rent, or knew its customers would travel the literal extra mile to visit. A flyer in the window of Gary's Fish Tank & Supplies featured a smiley purple face, which implied even those Turned were welcome. The nearby chip shop was not so neighbourly, with a sign proclaiming 'NO LAVS' taped to the door. You can buy fish, but you can't eat it, Eve thought, before remembering Duncan and feeling a jolt of anxiety on his behalf. Hopefully he was at least for now enjoying Simon's company, the ale and the anchovies.

Ahead of her, a denim-clad woman with a panting spaniel jogged out through the rusting cemetery gates clutching a large stick, which the dog's eyes flicked towards, ready for action. Once on the pavement, the woman stopped, taking deep breaths and gripping the wall with her free hand, steadying herself. The spaniel sat, watching her, the woman's face now of more interest than the stick. Distracted and facing the road, the woman didn't see Eve enter the cemetery behind her.

Eve hadn't been here for years but, as always with such places, found the tangled, overgrown greenery and crumbling headstones instilled a sense of calm rather than decay, the crunch of dry grass and sweet, sporadic birdsong scoring the stillness. This peace, respite from the adjacent streets, was encouraged by the high stone walls which circled the grounds, cloaked in perpetual fashion by stealth ivy. Eve stood for a moment, absorbing the tranquillity.

A hooded figure suddenly loomed from behind a tree – a man with mauve skin, dappled with acne – and Eve jumped, a hand to her fluttering heart. Was he lurking, intending to harm, or simply seeking refuge? He stood, eyes fixed on her, and Eve, briefly stunned, stared back. He took steps towards her, and Eve felt her knees weaken, wondered if she should scream – or if she could find the breath to. Aside from being, as intended, a most public curse, in circumstances such as these Purpleness could strike unquestioned terror. Here was a bell-clear warning, a telegraphed signal, a statistical likelihood that this person may do you harm.

'Can I help you?' said Eve, mouth dry but voice even.

Dappled moved closer with cocksure bluster, his neck craning forward so that the tip of his purple, pointy nose almost touched hers. Had she found herself in this position with someone of a more natural tint, Eve would undoubtedly have veered backwards, shrinking away from him. But instead she peered at his complexion, with its criminally-toned craters – pores for thought.

She wanted to ask: Why? Why Purple, why hiding, why here, why her, why frighten? Eve remembered the woman with the spaniel; she must have encountered him, too.

'What do you want?' Eve asked, voice less certain.

Dappled gave a mocking grin.

'Trouble, of course,' he said.

I can see that, Eve wanted to say, but given that he already seemed a loose enough cannon, held her tongue (and thinking of tongues, she wondered: if you were Purple on the outside, had you become Purple on the inside, too?).

'You alright, love?' shouted a man who appeared near the crypt, making his way towards them. His skin was agreeably brown, and running ahead of him was a Border Collie, who barked as she approached this strange encounter.

Relief washed through Eve's veins. The cavalry, in shorts and a Hitchhiker's Guide t-shirt.

Dappled hadn't scarpered, but instead started to take lethargic steps back, turning to half-look over his shoulder at the new arrival with a brassy smile that said, I'm going, but in my own time.

T-shirt tucked a cigarette back in his pocket as he reached

them; Eve noted the flicker of recognition in his face as he spied Dappled's damson-ness. Looking towards Eve, T-shirt raised his eyebrows in kindly enquiry. She gave a small nod.

'I know you, don't I?' asked T-shirt. 'From the Thistlemore Centre?'

Thistlemore was a local rehab facility.

'Do you?' said Dappled, who apparently couldn't care less.

'What're you up to, son?' said T-shirt.

'Nothing,' said Dappled, supercilious, still retreating.

'Didn't look like nothing.'

Dappled shrugged. 'What you going to do? Get me Turned Purple? Oh wait – ' a smirk – 'I already am.'

He laughed and continued to walk away, now facing his direction of travel, and picking up speed.

Eve thanked T-shirt.

'That was some timing. I wasn't sure what was going to happen next.'

'Are you alright? Can I do anything?'

'I think I'll be fine, but thanks.'

'I might follow our friend, see what he gets up to next.'

Eve nodded, stooping to pat the Border Collie before the dog followed T-shirt away through the gravestones.

Eventually Eve found what she'd come here for. A recently filled plot, with a simple plaque on which was engraved the name Luke Burns. Underneath the dates of his too-brief years on earth were the words:

Our sweet boy
May you find release from your demons
You will be forever in our hearts

Oh, Luke, thought Eve. Might you have survived in un-Purpled times? She considered the nurses' conversation when he'd been admitted to the hospital, of his role as curiosity, or, worse, present-day freak show. And remembered, with guilt, how she too had wanted to glimpse him.

'This can't be right, can it?' she whispered.

A bird flapped away from a nearby tree, startling Eve. She glanced about, half expecting to see Dappled. Had his Purpleness helped or hindered their encounter? Didn't he seem like just the sort ripe and right to be Turned?

But... Duncan.

Then: Stone Age. The policeman sprayed with paint.

It was one enormous Purple pickle, and still Eve didn't know what to think. Despite Duncan, and Helena, and – she hoped – an inherent sense of kindness, and fairness, if she was honest, *really* honest, Eve did feel safer because of the scheme. It wasn't a simple in or out, yes or no, all wrong, or all right. Could they finesse the Turning, who they targeted? Or was any collateral too high a price?

As she walked away Eve looked back at the plot – horrified to see that, already, the word 'Lav' had been daubed in purple paint on the back of Luke's plaque. So much for letting him, or his family, rest in peace.

Eve stood outside the back door at Duncan's house, watching a bird nabbing nuts from a feeder hanging nearby. There was the sound of a key being turned, and it wasn't Duncan who opened the door, but Simon.

'Hi, sis,' he said, with a nod.

'Simon,' she said, 'I wasn't sure if you'd still be here.'

'It's Eve,' he called to Duncan, stepping back to allow her

in. 'Shall I make us another cuppa?' As he ambled towards the kettle, Simon turned back to Eve, 'Tea?'

The water rushing from the tap filled the seconds in which she might have made a snippy comment about it being nice to see Simon doing something for someone else for a change; instead she managed to hold her tongue until the moment had passed. Eve left him rinsing mugs with haphazard squirts of Fairy Liquid – was it her imagination or did he lack some of his usual bluster? – and went to greet Duncan, who had his eyes on the doorway and was just standing up as she entered.

'There you are,' he smiled. 'I was contemplating whether there might be silent ninja warfare breaking out in there.'

'No, no.' Eve clasped Duncan in a hug, which he not only allowed, but reciprocated. Making progress, she thought. Both the boys seemed to be mellower than usual, and Eve sniffed the air. She couldn't detect the scent of any illegal substances, but there was the whiff of white musk.

'You've been doing some laundry,' she said, still tickled by the scent-assault of these appliances.

'Simon has,' said Duncan.

Eve turned towards the kitchen, where Simon was sloppily trying to gather three dunked teabags onto one spoon. Duncan stood behind her.

'You know how to work a washing machine?' Eve teased.

'Yeah. You may think I'm completely useless, but…'

Duncan winked at Eve.

'Yeah, well, alright. Maybe I hadn't used one like this before, this *model*, but Dunc told me how.'

'He can be quite the housewife when he puts his mind to it.'

'Steady on, mate!' Simon handed Duncan a mug, adding, 'Though your clobber smells lovely now, if I say so myself.'

They both chuckled.

257

Duncan glanced down at his tea. Simon noticed and looked at his own.

'Did I give you the sugary one? Sorry.'

They exchanged mugs.

'Poisoning me with sweet tea.'

'I know, I know. But if that's the worst thing I've done today, I'm doing alright, eh?'

'You say that, but that toast was a disaster.'

'Nah, it was just—'

'Well done!'

Eve watched them, their easy chemistry.

She wandered back into the living room, which was looking tidier, plus the curtains seemed to be open a fraction more than when Eve had first set eyes on damsoned Duncan. He followed her.

'How are you feeling?' Eve asked. 'You seem brighter.'

'Simon ended up crashing here,' Duncan said. 'It's been fun spending some time with him. He's been on good form.'

So he should be, under the circumstances, Eve thought.

'I'm glad you had some company,' she said.

There was a thud and an exclamation from the kitchen.

'You smashing up my house?'

'Yeah, sorry.'

Duncan looked at Eve. 'Would you see if Simon managed to find the biscuits?'

'The biscuits?'

'If you wouldn't mind...'

'Duncan wondered if you'd found the biscuits,' Eve said, uncertainly, standing in the kitchen doorway, thinking that she could do without a digestive right now.

'Uh, not yet.'

'Should I look for them?'

'Nah, you're alright. You sit down.'

258

Eve was about to retreat into the living room, when Simon added, 'Here. Sit here a sec.'

Eve pulled a chair out from the kitchen table, wiggling it to untangle a leg from a plastic bag on the floor. She sat down.

Simon twitched, fiddling with a spoon he'd just lifted out of the washing up bowl. Eve was finding it incongruous seeing him doing housework.

'Look, I uh, I'm sorry about what happened to Dunc, I am. I'd never want to get him, you know...'

'Purple.'

'Yeah. I'd swap places if I could. I'll do what you need to try and get him changed back.'

'Great, thanks.'

Eve watched Simon, soap suds on his wrists. The kitchen clock ticked.

There was a cough from the living room; Eve moved her chair back.

'Shall I dry?' she said.

Simon shrugged.

Eve reached for a tea towel, wonkily illustrated with the Wetland Birds of Britain, seemingly crowded in a rather small pond. The grumpy-looking geese were joined by a bow-legged heron and a mandarin duck with an unusual mohican.

Sponge in hand, Simon called, 'You alright, Dunc?'

'Yep.'

Simon nodded in satisfaction. He and Eve addressed the pots and plates, if not each other, oblivious to how much pleasure Duncan was taking from their quiet cooperation.

Duncan had got changed, into freshly-scented, freshly-laundered clothes, and sat on the edge of the sofa, mentally preparing himself to venture into the outside world.

'There's no rush,' said Eve, aware that she was back-tracking on herself, but feeling anxious as to what awaited him.

'I should go. Get it over and done with.'

'I'm gonna come too, and tell them what happened,' said Simon.

'Are you?' Eve asked.

'No,' said Duncan, 'there's no point risking you being Turned, and two of us being Purple.'

'He should come,' said Eve, firmly.

'Whatever you want, mate,' said Simon.

'You should come,' Eve told him.

'Eve, really… it's fine, it's noble of Simon to offer, but I think we should see what happens without getting anyone else into trouble.'

Eve looked at Duncan. Noble. Duncan was the noble one.

'Let's go,' said Duncan. 'Come if you want to, Si, but don't say anything 'til we get an idea of the lay of the land.'

Duncan got out of the car.

'Thanks for driving,' he told Simon.

'Welcome.'

'Actually, are you allowed to drive?' Duncan asked.

Simon grinned. 'Now that you mention it, nah, not really. My licence was suspended. But no one'll know.'

'We're at a police station!' Eve exclaimed, though feeling that in actual fact Simon's behaviour was providing some welcome light relief.

Under his hood, Duncan's eyes cast around. There were a handful of people nearby, some coming out of the shop across the road, others walking along the pavement that passed outside the station, but no one paying attention to them. The drive had been uneventful, too – Duncan in the back, hood up, while Simon and Eve had sat in the front ('I don't wanna look like a cab driver,' Simon had said).

Outside the building were glass-doored noticeboards, filled with leaflets about crime prevention, missing kittens, and not leaving dogs in hot cars, all held in place by drawing pins, at wonky angles, stabbed into the felt-covered board with varying success. Behind one glass door was a photocopied sheet featuring a blurry photo of an iguana wearing what appeared to be a small leather jacket. Eve peered closer. 'KEITH IS MISSING! Lost at the Parkside Festival. Reward available for information leading to his return,' said the notice. Eve pointed it out to Duncan, thinking it might make him smile.

'I'd run away too, if I was a lizard in a jacket,' said Duncan.

Eve imagined the iguana at a gig with the mohican-topped mandarin duck.

'How are you doing?' Eve asked him.

'Okay, I guess.'

'Sure? Ready to go in? We can wait for a bit if you want to gather yourself.'

'I think I'm as gathered as I'll ever be.'

They were walking towards the door when Duncan stopped and took a step back.

'What if I don't get to leave here? What if they put me in prison?'

'For a scrap in the street?' Eve replied. 'I shouldn't have thought so.'

'I suppose,' Duncan muttered. 'I'm under house arrest anyway.'

'You can go out,' said Simon. 'Who cares what people think?'

Eve jabbed her brother in the ribs.

'What?' he said, turning to her. 'It's true.'

'Shall we go in?' Eve asked Duncan.

He nodded and they moved towards the door.

In the corridor were what appeared to be cat's bowls of food and water. Eve was buoyed by that. Maybe this won't be so bad, she thought. Maybe we'll bump into Frankie or his dad.

The officer behind the main desk stared at Duncan expectantly, not saying a word, as he approached the counter. Eve's heart sank.

'Hi,' Duncan said hesitantly. 'I'm here to…'

The officer put her elbows on the counter, waiting for him to continue.

Duncan cleared his throat. 'I'm here to report an incident I was involved in.'

The officer nodded. 'Clearly. You'll need to complete these forms.' She looked to either side of Duncan, her head turning as though at a tennis match, taking in Eve and Simon. 'And you two?'

'I'm here for moral support,' said Eve, who couldn't help herself and added, 'He might be innocent you know.'

'There are no innocent people Turned,' said the officer.

Eve peered towards the policewoman's name badge.

'That's not actually true, Officer Geib,' she said. Simon looked at Eve, agog. 'I met someone who'd been accidentally Turned and was being Turned back.'

'Much as I'd love to stand here chatting,' said Officer Geib, her expression hardening, 'was there something else I can do for you?'

She cast her attention towards Simon.

For a moment Simon said nothing, staring stonily at Officer Geib, adamantine. Eve directed a Hard Stare at him, not that he was looking at her.

'Look, sunshine, I can tell you're not thrilled to be here, and honestly, neither am I. I could be at home, cutting the pattern for my friend's wedding dress, which is a relaxing way to spend some time, let me tell you. But here we are, so why not spit it out, eh? Before this one – ' the officer pointed at Eve – 'has kittens.'

Duncan nervously smoothed the creased form with his purple hand.

Simon may have caught this and felt a jolt of conscience, eventually admitting, 'I was at the same incident. Part of it.'

'Were you now.'

'Does he need to fill in a form too?' Eve asked (she knew if Duncan hadn't been standing between them, Simon would have kicked her).

Simon looked mortified, the police officer amused.

'Let's see, shall we. Now, you,' she turned to Duncan. 'What date did you find yourself Turned?'

Duncan was looking pale. 'On Saturday.'

'Right.' She made a note. 'You'll need to go with my colleague.' She called to a baby-faced officer hovering nearby. 'Rog, we've got another one.'

The young policeman came forward. 'This way, sir,' he said, giving Duncan a supportive smile, and leading him away.

Officer Geib watched them go, then turned back to Eve and Simon. 'You can both take a seat,' she said.

'What a witch,' said Simon, under his breath, as they made their way to the waiting area.

Eve smiled.

There were posters covering the walls, mainly mugshots of successfully caught or surrendered Lavs, interspersed with other notices, including a poster featuring pairs of comically darting eyes, shiftily advising you to be vigilant and watch your belongings at all times. In the most prominent position, underneath the clock, a low-fi sign – a board with movable characters, like the sort you'd see displaying a chip shop menu – proclaimed that recorded crimes in this area were down by fourteen per cent since the Purple initiative had begun. There's a sign that's been located in haste, Eve thought. There were no other Purple people in the waiting room; Eve guessed they must all be instantly escorted away, like Duncan.

Simon was agitated. His knee jigged up and down, and he jangled the car keys in his pocket. Obviously not the most calming environment for him, Eve thought.

'I can't believe you just dropped me in it, as soon as we walked in the door!' he said, not quite as nastily as usual; more incredulous. 'Old habits die hard, or something?' He sighed, resigned. 'You always got me into trouble.'

'You always got yourself into trouble.'

A pause.

'Dad liked you more.'

'What? Are you kidding me? He was equally disinterested in both of us.'

'Yeah. There was always another woman.'

'Or three.'

'Would've been funny to have a normal family, like Dunc's.'

'Yes,' said Eve. 'And just imagine, we wouldn't be the fine, well-balanced people we are now.'

With a tut, Simon said, 'There you go again, digging at me.'

'Actually, I did honestly mean both of us.'

'What? Miss Perfect having an identity crisis?'

'Simon, can we just stop? I can't be bothered, I really can't. And this is hardly the time or place.'

'Fine. Yeah.'

There was a crack and a whir as a fancy coffee machine (or a formerly fancy one: there were various pieces of tape holding bits together, and Eve guessed it might have been from the 'client-serving' private days) began spitting out some frothy liquid.

'I meant to say, by the way, it was great how you stuck at the hospital with Mum.'

'Yeah, well… I didn't have anywhere else to be.'

'She really appreciated it.'

'I know.'

The machine hissed.

'Dunc said you were wondering how they do it, Turning.'

Eve glanced around to see if anyone might have heard.

'I am. Which is tricky, when they obviously don't want anyone finding out,' Eve whispered, wondering if the station was bugged.

'Oh, right,' said Simon, whose interest, Eve guessed, must have been piqued at the idea of defying authority. Quietly, with chin down, he asked, 'So what can you do?'

Eve shrugged. 'Not much to go on. I need a blabbermouth or some amazing ISON footage.'

'Huh,' said Simon.

There was some yelling from outside, and then two officers entered, trying to control a man who was shouting and kicking, his feet barely touching the floor as he scrabbled, the officers each gripping one side of him and trying to keep him upright.

'Cells or straight to Turning?' said Officer Geib.

One of the officers replied, 'Given the knife he was waving about, Turning.'

'Right you are,' she said.

The scrabbling man bellowed an ear-piercing 'No!' as he was dragged along, flapping and flailing.

'You sure?' Eve heard one of the frogmarching officers question the other. 'He's off his face, and, well, Turning him

265

isn't going to help him kick whatever he's on, is it? Or what if he's mental health?'

Her colleague replied, 'Then they can Re-Turn him. But if he's going to be prancing about with a knife, he's as good a bet as any for people to be warned about.'

They veered towards the corridor Duncan had been led down, disappearing out of Eve's sight; shortly afterwards, a door slammed.

'You,' Officer Geib called, nodding towards Simon. 'Come back to the desk.'

Eve followed behind Simon.

'We won't be pursuing your activity at the scene of your colleague's offence.'

'Is that right…' said Simon, hesitating, as though this was a bluff of some sort.

'That's interesting,' said Eve. 'Do you have any information as to why?'

'No.'

'Just so we know,' Eve asked, 'could the situation change?'

'Not at the moment,' said the policewoman, pursing her lips. 'You're free to leave.'

'We'll wait for our friend,' said Eve.

They returned to their seats.

'Bloody hell,' said Simon, 'I wasn't expecting that.'

'Me neither. Curious,' said Eve. 'And lucky for you.'

The doors opened again and a woman raced in, a small, reptilian face peering out from under her arm. As she rushed up to reception, she announced, 'We've found Keith! I know you've been trying to find him, so I wanted to let you know. Tear down the posters, he's home, safe and well!'

'Spectacular,' the policewoman said, deadpan.

'At least there are some happy endings around here,' said

Eve, glancing at the clock, and wondering how long they were going to keep hold of Duncan.

'Right,' said Eve, 'tell us exactly what happened.'

She, Simon and Duncan were now sitting in the car outside the police station, Duncan having finally, after three hours, been released. This time Eve sat in the back.

'Well, first, as you saw, they gave me some forms to fill out. One had lots of questions about the crime I believed I was committing when I was Turned.'

'Believed you were committing? Your interpretation of what happened, whether you're innocent or not?'

'No, more like, was there more than one crime I was involved in. There were multiple pages, so you could list different incidents.'

'Why would someone list more than one? No one's going to own up to more than they need to, are they?'

Duncan shrugged. 'I think they must have a log or something, so you list where you were, how many people you were with, what happened, and then they compare notes with – I don't know, some sort of database maybe. They knew things about what had happened already, so whoever the police officer was who Turned me, he must have written up a report. They must have a list of the people they've Turned, and where, and then when you turn yourself in, they tick you off.'

'Did they have pictures, or ISON footage or anything?'

'They didn't say.'

'So how can they prove you've actually done anything? They must have evidence. What if you'd said that you were innocent? People must be saying that, denying having done anything wrong. And whose word would you be speaking against? They've not got an arresting officer, have they?'

'They didn't mention that, either.'

'So they don't show you any evidence, there's no police statement about what you did that you actually see, they just ask you to own up to something?'

'Right. But they behaved as though they'd already got the evidence, that it'd already been filed, no question. They knew what I'd done.'

'But what if you'd contested it?'

'Wasn't an option. The start of the form says something like "you have been caught committing a criminal offence", then "please state here all criminal or disruptive activity in which you participated prior to finding you had been Turned. Please be aware that your guilt is not in question; your offence has already been documented."'

'So some undercover officers are going round Turning people, then writing notes when they get back to the station. That's putting a lot of trust in their officers. It's inevitable that they'll get it wrong sometimes, if not a lot of the time. And also, if they have everything so well documented, how is it that they let Simon go, when he was there, and they must have seen that?'

Simon said, 'Dunno, it's weird.'

'Did they say whether any of the others who were involved have been Turned too?'

'The form asks you about that. I said I didn't know.'

'Did you mention Simon?'

Duncan shook his head. 'There didn't seem to be any point, and he hasn't been Turned, so I didn't need to put anything about him on the form.'

'Thanks, mate,' said Simon.

Eve considered this. If the scheme was being used as a deterrent, Turning any one of a group involved in an incident would surely affect how the others went on to behave. And if so, then obviously that was as effective as multiple Turns.

She gave Duncan's arm a soft squeeze of solidarity.

'What else happened?'

'They took me to an interview room. There were two police officers, one about our age, maybe a bit younger, the other quite a bit older. They looked over the forms, had me talk through my statement and say exactly what had happened. They asked if there were any other occasions when it might have been that I was Turned – I guess they're definitely trying to get people to admit to as much as they can while they have them there – and I said that I absolutely hadn't been involved in any other trouble.'

'Did they say anything about why you weren't just arrested at the time?'

'I asked about that, and they looked a bit surprised. The younger one said, that's not how this works. We can process more people this way, rather than stopping and arresting offenders and bringing them back to the station each time.'

'*Process?*'

'Yep.'

'What happens next, do you have to go to court?'

Despite having told him it was unlikely, Eve was fretting about the looming spectre of prison, but daren't bring another shadow into the conversation. So she was relieved when Duncan replied.

'No. They said mine wasn't a custodial offence.'

'Well that's good! That's something.'

'I have an appointment at court. As it was a fight and not something worse I don't have a trial.'

'That's a positive thing, isn't it? But if you're not going to prison and not having a trial, what are you going to court for? Might you be put on probation, or given community service?

269

And in the meantime, can you get an antidote, or whatever they use, to Turn you back again?'

Duncan shook his head.

'Oh,' said Eve, realising. 'Do you get sentenced to… time like this?'

'Yep. I'm sent before a judge who deems the minimum amount of time before I can be considered for being returned to normal.'

'Okay. So, what, a few weeks?'

Duncan's body slumped. 'Two years.'

'Two years?!' Eve was stunned.

'That's the minimum for everyone. I'm on probation in the meantime and can only be Turned back if I've shown perfect behaviour and passed a psychological test. I'll be kept on an anti-social database for another ten years. If I'm involved in any other crime or misdemeanour I'm Turned indefinitely and sent to prison.'

'For a post-pub brawl? Surely you can appeal?'

'I've admitted guilt, and they have proof of my crime, so no. That's how the chips are falling.'

'This is insanity,' said Eve. 'They can't do this. We'll find a way to sort it out, get you back to normal.'

'You're sweet, but there's nothing to be done. I just need to accept it.'

Duncan reached up to the hood of his sweatshirt, rubbing the soft material between two fingers, like a comfort blanket. Coincidentally, or not, this shielded one side of his face from the car window.

Eve opened her mouth, about to attempt further bright-eyed promises, when Simon, slowly shaking his head, gave her a look which implied: hold your horses.

Eve looked out of the window.

'To figure out how they're doing the Turning, I could get myself Turned,' she said.

'No way,' said Duncan. 'Absolutely not.'

In the rear view mirror, Simon looked at her.

'The last person in the world to get into trouble,' he said. 'Fat chance you'd have of being Purpled.'

'I could engineer it. You could come with me,' she told Simon.

'No,' said Duncan. 'Besides, if you get Turned that'll hamper your ability to investigate, won't it?'

That shut Eve up.

'We all know I'd be most likely to get Turned, anyway,' said Simon, evenly.

'No, Si,' said Duncan.

'If it helps though, mate,' said Simon.

'We'd need to get into an altercation,' said Eve.

'Shouldn't be too difficult,' said Simon.

They exchanged a smile.

'Then Eve still might get Turned,' said Duncan. 'I could come.'

'You're not ready to be out and about, though,' said Eve, gently.

'And I reckon we'd probably have more chance of getting Purpled at night,' said Simon. 'When you're tucked up with a Horlicks.'

Funny how Simon could make a comment like that – honest about Duncan's curfew, and yet it didn't seem to upset him; there was solidarity in it.

'We need three of us,' said Eve, thinking the plan through. 'Two to be in a dispute, and one to observe.'

She let out a satisfied murmur.

'You alright back there?' asked Duncan, amused.

Simon pulled a face.

'Finn,' said Eve, thinking of how he'd been proud to be Purple. And even if he's been Re-Turned, I've a feeling he'll be game, she thought. Plus his uncle... Well, best not to mention that some folk had a Get Out Of Jail Free card. 'He's a lad I met recently. I think he'd be willing to be Purpled. We should ask him.'

'I'm not sure about this,' said Duncan. 'It could go horribly wrong.'

'Dunc, all this grief – it gives me a chance to try an' make it up to you,' said Simon.

Duncan sighed.

'That's settled then,' said Eve. Surely, she thought, even if the consequence is someone being Turned, this had to be a foolproof plan?

Chapter Fourteen

It was Friday night, and Simon and Finn were in a pub, while Eve sat in Duncan's car, watching as the town's weekend shenanigans began to unfurl.

Finn had been only too happy to take part in a clandestine operation. He'd already been Re-Turned, and assisting Eve gave him the double whammy of a win: he was helping Jason (who naturally wanted scheme-unravelling justice for his brother Luke), and being Turned twice would, Finn believed, enhance his post-Purple, edging-towards-edginess reputation. Eve had been curious as to how he'd explained his reversal to a less mauve hue – preferential treatment seemed an unlikely crowd-pleaser – and Finn assured her that everyone had swallowed his tales of sweet-talking his way out of it. Eve worried, too, what the police commissioner uncle's response would be to his nephew potentially being Purpled for a second time, but Finn had responded with a youthful, cross-that-bridge nonchalance.

So, here they were, with the odd couple downing beers which Simon had insisted that *Say Fantastique!* paid for (though slightly peeved, Eve had to admit this did make sense), and Eve, perched in the car, writing extensive notes about those who passed by, her bare legs making a velcro-like de-suctioning sound each time she shifted in her seat.

Thus far, her observations looked to be a list of banalities, beginning with an assortment of workers – on their way home, carting groceries or a carrier bag betraying the shape of a single bottle of wine, or refreshment-ready, leaning in the pub door for a swift pint. Later came gals with the night-out sheen of hair lacquer and lashings of lip gloss; eager new couples, bright-eyed, and soon to be puckered up against the walls of darkened shops clutching at one another with octopus arms; and the bored or comfortable long-term pairings, who said little on their way to, or from, the bustling Thai restaurant a few doors from where Eve was parked. There were also dog walkers who ambled through the festivities, patiently waiting as their canine pals sniffed at the delicious stenches they found laid out for them like a banquet along the pavement.

All of these things appeared unremarkable, but of course, somewhere amidst this tableau of ordinariness lurked the lavendering truth. Such a scene would be replicated in towns across the country, and, come tomorrow, how many of the revellers would find themselves as damson and undesirable as Deadly Nightshade?

Eve wondered how the boys were getting on, and whether they had found any common ground. They were a Jack Sprat combination, contrasting in age, height and temperament. She imagined that Simon would be milking his impressionable audience, and guessed Finn likely to be lapping up his elder's tales of mischief.

A few feet away stood two women in matching denim shorts; one wore a blue top, and the other, the shorter gal, a tiger-print t-shirt. A loud and lively conversation between them had erupted into an argument.

'How dare you!'

274

'Excuse me?'

'I knew I should never trust you.'

'That's rich coming from you—'

'You're disgusting.'

'I'm not, you're the one—'

'You disgust me. You're a liar, a filthy liar!'

Blue Top was becoming increasingly intimidating, leaning forward, her face getting closer, crowding Tiger T-shirt, closing the space between them. Eve remembered, before the Repeal, seeing a heated row between two men in the street become physical, and how, instead of intervening, folk had stood by, entertained, filming it on their PortAbles. Right now, people simply walked past; this wasn't their business. But then Blue Top raised her arms, as though about to shove Tiger T-shirt, who was already standing near to the kerb, her back to the road. One push and she could fall in front of any oncoming traffic.

Eve swung open the car door, and hopped out.

'Hey!' she shouted.

It took the women a moment to extricate themselves from the enveloping fug of their brawl, but eventually they turned around.

'Are you okay?' Eve asked Tiger T-shirt.

'What's it to you?' said Blue Top.

'I wasn't talking to you,' said Eve. She looked at Tiger T-shirt, who stared back at her with disdain.

'Yeah,' she said, 'but you can keep your nose out.'

Blue Top raised a middle finger in Eve's direction, and they walked away, if not now reunited, to continue their argument elsewhere.

Eve got back in the car, a little shaken. She had long been aware of the unsettling frisson between tribes of different temperaments: the sensitive and non-confrontational versus the bolshie and antagonistic (like the woman on the train the other day and the lady she'd assaulted with such verbal acidity). Eve could feel it, crackling invisibly through the air. It frequently felt as though kindness made you vulnerable, and open to ridicule: a soft touch, easily manipulated, or dismissed; the chink of any helpful, non-judgmental aspirations just waiting to be crowbarred into a chasm filled with empathy-less exploitation and well-intentioned regret. Gentleness and compassion could paint a target on your back. Where was the justness in benevolence making someone easy prey? In spikiness – like a cactus, or a poisonous pufferfish – granting protection as a reward? And yet, did Eve appreciate the Purple prospect of the spikier, frequently toxic tribe being most likely to be Turned? Reciprocal protection for the temperate, like her?

Her train of thought returned to Tiger T-shirt and Blue Top. Eve realised that it might have been a qualifying Purpling incident, but her instinct to help had distracted Eve from what was happening around them. She sighed, frustrated, fidgeting in her seat, further annoyed as she unpeeled her thighs from the vinyl. Definitely don't wear shorts tomorrow night, she told herself.

The pub door was flung open, and the boys appeared, Simon with his usual confident swagger, Finn beaming, gleaming as though some of Simon's naughty lustre had rubbed off on him. Simon was smoking a cigarette, which Finn playfully reached for; Simon's retaliating swipe, with a sharp, accompanying 'Oi!', knocked the fag to the ground, so he swiped again, this time to Finn's head. The predetermined tussle was afoot.

Eve glanced around. A couple came out of the Thai restaurant, jackets on, about to head home, and only registered the boys' scrap with a glare of vague disparagement. 'They'll probably get Purpled,' Eve heard the man say. Here's hoping, she thought. A woman walked by with a yapping Jack Russell, which stopped to lick a littering crisp packet before it was yanked away. A trio of well-dressed lads strode purposefully along, laughing and clapping each other on the back. And an elderly man stood outside a phone booth, having a cigarette; the phone must have begun to ring, though Eve couldn't hear it – his head jerked up and he stepped inside the red kiosk, lifting the receiver, fag still in hand.

The pub door opened again and a woman leant out.

'Lads!' she called to Finn and Simon. 'Pack it in. You know as well as I do that you might get Turned, and I don't want that on my doorstep. Go home.'

The boys appeared to grumble, shoving each other a couple more times before wandering away and around the corner.

Eve started up the car engine.

Saturday night, now. Neither Simon nor Finn had become even the slightest bit aubergine, much to Eve's chagrin, so they were on Operation Purposefully Purple part two.

Another pub, in another town.

There were the usual comings and goings; people a little ritzier and glitzier, bouncing with elastic, relaxed cheer for having now fully unwound into the weekend.

Eventually the boys appeared, again orchestrating a scrap in the street. This time, a pair of police officers had passed a few minutes beforehand, but weren't in view when Simon and Finn began to fight. A man walked a pair of Boxer dogs, one black, one white. He'd taken a packet of cigarettes from his pocket, stopped to light up, before seeming to think better of it, drifting on as one of the dogs saw a cat and began to bark, tugging on its lead as it tried to give chase. A hen party dressed as beauty pageant contestants – with sashes such as 'Miss Guided', 'Miss Fortune' and 'Miss Taken' (a large badge identified the latter as the bride-to-be) – giggled as they conga'd haphazardly down the road, some with one hand holding a plastic party-favour crown in place or clutching the skirts of a cheap, voluminous gown so it didn't trail along the pavement. One of the women accidentally stumbled into Finn, mumbling an apologetic 'Oops' before hurrying onwards.

'How'd we do?' Finn asked, when Eve picked them up a few streets away.

'Great,' said Eve. 'Thank you, both of you, for this.'

'It might not work,' said Simon.

'I know,' said Eve.

'But it was a laugh!' said Finn. 'Right, Simon?'

'First time I've actually been asked to get into trouble,' said Simon.

'Are we out again tomorrow?' Finn asked.

'Let's see what happens,' said Eve, glancing in the rear view mirror. As far as she could see, the boys had got away surveillance-free. They'd soon find out whether or not that was a good thing.

Sunday morning, and Eve was back at Womble and Helena's. She had spoken to a still un-damson Simon, and while she had yet to get hold of Finn, was prepared for disappointment.

The phone had stopped ringing, but Helena's hand hovered over it; Eve watched her fingers wiggle, itching to lift the receiver.

'Womble must have got it,' said Eve, hoping it might be Finn.

'Yes,' said Helena, sitting down and resting her elbow on the table, her chin tucked into her palm.

'You okay? You look perturbed. You're not thinking about the silent calls again?'

'Not those, no. But Womble's had a couple of odd calls this week.'

'Odd?' Eve asked.

'I don't know. Secretive. He didn't sound as though he was greeting someone we know – sounded more business-like. He took them in another room.'

'Well, if it's business, maybe he's just trying to save you from a conversation about the school music curriculum or something.'

'I suppose so. But something doesn't feel right.'

'It'll just be boring school stuff.'

'Maybe.' Helena glanced again towards the kitchen door, this time to see if Womble was about to return. 'It's just… I've got a bad gut feeling about this. Women's intuition.' Helena leant over and whispered, 'What if he's having an affair?'

Eve almost laughed. 'He wouldn't,' she said, 'he's besotted with you. And besides, he's not the type. After growing up with my dad trying to charm every woman within lasso-ing distance, and then ten years of dating in New York, I think my philander-o-meter is pretty finely tuned. Nothing surprises me, as you know, but Womble cheating? Less likely than people turning Purple.'

'People *are* turning Purple,' Helena sighed.

'You know what I mean.'

'I know things have been tricky lately, but I don't want him running off with some other woman.'

'He wouldn't do that! Honestly, I can't imagine it, Hels, I really can't.'

'So he hasn't said anything to you?'

'Nope.'

Helena briefly glanced upwards, listening, before changing the subject.

'No word from your mum or dad?'

Eve shook her head. 'Nothing. They'll just carry on as usual, thinking it's all blown over. And knowing that me and Simon have been spending time together while we're keeping an eye on Duncan, they'll think everything's hunky dory.'

Mr Bailey, the Golden Retriever, ambled over to Helena and put his head in her lap.

'Hello, my lovely boy,' she said, stroking his ears.

'I keep thinking about that woman on the train the other day,' said Eve.

'That sounded dismal.'

'It was. Such anger, and nastiness – the kind you could feel in your bones. And I've been wondering about those children, how they are, and how they'll turn out, having a mother like that.'

'You have to think too, though, how did she become that way?'

'I suppose.'

'The mum's another layer of tragedy, and there are probably more before that,' said Helena. 'Doesn't excuse her behaviour, but it's so sad. Womble sees it at school, and you think, where does it end? Which reminds me, he'll tell you this, but they found out that one of the kids he teaches has been Turned.'

'No!'

'Yes. Hideousness,' Helena shuddered. She was quiet for a moment, then said, 'You're sure you don't think he's doing anything?'

'Absolutely. Why don't you ask him? There'll be a logical explanation, and then you can stop worrying about it.'

A few minutes later Womble ambled into the room. Helena smiled broadly.

'Who was that on the phone?' she asked.

'Work,' Womble replied, opening the fridge, and peering inside, rendering himself out of sight.

'A school thing? On a Sunday?' Helena continued, affecting a casual tone but looking intently towards the fridge door, as though if she concentrated hard enough she'd be able to see through it and capture his expression.

'Yep,' Womble mumbled, towards a bag of lettuce and the cheese dish.

'What school thing?'

'A boring thing.' There was the sound of plastic packaging being snapped. Womble closed the door, a yoghurt in hand. 'Mm, raspberry.'

Helena's eyes narrowed slightly, not that Womble noticed, his attention instead focused on the cutlery drawer as he located a spoon.

Helena turned to Eve, her expression silently questioning Womble's present behaviour.

'Hels said someone at school has been Turned.'

'Yes,' said Womble. 'We thought he'd been bunking off, which wouldn't be unusual, but no.'

'Isn't he a bit young to be Turned?'

'Exactly,' said Helena. 'It's criminal.'

'I don't know. Maybe it'll do him some good. He's always in trouble,' said Womble, who popped a spoonful of yoghurt into his mouth, then added, almost to himself, 'Can't imagine the purple goes so well with his blue hair.'

'That's an awful thing to say,' said Helena. 'How can you be so flippant?'

'Drew?' Eve asked.

'Yes,' said Womble, surprised at her knowing his name.

'Bob was talking to him that day I came in. When did he get Turned?'

'A week ago, his mum said. She was going to go on the rally, but when she got up that morning, he was sitting eating toast, Purple. Gave her a fright.'

'So he was Turned on the Friday?' Eve said.

'I suppose so.'

'That's the same night Duncan was Turned. The night we were in the pub. We saw him – or you and Bob did, remember? On the way there, when we bumped into Rory?'

Womble murmured in the affirmative as he scraped the rest of his yoghurt from the pot.

'How strange,' said Eve. 'Maybe it was the same police officer who Turned them?'

Womble coughed.

'Only you could choke on a yoghurt,' said Helena.

Eve glanced at them, trying to detect if there was any affection to this comment.

'This is a long shot, but maybe Rory saw something,' said Eve. 'He might have seen a police person near Drew.'

'Bit unlikely isn't it, Evie?' said Helena. 'If you saw Drew before you went to the pub, and Duncan got into the fight after you all left…'

'You're right,' said Eve, with a sigh. 'Drew was probably Turned much later on, like Duncan.'

'Worth asking, though, just in case,' said Helena. 'Right, I'm going to walk the pups.'

She called to Sven, who rushed into the room, tail wagging.

'I'm going to do some homework,' said Womble.

As she put on the dogs' leads, Helena watched Womble retreat from the room.

'You really don't think he's up to something?' she asked Eve.

'He wouldn't,' said Eve.

Helena nodded uncertainly and headed towards the front door, which clunked shut behind her.

Womble's behaviour had seemed evasively out of sorts. Eve didn't believe he'd be unfaithful – plus he was such a terrible liar that the jig would soon be up – but she wondered if something mildly fishy could be afoot. She frowned, and switched on the radio.

'Sebastian Dell, son of MP Alistair Dell, has been defending the behaviour for which he was recently Turned Purple. The twenty-five year old was heavily criticised for taunting a homeless man, and allegedly burning a fifty-pound note in front of him. Alistair Dell was said to be "saddened" by his son's behaviour and said he hoped having been Turned would give him cause for reflection. The prime minister commented: "I think this just goes to show that the Purple Initiative leaves its mark with regard to *all* repellent behaviour on our streets, whoever the perpetrator or whatever their crime". That was the news at one o'clock. We'll be back again in an hour.'

Eve moved her attention to the day's newspapers. Most of the headlines centred around a pair of Purple people, believed to be part of the trio who'd been snapped escaping the secure facility and triggering awareness of the scheme. Their mugshots scowled from the front pages; the shot of one of the men caught him with a curling lip, as though if you pressed your ear to the page you might hear him snarl.

These are two of the LAVENDER LADS whose astonishing appearance – caught on camera as they ESCAPED police detention over two weeks ago – launched the public unveiling of Theo Fletcher's INCREDIBLE Purple Scheme. Brothers Ritchie Hawking and Jamie Pratt had been Persons of Interest to coppers investigating a series of VIOLENT ATTACKS, where victims were set upon in their own homes.

Having been caught RED-HANDED during a raid on a home in Mansfield – during which the PETRIFIED owners triggered a panic alarm – the terrible twosome soon found themselves Purpled. Like original Lav, Lee Bowen, the pair had NO IDEA what had happened to them – and realised the tables had been well and truly turned now they were the ones FEARING for their lives.

The brothers – who have the same mum but different dads – are no strangers to being held at Her Majesty's Pleasure, having been NICKED for armed robbery at a post office. That offence caused elderly customer Doris Pugh – who was in the queue at the time – to have a HEART ATTACK, from which she later died.

'Those men killed her,' said Doris's daughter Toni. 'I said they shouldn't be let out, and look what happened. I'm glad they're Purple now and everyone can see them for the MURDERERS they are.'

Unbelievably, since their Houdini act, the duo were being harboured by a pal, Nev Paulson, who had also recently been Turned Purple – but had yet to turn himself in. Ironically, it was a postman who saw the three in Nev's back garden and called the police.

Arresting officer Gilbert Brown said, 'I think the general public can see the sort of people being identified by this scheme. We're very pleased that, due to their having been Turned, a passer-by alerted us to these men, and more importantly still, that three DANGEROUS criminals are now in custody. It's an excellent result.'

Eve sighed and turned the page, to yet more Purpleness – the Lav Line Up. There, she saw a familiar face: the young mother from the train. Dead-eyed and not even looking directly at the camera (one of the papers picked up on this, commenting 'a Lav who seems unable to even acknowledge, let alone respect, authority'), this was apparently Amber Brey, 23, who had been Turned for 'extremely offensive and upsetting anti-social behaviour'. No surprise there, Eve thought, though she was curious to know more about the incident that had caused her to be Turned. Now however, with so many new Purple people to be reported each day, there wasn't a huge amount of space to include more specific details about each one, unless it was a particularly outrageous or conspicuous case. Sebastian Dell, the MP's son, joined Amber in today's mauve rogues' gallery, along with:

Julian Tobey, 31, Loughborough – HEAD-BUTTED a shopkeeper, who gave chase after Tobey stole several bottles of wine and threatened to STAB him.

Maurice Webber, 19, Luton – threw lit FIREWORKS at a pair of volunteers collecting money for a children's CHARITY. The volunteers received minor burns but have been released from hospital.

Denny Henlock, 24, Glasgow – PUNCHED an unsuspecting dinner lady outside her school's gates, pushing her to the ground and stealing her bag in a VICIOUS mugging.

Tim Snell, Anthony Hyde and Snowy Langen, all 14, Worthing – in the first reported case of a GANG of people being Turned, this motley crew of boys attacked FIREFIGHTERS who they had despicably summoned as a JOKE – delaying the fire engine getting to another, genuinely life-threatening, call.

If it weren't for Duncan having been Turned, Eve was seriously unsure that she would've been able to maintain her resistance to the Purple Scheme. Despite the sensible arguments against it – the wisdom of exemplary people like Helena, and Magnus – there really wasn't any excusing such repellent behaviour. Was there? Maybe Julian Tobey was penniless, or an alcoholic; perhaps Danny Henlock was desperate, a drug addict. But that didn't negate the fear or the suffering of their victims. Even with naiveté, or peer pressure, the Worthing ambulance-summoners should have known better – and who on earth would throw lit fireworks at another living soul? As for Sebastian Dell, his obnoxiousness and jaw-dropping lack of empathy turned the stomach. Eve groaned; this conflict felt uncomputable.

The phone rang, then Womble called from upstairs, 'Eve, someone for you.'

Eve reached for the receiver.

'Hi, Eve, it's Finn.'

'Finn! How are you?'

'I'm Purple.'

'Oh, wow.'

After everything Eve had just been thinking.

'That's… great. Well, terrible, but great.'

Was it really? she thought. Eve had been there, watching, as he was Turned, yet, like a befuddling illusion, she couldn't say how it had happened.

'Yeah. Sorry I didn't let you know earlier. My mum's gone spare.'

'You will definitely be able to get Turned back?'

'Probably. Mum's saying we can't ask my uncle again. But honestly, I don't think he'll want it in the papers that his nephew's been Turned twice, so he'll agree, I reckon.'

'I do *really* appreciate you putting yourself on the line like this.'

The guilt, now.

'No worries. I told Jason. He's worried, but a bit chuffed, I think, that it might help.'

'I know we already went through everything, and of course I saw everyone who was around you both when you were outside the pub, but there's nothing else you remember, right?'

'Nope. Didn't feel anything.'

'Right. Let me see what I can figure out. You'll keep in touch and let me know when you're Re-Turned? And if there's anything else I can do?'

'Yep.'

'Great. Thank you again, so much… and I'm really sorry.'

'Don't be. All this has been amazing. Oh, and Eve?'

'Yes?'

'You'll tell Simon I got Turned, won't you?'

'I will.'

Eve tipped forward, resting her head in her hands. What had she done? And was it actually going to make any difference?

Chapter Fifteen

Rory was making his morning coffee.

'Hi, Eve,' he said, brightly. 'I didn't know we were going to have the pleasure of seeing you...'

There was a pause. Was he going to add something else? You never quite knew.

'Well actually, I wanted to have a natter with you,' Eve said.

'Really?' Rory finished stirring his coffee and tapped the spoon decisively on the counter. 'That sounds interesting.'

'I've a bit of a strange query. There was a boy who Womble teaches who was Turned Purple—'

'Oh. That's unfortunate.'

'I know. It seems to have happened that night we all went to the pub – do you remember? We bumped into you on the way?'

'Of course.'

'The random bit is that the boy who was Turned was in the area that afternoon – he was only a little way ahead of us when we bumped into you. He's quite distinctive looking – his hair's blue – and I just wondered if you might have seen him, or noticed anyone approach him?'

Looking doubtful, Rory said, 'Blue hair?'

'Yes.'

'I don't think so. What should I have seen?'

Eve sighed. 'Probably nothing. You definitely didn't see him, then? Or notice anything unusual?'

Rory's face wrinkled as he considered this. 'I don't think so, no.'

'Of course,' said Eve. 'Never mind. I should go and let you crack on.'

'*Au revoir*, then. Sorry I couldn't…'

'Help,' said Eve, under her breath.

Eve's veterinary pitstop had been made en route to visit Annie Morris, and aside from an obvious excitement at spending time with one of her heroines, she was glad of the distraction. She'd barely slept the night before, and wasn't sure if that was the night-before-Christmas-ness of seeing Annie, or the sanity-shredding confusion of the Purpleness. Despite the fact that it was the very outcome that she had desired, Eve was upset at the thought of Finn being Purple, again. Especially given that however many times, notes in hand, she'd replayed he and Simon's scuffle in her mind, she couldn't see how it had happened. Were the police officers who'd seemed out of sight actually involved, or had the apparently innocuous, satin-frocked hen been an officer in disguise and nabbed Finn when she knocked into him? Those were the only possibilities Eve could think of, but, even so, she hadn't seen *how* he had been Turned. No needle, no poisoned nectar, no sinister magic powder. It had happened right in front of her, and Eve still had absolutely no idea.

*

Eve's arrival at Television Centre was much later than she'd intended – her teenage self planned to have rolled up years ago, ready to clamber the corporation's news ladder – but it was still a thrill to be there. And professional path aside, the young Eve would have been more than impressed that her reason for being there now was to meet Annie Morris – and for a social engagement, no less.

Eve could have spent hours sitting in the lobby, feeling the hum of activity in the hub where meetings began and ended, as smartly dressed people with clipboards and firm handshakes strode purposefully about. From the walls, decades of broadcasting greats watched the new faces coming and going as the revolving door spun, secure (at least for now) in their place in history.

So far Eve had seen a pop duo dallying, one of them carrying a not insubstantial synthesiser case under his arm which, as he turned to greet a clipboard carrier (from the recently reinstated chart rundown show, Eve presumed), just missed knocking into a renowned wildlife presenter who was passing behind him. There was also a news reporter who the night before had been on location for a French election, and was carrying a duty-free bag.

Eve had been so transfixed by the bustling activity that she hadn't noticed Annie walking towards her. She was wearing a silky blouse with a high, gathered collar, and Eve couldn't help but smile.

'Eve!' she said. 'So lovely to see you.'

'Lovely to see you too.'

'I thought you might like to have lunch in the canteen,' Annie said, 'but we can go out to a restaurant if you prefer.'

'I'd love to have lunch here,' said Eve, with a laugh. The infamous canteen. Which legends would they spot in there today?

'Shall we just spend a few minutes in the sunshine? I think it's always sensible to get out and get some air,' said Annie, heading towards the door.

They walked along the street, past cafés and convenience stores, a newsagent's, dry cleaners, a nail bar and a tanning salon. Eve thought of InTan. She'd been hoping she might hear more from Mina, but no. Another dead end.

There were shouts from further along the road suddenly, and Eve looked over to see a Purple man being set upon by a trio of lads.

A waiter from a nearby restaurant ran outside, flapping a menu, as though they were pigeons who could be shooed away.

'What do you think you're doing?' he shouted.

'He deserves it,' said one of the three, kicking the Purple man.

'They're all scum, thinking they can do as they like and get away with it,' said the second.

'Yeah, causing trouble,' said the third, spitting at the Purple man but missing, and instead sputtering into the gutter.

'And what do you think it is you're doing?' said the waiter. 'Making the world a better place?'

'Exactly,' one of the lads said.

The waiter stood his ground.

They shrugged, and then, as quickly as they had appeared, skulked off.

'Thank you,' said the Purple man. 'I appreciate it.'

The waiter nodded before marching back into the restaurant, shaking his head.

The Purple man stood for a moment, watching him go. Wondering if he despised him too, Eve thought, despite the rescue. He had looked unassuming, normal, and was dressed quite smartly – not a stereotypical mischiefmaker or

resembling most of the mugshots found in the Lav Line Up
—so how was it that he'd found himself Turned? The man
dusted himself down, glanced around. His gaze met Eve's. She
blinked. The man walked away.

Thinking of Duncan, who, since visiting the police station,
still refused to leave his house, she shivered. Was that what he
would be subjected to if he went outside?

'Are you okay, Eve?' Annie asked.

'Yes, of course, I—' Eve stopped. He may have been through
it before, but she'd lined Finn up for reactions like those, too.
'What a mess,' she said.

'How's your research going?' Annie asked. 'You were
looking into that, weren't you? You seemed intrigued.'

'Well,' said Eve. 'Slow and frustrating progress. Like pogo-
ing through treacle. Plus to be honest, I feel so conflicted. And
I shouldn't, should I?'

Annie linked her arm through Eve's. 'Go on.'

'One of my friends has been Turned. He's a good guy. A
really good guy, I think. And I—' Eve wasn't sure she could
bring herself to confess about Finn, yet.

'You can rarely stop bad things happening to good people,'
said Annie. 'Maybe your looking into the Turning could help
him?'

'But there aren't even any crumbs of clues to be found. I've
been scouring the news wires and other bits on the Portal,
I've spoken to people who've been Turned, I've even…' How
could she put this? 'I was with someone the night they were
Turned, and I saw nothing. No police, they didn't have a
drink that could have been spiked, we didn't see anyone –'
she shrugged – 'I don't know, stick a syringe in them, or
something. And there was one crazy lead, which I tried to look
into…'

Should she tell Annie about InTan? Eve bit her lip.

'You are being careful?' Annie asked.

'Yes, don't worry,' said Eve, deciding to hold her horses, for now, on the InTan front. 'But no one – me included – seems to have seen, or felt, anything out of the ordinary. It's incredible. If it turns out that Theo Fletcher's got the Invisible Man Turning people, I won't be surprised.'

'Maybe he has,' said Annie.

Eve looked at her. 'You haven't heard anything?'

'No.' Annie shook her head.

'Journalists don't seem to know anything. I've spoken to some criminal defence lawyers with Purple clients – a lot of them are steaming about the scheme – but they don't know anything, the police aren't saying anything—'

'You've been talking to the police?'

'Just one PC, an old friend. He couldn't say anything, and said to be cautious about looking.'

'I agree.'

'And if I saw someone Turned in front of my own eyes and still don't know… it seems an impossible riddle. But they're doing it somehow. I just wish I could find a loose-lipped somebody in the know.'

'Unfortunately, I don't think there'll be a queue of those,' said Annie.

'I'm not being ridiculous though, am I? Honestly, if it weren't for Duncan—'

'He's your friend who's been Turned?'

'Yes,' said Eve, before asking, 'Do you still think it's worth investigating?'

Annie gave a nod. 'It's funny, I was asked to be part of a committee brought in to consider options for curtailing crime, which ended up not happening. I'd never have imagined this initiative as one of the options.'

'Crikey, that sounds high-flying. When were they supposed to have it?'

'Not that long ago, maybe a year. I wasn't sure if I'd be able to participate, anyway – having to be careful with professional political neutrality – ' Annie smiled – 'which was a potential relief. I wasn't sure if it would be productive or dreadful. I imagined it would be all the usual suspects that take part in those sorts of things, that I was there to round out the numbers, be a token thinking woman.'

'Theo Fletcher's pretty tip-top on equality though, isn't he? Even if so many things feel backwards, with the Repeal.'

'He is, yes. Some of the others though… whatever strides are made, they can still only see a woman's role as being to pretty up the proceedings. I encounter more of them than I expect, still stuck in a timewarp. It's astonishing.'

'This country, stuck in a timewarp?' Eve laughed.

'Come on,' said Annie. 'Let's get back and have some lunch.'

There was something quite funny about being in another television studio canteen with Annie Morris. Eve thought about Simon graffiti-ing the table, all those years ago.

'Thank you for inviting me,' said Eve. 'It really is a treat to be here.'

'You're welcome.'

'And I appreciate your encouragement. It means a lot.'

'Don't mention it.' Annie reached into her bag. 'I found something I thought you might like to see,' she said, producing a paper wallet branded with the logo from a high street camera shop. 'Some photos from my early broadcasting days. Try not to laugh – some of the clothes and hairstyles are really awful!'

Eve opened the wallet and took out the pictures. She laughed and held out one where Annie, wearing a zebra print jacket, her relaxed hair lacquered firmly in place, glanced up from her notes. She was in the studio where Eve had made her birthday visit.

Annie groaned. 'I tried to wear that jacket on air! They weren't having any of it.'

In another, Annie and her husband were on a boat, the Statue of Liberty behind them.

'On that trip,' Annie said, 'I'd been flown over for a job interview, to be a news anchor on one of the networks.'

'Wow,' said Eve.

'I know, it was exciting. We'd decided we really wanted to start a family – though actually I didn't fall pregnant with Robin until a while after that – plus Robert had a good job he was enjoying, so it didn't seem like the right time. That was one of those situations where you think, well, if I've been offered this now, it could come round again...'

'Did it?'

'No.' Annie shrugged.

Eve studied the picture – the blue sky, Annie's skirt blowing in the river-crossing breeze. Hats off to Annie, she thought, for being so at ease about what might have been.

When Eve had finished scanning through the snaps, she looked over at Annie, who was re-reading that night's notes for the news analysis show which she presented.

'Do you get nervous about doing interviews?'

'A little, of course. What if something goes wrong... what if the interviewee is difficult. But I try to overdo my research, so I'm prepared. Being a pre-record is less nerve-wracking, too. It's the live ones that give me palpitations!'

Eve tried to imagine what it would be like if she were about to interview, say, Theo Fletcher. What would she ask? How would she try to subtly squirrel information out of him? And how would anyone become such an eloquent, effective interviewer that they could tease the responses they wanted from their subject, like charming a wary, wily snake from a basket?

'I'm sure I would've been a disaster at it, but I really wish I'd tried to do what you do.'

'Really? But what you do is so joyful.' Annie paused. 'What's particularly appealing about it, do you think?'

'Telling stories.'

'You do tell stories.'

'Important stories. Sharing things that are worthwhile.'

'I'd say you already are. It makes me happier, having *Say Fantastique!* to brighten my mornings.'

'Thank you,' said Eve, awkward with the compliment. She was wondering how things might have been different, between that previous TV canteen moment and this one.

With her fork, Eve pronged a couple of pasta shells and a mozzarella ball.

'What's the prime minister like?'

'Theo Fletcher? As you might imagine, really. He's always been decent, I think,' said Annie.

'Charming?'

'Yes. A lot of people think he plays on that, I know, but I don't think so. I find him quite earnest. And – I could be wrong, but – from my experiences of spending time with him, I'd say he's not much different in person to how he is in private. Though obviously his family and friends might disagree.'

'What does he do outside of being PM, do you know?'

'I'm not sure... he always gives the impression of being absolutely committed to the job. Rather consumed by it all.'

'He does, doesn't he? As though if he had any down time, instead of playing golf, or lazing around in his pyjamas watching telly, he'd be sitting gazing out of the window thinking about economic strategy, or something.'

'Quite!'

'I wonder if he'll ever get married?'

'He may well be exceptionally good at keeping his private life private, but he doesn't appear to have time for that either.'

'The drinks receptions and fundraisers he goes to must be a hoot, then, mustn't they? Women lining up trying to nab Britain's most eligible bachelor.'

'From the times when I've seen him at those events, yes. It's made me feel a bit sorry for him, though.'

'I wonder how much of an impact his fiancée's death really had on the Purple Scheme.'

'Indeed,' said Annie. 'I've wondered that.'

A mozzarella ball fell off Eve's fork, splashing back into the tomato sauce. Eve glanced down at her blouse – no rogue red stains. When she looked up, she could see a handful of people gathered around one particular table, laughing and fawning in a way that implied they had an audience with a particularly notable celebrity. Though given that the canteen had a healthy smattering of them eating their lunches in peace, including renowned TV chef Abigail Hitchcock, some of the *Victory Way* cast, and a legendary actress best known for a Technicolor musical which was always shown on Christmas Day, it was hard to think who'd caused a stir. As the people began to move away, Eve caught a glimpse of the figure responsible for the furore: Carla De Lora.

'Oh my God,' she said.

'What is it?' Annie asked, her back to Carla's table.

'Carla De Lora.'

'Oh,' Annie said, without turning round. 'She doesn't strike me as someone you'd be impressed to see.'

'No, it's not that. I think she might know something.'

'About what?'

Her focus on Carla's table, Eve said, 'Do you mind if I hop

over there and try and speak to her, before another crowd descends?'

'Of course not,' said Annie, slightly surprised, before turning again to her notes.

'Miss De Lora?'

Carla was as striking as she appeared in pictures, despite being make-up free and low-key, dressed in a simple cotton top, a delicate silver locket swaying gently against it, and her hair-care millionaire mane tied back – about as incognito as she managed to be, Eve guessed. She looked up, wary, but ready to charm.

'Yes?'

'I'm so sorry to bother you. I'm a, um, big fan of your work.'

'Oh,' said Carla, with perfected politeness. 'Thank you. It's just standing about in posh frocks, really!'

'I'm Eve Baxter, I write for an agency called *Say Fantastique!*, we write fun news stories.'

Eve could see Carla was unsure how best to process this; her expression had hardened a little at Eve's mention of writing – journalist alert – but eased again at the word fun. Carla would most likely be calculating this to equate Eve with being harmless.

'This is a bit of a silly question, but we were writing a piece about funny tanning stories, and we found a press release for InTan – this is ridiculous, I know, but it sounds amazing! I really wanted to try it, but apparently its release is on the shelf now... I'm still desperate to know though, how does it work?'

Carla cocked her head to one side, considering Eve. 'I'm sorry,' she said, 'but while it's on hold I can't talk about that.'

'Really? Rats!' said Eve. 'Not even a clue?' She gave a sisterly smile.

'It's a drag, I know,' Carla apologised, 'but I'm duty bound to keep my lips sealed, I'm afraid. To some it may seem like a little bit of bronzing, but to others it's a secret to be guarded like a Pharaoh's tomb!'

Eve had once seen a travel programme where Carla was on a Nile cruise. You wouldn't need InTan there, she thought.

She sat down in the chair opposite Carla. 'I really need to find out how it works,' she said, 'and I would be incredibly grateful for any details.'

Carla tilted her head again, her ponytail swinging behind her. 'It's funny, you don't look like the sort of woman who tans a lot.'

Apparently Eve's scarlet lipstick and pale skin, a complexion more Snow White than golden goddess, had given her away.

'I haven't found the right product,' said Eve, both of them now knowing Carla didn't buy this line of questioning in the slightest. 'Can you just tell me – nod, wink, whatever – how it's administered? Is it a pill, is it—'

'I can't talk about it, I'm sorry,' Carla insisted. 'It's just a tanning thing, truly not that exciting.'

'Please,' Eve pleaded. 'I know it seems bonkers, but—'

'I'm so sorry, but you need to move away now.'

'All I want to know is how a tanning product works…'

Out of the corner of her eye Eve could see Carla's companion arriving back at their table, ready to intercept this exchange.

'Are you okay?' Eve heard him ask.

'Fine, thank you, Magnus,' said Carla.

Eve was quite certain her heart had stopped. She turned, momentarily silenced at the shock of seeing him.

'Eve,' he said. 'What on earth is going on?'

'You know her?' Carla asked.

Magnus didn't respond, and Eve wasn't sure whether to

interpret this as his not wanting to acknowledge their acquaintance, or being distracted and not listening to Carla. Instead he was looking at Eve with astonished confusion.

Eve couldn't think where to begin, and her brain was scrambled with horror; all she could think was this was far, far worse than Simon graffiti-ing the table. And then she remembered: it could yet be more mortifying, as Annie was here too. Eve daren't look over to see if she had witnessed this debacle. Utter humiliation.

'Eve,' said Magnus. 'What's going on here?'

'She was asking about a product I did some promotion for,' said Carla.

Magnus looked surprised, and relieved. 'A product?'

'A tanning product,' said Carla, nodding her head.

'I had a question about it,' said Eve.

'Really?' he now looked slightly bemused. 'You were never one for tanning.'

'That's what I said!' Carla exclaimed.

'I think how it works could be important.'

'Important to what?' Magnus asked.

What should Eve say – a little, a lot?

'I'm looking into something for a story...' Eve could have cried. To be so shamed in front of Magnus, of all people.

Then she noticed Annie approaching – scanning the group, trying to read the situation.

'Hello, Carla!' she said brightly. 'I'm Annie, I wanted to come and say hi. I see you've met my friend Eve. And you must be the infamous Magnus Jones.' Annie extended a hand. 'It's a pleasure to meet you.'

'It's great to meet you, too,' said Magnus, then, with a question directed to Eve: 'You two know each other?'

'Ah yes, I'm a big fan of Eve's work. Just call me Pam Fox-Jones!' Annie intercepted, with a laugh.

'You write that?' said Magnus.

Eve nodded. She turned to Carla. 'I'm so sorry to have upset you. I'm just… trying to solve a puzzle and thought you might be able to help. I really didn't mean to cause any trouble.'

Then she looked at Magnus.

'Magnus, I… this isn't as loony as it seems, honest.' She attempted a small laugh. He was gazing straight at her, clearly baffled by this bizarre episode. She glanced away, thinking of their last encounter, all those years ago. How could she explain this, and that?

'I…' Eve took a breath, and thought of the four hundred and one things she wanted to say to him – that for so long she'd wanted to say to him – things that were now jumbled in her brain like socks in a tumble dryer.

Magnus tipped his head forward, sweetly waiting.

'I…' Eve faltered, wondering how she could say anything of significance, right here, right now, concisely, and in front of Carla and Annie. She swallowed.

'I should get back to lunch.'

Oh Eve, you idiot, she thought. You half-wit of prize-winning proportions. Magnus must have been mystified (again). He nodded, and gave an affable smile that only made her feel worse.

'Lovely to meet you both,' said Annie.

She and Eve returned to their table.

'Are you okay?' Annie asked.

White as a sheet, or red as a beetroot?, Eve wondered, trying to recall when she'd ever felt so humiliated. Possibly the only other incident where self-combusting on the spot would have been more preferable was the last time she'd clapped eyes on Magnus. Feeling faint, she pictured their doorstep embrace, and then the one Magnus had later found her in with the gobby Globe bloke; their final encounter. Her current

301

mortification would have been more pronounced – woeful wailing, rubber-faced gurning at the gobsmackingness of it all – had she not wanted to avoid further letting herself down in front of Annie.

'What a flailing, embarrassing fiasco, I'm so sorry,' Eve said. 'And of all the people...'

'It wasn't that bad,' said Annie. 'Plus, a not-so-talkative model is hardly the end of the world. What was she being so reticent about?'

Quietly, Eve said, 'She might be the one person who could shed some light on a Purpleness lead. Well, bonkers but hopefully possible lead. And there I was, just saying what a disastrous journalist I'd make...'

'Not at all,' said Annie. 'Now, why don't I show you around the studio. And if it helps, we can mull over your investigation.'

Eve nodded, trying desperately not to look at Magnus as she followed Annie towards the door.

Eve was back at Duncan's, and almost ready to disembark today's rollercoaster. She re-read the letter, written and re-written in scribbled biro on the train, but now on a glowing screen, ready to scurry through the Portal's virtual postal pipes.

Dear Magnus,

Um, hello. So, it was a wholly unexpected treat to bump into you today, though you can possibly imagine how red-faced I am. If I'd ever imagined we might meet again, I certainly wouldn't have anticipated today's encounter – yikes. I'm so sorry for any weirdness, and I do hope Carla doesn't think too badly of me.

I should explain. I've been trying to look into one of the aspects of the Purple initiative. I find just how folk are being Turned particularly perplexing. I know everyone has the bigger picture in mind, either for or against, but it does seem odd that there's not more questioning about that – who's doing it (which I had presumed to be the police), and how, physically, the change is administered. A friend had a suggestion as to that (which may be a remarkably astute hunch, or completely bananas) which I wanted to investigate, but initial research has thrown up a block, which I think Carla may be able to help with, though obviously, and understandably, that potentially puts her in an awkward spot. If this seems at all intriguing, perhaps we can have a chat or a cuppa (and needless to say, this is confidential).

I should probably add a note here of what I've been up to in all these years: was bobbing on the peripheries of proper news, before being invited to New York to set up (as Annie mentioned) the somewhat jollier news bureau, 'Say Fantastique!'. Not sure if that's been keeping me in or out of mischief (!), but I've been there a while now, and love it. It's been funny being back in Blighty – if all goes well I'll be returning to NYC soon, but in the meantime seem to have embroiled myself in this Purpleness, and have some unfinished business with it.

Anyway, I hope all's well with you. Having spotted you during your recent telly/rally/newspaper appearances, all appears well, and exceptionally busy. You'll be achieving world domination next (I told you so!).

Best (sheepish) wishes,

Eve

What must he think? What would he say? What if he didn't respond at all?

Before she could convince herself otherwise, Eve pressed *Send*.

Duncan was just out of the bath, his skin scented with lavender while his pyjamas smelled of white musk.

'What's up with you?' he said, glancing at Eve's wrinkled nose.

'You are very… fragrant,' said Eve.

'Great, thanks.'

Duncan turned, pretending to be miffed, but sat down on the sofa and leant back against Eve. He seemed comfortable, and after the horrifying encounter with Magnus – the reminder of her romantic failings – Eve appreciated the feel of him, a human touch.

Duncan put the television on.

'I shouldn't let you watch films when I'm here, you're watching so much telly that your eyes will go square.'

'Square eyes *and* Purple skin,' he said. 'I'll be a medical marvel.'

Eve squeezed his shoulder and then, her sight roving to the uncovered patch of skin above his collar, without thinking, she stroked his neck. Duncan's unwittingly sleeve-less hand immediately shot into place to cover the bare spot; Eve shielded it with her own.

'It's okay,' she said.

'I can't see it, and I don't want you to see it.'

He sighed, fidgeting, shifting position so he was now facing her. 'Do you want to go and look at something more interesting?'

'Sure.'

Eve followed Duncan to the back door. He raised the hood on his sweatshirt.

'Is there anyone out there?' he asked.

'Not at this time of night, I shouldn't have thought,' said Eve, opening the door and peeking out. 'Nope.'

They crossed the garden to his shed, which was almost as wide as the lawn. Inside, a workbench took up one side of the room, covered in tools and blocks of wood. To one side was an armchair, a birdwatchers' guide, and a pair of binoculars.

'This is cosy,' said Eve.

'I can spend hours down here,' said Duncan. 'It's very relaxing. Though now, what with the windows... I've not really come down as much.'

'You could put something up, some net curtains.'

'Not so good for seeing the birds.'

Duncan leant towards the window. 'Look.'

Eve peered out, towards a hedgehog shuffling across the grass.

'Oh, sweet,' she said. 'I can't remember the last time I saw one of those.'

'He's called Spike,' said Duncan.

Eve laughed.

'Not my idea, I might add. The girl next door christened him.'

'It's the same one?'

'I think so. Though it could be another Spike. I hear it's quite a popular name in hedgehog circles.'

'I'm sure it is.'

Duncan turned his head, as though listening for something.

'Can you hear it?' Eve asked.

'The hedgehog? Oh no, they're very quiet. I was waiting for you to regale me with a funny hedgehog story.'

'I see.' Eve considered this. 'Do you know, none are coming to mind.'

The only tale Eve could remember was inappropriately prickly for this conversation. It involved a poor hedgehog who'd been rescued after being used as a football, kicked about by some irredeemably unkind soul who she couldn't bear to imagine (she guessed even Simon wouldn't do something so cruel). What on earth must the wee creature have thought, Eve had wondered, to be subjected to such an astonishingly awful attack, as it pottered about, being a hedgehog and minding its own business. She'd been particularly struck by that story, had kept meaning to contact the sanctuary that took it in, to ask about its recovery. And what had happened to the person that treated it so? (This was hardly the time or place to think such a thing, but were they off colour?)

Eve leaned against the bench.

As if there weren't enough things to be confused about, Duncan now seemed to be behaving in a notably tactile way; Eve couldn't tell if this was the result of his understandably conflicting needs – appreciating some comforting contact but keeping any potential intimacy at fully-sheathed arm's length while he negotiated the emotional labyrinth of having been Turned (raising the drawbridge to emotional entanglements. There was something Eve knew well).

If she was honest, she'd felt an attraction to him since their unexpected meeting at The Shifty Fox; he was calm, certain, kind, and in spite of the discomfort of his current situation, remained perfect company. He also had that uncanny quality of putting people at ease, of making you feel like the truest, shiniest version of yourself. No wonder Simon liked him so much, Eve thought. She remembered this to be a super skill that Magnus also had. Eve winced at the thought of their canteen encounter, and closed her eyes.

'You okay?'

'Yes, sorry,' said Eve.

She put a hand on Duncan's chest.

He looked down – an automatic, shame-filled response these days, which only put them in closer proximity. Eve tilted her face towards his, and kissed him.

Duncan's head hovered forward. 'I don't think you want to—'

'Oh, pipe down,' said Eve, lacing her fingers through his.

Duncan kissed her, their hands untangling as she reached up to his shoulders and he put his arms around her, pressing her against the bench. The proceedings were interrupted by a rattle as Eve's elbow knocked against a part-whittled piece of wood which teetered on the table. Eve gasped as Duncan grasped this work in progress, his Purple hand in view, just stopping the carving from toppling over.

'Close,' she said.

'But no cigar,' said Duncan.

'As you were,' Eve whispered, as they puckered up.

His hand returned to the small of her back. Hers ran along the hem of his sweatshirt before she slid both underneath, fingertips running along his torso. He didn't flinch, which though distracted, she half-registered as progress. A hint at removing the shirt, sliding the fabric upwards as they busily embraced, didn't work so well. Duncan pulled away, reaching round and tugging at the material, ensuring he was fully covered.

Eve bit her lip, again placed a hand gently on his chest. 'Are you thinking we should show some restraint at this point, or attempting to combat any sight of yourself unwrapped?'

Duncan tilted his head as though trying to discreetly shake a thought from it.

Eve said, 'I don't want you to feel...' What? Weird,

desperately uncomfortable, undeniably Purple? Easy for her to say. 'I just see you, you know.'

Duncan opened his mouth to protest, but then stopped, resting his forehead against hers.

Eve said, 'Shall we go indoors?'

Chapter Sixteen

Eve had woken up in the night, lying next to Duncan in his indigo entirety, a vision in slumbering plum. She'd touched his arm, his chest, almost expecting the colour to rub off, to see it transferred to her fingertips. Every part of him was Purple: head, shoulders, knees and toes, and unlike fables involving frogs and kisses, no fairytale caress could fix it.

Now, then, waking to an empty bed, she almost wondered if this development had been a hallucination, if a mauve fog was clouding her dreams. But no, the strangeness, and unexpected familiarity, had been intensely real. Such sudden intimacy with someone whom she'd known through her formative years, and then barely seen at all, could have been a garish mistake, but had felt both safe, and new. Perhaps Duncan wouldn't feel the same. Maybe she was grasping a passing rock, trying to avoid the churning romantic rapids she usually flailed in, the ones just the thought of Magnus always reminded her of. Safety net, port in a storm, true object of affection? Eve sat up, in the shadow of the closed curtains, and told herself that she was sure this attraction to Duncan was pure, and well-intentioned.

Hearing clattering in the kitchen, she wandered downstairs.

'Good morning,' Eve said.

Duncan was prodding the contents of a frying pan with a utensil. Eve took a breath at the sight of him, relieved to see the unruffled, assured Duncan in this unguarded moment, where, purposeful, he'd forgotten about his Purpleness. She sidled over to him to deliver a morning kiss. Before returning his attention to the pan, Duncan lightly touched Eve's cheek, gazed at her briefly, his face glazed in an expression she couldn't quite read.

'There's a cup of tea ready for you,' he said.

'Ah, my hero, thanks. I'd have joined you earlier, but I didn't hear you get up, sorry,' she said. 'Have you been awake for ages?'

'A while,' Duncan said.

He slid pieces of egg-dipped bread onto a pair of plates and dunked the empty pan into the sink.

They sat on the sofa, her legs stretched across his lap.

'Delicious,' said Eve, licking her lips appreciatively.

They ate quietly, before placing empty plates on the coffee table. Duncan tipped his head back, staring at the ceiling. Eve reached into his sweatshirt sleeve and clasped his hand, which he squeezed in return. She said nothing, waiting for him to speak.

Eventually Duncan said, 'Last night... I—' He stopped.

'Go on...'

'Nothing.'

Eve yawned and leaned against him, wanting for this to feel normal, to ease any pressure.

Duncan spoke again. 'I hate the way I am. Hate it.'

'I wish I knew a spell that would make it go away,' said Eve.

Head resting on his shoulder, she slipped her free hand under his sweatshirt, fingertips touching his torso, gently caressing his hidden skin.

'Last night,' he said, 'was a distraction. A good one.'

'I know,' said Eve. She thought, oh, I know.

'I wasn't thinking about being this. But…'

He was quiet again; cogs silently turning.

'But?' Eve nudged.

'Pity?' Duncan asked. 'Curiosity?'

'What?' Eve sat up, smacking his chest with a kitten-soft punch. 'Neither!'

'That you saw…' Looking pained, Duncan swung a hand loosely in front of him, implying *this body* as indirectly as he could. 'Doesn't it disgust you?'

'No! I like you, Purple or not.'

Duncan let this sink in. Uncertainty cautiously converting to pleasure.

Eve prodded him, teasing. 'Are you fishing for compliments?'

A slow laugh; a smile. 'Definitely not.'

'Good. Stop fretting and kiss me, would you.'

Duncan obliged.

'Anyway,' said Eve. 'There is another problem.'

'What?'

'Simon might be a smidgen annoyed about this.'

'He'll be fine.'

'Really?'

'It won't be his favourite thing, sure. But he wants me to be happy. And, um…'

'Right. He owes you.'

'I wouldn't put it like that.'

'I know you wouldn't.'

They sat still, cosy, Eve believed, though Duncan's heart rate was less sedate. Outside traffic passed, then the postman; they heard his conversation with a neighbour before the rustle of mail through the letterbox.

With a look at the clock, Eve said, 'I suppose we should hop about and get ready.'

'Maybe we shouldn't go out,' said Duncan.

'Whatever you like,' said Eve, noting that the one third of open curtain that had been letting in light yesterday had now been reduced to a quarter. 'Though you said you wanted to. And you've arranged to meet your dad.'

'My first proper appearance in public.'

'It wasn't so bad when we went to the police station, was it?'

'It went as well as could be expected, I guess.'

'And I'll be there.'

'I know.'

'We could get a bottle of wine, something nice for dinner. Or go to a restaurant, even, if you feel like it.'

Thinking of the man who'd been accosted near the TV studio, Eve instantly regretted saying this.

'Hm,' said Duncan. 'One step at a time.'

'It's going to feel daunting, of course it is,' said Eve. 'But it'll be okay.'

'We could just stay in.'

Eve laughed. 'Nice try, Romeo. Come on, let's go out and have a change of scenery. You might feel better for it.'

Suspicion clouded the newsagent's face. Frowning slightly from where he stood, he was framed by the rows of cigarette packets behind him. He laid his hands solidly on the counter, as though readying himself for action.

An elderly customer approached the till with a couple of magazines – a women's weekly and a puzzle compendium – exchanging familiar pleasantries with the shopkeeper. He was chipper with her, but kept glancing towards the potential troublemaker in their midst. The old lady turned to leave, bidding a cheerful farewell, before spotting the Purple person. Her eyes narrowed – possibly in curiosity, probably in disapproval – as she made her way back through the shop, inadvertently knocking a couple of greetings cards onto the floor with her boxy shopping bag as she did so. A burly man in a straining t-shirt paid for a loaf of bread and some tobacco before grunting towards the door. He gave the mauve man a disgusted look.

'Ought to be ashamed of yourself,' he said, so focused on commenting that he almost clonked into the elderly lady on his way out (she was hovering, goggle-eyed, near the exit).

The doorbell chimed, signalling their departure.

Duncan stood holding a wildlife photography magazine, appearing to be transfixed by a feature on pelicans, while really seeing nothing at all.

'Do you want to get that?' Eve asked, gently.

'What?' Duncan replied. He looked down at the magazine, almost surprised to see it in his hands. 'No,' he said, returning it to the shelf.

Eve steered him alongside her to the till. She smiled at the shopkeeper, placed a couple of newspapers on the counter, then looked to Duncan.

'Do you want anything?'

Duncan was looking down, avoiding the newsagent's gaze, but he needn't have worried – the shop owner was avoiding eye contact too.

'No, thanks,' he said.

'Just me then,' said Eve, placing a Texan bar and packet of mints on top of the papers. It was heartbreaking to see him so dejected and rejected, and as she handed a five-pound note to the shopkeeper with another friendly smile, she willed him to say something to peaceably acknowledge Duncan, but he did not.

Who knows what trouble he might have experienced here, Eve thought. There had been plenty of stories about the increase in shops being robbed over the last few years, and a Purple person might seem to be more of a threat to the newsagent than people on the street who could walk past and tut. But still, surely he recognised Duncan as a regular customer, knew him to be dovish and perfectly polite.

They left the newsagent's and made their way towards the main drag of the town centre, keeping away from the high street itself. It was strange experiencing the public reaction, where everyone clocks you, whether they attempt to conceal their reaction or not, making for a never-ending conveyor belt of double-takes and wide-eyed stares. Eve hadn't expected this to be so extreme, so relentless. At one point she stopped to show Duncan a display in an electricals shop window – not that she was truly interested in it, but figured even just a moment of distraction, seeing something other than all eyes on you, had to be a good thing – and noticed that people who they'd just passed would stop and look back, watching Duncan, waiting to see him go on his way. It felt like an inescapable B movie, where folk froze upon seeing the spaceship or aliens, incapable of shifting their attention elsewhere.

A young boy wearing a superhero costume and painted face was so astounded by Duncan's appearance, mini mouth agape, that he nearly tripped over the family dog (Eve noted that so far the puppy was the only being unfazed by the Purple skin; it glanced at Duncan briefly before sniffing a nearby crisp packet). The boy's mum, holding the pet's lead, stopped to whisper to her son not to gawp, but Eve could see that she herself was almost as agog, though from the apologetic look she shot Eve (interestingly not to Duncan himself, Eve thought), it was obvious that she was one of the anti-Purpling brigade, if still amazed when encountering one in person. Before they walked away, the little lad stopped, taking a step towards Duncan and pressing a tiny fingertip against his hand; to see if this was crayonned colour, like his own, or real, bruised and tender, Eve couldn't tell. Duncan mustered a smile, which the boy returned as he was led away, peering back over his shoulder, his costume's cape bobbing. But Eve saw Duncan's eyes glisten and a pained gulp that implied such an occurrence was impossible to swallow.

A couple more people muttered insults, and then one skinny scally gave Duncan a smirking nod of approval. Eve saw Duncan was as disturbed by this leer as the looks of disdain. And to all of them, whether they commented aloud or with an uncloaked observation, she wanted to say: he's a good 'un, really, he's done nothing wrong. She gave Duncan's hand a squeeze in solidarity, but he pulled it away.

The café where they'd arranged to meet Duncan's dad had been quiet when they arrived, but was getting busier. Eve had watched as Duncan picked the least visible spot to sit, away from the window, with his back to most of the other tables, facing the wall, trying to minimise his ordeal as the resident freakshow. Thankfully this was homier than some other local establishments, more sentimental tea shop than greasy spoon, which Eve hoped would mean that its ambience might be a little calming. Old tea tins and caddies lined the walls, nestled next to coronation mugs and commemorative plates, while the teapots wore no-two-the-same hand-knitted cosies. Theirs had blue and white stripes, with a scalloped frill at the bottom. Eve touched the soft, and warm, wool. A waitress came over with their food. She tilted her head to address Duncan as she placed his plate before him, pulling back slightly as she saw his off-kilter shade. He sensed rather than saw this, and his shoulders sagged.

The waitress leant forward again and, looking him directly in the eye, said, 'Can I get you anything else? Any sauces for your chips?'

Duncan smiled gratefully. 'Some ketchup would be great.'

She nodded. 'Right you are.'

Duncan looked at Eve. 'We could just go home.'

'Whatever you want,' Eve said. 'We should wait for your dad, but it'd be perfectly understandable if you want to give all this a break. People's behaviour just boggles the mind. I'm sorry I said we should come out.'

Duncan shrugged. He didn't look at her, but said, 'It's not your fault. It had to happen sooner or later.'

Eve was about to try and conjure some words of encouragement when a cup and saucer landed on their table, deposited by Pete, Duncan's dad.

'Hello there, you two. Alright, son?' he said, giving Duncan a hearty pat on the back.

'It's been an interesting morning,' said Duncan. 'If I'd known how welcoming the streets would be I'd have stayed at home.'

Eve and Pete exchanged a glance.

'People are idiots,' said Pete. 'We know that. Never be surprised by how stupid they can be. That's how this whole poxy scheme got started in the first place.'

A young woman at the counter saw Pete and waved hello. She picked up her tray and came over to the table.

'Pete!' she said, 'Howdy. How are you?'

'Hi, Olivia. Good, thanks. I didn't know you were home. How's university?'

The young woman beamed.

'Brilliant!' she said. 'I'm having a great time.'

'Come home to do your washing, eh?' Pete teased. 'Oh, and this is Eve. Eve – this is Olivia Price, who grew up next door to us.'

'Hi,' said Eve. 'Nice tea cosy.'

Olivia's teapot warmer was a fluffy honeypot adorned with appliquéd bees.

'Yes, isn't it something?' she said, with a laugh, turning to introduce herself to the table's third musketeer. 'Hello,' she began. She happened to spot his hands first, then saw his face, and neatly covered her surprise. 'Oh, hello, Duncan.'

Duncan nodded a hello, barely looking at her, clearly mortified at seeing someone they knew.

'This is nuts! Whatever happened?' Olivia asked, sensing Duncan's distance, and putting a hand on Pete's shoulder, support disguised as that of a balancing kind as she leant gently forward.

'I'm a bruise on society, don't you know?' said Duncan.

'Oh, Duncan,' said Pete. 'I'm afraid he's been having quite a day of it so far, so not feeling too chipper, are you, son?'

'Can't you appeal or something, do they do that?' Olivia asked.

'No,' said Duncan.

'Well, that's rotten luck,' said Olivia. 'Keep your chin up, though. And shout if I can do anything. I'm finished for the summer, so I'll be around, eating crisps and getting under everyone's feet.'

'Very kind, Olivia, thanks,' said Pete.

Olivia nodded. 'Right then, I'll buzz off,' she said, indicating towards the tea cosy with a sheepish smile.

'I can only imagine what kind of morning you've had,' Pete told Duncan, 'but try not to let it get to you. People can be right mean-spirited bastards, but no use letting them make you feel more miserable.'

'I shouldn't have pushed you to come out today,' said Eve.

'Too late now,' said Duncan.

'It had to be done, son,' said Pete. 'You can't stay indoors all the time, you'll drive yourself mad.'

'It'd be better than this. You should see the way everyone has looked at me this morning. They don't even try to hide it.'

'It'll get better.'

'Really?' said Duncan, with no hope.

317

Another woman bustled over to their table, taking a deep breath as she approached, gathering her energy towards something. Please, no, thought Eve, bracing herself.

'I just want to say,' she said, 'that I think it's disgusting. You got what you deserved.'

'How do you know what he deserved?' asked Pete. 'You don't know what happened, you don't know anything about him.'

'Leave it,' Duncan told his dad, 'you don't need to get dragged into this.'

But the woman was already responding. 'But I know very well what happened!' she said, triumphantly, thrusting a newspaper in front of them. 'It's all right here.'

'What is this rubbish?' Pete snatched the newspaper, cast a glance over it. 'A right load of bandwagon-jumping clap-trap.'

'They print the facts!'

'Nonsense! You weren't there, what do you know? About the circumstances, about his background.'

'Here we go,' the woman said. 'Here come the violins for some woeful story that is his background! Was he a poor boy, deprived and just didn't have enough toys? Got into trouble but it really wasn't his fault?'

Pete stood up. 'Lady, I don't know what your *background* is, but there's clearly something wrong with you if you don't have the manners to let people just go about their business without judging them or insulting them. It's a pretty poor show to march up to someone, shouting at them about their behaviour, when in fact you know nothing about it. So I'll *respectfully*' – he spat this word out – 'ask you to keep your opinions to yourself.'

Eyes bulging, the woman opened her mouth to speak.

But Pete said, 'Button it, love. And jog along, will you. We're trying to eat our lunch here.'

'Well!' the woman blustered, only to be intercepted by the waitress.

'Are you alright there, madam? Is there anything else I can get you – more tea?' she said, guiding the woman back to her table.

'Ignore her, son,' said Pete. 'And excuse me for a sec. I'll be right back, I'm just going to pop out, for a bit of air.'

Duncan watched him go. Outside, Pete paced back and forth, eventually striding past the window, out of view. Duncan picked up the newspaper, folded on the Lav Line Up pages. His own purple face gazed balefully back at him, above the line: 'Duncan Miller, 39, Tellingley, part of an UNRULY mob scrapping in the street.' For a few minutes he stared silently at the page.

'Don't look at it,' said Eve, trying to prise the paper from his hands. 'It's a load of nonsense.'

'You love newspapers.'

'I read them, yes – that's not the same as thinking everything they print is right.'

Duncan put his crumpled napkin on the table.

'I don't think we should do this,' he said.

'You want to go home?'

'No, I mean, I don't think we should do *this*. Us.'

'I don't care what people think.'

'I do.'

'Well, you're overruled. You're not getting rid of me that easily, you know.'

'It's not going to work.'

'But—'

'Look, I'm sorry, but I just want some time on my own. I thought I could deal with this, with this stupid skin, with us, but I don't think I can.'

'You can't go through it on your own.'

'I can. And you're only going to leave anyway, aren't you?'

Eve blinked, her breath catching in her throat. 'That's not fair.'

'But it's true. You knew that, so I'm not sure what this is all about anyway.'

'I like you.'

Duncan focused on his plate. 'Well, I'm sorry. Whatever this is, there's no point.'

Depositing some money next to his napkin, he stood and went outside, disappearing in the same direction as his dad.

Eve lay on her bed, the radio playing quietly beside her. Having already been fretting about Finn, she now felt wretched about Duncan, distraught that their entanglement had seemingly caused him more grief, and rather than providing increased support, had instead deprived him of a companion. You should have known better than to think you could navigate sailing into anything other than choppy relationship waters, she told herself. Had Magnus's reappearance taught her nothing? And as a minor rotten cherry on this collapsed sponge, so far there was no reply from him, either. Eve folded a pillow over her face, absorbing her frustrated tears. If she could make some headway with her supposed investigation, that might improve the situation, but she could practically feel her forehead being grazed as she bashed it repeatedly against a figurative brick wall. Should she harangue Frankie, though he'd already said he didn't know anything? Or plead with Mina at Crayne Industries, despite the fact that Eve barely knew her? These weren't the most sensible, or productive options, and seemed unlikely to yield results.

Eve watched a spider nimbly crossing the ceiling. Her window was open and outside she could hear the tinny melody of an ice cream van. School must be out, she thought; Womble would soon be home. She rolled onto her side, her attention turning to the tail of the news bulletin.

'...Theo Fletcher is said to be "delighted" at results of a newly published poll which gives the Purple Initiative a 47 per cent approval rate. Though he didn't comment on controversial reports that a sixteen year old had been Turned for disturbing other tram passengers with loud music played on her personal stereo. Meanwhile, campaigners have claimed that another survey shows a high number of those Turned are sufferers of mental illness and drug or alcohol addiction. They're requesting Re-Turning exemptions for those who require "treatment and intervention". Stay tuned for more news in an hour...'

Before the Repeal, people played loud music on their PortAbles all the time, and it used to drive Eve bananas. So thoughtless, and self-involved. Milton Hardy hadn't been far wrong; PortAbles did seem to have encouraged a selfishness and narcissism which left little room for common decency. Did that deserve Purpling?

Eve looked up at the spider, now resting on the other side of the room.

'Don't you get dizzy being upside down all the time?' she muttered, thinking of the rollercoasters Simon had loved to go on when they were teenagers. 'Though to be honest,' she said, 'I'm beginning to feel as though I'm hanging upside down myself.'

Of course, the spider didn't reply.

Womble had been home long enough to have a cup of tea and watch his favourite quiz show, but had now changed into a smart shirt and was checking his pockets for his wallet and keys.

'I'm going out,' he said. 'See you later.'

Helena had just fed Sven and Mr Bailey, and was now reaching under the kitchen table to retrieve a rubber ball. 'You're going out?'

'Uh, yes. Won't be long.'

'Where are you going?' Helena was still kneeling beside the dogs, her head and shoulders just above table height, which made for a strange interrogation.

'Meeting Bob for a coffee.'

'A coffee? You never meet people for coffee.'

'Well… now I am.'

Helena began to stand. After a pause, she said, 'Are you having an affair?'

'What?' Womble looked horrified, then said, 'I can't believe you would ask me that – and in front of Eve.'

'She doesn't mind, and I already told her I was worried about you.' Womble looked even more mortified. 'Besides, you're not answering the question. Are you?'

'Of course not!'

'Then what's with all the secretive phone calls and meetings?'

Womble looked pained. 'It's nothing, just school stuff,' he said feebly.

'I don't believe you.'

Womble said nothing for a moment, then, 'It's something I…'

'Yes?'

'I'm not supposed to talk about.'

'Not supposed to? Says who?'

'The thing is, I've been sworn to secrecy,' Womble said, groaning at how ridiculous that sounded. 'I could be in serious trouble if I say anything—'

'You'll be in serious trouble with me if you don't.'

Womble's face contorted in anguish.

'Whatever is it?' Helena looked worried. 'What are you involved in? Is there something illegal going on? At school?'

'No, absolutely not, no.' Womble looked down at his feet.

'Fine. If you don't want to tell me, you can go out, and stay out until you do.'

'What?'

'You heard me. I'm not having secrets in this house.'

'I can't…'

'Don't be ridiculous, of course you can. Come on, spit it out.'

Womble looked exceedingly peaky. He took a deep breath.

'What it is…'

'Yes?'

'What it is,' he said, 'is that I was approached to, um, become involved in the Purple Scheme.'

Helena was silent for a moment. The air thickened with the sense of her disapproval.

'The Purple thing?'

'Yes.'

'Become involved how?'

'I'm not quite sure yet, and I was told not to say a word to *anyone*—'

'Are you kidding me?' Helena shouted. 'You're not supposed to have any secrets from me, and certainly not be involved in some political insanity like this. Are you out of your mind?'

'I agree with the Purpleness. It's decisive action.'

'Well, as you know, I absolutely don't. If you want to be involved in it, you can leave.'

'What?'

'You heard. You know how strongly I feel about it. It's immoral. It's dangerous. It's detrimental to our society. I'm still trying to grasp the fact that you actually agree with it…' Helena shook her head angrily, and concluded, 'You won't be involved with it while we're together.'

323

Helena looked furious; Womble, frustrated.

'I'd almost rather you had been having an affair,' said Helena.

Eve saw the hurt in Womble's face as he turned to Helena, aghast, and said, 'You don't mean that.'

Helena, jaw set, looked towards the window, her expression hidden. When she eventually turned back she stared straight ahead at the wall (and the Svengalis).

'Perhaps I should leave you two to talk about this...' said Eve.

'No,' said Helena. 'Stay. Please. We might need a mediator.'

'Referee,' said Womble, despondently scraping a chair back from the table and sitting down. Helena remained standing.

Super, thought Eve.

'What exactly were you asked to do?' said Eve.

'At the moment I haven't really been asked to do anything...'

'Apart from lie to your wife,' said Helena.

'They seem to be sort of sounding me out before they maybe give me training.'

'Training to do what?' said Eve.

'Turning people?'

'*You* would be Turning people?'

Helena looked as furious as someone could without steam coming out of their ears; Eve was worried she might self-combust with fury, leaving just her shoes smouldering on the kitchen floor.

Womble cleared his throat. 'I think so.'

'I thought you meant you were going to photocopy files or something, help support the cause,' Helena blustered. 'You can't go around Turning people – who are you, God?'

'Of course not.'

'And what on earth are they doing, recruiting school

teachers to do this – who should know better. Are they just picking random people off the street?'

'Yes, that is odd,' said Eve.

Now Womble turned his sad gaze to her.

'I mean,' Eve said gently, 'you'd think they'd just be getting the police to do that. Such a colossal responsibility and everything. Did they definitely tell you that you'd be Turning people?'

'Yes. Well – they asked if I'd be willing to, and I said yes.'

Helena made a noise which Eve couldn't quite identify.

'Did they say how?' Eve asked.

'No, not yet.'

'And who was it that approached you?'

'Some guy rang from an office at the Department of Corrections.'

'Had you contacted them?'

'No.'

'Then how did they know to contact you?'

'That's a bit of a mystery. I'm not sure. The guy who called said he was part of the initiative's enforcement department, that they'd been advised that I might be sympathetic to the scheme. I said I was.' At this point Helena pursed her lips and looked back towards the window. 'And he asked if I'd be interested in discussing how I could assist. I did ask how they'd got my name, and he said that was confidential, that for security reasons they had to be cautious about revealing sources.'

'How can you think of doing that to people? You as someone who's supposed to be nurturing the nation's kids, setting them a good example.'

'I do try and set a good example. You of all people know how much I want them to do well. But seeing the behaviour we do, the way some of these kids are already…' He shook his head. 'It's damage limitation, at best. I look at some of them and

325

just hope they can't be bothered to go out and act on the anger, and the complete lack of empathy, you see bubbling inside them. I really want everyone to be happy, and safe, and for there to be tulips for us all to skip through, but I look around and it depresses me. I don't want *our* kids to grow up in a world where people have so little regard for others, where there's so much pointless violence, and no deterrent.'

'If we have kids,' muttered Helena.

'You think everything's fine and we don't need to do anything?'

'I don't think we need to turn people Purple, no. And I certainly don't think *you* need to turn people Purple. Right now I just don't see how we can do this.'

'Do what?'

'Us. Be together. Consider yourself lucky to be on the sofa tonight, because honestly, if Eve wasn't here you'd be on the street.'

Womble blinked – Eve could see tears in his eyes – but instead of characteristically keeping quiet, or taking a tack that might be most likely to keep the peace, he said, 'Why is it that you're always right, and you make a final decision? This is my house too. And I'm not going anywhere.'

'Is that right?' said Helena. 'Then why don't I leave?'

She marched out of the room. The front door slammed behind her.

Sven ran into the hallway, whining.

Eve looked at Womble. 'Should I—?'

'No, leave her. She'll calm down. She'll come back.' He leant forward, face down on the table.

Eve put a hand on his back.

'This is the bit where you're supposed to tell me it will be alright,' said Womble.

Eve sat down beside him.

'It'll be alright,' she said, desperately worried that it would not, and feeling far more affected by this fight than any her parents had had.

Some hours later, Eve and Womble were perched on the sofa, trying to keep their eyes off the clock and on whatever nonsense was flickering across the TV screen. So far they'd sat through a detective show, the week's edition of future-technology programme *Tomorrow's World* (featuring new self-cleaning sports kits and school uniforms that Eve had already seen on television in America, and a hot-drinks-making robot created for use in hospitals, which Womble had remarked was 'a teasmade on wheels'), plus an episode of *Victory Way*, one of the nation's most watched soap operas. A popular but troubled *Victory Way* character had just been Turned, which was proving to be controversial. At the end of a recent programme she was seen getting into a brawl outside a nightclub, and in the opening moments of the next instalment, clambered hung over out of bed, noticing as she passed a mirror that she was now Purple. The station's switchboards had apparently been swamped with calls, mostly complaining that this should happen to a likeable character. In response, the show's producer had appeared in a brief interview at the start of this evening's episode.

'We're really pleased that Kayleigh's being Turned Purple has had such a passionate reaction,' the producer said. 'At *Victory Way* we've never shied away from the big issues, and we try to reflect what's going on in our homes and communities, and of course at the moment this is something that everyone feels very strongly about. It wasn't a decision we took lightly for it to be Kayleigh that is Turned... Not only is this part of an ongoing storyline about Kayleigh's battles with drinking, drugs and increasingly anti-social behaviour; we felt it important that if we Turned a character, it be one that viewers sympathise with, and are rooting for, not a typical villain. As many people in this country are experiencing, finding yourself Turned is something that can happen to anyone who's behaved outside acceptable boundaries, so hopefully this will not only help people imagine the experience of being a Purple person, but will also serve as a caution that it can happen to anyone, not just the stereotypical "yobs" we associate with crime and anti-social behaviour.' When asked how the character was Turned, he added, 'Ah, well of course we don't actually know about that. So, as seems to be the way, it happens offscreen, and we find out about the change afterwards, at the same time as Kayleigh.' 'Will she get Turned back?' the interviewer asked. 'Not before anyone else does.'

Eve imagined the actress playing her must be thrilled about that. Though at least she could wash the Purple off at the end of the day.

Eve looked at the clock.

'Should we call anyone? Where might Hels have gone?'

'I don't know. There are a few friends I could ring, but I'm going to be persona non grata, so they're not going to be thrilled to hear from me.'

'I could call.'

'That'd be worse – getting you to ring instead of doing it myself. Hopefully she'll be back soon. Maybe we'll just wait a tiny bit longer.'

'Just a bit, then.'

'What should I do? About the whole thing.'

'I don't know what to say,' said Eve. 'If I was any good

328

at knowing the best way to conduct relationships, I wouldn't have been on my own for a hundred years.'

'I am allowed to have an opinion.'

'Of course. It's just tricky that the one thing you're so passionate about besides the Svengalis—'

'And Helena,' said Womble.

'Is the one thing that she's so adamantly against.'

'So I should just keep quiet then? Even if I don't say anything, I'm still going to think it. And why can't she ever see things from the other side?'

'But you need to do that, too, don't you think? She feels so strongly about this.'

'I know, and I see what she's saying, but I think there's something else at stake here. I want to be respectful, I really do, but this scheme has a strong purpose, and I believe in it. I think the negatives are outweighed.' He sighed. 'Sorry, I know that what with Duncan…'

'But even if you can agree to disagree about the scheme itself, of course she was going to be furious about you doing the Turning, wasn't she?'

'I know. I shouldn't have carried on talking to them. I kept thinking, I'm not going to be able to do this, if Hel found out she'd go mad…' He looked at Eve.

'Rightly observed.'

'But I liked the idea of getting to be part of it, of being involved in something I really believe in, feeling I'm doing something important. Worthwhile.'

'Your job is that, isn't it?'

'It can be. But it can be frustrating,' Womble said. 'Anyway, I couldn't imagine what would happen if I actually did it… But it hadn't got that far, so I'd think, oh, I'll just talk to them, and then maybe I'll meet them… And so far I hadn't got to a point of no return, if you know what I mean.'

'But would you want to do it if it caused irreversible damage with Helena?'

Womble gave a long sigh. 'No,' he said, 'Of course not. I can't say I wouldn't have an opinion, but I can see it was dangerous to think about Turning people.'

'Dangerous?'

'Stupid,' said Womble, with a smile.

'Have you really not got any idea how they might have got in touch with you?'

'No, I thought it was unusual. At first I wondered if it was a hoax.'

'That's what all the silent phone calls were about – because they didn't want to speak to Helena.'

'I think so, yes.'

'Could you trace the number?'

'I tried it, no.'

'And they didn't give you any contact details?'

'No, they always called me.'

'And you hadn't met them.'

'No, that was supposed to be today.'

'I'm surprised they haven't called to find out what happened to you.'

'That's true, I hadn't thought of that.'

'Where were you supposed to meet?'

'I was supposed to go to a phone box, and they'd call with instructions.'

'Blimey! It's just like a spy film. Of course this wouldn't be staff room chit-chat, especially if you've been sworn to secrecy, but you've not heard of anyone else being approached, have you?'

'No.'

'It just seems to get more bizarre and tangled. There's no

logic to any of it. And if random local folk are doing the Turning, how would no one know about it?'

'I don't know.'

'I almost wish you were going to go through the training, so we could find out what's happening.'

'Helena would kill me.'

'If I was encouraging you to do it she'd kill us both. It would be amazing though, having you on the inside.'

'But if you knew the truth, you'd want to expose it, wouldn't you? Which would jeopardise the whole scheme. I wouldn't want that.'

'You really wouldn't? You don't think people should know?'

'Then the scheme wouldn't work, would it? If everyone knew how it was happening. Besides, if it got traced back to me, the government would kill me, if Helena hadn't already.'

'Maybe you can recommend me! In your place.'

'And then what? You'd find out the truth and expose it, and then you'd be in massive trouble, and I'd be in trouble, too, for suggesting you.'

'This is such a huge piece of information though, knowing they're using ordinary civilians to Turn people.'

'We don't know that.'

'Why would they ask you if you weren't going to be doing it?'

'Maybe it was to test how committed I am.'

'I can't believe we're not going to infiltrate the scheme. This feels like such an opportunity.'

'I'm not getting into more trouble with all this, and I'm not letting you, either.'

'It would transform my career, and get you back in Helena's good books,' Eve teased.

Womble looked at her.

'You could do it,' Eve said.

'No. For Helena's sake, assuming she speaks to me again, I'm not going to Turn anyone, or be trained to do it. But for the scheme's sake, I'm also not going to go ahead with it for the wrong reasons. Sorry.'

'That's understandable,' said Eve. 'Frustrating, but completely understandable.'

She wished the fine threads of speculation and information – Carla De Lora and InTan, Womble being approached – could somehow be spun into something more illuminating. But just now there were more important things to worry about.

'Is it time to make some calls, do you think?' Eve asked.

'Maybe,' said Womble.

Then the dogs ran towards the door, pre-empting the sound of a key in the lock. Helena was home. She stood in the hallway, wearily dropping her keys on the table.

'Here I am,' she said, 'still not happy.'

'I'm glad you're back,' said Womble.

'Me too,' said Eve, giving her a hug before glancing between them. 'I'm off to bed now, I'll see you two in the morning.'

Womble having been approached was quite the revelation. Eve had yet to figure out how – if – his recruitment experience could be harnessed into something more useful. That required further thought. But that random citizens were involved... Well, on the one hand it explained why more police officers hadn't been seen on the scene when people had been Purpled, and why those who were there appeared so innocuous. And yet, it didn't provide any insight as to the *how*. Take Finn – was it the hen who'd Turned him, then? Eve pictured her, tried to recollect even a fleeting glimpse of some kind of Turning device, but all she could remember were hands clutching tiaras and swathes of trailing satin. Why was it that none of these jigsaw pieces fitted together and that every one was blank? No snatches of shapes, bursts of colour, or suggestions of an outline. It seemed unfathomable that all these clues could be thrown into a pot and yet, however long they were left to simmer, still boiled down to a big fat zero.

Having got little sleep, Eve was up early, scratching her head and ruminating on her notes about the Purpling. She examined the details of those she'd met who'd been Turned, searching for a pattern, some link that she might have missed.

Finn (2nd time)

Where: Outside pub

Incident: Fight with Simon

Police: Not right there, but had recently been on the scene.

Hen an undercover officer?

Witnesses: Hen party, couple leaving restaurant, man walking dogs

Duncan

Where: Outside pub

Incident: Is attacked after stepping in to back up Simon, who had provoked fight

Police: Not that he noticed

Witnesses: Four friends, other blokes involved in altercation, pub neighbours who shouted out of window, people who'd come out of pub and were further up road, man with dog outside fish and chip shop, woman who walked past and was harassed (ugh, these blokes...)

Mr Rees, the Cardiff cabbie

Where: Outside pub

Incident: Steps in to help gal being harassed, is attacked

Police: Not that he noticed

Witnesses: Friends, pub landlord

Bike thief, talking to Humane rep at rally

Where: On street

Incident: Bike theft

Police: No

Witnesses: Blokes outside nearby pub, a dog walker (maybe), man using a pay phone (none close by)

Finn (1st time)

Where: In pub

Incident: Theft of charity collection box

Police: No?

Witnesses: Other people in pub?

Luke

Where: In prison

Incident: Was Turned post-arrest

Police: Yes

Witnesses: No (?)

There was also Drew, Womble's student. Eve didn't yet know the definitive details of where or when he thought he'd been Turned, though experience thus far had taught her not to expect any enlightening revelations. She stared at her words on the page, as though they might animate themselves, speech bubbles appearing with a *pop* and filling with scribbled secrets.

I need coffee, Eve thought, padding downstairs. The duvet strewn across the sofa betrayed where Womble had spent the night; he and Helena were in the kitchen, silently making breakfast and preparing packed lunches. Both mustered overly bright greetings when Eve appeared, then, after a curt exchange with one another, they left for work.

Eve told herself that getting some air would be just the ticket, invigorate her flagging brain cells. Outside, neighbours wearing their best summer take on smart casual climbed into cars for the morning commute, some shooing school uniformed children trailing backpacks and munching slices of toast into the back seat. An early bird older gent watered his garden, a woman walked a rather tubby Bassett Hound, and the a-while-after-dawn chorus was the clink of milk bottles being deposited on doorsteps. There was a whir as a milkfloat trundled past; the milkwoman gave Eve a friendly wave, and

Eve smiled, waving back (some elements of the Repeal were kind of nice, she thought).

Reaching the local shopping parade, Eve ducked into the newsagent's to buy the day's papers.

Stepping back into the street, she took in the headlines.

'LITTERBUG LAV!' shouted one, showing an accompanying photo of a lilac lad holding aloft an empty crisp packet.

A student was shocked to discover he'd been Turned – for DROPPING LITTER. David Smith, 18, from Darlington, woke to find himself Purple, but had no idea why.

'I hadn't been in any fights or anything, so I thought there must have been a mistake,' he said. But when David went to his local police station to explain, and ask to be Re-Turned, he was told there was no error. 'I couldn't believe it,' he said. 'Since when was dropping a bit of rubbish such a big deal?'

A government spokesman said: 'It is unfortunate that David has been Turned, but everyone should remember that the Purple Initiative isn't solely concerned with criminal and unlawful acts, it's also about anti-social behaviour, and not showing respect to your community and your environment. Already many vandals have been Turned, and rightly so. I would imagine that David will serve a short term, and will have learned his lesson – I shouldn't think he'll drop litter again!'

Bonkers, thought Eve, tucking the news fix under her arm and trotting along, taking the short-cut down an alley. Which was where she felt someone tightly grab her arm, and their grasp didn't feel very friendly.

Chapter Seventeen

With an arm now twisted uncomfortably behind her back, the mystery man frogmarched Eve towards the middle of the alley. She considered screaming, but despite a scolding from the sensible half of her brain, first wanted some inkling as to what was going on before she attempted to exit the proceedings (also, she asked herself: what would Annie do? Immediately shout for help, or try to stick with the story? Surely she had to try and be brave?). Plus, the man was dressed in beige slacks and a blue striped shirt, a sartorial choice so bland she just couldn't convince herself that he could be deadly.

They stopped, and he pushed her, not very forcefully, against the wall. A lock of dark hair flopped in his eye; he looked annoyed as he moved it away.

'Miss Baxter,' he said, his face contorting into a lemon-sucking configuration.

'Who's asking?'

'I am.'

Clearly, thought Eve, imagining Saffron rolling her eyes and saying, 'Oh, man,' at the lacklustre commencement to this interrogation (Eve could have guessed though, from the trousers).

'Miss Baxter, you don't seem to realise that you're on a very unwise path. What you're looking into right now is none of your business. It seems you need me to spell out the seriousness of what you're doing, and the penalties for the breach of security that you seem so keen to make.'

'I'm not sure what you mean.'

'Is that so?'

Eve was watching him twitch, frustrated as the lock of hair drooped back in his eye, and so wasn't expecting the tightening squeeze on her arm.

'Ow!'

'You've been asking a lot of questions, enquiring about things that are none of your business.'

'I think you'll find anything I might have been asking about is very much in the public interest.'

'I'm going to have to disagree with you. Such behaviour falls under the Landell Responsible Reporting Act, as I'm sure you're well aware.'

'That's a bit of a stretch,' said Eve.

'It's only one part of your investigation's unlawfulness. You'd also do well to remember that private companies are entitled to keep their operational information private.'

'Like Crayne Industries, for example? That's handy to know.'

'This is very, very serious. I'm advising you, in the strongest possible terms, that you need to cease your amateur hour investigation or there will be dire consequences.'

'Is that so?'

Beige didn't appreciate the mimicry, and actually Eve was wondering if, in a case of double-bluff blandness, she'd underestimated him. But still...

'Don't underestimate us, Miss Baxter, please.'

'Who is "us"?'

'Still asking questions...' Beige leaned in. 'As they say,

curiosity killed the cat. And I believe you know plenty about cats.'

Harsh, thought Eve.

'You'll do best to remember what I've said. I hope we don't need to meet again.'

Beige released her arm, which was now red and blotchy. She watched him walk away, then leant back against the wall, heart pounding, arm throbbing, and flutteringly out of breath.

Despite Frankie and Annie's warnings, quite honestly Eve had considered herself to be too small fry to really rattle anyone further up the chain. It was almost a compliment to be considered a threat, though more likely there were some pen-pushing government types who enjoyed the occasional opportunity to flex their muscles (how nice for Beige to get out of the office, she thought, with fleeting bravado; he looks like the sort who often loses a fight with the snack vending machine, trying to release a Wagon Wheel he's just paid for that's stuck, still behind the glass, torturing him).

This raised some quite serious questions, though, such as: who had ratted on her? There were limited suspects. Perhaps Finn had to confess the true reason for his second Purpling to his police commissioner uncle? Could a less-than-impressed Carla De Lora have let something slip about a pale lass investigating InTan? Maybe Mina or François from Crayne Industries had shared Eve's curiosity with the corporation's big cheeses? Would the nurses at the hospital have spoken to anyone? Might Frankie have felt he had to protect the police force's Purple work? Surely Annie, Eve's idol, wouldn't have said anything?

Eve was feeling tetchy, now. The Purpleness is all snakes and no ladders, she thought. She'd been surprised at herself, though, having always considered that her dad was right – that she would hide in a cupboard at the first sign of danger. And surely this type of encounter could only ever have one outcome?

A hardened resolve.

Eve turned the tap, her hand shaking as she held the kettle beneath the gushing water. Never mind a calming cuppa, I need a large brandy, she thought.

As soon as his office opened, she was going to call Magnus, but first…

'Hello?'

'Ad, it's me. I didn't mean to wake you.'

'Hi, doll. You alright? You sound a bit… breathy. Are you practising dirty phone calls?'

'I've just been threatened by some bloke in disconcertingly unassuming trousers.'

'Bugger. Are you okay?'

'I think so. Just a bit shaken.'

'You're not hurt?'

'No.'

'Good, that's a relief. And obviously an equally important question: what sort of trousers?'

Eve gave a gasp of a laugh. 'Beige slacks.'

Adio let out a low whistle. 'This sounds serious. What happened?'

Eve elaborated.

'I have to say, when you said Annie had told you to be careful, I thought that seemed a trifle melodramatic.'

'Me too. But we must be on to something if they're so riled up, don't you think? Even though I can't see how anything fits together.'

'The pieces of the puzzle we have again are… ?'

'InTan, even though we don't know how it's administered.

Womble being approached – so, civilians potentially doing the Turning. And... that's it. I keep trying to think through all the things I've read and heard, to see if there's some clue that I'm just not picking up on – something that seems tiny and irrelevant but actually is going to be the thing that cracks it. But I just can't see it.'

Outside, a car blaring an old Eddie and the Hot Rods tune drove past; Sven started barking.

'Dogs!' said Eve.

'Say what, doll?'

'Dogs. I wonder...'

'Wonder what?'

'Though I don't know how that would fit in. Maybe it doesn't, maybe I'm delirious. A rush of blood to the head and all that.'

Eve was quiet for a moment, thinking.

'Spill it sister, the suspense is killing me.'

'Well, in a lot of the cases of people being Turned, they've mentioned there being a dog nearby. Duncan said there was one, outside a shop near where the fight happened. There was a man with two dogs going past when Finn was Turned. And a guy who was talking to Humane at the rally... I'm sure even the cabbie said something about a dog.'

'Not unusual.'

'I know.' Eve sighed.

'I mean,' said Adio, 'what *could* it mean?"

'Probably nothing. It must be delirium after all.'

Eve's arm was aching; she examined the bruising, already darkening to a ring of green-tinged plum.

'Do you think I should back off?'

'Do you?'

'I don't know. I was feeling all invincible, but that might have been the shock of it, I suppose, the adrenaline. You're right that it seemed preposterous that the warnings were justified, that anyone would really do anything – whoever "they" officially are. But what might they do, what would be next?'

'Hard to say. You'd have to suppose at this point they're just trying to frighten you.'

'Maybe they'd Turn me? What could they officially charge me with?'

'No doubt they can do some sneaky twisting of the Landell legislation.'

'But we haven't actually reported anything.'

'Common sense and fair trials don't seem to be immediately to the fore at the moment though, do they?'

'The news folk we admire wouldn't back down.'

'I know, but you don't have to go for the most daring option. It's alright to be sensible, doll.'

'We both know I'm no daredevil. But just imagine – *imagine* – if we could crack this.'

'If *you* could crack it. I'm presently at home, in my pants.'

Eve smiled, then looked again at her mottled arm. 'If I knew what they would do if they got hold of me again, if I could picture it, whatever it was going to be, I'd be more terrified. Not that I'm not at all terrified, but…'

'Do what you think's best. Go for it if you want to, but don't feel you've got anything to prove. We've got an empire of sorts, however jovial and cat-packed it is. You don't need to put yourself in harm's way. You don't have to solve the puzzle.'

'I know.'

'I'm here when you need me.'

'In your pants.'

'Always,' Adio said, and laughed.

What a morning, Eve thought. What a tangled web. What an avalanche of insanity. And now it was time to ring Magnus. Eve looked at her cup of tea, then poured herself a whisky. She took several gulps before again picking up the phone.

'Lit, good morning.'

'Magnus Jones, please.'

'Can I ask who's calling?'

A deep breath.

'Um, yes. Eve Baxter.'

'Hold the line.'

Eve inspected her arm, thinking of how it would feel being Turned, seeing this first island of colour appearing on your skin.

'Eve?'

She almost dropped the phone.

'Magnus!'

'Hi.'

'Hello. Did you get – I hope you saw my message.'

'Yes. Everything's been so hectic, sorry, but I've been meaning to call. I told the office to patch you through if you rang.'

'I'm so sorry about the other day. I didn't—'

'Don't worry! I thought it might be Carla being a bit – well, temperamental. Obviously I figured you for an unlikely harasser, then when I saw your message...'

This is such a strange conversation to be having, Eve thought. After all this time, the topic – before anything else, even the pleasantries – was Eve's unlikely encounter with the world's number one shampoo saleswoman, and some bonkers espionage. It wasn't quite the apology she had imagined she'd be making, either.

'There's a bit of an update,' said Eve, 'which best guess says

343

must be related. I was – not quite attacked, but approached in a pretty, I suppose threatening isn't over-egging it, way—'

'What? Are you alright?'

'Yep. I was a bit spooked, but also, I think it means—'

'You're on to something. Where are you?'

'In Belton, at Womble and Helena's.'

'Oh! I saw Helena recently, at *Question Time*—'

'I know. I was there, too.'

'You were?'

'Yes. Bit of a story, sort of. Anyway…'

'I see.' Was Eve imagining it, or did he sound slightly dejected? 'Well, I shouldn't be here too much longer, I can swing over and get you and then – well, there's somewhere I thought we should go.'

'Oh.' A bar? A restaurant? 'Is it not easier for me to meet you?'

'It's a bit out of the way.'

'Well, if you're sure.'

'I'll be there in a couple of hours.'

'Okay. Super.'

'Oh, and Eve?'

'Yes?'

'How are you?'

That warmth. That smile.

'I'm very well, Magnus. How are you?'

He chuckled. 'Marvellous, thank you. Now sit tight and try and keep out of mischief.'

'Will do.'

Eve took another gulp of whisky.

After the fundraiser, Eve and Magnus had continued to cross paths – two social circles happily colliding, like the centre of a

Venn diagram, she liked to think (this thought occurred to her after a few conversations with Magnus; 'He's so unassuming, but his braininess seems to rub off on you,' she told Helena, who responded, 'What, like dog hair?').

With Doug as go-between, Eve had invited Magnus and Greg to her household's Christmas party. Greg arrived slightly tipsy ('He's celebrating finding his bike,' Magnus winked), which to Eve's disappointment, didn't grease the wheels of conversation between them. She did, however, enjoy an exchange with Magnus. Firstly they'd found themselves discussing famous fictional rodents.

'What about the ones that spread the plague?' said Eve.

'Ah.' Magnus smiled. 'Apart from not being fictional, were any of them well known?'

'There was Reg.'

Magnus's face creased in amusement. 'Reg?'

'Yep. He was the one who led the charge.' Eve cleared her throat. '*Right boys, I've got a map, so let's go.* She giggled, adopted another, squeakier, voice. *But Reg, aren't we a bit, um, contagious?*' Back to the first, gruffer, voice. '*Pipe down, me lad, apparently them streets are paved with gold.*'

Magnus, now midway through a mince pie, snorted with laughter, before starting to cough.

'Oh no!' said Eve. 'You're not choking, are you? Shall I thwack you on the back?'

Magnus shook his head, and took a long glug of beer. He swallowed. 'All good,' he said. 'Though I still don't think Reg qualifies.'

'Poor Reg,' said Eve, nibbling on her own mince pie. 'I wonder what we'll all be doing this time next year. Somewhere out in the world, working.'

'What do you want to be when you grow up?' said Magnus.

'The dream would be...' Eve wrinkled her nose, embarrassed.

Magnus leant forward, intrigued.

'I don't know...'

'Oh, you do. Try me.'

Eve elaborated as to her newsreading, Annie Morris-esque plan.

'That's amazing!'

'You think so? It's daft really. I mean, how many people get to do that?'

'Some people. And why shouldn't you be one of them? You can't give up before you've even had a crack at it.'

'What about you? What are you going to do next year?'

'I'm not quite sure. Something less ordinary, I hope,' Magnus said.

'You're going to go to the moon or something, aren't you?'

Magnus laughed. 'Ah, I don't think so. I do wonder what it'd be like to visit the planets though. Just imagine. To fall through the clouds covering Jupiter...' He paused and held his arms up above his head. 'I sometimes think about it, falling feet first, and you're up to your waist in cloud,' he laughed, 'you can't see your legs, and you're waiting to see what your feet will touch.'

'What will they touch?'

'I don't know if anyone's really sure. There's miles and miles of cloud, and then it gets too hot for anything to survive finding out.'

'You'd be a bit crispy then.'

'Yes.'

'Your mum probably wouldn't be very pleased.'

'True.' Magnus lifted an imaginary phone receiver to his ear. *'Hi, Mum. Er, I know you said to be careful, but I'm a bit... deep-fried... Here's another space fact I love – sorry, just punch me* if I'm getting boring – on Mercury, one day lasts two earth years!'

'Crikey,' said Eve. 'Not a good day to be the only one in the office.' She took a bite of mince pie. 'I bet space novices ask you this all the time, but do you think there's life on other planets?'

'It'd be amazing to think so, wouldn't it? And pretty arrogant to assume we're all there is—' Magnus was interrupted by a loud crash.

This was caused by a very drunk Womble, who in the process of re-enacting a scene from a Svengalis video, had jumped down the stairs and lay crumpled on the floor.

'Good job you raised that money for A&E,' said Eve.

A week later, with a hobbling Womble in tow (his Svengalis stunt having earned him a fractured ankle), Eve attended a Magnus-lit (but unfortunately Greg-free) gig at the student union.

'The blue lights were excellent,' Womble told Magnus as they had a drink after the show. 'Very icy.'

'Amazing what you can do with a few Quality Street wrappers,' said Magnus, with a laugh.

'What a lovely chap he is, and quite properly brilliant,' said Eve, as Magnus went to greet some other friends.

'Top bloke,' agreed Womble, wincing as a guy nearby nearly trod on his good foot.

'If he was single, we'd have to set him up with someone.'

'What's his girlfriend's name – Chloe?'

'Yep. Studying at Edinburgh, dad's a human rights lawyer.'

'Impressive,' said Womble.

'Isn't he,' said Eve, though still pointlessly attached to Greg, or an idea of Greg.

A few days after the end of their final term, Eve and Magnus had met on a pedestrian crossing in the centre of town. While waiting for the traffic to stop, they'd waved hellos from opposite sides of the road, and, uncertain as to which side to convene on, laughed as they both started to cross, then stopped, then started, while the driver of a blue Vauxhall Astra looked increasingly unimpressed.

'Wait there!' Magnus had said, striding across the crossing with an appreciative nod to the Astra driver.

'Hi, Eve Baxter,' he said with a smile, upon reaching Eve.

'Hi, Magnus Jones.' Eve smiled back.

'How goes your week?'

'Um, uneventful.'

'Can't complain about that I suppose. But perhaps a little festiveness wouldn't go amiss?'

'Possibly. Do you have any suggestions?'

'I'm lighting a gig tomorrow, which should be fun. Though the band are quite unpredictable, so we'll see how that goes. Molotov Marmalade, have you heard of them?'

'Is the singer the guy who wears a boiler suit to lectures?'

'That's the one. I was going to call you – come along if you fancy it. Though you might not. Most of the gang'll be there, so the company should be good, even if the music's questionable. Bit of a last hurrah before everyone disperses.'

'You and Chloe are going off travelling again, aren't you?'

'Ah, no. Well, she is, but now she's going with one of her dad's law protégés.'

'Oh,' said Eve. 'Yikes. Sorry.'

Magnus shrugged. 'I've been asked to go on tour with a theatre company – they do rather anarchic Shakespearean productions—'

348

'Not the Never Mind The Bard folk? They've won some awards lately, haven't they?'

'Yep, that's them. I'll be doing their lighting, so that should take my mind off things and keep me occupied for a while, be a change of scene. Though I'm not quite sure what I'm letting myself in for... To be or not to be, in bondage trousers.'

'Fun for all the family,' said Eve.

'Quite,' said Magnus, with a laugh.

The Molotov Marmalade night had been suitably raucous. The boiler-suited frontman had almost electrocuted himself after biting into the microphone cable, but survived and proceeded to partake of a stash of absinthe found behind the bar; Greg also tried some, though a little too much, and was later found being sick in the quadrangle. Eve had bought Magnus a good luck card featuring a googly-eyed black cat (inside she inscribed, *Fare thee well*), and a pack of large safety pins.

The next morning, hung over, Helena had told Eve, 'Greg was in a bad way last night – was it me or did he actually look green? I'm glad you gave up on that, I don't think he was a match for you at all.'

'You're right,' said Eve from behind a cupboard door, as she gathered sauces for the bacon sandwiches Womble was making. 'Have you seen the ketchup?'

'I don't know why you're not on Magnus's trail now he's single. You two always seem to get on so well.'

Almost knocking her head on the door, Eve reappeared brandishing the condiments, mouth agape. The notion had hit her like the surprise ending in a whodunit. She pictured a jackpot whirring into place: when he called she could hear him smile. *Ding!* A bunch of cherries. They had long conversations, which could involve anything from dire political developments

349

to *Danger Mouse*. *Ding!* Another bunch of cherries. When he looked at her, she felt he really saw her, saw her with those eyes that twinkled and – *Ding!* Cherries. *Ding! Ding! Ding!*

Seeing her reaction, Womble said, 'That's good timing. Now that he's just gone on tour, with a group of theatrical punks.'

Back in the kitchen, a year later. Womble and Helena were playing music, loudly, but Eve could still hear Helena giggling and saying, 'You can't dance to this', as Womble tried to convince her that there was a way to coherently cut a rug to the Svengalis' latest offering (that morning they'd been having a conversation about former flames. 'First love?' Doug had asked. 'Helena,' said Womble. 'Smooth!' said Helena, adding, 'I thought I was second.' 'I'm not sure,' said Eve, wondering if it was – sort of, not quite requitedly – Magnus). Eve was on her way through the living room to answer the front door. She glanced in the hallway mirror, pursing together her lipsticked lips and running a hand through her hair. Butterflies.

'Hello,' said Magnus. He handed her a bottle of wine. It was wrapped in tissue paper which was fanned fancily around the neck.

To Eve, taking wine to dinner still had a new, slightly grown up thrill to it. 'Why, thank you,' she said.

'Evening, Annie,' said Magnus, towards the television, where Annie Morris, resplendent in a peach blouse, wished everyone a pleasant rest of their weekend before handing over to the weather centre. The outlook was sunny.

'I'll just take this to the kitchen,' said Eve, expecting to have a moment to hop up and down in front of Womble and Helena, a bouncing ode to excitement, but Magnus hovered in the doorway behind her.

Helena had been laughing, enjoying the merry idiocy of the dance she and Womble were attempting, and now, seeing Womble's face as Magnus caught them mid-step, she tipped back her head as a further ripple of giggles engulfed her.

'Magnus, hi,' said Womble, now standing stock still, stalled by their visitor's sudden appearance.

'Hi Womble, hi Helena,' Magnus grinned.

'Um, dinner is going to be a bit late,' said Womble.

'No problem,' said Magnus, though his stomach grumbled.

'Poor Magnus!' said Helena. 'Arriving ready to eat and we're being awful hosts and starving him.'

'Let's open the wine,' said Eve, unwrapping the tissue. She turned to Magnus. 'It's still warm out, isn't it – we could sit by the garden.'

With an apologetic smile, Womble held up a party-sized bag of crisps. Eve took them and she and Magnus wandered back through the living room towards the patio doors, sitting on the step that led out towards a shaggy haze of grass and an accompanying tangle of bedding plants.

'Thank you for the wine,' said Eve, taking control of the corkscrew and hoping she wouldn't make a hash of opening the bottle in front of Magnus.

'You're welcome... though you might want to wait until after you've tasted it.'

'So, welcome back,' she said.

'Thanks, and cheers,' Magnus chimed his glass against hers in a toast. 'Thank you for coming to the show the other night.'

Eve took a sip, and nodded appreciatively (not that her wine-tasting skills were any more advanced than her bottle-selecting abilities). 'Oh, of course. It was a treat to see you. It's been quite a while since that Molotov Marmalade gig, though I have enjoyed the postcards.'

'Good.'

'The Milton Keynes one was pretty special.'

'Like the place itself.'

'Don't you get wobbly, having to be clambering about so high with all the lights? Do you have helper sprites for that?'

Magnus laughed. 'I don't notice, really. And for the time being, I am the sprite.'

'"For the time being..." I see, you have your empire in mind.'

'Absolutely. No sprites, no comment.' Magnus lifted his wine glass.

'So what's next?'

'I've had offers to do a couple of bands' tours, which could be good. I'd get to do some more travelling.'

'You want to go further than Milton Keynes?'

'Absurd, eh? And, I don't know... I've had some ideas for things further down the line – a fundraising enterprise for charities that deserve more support – so if I can get experience on bigger music tours, prove myself there, that might—'

'Open some doors?'

'Exactly. We'll see. Might be too ambitious and come to nothing.'

'So you might bob away on tour again?'

'Probably not immediately. It'd be nice to stay in one place for a bit, for a change. Anyway, enough about me. How was your week at *The Globe*?'

'Terrifying, and fascinating. They're such characters... and the stories! They know *everything*. The scandalous stuff, anyway. It boggles the mind.'

Eve bit her lip, then leant over and whispered in Magnus's ear.

'No!'

Eve nodded. 'Who'd have thought, right?'

Magnus took a sip of wine. 'I have to say, I didn't imagine you at a tabloid.'

'Me neither! Sometimes I think I could hide in a cupboard. And other times, that I could do it, be all gung-ho, if I believed in it. But really, it's all one big ruse. Telling elaborate stories, just because you can.'

'It does seem questionable.'

Eve nodded, bashful, thinking he disapproved of what she was doing, of her accepting a tainted opportunity.

'I know that mostly it's not the real news, or a sensible explanation of the real news. Everyone knows that. It's football-thing this, or telly-star that. Or if it's, say, some MP scandal, they'll over-egg it, being all theatrical about the gory details, obviously. But then sometimes it's interesting seeing what they pick to ramp up into a front page, or how they turn on the outrage. And it can seem a bit chicken and egg – do they condition people into feeling so outraged about something, or is it that they pick things which are sure-fire—'

'Crowd-pleasers?'

Eve smiled. 'Exactly – to begin with at least. But *occasionally* I suppose they're right, they're reflecting what people feel, when there's some really terrible thing happening – remember that young boy and the dog, and then the little neighbour down the road? – and everyone else is being quite matter of fact. The proper news people will say 'Such and such happened'. And the tabloid people will say 'HOW COULD THIS HAPPEN?' It's surreal, and cartoony, and a lot of the time not very helpful, but it is… digestible.'

'Eve, are you saying you're going to the dark side?' Magnus teased.

'It's definitely the last place I'd have expected to be, but… being recommended got me in the door, and I couldn't pass it up. I figured, in at the deep end – that it'll prepare me for anything, and I'll learn a lot there, if I don't pass out from fright first. They are intimidating, and fearless. It can feel a bit like the Wild West sometimes – these larger than life editors, gun-slinging gossip. It's a real – get swept up in it, or...' She faltered, looking uncertain. 'I don't know. I wonder if you can be there and avoid the dark side? Though surprisingly, as a comical bonus, for once my dad is really proud.'

'That you're hob-nobbing in the big leagues?'

Eve shook her head. 'That he thinks I might be hob-nobbing with glamour girls, more like.' She looked down, watching an ant making its way across a patio slab, briefly losing sight of it as it marched nimbly under her leg.

'Did he say that?'

'Not quite.'

The ant disappeared down a crack between the slabs. Eve turned to Magnus, who was looking at her, thoughtfully. Her hand was resting on the step, beside her wine glass. Magnus put his hand over hers and gave it a squeeze. A tingle of electricity fizzed from her fingertips up her arm – an unexpected shock given that she hadn't assumed he might like her (wasn't she too hen-witted, too trifling?). It addled her brain and she couldn't think what to say.

His hand still touching hers, Magnus said, 'How goes the grand plan?'

The glass, now rested on her knee, felt light in Eve's hand. She looked at him, at a small graze on his arm, at the soft, touchable cotton of his t-shirt... he could conquer the world, she thought. Maybe she could conquer the world with him.

'I'm not quite sure. I guess at the moment I just want to learn – this *Globe* thing is a bit crazy, and not what I'd planned, but it's good to get experience of all angles, isn't it? Grabbing opportunities, and all that. Then I was thinking if I could maybe get behind the scenes in a newsroom somewhere – you know, probably regional stuff – and work my way up, get to do some reporting.'

'If you're already at *The Globe*, anything must be possible. And naturally, where there's a will…'

'Here's hoping.'

Eve raised a hand to shield her eyes against the setting sun, currently poised, picture-perfect, on the peak of a neighbour's shed roof.

'Look at that sky,' said Magnus. 'Beautiful.'

'Right you two,' called Helena from the kitchen, 'dinner's ready.'

Eve was about to stand when Magnus said, 'Wait,' and reached into his jacket pocket, pulling out a camera. As he held it up, Eve leant away, out of frame.

'What are you doing?'

'Moving so you can get the sunset.'

'With you in it, dummy.'

Eve groaned and held a hand in front of her face.

'Kids!' Helena called. 'Dinner!'

'Quick!' said Magnus. 'The light is great.'

Hand down, and after a couple of clicks, with a face not gurning into camera-shy contortions, Eve looked towards the camera – *snap, snap, snap* – before self-consciously glancing away. She wanted to say something, but she wasn't sure what.

'I—'

Eve could hear cutlery clattering through the kitchen window.

'Yes?' Magnus leant forward, the way he always did, ready to really listen to whatever you wanted to say.

'Dinner time,' Eve said.

They picked up their glasses and went inside.

Eve still had the copy of the photo he'd given her. Mostly she didn't dare to look at it, but now she stared at her younger self, glowing in the sugar-pink and sherbet-orange sunlight, smiling while glancing just out of frame. She found it ironic that the photo she had was one where she was looking away from the camera, away from Magnus, a memento of the sorcerous moments before she turned away completely. And before the time when, their moment on the cusp just about to pass, with Eve feeling scared and meaning, but not managing, to call, she found herself in a lechy clinch with an idiot from the *Globe*'s newsdesk, at a party attended by (what were the chances?) Magnus and a band he'd lit. It hadn't been what it looked like – Eve could imagine what it had looked like – but (as if she didn't already need to explain herself) mustn't Magnus just have thought she'd gone to the dark side after all?

Eve tucked the photo in the back of a notebook, out of sight, but not out of mind.

Eve was scouring the Portal, searching for crumbs about Crayne, when the doorbell rang. A wave of nerves rose and crashed in her belly. On jelly legs, she headed towards the door, briefly glancing at her reflection in the hallway mirror and running a hand through her hair. Butterflies.

There he was.

'Eve!' Magnus gave a broad smile.

'Hello!'

'You look exactly the same,' he said.

'As on Monday?'

He laughed.

They exchanged a brief glance, which seemed to Eve to say, well, here we are, unexpectedly. She was thinking: should they hug, if she was awkward now would that set the tone, had she put too much lipstick on?

Magnus's expression clouded. Eve was about to panic when she saw he was focused on her arm.

'Is that... ?'

'From my friendly warning this morning? Yup.'

I think we've missed the hug moment, she thought.

Magnus shook his head. 'Mind-boggling, isn't it?'

'It's an adventure,' said Eve.

'Speaking of that,' said Magnus, turning to indicate towards his car, 'your carriage awaits.'

They made small talk, condensing more than a decade into easy, breezy kernels of drive-time chat: updates and anecdotes about what they'd done, where they'd been, how they first heard about the Purpleness. It felt comfortable, convivial... lovely, actually. Though Eve was aware of what wasn't being said; past times and near misses hiding in the glove compartment, behind the sun visor, under the seats.

'When do you go back, then?' Magnus asked.

'Hard to say,' said Eve. 'It depends on all this Purple stuff.'

'That's what's kept you here?'

'Mostly.'

'It's funny that we should bump into each other then, you being here so rarely and then we meet because of the Purpling. What's it been – fifteen years?'

'Mm,' said Eve.

'The infrequently seen Eve Baxter, eh.'

'What can I say,' she said. 'I'm just like a comet.'

Magnus slowed down as they reached a set of traffic lights, and checked his watch. 'We're a bit early. She'll be back at four.'

'Who?' Was he taking her to meet his wife?

'You'll see. How about a pitstop – are you hungry?'

Eve's stomach had been rumbling, but she'd put it down to nerves.

Magnus pulled up at a Chef Jeff's diner. A family wandered across the forecourt towards their car, one of the children skipping and waving a lolly. Eve remembered she and Simon getting those at one of these diners once; there had been a bowl of them hidden under the counter, and they'd been given them as they left. Simon had dropped his on the ground – he'd already licked it so it got coated in car park grit – and then tried, unsuccessfully, to force Eve to swap it for hers. Linda had gone back to the restaurant and procured a replacement.

They walked towards the entrance. A poster in the window set an exclamation-fuelled challenge: 'TRY THE CHEF JEFF'S BREAKFAST BUSTER!!! A hearty way to start your day!'

'What is this, Magnus Jones? Become accustomed to all the fancier things now, have you?'

Magnus laughed again.

They took seats in one of the cream and yellow coloured booths. The walls were painted a peachy tangerine, and on them were framed posters of Chef Jeff, who always seemed tickled by something – rounded cheeks and eyes crinkled with laughter.

A television set was mounted above the bar. A news bulletin was in progress, currently showing Theo Fletcher at a newly opened hospital; the staff looked pleased as punch, and the prime minister paid close attention as they showed him machines that could deliver the latest medical wizardry.

Magnus glanced at the TV with mock exasperation.

'Not your favourite person,' said Eve.

'Hardly,' said Magnus. 'Though it's incredible to witness just

358

what he can get away with. Do a few good things and the Great British public are putty in your hands.'

Eve nodded. 'He *has* done some good things though. And if you think what it was like before…'

'That's what he's counting on everyone thinking.'

'But aside from the Purpleness?'

'Before that I liked him. But the Purpleness is unforgivable.'

You should talk to Helena, Eve thought, almost saying so, but knowing that might lead to having to explain her own conflicted feelings about the scheme.

'So, where are we going?'

'It's a surprise. I think you're going to like it.'

Back to a doorstep fifteen years ago? Eve thought. If only.

A waitress came over and they placed their orders.

'A *salad*?' said Eve.

'I'm not that hungry, I've been scoffing all morning.'

'Don't tell me you're on a model diet, now you're a pin up?'

'I'm nothing of the sort, cheeky. We stopped so *you* could eat. And so we could talk.'

Eve swallowed.

'Tell me more about this theory,' said Magnus.

Eve pondered for a moment, mulling over how best to present it.

'Well… as I said, I've been trying to look into how the Turning is occurring, and I was really hitting a brick wall. But then, with what happened this morning, it seems that what I thought could easily be just a fanciful conspiracy theory is definitely more than that.'

'A conspiracy theory, eh? Try me.'

Having already made a fool of herself in front of him once in the last couple of days, Eve considered how she could best avoid doing that again.

Magnus took a sip of coffee, looking at her expectantly.

'Well, you may well think this is bonkers. I thought it was bonkers, but… possible. Possibly.'

'Go on.'

Eve regaled him with Bob's InTan speculation.

Her explanation almost complete, Magnus looked thoughtful.

'Was it unsafe?' he asked.

'Nope. Bob couldn't find a record of any questions or complaints about its safety, and not only was there no trace of any negativity about it, suddenly the company's share price went up.'

'Interesting.'

'Exactly. Our research into how InTan worked wasn't going anywhere. There's no information on the Portal, so I went to try and get some information from some folk there – friends of a friend – which similarly went nowhere. Then today the dodgy guy threatens me and says I need to stop looking into the Purpleness, and makes a reference, I'm pretty sure, to Crayne.'

'Very interesting,' said Magnus, 'and I think our mission this afternoon is going to prove fruitful.'

'Good!' said Eve. 'And also curious.'

The waitress brought over their food.

Eve acknowledged the salad with a smile.

'Button it, Baxter,' said Magnus.

'Did I say a word?'

As Magnus loaded a fork with lettuce, he started to laugh.

'So,' he said. 'How are Womble and Helena? I always liked them.'

'They're very well,' Eve said. 'Helena's a vet, and Womble's a music teacher.'

'They've been together a long time.'

'Yes,' said Eve, picturing the four of them having dinner, all those years ago.

At this point she should have been polite and asked about his wife, his children, but she wasn't sure she'd keep her tortured twitches in check. Yes, there were rivers of water under this bridge, and her expectations for this encounter were no higher than managing not to humiliate herself – and maybe, if she was honest, catching a glimpse of their old rapport, if only to prove it had ever existed, and not been just a highly rose-tinted, retrospective figment of her imagination. But still.

'How do you know Annie?' he asked.

Phew.

'Bit random, really,' said Eve. 'We bumped into each other at the Anti-Purpleness rally, happened to get talking. I almost had a heart attack when I realised it was her.'

'Of course, one of your newsreading idols.'

'We got talking, and it turned out, astoundingly, that she loves Pam Fox-Jones.'

'Everyone loves Pam Fox-Jones!' said Magnus.

He must be wondering, Eve thought, how it is that instead of partaking in the world of real news, I write a cartoon about someone who does.

'What did you think to the rally?'

'I saw you speak,' said Eve.

'That was terrible…'

'No, you were great. You kept things going admirably, I thought.'

'Of all the things to happen. Idiots. The pro-Purple brigade couldn't have wished for a better outcome. I know they're angry, but honestly. That's an impressive case of shooting yourself in the foot.'

'Do you know what happened to the policeman?'

'He's still being treated. I went to see him. Wouldn't you know, he'd been against the Purple Scheme himself.'

'No!' said Eve. 'How awful. How does he feel about it now?'

'Still against it. Not so supportive of the guy with the paint though.'

'Of course.'

'I talked to him about being in one of the portraits I've being doing – I've been taking pictures of people, filtering them so they look Purple.'

'I've seen some of them.'

'Have you?'

'Yep. I saw the one of Carla.'

Magnus said nothing.

'So is the policeman going to do one?'

'I'm not sure. Professionally he shouldn't be seen to be supporting the anti-Purple campaign.'

'With what he's been through he should be allowed to do what he wants.'

'True. But never so simple when there's politics involved, and when him being against it could be so effective.'

'Does he know how they're doing it, the Turning?'

'I did wonder that, but I didn't ask. I figured if he wasn't sure about a photo, he'd be even less sure about spouting confidential information. But if he decides to do the picture…'

'I tried to ask a friendly policeman,' said Eve.

'Did you? That's throwing caution to the wind.'

Eve felt a hint of pride at hearing that.

'You don't think… it wouldn't have been him who said anything?' Magnus asked.

'I don't think so,' said Eve, 'but it crossed my mind.'

Uncertain, she bit into her sandwich.

A little later, they were back on their mysterious mission. Magnus pulled up outside a shop, whose sign, in classy gold paint, declared it to be De Lora Antiques.

Eve swivelled to face Magnus.

'Is this—?'

'Let's go in,' he said, 'Carla's waiting for us.'

Chapter Eighteen

A smart, middle-aged man with rolled-up shirt-sleeves and glasses pushed down his nose turned as the bell above the door rang.

'Hello,' he said, lifting the specs up and adding, 'Magnus, is it?'

'That's right, hi,' said Magnus, stepping forward and shaking the man's hand.

'I'm Al. We've seen you in the papers, of course – and on the telly. Very impressive.'

Magnus shrugged. 'Ah, I don't know about that, but thanks.'

Al pushed his glasses back down. 'Nine across is a tricky one.' He looked about to read them the clue, then said, 'But you're not here for cryptic crosswords. Follow me.'

They walked through the shop, weaving between polished pieces of refined furniture – solid Victorian desks, Art Deco lamps and teak side tables, with glass vases providing bright bursts of colour. There were also plenty of random treasures – old cigarette machines, a gumball dispenser, and a beautifully restored rocking horse.

Al opened a door at the back of the shop. Further back

looked to be a stock room, but to one side was another door, which he opened.

'She's upstairs,' he said.

Eve followed Magnus up a staircase to a sitting room with a soft green carpet and floral wallpaper. In the middle of the room was a sofa, and on it sat Carla De Lora.

'There you are,' she said, hopping up and giving Magnus a hug hello.

'And here's Eve,' said Magnus.

'Hello again,' said Eve. 'I'm sorry about the other day.'

'It seemed pretty weird,' said Carla, 'but then Magnus said there was more to it, why you needed to know.'

'I completely understand that it puts you in an awkward position—'

'An illegal one,' said Carla.

'Well, not quite,' said Magnus, affably. 'It is, technically, breaking a confidentiality clause on a contract, which I would never usually ask anyone to do. But that was signed long before what's happened with everything else. Besides, I promise you that neither of us is going to say anything that could incriminate you – right, Eve?'

'Absolutely not.'

'And in fact she's more likely to get into hot water than you are,' Magnus said, pointing to Eve's arm.

'Ouch,' said Carla. 'Who did that to you?'

'I'm not entirely sure,' said Eve.

'People who don't want the Purpleness being thwarted,' said Magnus. 'You don't support the Purple Scheme...'

'I definitely don't,' said Carla.

'Then go for it. Can you tell Eve what you told me? How InTan works.'

Carla tucked one leg underneath her; her toenails were

painted in the same coral as her manicured hands. She pursed her lips.

'They inject it.'

Eve glanced at Magnus, then back to Carla.

'You're sure? And that's the only way they do it?'

'Yes.'

'How many times did you use it?'

'Only a couple. I had one injection to try it, before I agreed to be spokeswoman, and another a few months later, before the photos.'

'How long does it last?'

'It was three months when I used it, but they were working on six-month doses, so if you used it you could be tanned for the whole summer.'

'This doesn't make any sense though,' said Eve.

'Why?' Magnus asked.

'No one felt anything. No one had anyone close enough to them to inject it.' Eve thought about this: did they? Couldn't it have been one of the guys Duncan was caught in the midst of, and the hen? If Womble had been approached, could it be that members of the public were being planted, to be victims who then Turn those who act against them? Wasn't that too far-fetched? But then, was anything, these days?

'What are you thinking?' said Magnus.

'I don't know,' said Eve. 'It has to be InTan, it has to be. But it doesn't make any sense. I feel like such a dunce. Why can't I work this out?'

'Humane have got a team of people compiling information and they haven't come up with anything. You seem to have got further than anyone else.'

'Thanks to Bob.' Eve frowned. 'How many people would have known about InTan, about how it works?' she asked Carla.

'I've no idea,' Carla shrugged. 'Not many. They were pretty strict about me talking about it. They really didn't want any rival companies knowing about it, wanted it kept a hundred per cent under wraps. I wasn't allowed to tell anyone, not even my manager, who did the deal. So most of the time I didn't know who knew, because I never brought it up. The photographer who took the pictures for the campaign hadn't a clue.'

'How do you know?'

'Because he kept asking, saying how mysterious it was. He thought it was really funny, it being so secret.'

Magnus looked at Eve, whose forehead was now cradled by her palms as she considered all this, frustrated.

'I don't see how they can be using it. Unless they follow people away from the scene, or – ' she shrugged – 'radio ahead to someone who finds them and injects them. But no one remembers being injected, or feeling anything that could have been an injection. And they couldn't have done that with Finn, because I was there.'

'So I haven't helped?' said Carla.

'No, you have, you definitely have,' said Eve, as positively as she could. 'There has to be something in it, I just need to work out what.'

The return journey had been quieter, Eve's brain cells like bumper cars, bashing into one another as they tried to steer a clear path to some answers, to finding a credible place for InTan in this mauve maze. Was it a red herring after all? Plus, the drive from De Lora Antiques made the car feel like an hourglass, the miles of road the grains of sand slipping through. Should she acknowledge what had gone before, before they ran out of time?

Magnus pulled up outside Womble and Helena's.

'Thank you,' said Eve, 'I really appreciate you arranging this, convincing Carla to talk to me.'

'It hasn't helped though.'

'It has. I'd never have found out how InTan worked otherwise.'

'Do you think they *are* using it?'

'I can't see how. But there must be a link somewhere.' Eve sighed.

'Are you okay?'

'Of course,' said Eve, brightly.

'It's been good to see you,' said Magnus.

'You too.'

'See you in another fifteen years,' he smiled.

'Do you want to come in and see Womble and Helena?'

'I shouldn't stay long, but yes, it'd be good to say hi.'

They entered the house, Eve calling a hello. There was no answer, except for the barks from Sven and Mr Bailey, who ran to greet them. On the kitchen table was a note.

Evie –

Hope you've had a good day.

We're going out for dinner this evening – send harmonious thoughts our way…

H x

Eve looked up from the note. 'They've gone out to dinner.'

'Ah, the romance is still alive!'

'Mm.' Eve nodded. 'I, um…'

Magnus leaned forward, listening, as ever.

She looked at him, acutely aware that he was just as she had remembered.

'I… Would you like a glass of wine?'

'I shouldn't,' he said, 'driving.'

'Oh, of course. Tea?'

'Sure.'

Eve put the kettle on. She felt sick. I shouldn't say this, she thought. Why would I think about saying this? Not a good idea. But then, what if she didn't get another chance?

She reached into the cupboard for a pair of mugs, then putting one on the table, said, 'I'm going to have wine.'

'Go for it. After the day you've had… How's your arm feeling?'

That wasn't what she'd meant, but remembering the bruise, looked down at it. 'Not too bad.'

She opened the back door to let the dogs into the garden, and to get some calming air.

'Shall we sit outside for a minute? Before you have to be stuck in a car again.'

Nearby someone was having a barbecue, the smoke and the scent of grilling meat wafting over the fences with the sound of the party's chatter.

Eve handed Magnus his tea. They sat on the patio wall. She was quiet.

'Pondering on another conspiracy theory?' Magnus said, though Eve was pretty sure that wasn't what he was anticipating.

'Not quite,' she said. She looked at her wine glass, gave a near invisible shake of her head. Now or never?

'I'm sorry, by the way.'

'For what?'

'For being a moron, back through the mists of time. Not

that… I know it was hundreds of years ago, and I'm sure you haven't thought about it again since then – I mean, why would you – but… I have, and I'm sorry.'

Magnus was still for a moment, gaze directed out across the lawn.

Eve was about to stand, to apologise for this too, now, but Magnus said, 'What happened? I was never really sure.'

Eve thought she might cry. What was the point in saying all this, dredging it up? Why put Magnus through it when it wasn't his redundant lunacy to deal with? He wasn't the one who'd struggled since, who'd failed, who needed to stop coming back to this and dwelling on it (although, she countered, hadn't she lingered less before he was in the news and plastered everywhere, a perpetual reminder?). Sleeping dogs, she scolded herself, imagining a snoozing cartoon canine, with zzzzs floating above its head, before being rudely and grumpily awakened. Eve glanced at him, but couldn't read his expression. In her head, they'd had this conversation many times before. Now she'd got the ball rolling, with the real and not an imaginary Magnus, she didn't know where to start. Didn't she just get the one shot? Should she have just said nothing after all?

'I liked you so much.'

Magnus put his tea down on the wall. 'Back at you.'

Eve didn't know what to say to that, scurried away from the compliment.

'I was much too daft for you,' she said.

He shook his head, though not so much exasperated, she thought, as slightly bemused, despite himself – plus maybe (and she might well have been imagining this), the tiniest bit sad?

'When we first met I remember thinking how brilliant you were, and lovely – one of the most tip-top, best people to spend time with – and that if you were single I'd have to set you up with someone. And then we were all at that gig before you went away—'

'Molotov Marmalade.'

'Yep, by which point you were single, and afterwards I must have been rabbiting on about something—'

'You liked Greg,' said Magnus.

Eve blushed, and covered her face with her hands, muffling a sound somewhere between a groan and a caught-red-handed giggle.

'Stop interrupting!'

'Sorry.'

'So it was after the Molotov Marmalade gig, and I was talking to Womble and Helena, and she said, I don't know why you're not chasing after him, and – *ding* – ' Eve used her hand to represent an imaginary lightbulb flashing beside her head – 'I realised I liked you. But you were already going, so… We'd still talk sometimes…'

'You'd call to see how I was.'

Eve nodded. 'I loved those calls. We always seemed to chat for a while, about nonsense, and I thought you must think I was dopey and couldn't believe you'd carry on humouring me.' She smiled. 'Anyway, I thought that was that. And then a while later, I was going into the tube station – I think Womble and I were going to a gig – and I thought I saw you. I figured I must be imagining things, willing that you'd be around again, and then a few nights later I got home and there was a message from you. And when we made a plan to meet, you said, it's a date, which I thought was funny because, you know, it couldn't really be a date. We hadn't seen each other in ages, and things had always been so… platonic.'

'It was a date.'

'Right. Crazy! I couldn't believe it.' Eve paused. 'Look, I know this is all stupid, and irrelevant now, but you should know how much I appreciated… you had this way of making me feel as though I was the me I hoped I could be.' She winced. 'That sounds ridiculous, and horrifying, I know. Honestly, if you knew the hours that I'd bored poor Womble and Helena with it all, up 'til late eating biscuits, and going on and on. Then here you were. Back. Calling about a thing that might be a date—'

'And then?'

Eve took a gulp of wine, then another.

'Then that last time you came round… I got home that evening and Helena's cousin was there…'

'Ah, yes.'

Magnus's face said, how could I forget?

'I'd told him all about you, and said you were coming, and he said he'd help me cook the most fantastic dinner to impress you.'

'You seemed impressed by *him*.'

'I know! I know, which I was, sort of, but in a puppy dog kind of way. He wasn't like anyone we knew, and I adored him, but not in any – it was a daft little sister kind of crush, I didn't have any romantic aspirations there.'

Magnus raised an eyebrow.

'I didn't! Honest. Though I can well imagine what it must have looked like. I always told myself that's where I went wrong, that it must have looked to you as though I wasn't interested, that I was easily distracted – especially later, with that awful guy – and so that was it. I don't think I could admit that maybe after all you might just not have been interested in me.'

There were some shouts and peals of laughter from the barbecue garden.

'Anyway. There you were, but I could feel myself retreating.' She held her hands in front of her, a mime touching a wall. 'I started to tell myself I wasn't sure… which was ridiculous – all that time, all that hoping, enjoying someone's company so much, getting this opportunity, and… Of course, I didn't twig 'til later – months later, when it was much too late – that the reason I told myself that was because I was – ' she paused, took a breath – 'scared, and inexperienced, and instead of just saying that, instead of saying, I really like you, but I'm feeling slightly terrified—'

'Terrified of what?' Magnus asked.

'Getting hurt. Being vulnerable. Getting things wrong.' She shrugged. 'And so then after we were on the doorstep…'

Eve became silent, recalling again what was to her the point of no return; the moment that, if she was given a time machine, she'd rush to faster than the speed of light, and change those minutes when they'd said goodnight.

'I said I'd call, and I didn't. And you didn't – and why would you have done, after that night. And when I finally called, all that time later…'

Magnus nodded. He rested his hands on either side of him on the wall, and his wedding ring glinted in the fading sunlight.

Eve took a sip of wine. 'So, that's my ridiculous story. You'll be pleased to know that I learned my lesson, and in every subsequent endeavour have managed to do too much rather than too little, not wanting to have anything else to kick myself about. Though I've managed to pick a succession of wrong 'uns,' she said, with a laugh.

'And now?'

'Ah, best not to ask.'

'I don't know what to say…'

'There's nothing to say.'

There were more roars from the barbecue.

'I'm glad we got to meet up, today,' he said.

Eve nodded, wondering if in fact tomorrow she was going to feel better or worse.

They sat quietly for a moment, the scent from the barbecue filling the air; the smoke trying to cloud the momentary lull in conversation.

'I should probably go,' said Magnus, 'say goodnight to the kids.'

Eve felt her chest tighten.

'Of course. I'm sorry. I shouldn't have said anything. I knew I shouldn't say any of this, I'm so sorry.'

'Don't be sorry. Please, don't be.' He smiled. 'I mean, if you can't clear the air every fifteen years... And it solves the mystery. I did wonder what had happened.'

He gave her a hug.

'Don't fret about this – promise?'

'Mm,' said Eve.

'Let me know how you get on with the Purpleness?'

'Sure.'

They went into the house. A moment later Magnus was walking down the garden path towards his car, and Eve watched as he drove away.

Eve refilled her glass of wine, went upstairs, and got into bed. She was still fully dressed but wanted to hide away from the world for a bit. If there was a sliver of light to be found in today's encounter, it was that the much-magnified rapport had not been a figment of her imagination. But she didn't forgive herself for failing with Magnus, however fleeting whatever could've been might've been. Now's not the time for flagellation, she told herself; just try and focus on InTan.

Eventually her agonising was interrupted by the sounds of Womble and Helena arriving home. Eve went downstairs.

'Evie!' said Helena, seeing her red-eyed. 'Whatever's wrong?'

'And what happened to your arm?'

Eve gave the most upbeat, condensed version of her day that she could muster.

'He shouldn't be allowed to get away with that,' said Womble. 'We should take you to the police.'

'I'm fine,' said Eve. 'Plus he's no doubt connected to the police. But thank you. And anyway, how are you two doing?' she said. 'How was dinner?'

'We had a good time, didn't we?' said Womble, looking optimistically towards Helena.

'We did,' she said.

'Nightcap?' said Womble.

Eve nodded.

'I might turn in, if you two don't mind?' Helena said.

Womble leant over and kissed her goodnight.

Eve followed Helena upstairs.

Helena lightly touched the skin below the bruises on Eve's arm. 'Are you sure you're alright?'

'Yep. Thanks.'

'Not just the bruise…'

'It's nonsense, really. Poor Magnus, he must think I'm a lunatic. *I* think I'm a lunatic.'

'You're not a lunatic.'

'And I haven't even told Bob about InTan! I've been so caught up in feeling sorry for myself. But much more importantly, how's everything with you two?'

'We're trying,' said Helena. 'The Purpleness is still unresolved, but… I don't know. It's exhausting.'

'Where there's a will…'

'I know, but,' Helena sighed, and waggled her finger, indicating going around in circles.

When Eve, now clad in her pyjamas, went back downstairs, Womble was in the lounge, headphones on, playing records; his body bobbed to the music, his form of meditation. He looked up, sensing her arrival, and pointed to a pair of whisky-doused tumblers.

Eve sat down across from him, took a sip of whisky. She closed her eyes. When she opened them – maybe twenty minutes had passed – she saw Womble stop bobbing and remove his headphones.

'You okay?' he said.

'Yup. You?'

'I think so.'

Womble knelt beside the record player, switching it off, before picking up the record sleeve.

Eve said, 'If you think of the me you first met, and think of me now, would you think I've let myself down?'

'What?'

'Would you think I've... not reached my potential. That I had potential, or ambition, but I've... failed?'

Womble's eyebrows manoeuvred into a deep frown. In one hand was the LP he'd been playing, held aloft, suspended in surprise.

'What would make you think that?' He sighed. 'This is the Magnus effect again, isn't it?'

Eve rubbed her nose. 'That was a starting point. But it's not just that, of course not. It's been great spending time with you and Helena, but I've no idea what I've achieved, coming here. I feel as though I'm just making everything worse, going backwards. Not just Magnus, but my dad, Duncan, Finn... And I've been thinking, in some dopey, deluded way, that I'm going to find out something significant about the Purpleness – but what? Me and Bunsen Burner Bob against the world?

It's bonkers. I always really believed I was going to achieve something, and now I think that's just not true.'

'Don't be daft! Look at you, you're a founder of a very successful company, living in New York…'

'I write about dogs on buses. I wrote a whole piece not that long ago about the wacky and unusual snowmen that people have built.'

'I loved those snowmen.'

Womble laughed, put the record down carefully beside him on the floor.

'I'm ridiculous and I always get it wrong.' Eve paused, sniffed, her nose was about to run and she didn't have a tissue. 'What if I've wasted my life?'

'Oh, Eve,' Womble said, putting his arms around her.

'Careful,' she said, 'I might leave snot on your shirt.'

Womble laughed again, which reverberated through their hug.

'You're not that old, Grandma,' he said. 'You've got plenty ahead of you. And everything will seem better in the morning.'

Eve wasn't entirely convinced about that.

Chapter Nineteen

There was a loud buzzing noise. The telephone. As Eve woke, the previous day's events began to reload in her brain. She groggily opened her eyes, twisting her head to look at her arm. The bruise was there, now a darker, more violent violet. She looked over at the neon numbers of her bedside clock; it was already nearly lunchtime.

Eve was padding downstairs when the answer machine kicked in.

'Hi, this is a message for Eve. It's Deb. We've got some ISON footage you might like to take a look at, if you're passing. We're here all the time, as usual!'

Having reached the kitchen, Eve picked up the receiver, but Debs had already hung up. She tried to call back but the number was engaged.

Curious, she thought, as well as, I'd best spring into action, then. Her stomach rumbled, and she decided: but first, toast.

Womble had left the radio on, and the news was in full flow.

'Dozens of students in Japan, including one Briton, have been hospitalised after taking an animal tranquillising drug. Said to be the result of "recreational misadventure", there have been no such cases reported in the UK, but manufacturer AnimolPharm have announced that, as a precaution, they will recall all recent batches for further testing… Shadow MPs have demanded an enquiry after reports that the attacker in an attempted rape case was Turned, yet not taken into custody until he arrived at a police station to turn himself in. Meanwhile in other Purple news, the prime minister is said to be considering designated seating areas on public transport, with additional ISON monitoring, for those who've been Turned, plus a reduction in benefits for any Turned person who usually receives them. That was the news at one o'clock – your next bulletin is in an hour.'

It just gets madder and madder, Eve thought, reaching for a jar of marmalade and wondering what it could be that Debs wanted to show her.

As she left, Eve collected up the morning's mail from the doormat, and was surprised to find a postcard addressed to her. It was from her mum.

Hi Eve,

Just a quick note about a couple of things.

Glad to hear you and Simon have been spending time together! I always wanted you two to get along.

Your dad's doing well – such a good recovery. We thought we'd have a little family gathering – and we have an announcement!

Hope you're having fun.

Love,

Mum
xx

That'll be news that surprises no one, thought Eve, wondering, doubtfully, if it might be different this time. She tucked the postcard into her pocket and headed out the door.

There was a ripple of warm air, which caused the leaves to shimmy on the trees, and the shifty fox, paw aloft, swayed ever so slightly.

'Afternoon,' said Debs, clutching a glass and a tea towel.

Frankie was seated at the bar, drinking orange juice.

'Hiya, Eve,' he said.

Debs put down the glass and retrieved the portable ISON unit.

'Simon thought you might like to see this.'

'Simon?'

'Yes. He knew of someone being Turned here, and said you'd probably like to see what the ISONs caught.'

Eve looked at Frankie.

'Officially, I'm not here,' he said. Then winked. 'But Simon and your dad were in last night, and Simon came over to Deb, said he knew this bloke, and would we let you see the footage.'

'But you don't want me looking into this. What's changed?'

'He doesn't agree with it.'

'Deb!'

'Well. He doesn't. Of course, he doesn't want to get into any grief, and he doesn't want *you* getting any grief, but...'

'It seems to be getting a bit out of hand. Turning people for minor offences that usually wouldn't even warrant a caution. And the segregation thing Fletcher's started talking about...' Frankie shook his head. 'I don't know if you've carried on with your investigation...' From the look he gave her, Eve could tell he guessed she had. 'Or if you managed to dig anything up...'

'Not much,' said Eve, thinking, what if it *had* been Frankie who'd tipped someone off that she was looking into it? What if this change of heart was a bluff? Here was a chap who'd grown up in a staunchly pro-law-enforcement household, and followed in his dad's footsteps, so would he really be willing to spill any beans – although she'd instinctively trusted him enough to ask him, hadn't she?

'Is there anything you can tell me?'

Frankie shifted on his bar stool. 'Here's a weird thing. Not everyone – police officers, that is – knows what's going on. A few from our station were sent on a course, it wasn't specified what for, before the initiative was announced. When they came back, they were vague about the training, casually dismissive about it, saying things like, you know how it is, they showed us a new way to fill in forms, ha ha. After the initiative became public, they had mostly patrol shifts, but wouldn't come into the station before or after, which was odd. I mean, usually you'd at least come in to change into your uniform, you wouldn't leave home in it.'

'But if they were out and about Turning people, they'd be in plain clothes, wouldn't they?'

'Exactly, you'd surmise that. Now, when they're at the station, they'll be in the office, never out on the front desk.'

'Do they go into the interviews with Turned people who come in?'

'Never.'

'Strange. Unless that's in case they risk being recognised. Though people would expect it to be police officers doing the Turning, wouldn't they, so hardly a surprise. What do they say about it? Do they talk about doing the Turning?'

'Nope, they say nothing.'

'Does your dad know anything?'

'He's heard rumours that apparently those who've had the

training aren't allowed to discuss any operational details even with each other.'

'So one officer who was doing the Turning wouldn't be able to say anything to another officer who was doing it?'

Frankie gave a nod. 'All tied up in confidentiality agreements, he heard.'

'So, if not all of you are doing the Turning, and those who are probably doing it aren't talking about it, do you know how they're doing it?'

'No.'

'That's ridiculous! They must tell you.'

'They haven't.'

Could that really be true, Eve wondered?

'Nor your dad?'

'No. He's fuming. *After all my years of dedication to the force...*'

'It's barmy,' said Debs. 'And don't even get him started on officers being made to keep secrets from each other. He's livid, isn't he?'

'Yep. They say it's for security purposes, and our own safety. That if no one knows everything then we and the scheme are all more secure.'

'Okay,' said Eve. 'So if the officers probably doing the Turning aren't interviewing the folk who've been Turned, how do the officers doing the interviews know what to say?'

'There's footage of every incident.'

'ISON footage?'

'No, it's at the wrong angle to be that. Looks more as though it was filmed by a bystander. Perhaps wall-mounted with remote access, though that would mean they'd need a lot of cameras, plus views would be restricted, and stilted.'

'Does any of it show anyone being Turned?'

'No. At least not that we get to see. And from doing the

interviews, there's a pretty uniform lag between any incident and when the Turning starts to occur. At least six hours, usually.'

Debs was busy scrolling through footage on the portable ISON screen.

'Here we are,' she said. 'This is the guy Simon said has been Turned.' She pointed to a man wearing a tracksuit with a stripe down each side.

'What did he do?'

'Head-butted a guy in the garden, broke his nose, apparently.'

'And Simon knows him?'

'I suppose so. He knew about him being Turned.'

'Curiouser and curiouser,' Eve murmured. 'Did you see it happen, the fight?'

'No. I don't really remember seeing the guy,' Debs said, looking at the screen with frowning concentration, like someone scanning mugshots, waiting for a face they recognised.

On the edge of the screen, a small dog wandered into view.

'Wait,' Debs said, 'that must have been the night that dog ate a chocolate pudding. Yappy little thing, it was. The owner was hyperventilating about it eating chocolate. But then a bloke stepped in, said he was a vet. He took it outside, and thankfully somehow got the dog to...' Debs mimed the dog retching.

'A vet?'

'Mm.'

'Would you remember what he looked like?'

'I don't know. Possibly.'

Eve zipped forward, skimming the action – punters going back and forth to the bar, their faces to camera as they walked away, their speed dictated by how many drinks they were carrying and how refreshed they already were. A pair of women, arms linked, laughed and clinked glasses as they tottered back to their table, the sequins on their tops glinting against the lights; a sweet couple sneaked glances at one another as they waited to order, hands entwined; a man studiously balanced four drinks, before turning doubtfully to the bar and moving away again a moment later, now loaded with just three. And then, a familiar face. Eve squinted at the screen, wanting to be certain. She was pretty sure it was... Rory.

'Was this him?'

Debs looked at the paused footage. 'It could be,' she said, pulling an indecisive, apologetic face. 'I really don't remember, I'm sorry. I was paying more attention to the owner, who was having a meltdown. Do you know this man, then? Would it help if it was him?'

'Yes, I think so,' said Eve. To Frankie, she said, 'One more thing. Have you noticed any new bits of kit at the station? Needles or anything that could be used for Turning?'

'I haven't, no. Though they emptied an old stationery cupboard recently, put a new door on it, and now it's like Fort Knox, so there's obviously something in there...'

'You don't have access to it?'

'Chance'd be a fine thing. What do you think, are you making sense of any of this?'

Cogs whirring, but playing it cool, Eve said, 'I don't know. I'll mull it over, see if lightning strikes.'

Eve stepped outside, taking a seat on a bench and raising her face to the sun, thinking. After so many blazing hot days, the breeze was a welcome treat, and at this precise moment, hopefully fanning her overactive brain. She pictured a one-armed bandit, wheels spinning, then slowing, one by one: *Ding!* Cherries. *Ding!* More cherries. There was now just a single reel still whirling, but she was pretty sure who'd be able to help bring that final bunch of cherries into view.

Eve looked at her watch. Hopefully she could get to the surgery not long after it had closed. On her way to the bus stop, she hovered by a pay phone. Should she, shouldn't she? Eve lifted the receiver and dialled Duncan's number.

'Hello?'

'Hi, it's me. Look, I know you think we shouldn't be seeing each other or speaking to each other or what have you, but I needed to talk to you.'

'Oh.'

'I'm sure the last thing you'd want to be talking about is the Purpleness, but as you know, I've been trying to work out how it's happening. Bunsen Burner Bob—'

'Who?'

'You'd have met him at the pub, briefly. A friend of Womble's, who had a theory about a tanning product that got pulled before it was supposed to come out.'

'That doesn't make any sense.'

'I know, bear with me. I was trying to look into it, but in a secretive way because Frankie and Annie said to be careful—'

'Annie Morris? Frankie the policeman?'

'Yes, yes, but then I got approached by a bloke in the alley – that was just after we found out Womble had been asked to do the Turning—'

'He was what?'

'Don't worry, he didn't do it. Anyway, when the bloke threatened me—'

'He threatened you? Did he hurt you?'

'No, I'm fine, but then I knew something was up, and Bob had hit on something with his theory. And then Magnus—'

'Magnus the campaigner, from the telly?'

'Yup, he—'

'You've been seeing that Magnus?'

'Just the once. Well, twice, sort of. Why? Would you be—'

'Jealous? Yes, I would actually.'

'Well, it's not like that. He's married, for a start. Anyway, he asked Carla De Lora—'

'The model?'

'Wait, did you say you'd be jealous?'

'Yes.'

'Really?'

'Yes.'

'Oh… Where was I?'

'Carla De Lora, the model.'

'That's the one, she was the spokesperson for the tanning product, and it turns out it's injected!'

'Injected? How? I don't remember being injected.'

'Mm… that bit I'm still working on, the dratted missing piece of the puzzle. But I think Rory—'

'Did I meet him at the pub too?'

'Yep. He works with Helena at the vet's. And he just appeared in some ISON footage from a night a man was Turned.'

'Okay…'

'And he said he didn't see anything, but I've a feeling he might know something about the night Drew was Turned.'

'I don't know who that is.'

'Don't worry, you don't need to. Anyway, then I twigged that in many of the accounts by people who were Turned, they mentioned that there was someone with a dog.'

'Lots of people have got dogs.'

'Exactly! And you don't pay any attention to them – they can be anywhere, unnoticed, they're just walking a dog. It's genius! If I'm right. Who knows, maybe I'm just loopy.'

'So police officers are borrowing dogs and injecting people?'

'Yes. No. Well, all sorts of people might be doing it, it seems. Anyway, that's not the point of me telling you—'

'It's not?'

'Well, actually it is. Because Rory is involved, I think. He has access to dogs, and people with dogs, which I'm sure is important. And he was at The Fox when this friend of Simon's was Turned. *And* I think he's the one who suggested Womble to be trained. He got all pally with Womble after the debate, and it was after that when the phone calls started. But I can't tell Helena or Womble, because they're friends with him, and what if I'm wrong?'

'Quite.'

'And if I tell Bob – well, he's lovely, but overexcitable.'

'Ah.'

'I could tell Annie, or Magnus, but I'd like to be sure first.'

'Of course.'

'And I will tell Adio and Saffron.'

'Good.'

'But I, um, thought I'd tell you.'

'I see.'

'So here I am.'

'Hello.'

'Hi. So, I think Rory is involved in all this, I just need to find out for certain.'

'Right. How?'

'I'm not quite sure. I'm going to try and find him, and ask him. I'll ring you when I know more.'

'Eve?'

'Yes?'

'Be careful.'

'Aren't I always? Caution is my middle name.'

Eve hung up the phone, and muttered to herself: but time for a change, and all that.

Chapter Twenty

Eve arrived to find the side entrance to the surgery unlocked.

'Hello?' she called, as she went inside.

There was no answer. Now what to do? She hadn't thought about this. She supposed her vague un-thought-through plan would be to subtly try and see what information she could get out of Rory, but with no one around… Eve walked down the main corridor, past posters for cat neutering and doggie vitamins, peering into each room she passed. Still there seemed to be no one about, and a second shout to announce she was there got no response either. Odd, she thought. When she reached Rory's office, his door was open. Eve glanced up and down the corridor, then went inside.

The room was sparse; a desk, an examining table, a few neatly laid out pieces of equipment, and a tidily stacked pyramid of dog food tins (all labels facing centre forward, a triangle of happy Chappies panting their approval). Thinking she heard a noise in the reception area, Eve jumped, knocking a pack of cigarettes on to the floor. She ducked behind the desk to retrieve them, listening for any sounds elsewhere in the surgery. If there was anyone about – and there had to be, if the door was unlocked – it would be tricky explaining why she was in Rory's office, though as she considered this, she realised it would be trickier still being found crouched behind his desk.

She reached towards the cigarette packet, and was surprised to find that it was plastic, and heavier, more solid, than it should be. What brand is this, Eve wondered, not recognising the name and guessing it must be something exotic bought at duty free. But then she noticed that one of the cigarettes had rolled out. She picked it up, found that too seemed a smidge weightier than it should be. It was also plastic, with what appeared to be a button, the sort you'd find on a retractable biro, at the filter end. What on earth was this – some new-fangled, habit-quashing faux fag? Eve was puzzled. She was about to peer more closely at the other end when the door opened. Eve sat up, banging her head on the edge of the desk.

'Who's there?' snapped a male voice on the other side of the table. Rory.

Eve winced as she stood, raised a hand to check the back of her head. Ouch.

'Just me,' she said, giving an awkward wave. 'Hello.'

Rory faltered, rightly surprised.

'What are you doing here?'

'I – oh,' Eve cleared her throat. 'Helena left a thing here, I came to get it.'

'She left it in my office?'

There was a brief pause as Eve opened her mouth to respond, hoping a plausible excuse would conjure itself as she began to speak. 'No, I—'

She was silenced by the sudden expression of shock on Rory's face, and followed his gaze to her left hand, still holding the strange cigarette.

'What the—'

'Getting some assistance with trying to keep off them, eh?

389

It's a very odd-looking thing. How does it work?' She asked, squinting again at the button.

'No!' Rory lunged towards her.

While she could usually be trusted to do as she was told, Eve was made even more curious by Rory's reaction, and, ignoring signals from the sensible side of her brain, couldn't help herself. She clicked the button. Rory seemed almost as surprised as Eve when the small, clear sliver shot out of the end and straight at him. He blinked down at his chest, staring in shock at the neat blue stripes between which the dart had landed. When he lifted his head, his face was a reddened mixture of rage and terror.

Eve looked down at the 'cigarette' in her hand, and then back to Rory.

He raised his hands in front of him, as though inspecting them for something.

And then Eve knew. She had just Turned him Purple.

The desk still separated them, but Rory was rounding it, arms outstretched, to grab the device. She remembered the inspector's conversation overheard on the night of the debate: this was the thing that could jeopardise the entire scheme. The thought flashed through her mind as to how improbable this was – a Saturday afternoon, being chased around a table by a seething, about to be violet, vet, when back in New York she'd have been in the thick of hungover diner stodge and mimosas with Adio and Saffron – but she dashed out of Rory's office and, on auto-pilot, towards reception, immediately realising her error and wondering if the front door would be open, or if she was about to back herself into a corner. But she didn't get that far: before reaching the reception desk she was shoved from behind and fell to the floor. Eve scrabbled to stand, but Rory was beside her, trying to grab her arm, which she held tightly under her chest.

Eve groaned as he shoved against her left shoulder, pinning

her to the floor. She had the device clenched in her right hand, not sure which was more likely to happen first: Rory getting hold of it and using it against her, or accidentally stabbing herself as she clung to it. Such a shame it's not a multi-tasking instrument, she thought, with a tranquillising dart so she could have had Rory helpfully unconscious by this point.

Eve wriggled as furiously as she could, trying to jerkily manoeuvre herself in a way that would knock Rory off balance. Now I wish I'd spent more time in the gym than the deli, she thought, scrambling for a plan. She twisted her head to get a glimpse of his position; he was leaning over, gripping her bruised arm as she pressed her body against the ground, determined to keep her hand hidden. He had a foot on either side of her, was dipping into a squat that would leave her completely defenceless. Using the only part of her body she could move, and with as much energy as she could muster, Eve gave a full-force donkey kick towards Rory's groin. He moaned, tipping onto his side, now rather less likely to sit on her. Eve tried to stand, but he grabbed her leg, tightly. (Thinking about this later, she would marvel at such a cheesy horror film move.)

'This is crazy,' Eve croaked.

'You were warned…'

'Then let's just go to the police,' Eve spluttered.

'That's no fun,' Rory snorted. 'If I'm Turned, I don't see why you shouldn't be.'

He was rising from his crouched position, still gripping onto her leg, moving forward, as though about to pin her down again. While holding the device, Eve only had one hand free to try to grip Rory, or anything else, which was proving fairly ineffective. She swatted at him, at one point putting her hand across his face, trying to block his view and push him away, but his unlikely reaction of licking her palm made her squeak with surprise and pull it away. She glanced around. The hopeful eyes of a guide dog collection tin peeked at her over the reception desk. *Please give generously.* Eve hoped people had. She reached up and grasped the dog, relieved to find it fairly full, and with as much might as she could manage (and the infant school orchestra sound of cascading coins), whacked it against the back of Rory's head. He grunted and fell at her side.

Eve clambered to her feet. Assuming she hadn't killed him – oh God, I hope not, she thought, and surely, being such a virtuous object, there was only so much damage a charitable weapon could cause? – he could come round at any second. Eve scanned the room for something to keep Rory in place. On the coat stand was a fabric dog lead. Clutching that, she gingerly approached the tumbled vet, now face down on the floor, squeamishly tying his hands together as tightly as she could. But now his feet... She reached across the reception desk to the telephone.

'Hello?'

'You're home! Where are the dog leads? At the surgery?'

'The what?'

'The dog leads. I'm at the surgery. Rory is unconscious and I need to tie him up.'

'I didn't even know you liked him...' Helena teased.

With increasing panic, Eve said, 'I'm serious. He attacked me. I know how they're Turning people, I think I've accidentally Turned him, and he turned on me, and now he's only half tied up and what if he—'

'Woah,' said Helena. 'We'll leave now, we'll be with you in a few minutes. And there should be some leads in the bottom drawer of the desk.'

Eve had just replaced the receiver and was about to turn to

check on Rory when her legs went from beneath her, Rory having hooked a foot behind hers so she tripped backwards, falling against the edge of the desk with a large crack. Winded, she shrieked, slightly feebly, with pain.

Rory was on his knees, and then up, drawers crashing as he tried to find something with which to cut the tightly bound dog lead.

Slumped on the floor and feeling dizzy, Eve tried to focus. How could she incapacitate Rory? And – glancing down at her empty hand, and panicking – where was the injecting cigarette, which she appeared to have lost in this latest scuffle? There was one good thing, at least, she thought – it would be hard to shoot it at her with his hands behind his back.

'I'm going to get you,' Rory shouted, frantically running about (Eve hoped maybe he was concussed from the guide dog tin), 'and I'm going to Turn you!'

'Not if I get you first,' said an unexpected voice from the hallway. And with a large block of wood, Duncan gave Rory another hearty thwack to the head.

'Duncan!' said Eve. 'Fancy seeing you here.'

'Well, I wasn't quite sure what you were talking about, but I definitely didn't like the sound of it,' he said. 'You alright?'

'I'll survive.'

Duncan unwound some of the lead from Rory's arms so he could use it to tie his ankles.

'Blimey, where'd you learn to do that?' Eve asked, taking in the partially folded Rory.

'Amazing the rope tricks you learn when you're living up a tree,' said Duncan.

There was the screech of a car pulling up outside and then Helena and Womble pelted into the room.

'Eve! Are you – oh, Duncan. And what is—'

'I think Rory has some explaining to do,' said Eve.

Eve and Womble stood around the operating table. Rory was tied to it, and what with his being a little over six feet tall, and rather longer than any of their largest animal patients, his legs dangled over the end. He was conscious, and furious.

With Duncan following behind her, Helena entered the room, studying something in the palm of her surgically gloved hand.

'I think I've found it,' she said.

Eve peered at the small piece of plastic. It was about an inch long, and slim, with a sharp point at one end. If found on the street, if you even noticed it, you'd consider it as innocuous as any of the other bits and pieces of litter.

Addressing Rory, Eve said, 'Tell us what you know, why don't you?'

Rory gave a snort of a laugh. 'You can't seriously think I'm going to tell you anything. If you don't release me I'm going to start...'

There was a pause, and they all leaned forward. Rory wriggled in his constraints before finishing this sentence.

'Screaming.'

'Like a wuss?' said Womble. 'That would be a bit ungainly. And anyway, do that and we'll gag you.'

'And then how will he tell us anything?' said Helena, with a roll of her eyes.

'So,' said Eve, 'here's what we know: people are being Turned by the use of these darts. Which I suppose are laced with whatever variation of InTan that does the Turning. Undercover police, and whoever else—'

'That could have been you,' said Helena to Womble.

'And it was you who suggested him, wasn't it?' said Eve to Rory.

'No!' said Helena. She gave Rory her most quake-inducing Hard Stare. 'Is that true?'

Rory swallowed, but said nothing.

'I can't believe you were such a sneaky snake in the grass,' said Helena. 'That's disgusting.'

'I thought we were friends,' said Womble.

To Womble, Eve said, 'Did Bob mention the InTan theory that night at the pub? After I'd been into your school to see him?'

Womble nodded. 'Yes, after he'd had a few beers he did hint at it. Why?'

'That's how Rory knew about the connection. And did you mention I was looking into Crayne Industries?'

'No. Though I might have said you went to Cardiff... I'm sorry, I didn't realise...'

To Rory, Eve said, 'So you were also responsible for my visit from the chap in the alley. Am I right?'

'As if I'd tell you,' said Rory.

'Suit yourself,' said Eve. 'But I'd say I'm on the money. Anyway, back to the recap. The agents doing the Turning include specially selected members of the public, who are trained up, and sent off onto the streets,' she cocked her head to one side, 'most likely with dogs, wherever possible, as what could be more inconspicuous than someone out walking a dog?' Eve thought of Rory with the borrowed pug, and the former officer with the whippet that she and Frankie had passed.

'You sound mad,' said Rory. 'No one would believe it.'

'We'll see, won't we?' said Eve. 'Then at the sign of trouble, the agents, whoever they are, take out one of these cigarettes – again, something which seems completely insignificant. I wonder how much they relate to all the increased tobacco advertising?' She looked questioningly at Rory, but he turned away. 'So having spotted someone to Turn, they just need to point and shoot.' She examined the dart. 'I have to say, it looks a bit weedy though. Wouldn't you have to be fairly close? Would it be able to get through more than a shirt? What about in winter, when folk are wearing coats? And how do people not feel it?'

'It's quite long. And pretty sharp,' said Helena. 'Did it leave a mark?'

Eve shrugged. Helena unbuttoned Rory's shirt.

'Steady on,' said Womble.

The girls tipped forward.

'Nothing,' said Helena. 'No visible puncture wound.'

'Maybe there,' Eve pointed at a tiny red speck.

'Mm, maybe,' said Helena.

'He's not very Purple,' said Womble.

'It takes at least six hours,' snapped Rory.

'We know that,' said Eve.

Rory scowled at her, before concluding, 'Which is why I need to leave, get an antidote.'

'You'll be lucky, sunshine,' said Helena.

'I still don't understand how they wouldn't feel it,' said Eve. She turned to Rory. 'Did you feel anything?'

Rory grunted.

'For someone who's been Turning other people, you're being very grumpy about it,' said Helena. 'After all, do unto others…'

'Just shut up all of you, and get me…'

Rory's satellite link-up was down again. Eve and Duncan glanced at one another, and she giggled.

'Get me out of here!' said Rory. 'It's illegal for you to hold me like this.'

'It's illegal for you to try to Turn me without good reason, I think you'll find,' said Eve.

Rory banged his head frustratedly against the table, and then flinched. 'Given the circumstances, I'm pretty sure it would be allowed. There are people who'll have you locked up for this. People high up.'

'Really?' said Eve. 'I'd be amazed if anyone seriously thought they'd be able to keep the lid on all this. After all, you'd have to get to them before we can release our story and get to everyone else, and given your present position, I'd say you're a bit too tied up to manage that.'

'So you want to put the safety of the British people at stake?' Rory asked.

'That old chestnut,' said Helena.

'It's very obviously in the best interests of the people,' said Rory. 'You're just being stubborn if you can't see it. This scheme has made the streets safer, made people feel safer, made criminals and hooligans think twice about their behaviour – isn't that worth keeping quiet for?'

Womble gazed across the table at Eve and Helena.

'You agree with me,' Rory told him.

Womble peered at the dart, as Helena placed it on a tray next to the operating table.

'You can't still think this is right,' she said to Womble.

'I don't know. Maybe not the method, but…'

They exchanged an unwavering glance.

'Now then,' said Eve, 'we've got nearly five hours at least before he starts to Turn. I think I may have a quite nifty idea.'

When he arrived at the surgery, Bob was absolutely beside himself. 'This is beyond my wildest imagination,' he said.

'Who knew there was such a thing,' Helena whispered to Eve.

Bob set up a tripod in the corner of the room.

Eve stood next to Rory. 'So, here's what's going to happen. Bob is going to film pretty much everything that happens from now on.'

Bob gave an enthusiastic thumbs up.

'You're going to partake in a chat – an interview, if you will – giving a detailed account, explaining exactly how people have been Turned. So everyone knows, straight from a horse's mouth, what's been going on.'

'I've got no reason to help you. I am completely committed to the Purple Initiative. I'll say nothing. And then what have you got? Fanciful theories with no proof. From someone well known for silly stories.'

Harsh, thought Eve.

'We've got the cigarette thing.'

'How can you prove what it is without using it again? I don't suppose any of you want to be Purple.'

What other evidence did they have? There was no concrete link to InTan, and even if there were, Eve couldn't betray Carla De Lora's confidence. Announcing that she'd been threatened for investigating would be her word against the government's, and if anyone did believe her, the powers that be would just proclaim the incident as a security-related and justified muzzling of the press. She couldn't prove Womble had been approached without being able to identify the man who'd contacted him. And though Frankie seemed to be on their side, even if he was willing to jeopardise his job, he didn't have any light-shedding facts he could share. The faux fag was all they had.

Helena broke the silence. 'Turn me,' she said.

'Hel, don't,' said Womble, horrified.

'If that's what we need to do…' she replied.

'I don't think you should,' said Duncan. 'Who knows what

will happen after this? There's no guarantee you'll get Turned back...'

Helena shrugged. 'I can take that chance.' She picked up the cigarette, and shooting Rory a look of defiance, handed it to Eve. 'Here you go, Evie. I'd guess there's more than one in there. Hit me with your best shot.'

Eve had a light hold on the device, her fingertips hovering over Helena's still outstretched hand. 'There has to be another way,' she said.

'Good luck with that,' said Rory.

Bob was busy tinkering with camera angles, humming as he did so. Trying to recognise the song, Eve played a subconscious game of *Name That Tune* while she mulled over their options; she was pretty sure it was an old record called 'Turning Japanese' by the Vapors.

'Got it!' she said. 'Hels, didn't you say you've got a package of the tranquilliser that had been recalled?'

'Yep.'

'Have you sent it back yet?'

Helena smiled, letting the 'cigarette' drop back onto her palm. 'No.'

'So we could give Rory a dose, couldn't we? See how he finds it.'

'Oh dear,' said Bob, 'the side effects with that are supposed to be really something. I'll bet what was reported isn't even the half of it. They said first there's euphoria and hallucinations, then vomiting and diarrhoea...'

'Followed by sweating and shaking,' said Helena.

'And in some cases, permanent paralysis,' said Bob.

'You wouldn't dare,' said Rory.

'Try me,' said Eve.

'Fine. Go ahead. I'm not telling you anything.'

Helena nodded. 'It's your choice,' she said, then left the room.

Rory's head and shoulders bobbed up and down violently as he tried to shake himself free, and the table began to wobble.

'Maybe he needs another tie across there. I'll go and see if I can find one,' said Duncan, leaving the room.

'I've told you,' said Rory, 'I'm not saying anything. Do you realise just what you're jeopardising? One of the most effective crime control methods modern society has ever seen, and you want to expose its secrets? You want to help the scum?'

'They're not all scum.'

'Most of them are. And you're going to rue the day you did this. When you can't walk down the street again in safety, think of this moment.'

Eve and Womble locked eyes, considering this.

Helena poked her head in the door, beckoning Eve into the corridor.

'When you arrived, you didn't notice a small brown box behind the reception desk, did you?'

Eve shook her head. 'By the time I reached reception I was a bit preoccupied.'

'Hm.' Helena wandered away.

'Aren't we going to be on a sticky wicket if we do this?' Womble whispered to Eve as she re-entered the room. 'Holding someone against their will, particularly a person who's a government agent, or whatever he counts as – isn't this kidnapping, or something?'

'I would think the police will have other things to worry about, given that we now know the crux of what they don't want us to know. We've got a pretty good bargaining chip.'

'What if he's right? What if we do regret this? You know how I feel about the Purple Scheme.'

'But you're here.'

'Because of you, and Helena, and… Look, I think it works. I think the good it does can outweigh the bad. I know you're doubtful, especially since what happened to Duncan, but you weren't entirely against it before, were you? You've wanted to know how they do it, and now you do. But does everyone else need to? If we do this, it's ruined.'

Eve turned to Bob. 'Could we borrow you for a second?'

'I know what you're talking about!' crowed Rory. 'You're seeing sense, aren't you? You know I'm right.'

'Pipe down,' said Eve.

Bob joined them, now a whispering circle. Down the corridor there was a thud and a 'dammit' from Helena.

'Bob, do you think the Purple Scheme is right or wrong?'

'I know it gets results, and it targets those who deserve to be punished.' He looked at Eve. 'Mostly, anyway. But I don't agree with the way they've gone about it, or how they're doing it, that's wrong. It's unjust, undemocratic.'

'But is it unjust, really?' asked Womble.

'I'll re-phrase the question,' said Eve. 'Is what we're doing here right or wrong? If the Purple Scheme implodes because of us, will we regret it?'

'Well,' said Bob, 'do we have to make that decision now? We'll be armed with the information, we can do what we want with it. We'll be ready to negotiate, and we'll have the upper hand over the governmental dark forces, won't we?'

'Found it, finally.' Helena returned with a cardboard box, and began unsealing the packing tape. She clocked them huddled together. 'What are you three talking about?'

'They know what they're doing is wrong!' said Rory.

'Zip it, Chatty Cathy,' said Eve. She turned to Helena. 'What if we are wrong?'

'Would you say that to Duncan?'

Eve closed her eyes. For all the bad eggs banished from the

streets, deterred by being Turned or the fear of it, could that justify people like Duncan – kind, unwitting, in the wrong place at the wrong time – or those committing increasingly minor offences, like the boy who'd dropped the crisp packet – from being collateral? Could the questionable good that came out of this qualify the bad? If she believed so, what had her investigation been about – simply solving the mystery, being the riddle-busting, news-making gal who could? Or proving her sleuthing-ness while also genuinely wanting to protect and de-lilac Duncan?

Helena took a bottle filled with clear liquid from inside the box, and filled a syringe with it.

'Right,' she said, 'shall we start?'

'Hel, we should be sure about this…' said Womble.

'Think carefully about what you want to do here,' Helena told him. 'Now, shall I?'

There were quick, shared glances around the room. Eve nodded.

'Okay,' said Womble, conflicted, but looking Helena in the eye.

'She won't do it,' said Rory.

'Really?' said Helena.

'Argh!' Rory let out a scream as Helena stuck the needle in his arm. Her thumb was on the plunger, ready to inject the liquid. 'Alright, alright,' he said, 'I'll talk.'

Bob hit *Record*.

Chapter Twenty-One

They all sat around the kitchen table: Eve, Womble, Helena, Bob and Duncan, plus the recently arrived Annie and Magnus. Rory was on the sofa, still tied up, and thankfully, due to a sneakily administered sleeping tablet, snoring quietly. He was also now quite Purple.

Eve had explained the day's events to Annie and Magnus, who had then watched the parts of Bob's video which most clearly showed Rory's change in colour. Duncan had winced at this, but the others, despite having already seen it happen once before their eyes, watched again, still agog. Patches of Rory's skin began to slowly change shade, his pale olive tone giving way to islands of a very slight, light mauve, which gradually darkened as it spread, the pools of colour merging into one another, like continents colliding on a map. From initial blotches to top to toe colour took four hours.

Duncan had squeezed Eve's hand as they watched.

'Incredible,' said Annie.

'He was rather reluctant to give us any information,' said Eve.

'Despite the threats of the dodgy tranquilliser,' said Womble, looking in his wife's direction.

'But eventually he realised resistance was futile,' said Helena.

'And he – very belligerently – answered all my questions,' said Eve. 'So, we have gathered that aside from police and military personnel, the scheme recruits sympathetic members of the public, who are given multiple assessments, background checks, and then six months' training – part-time, that is, so as not to arouse suspicion. They're then armed with these 'cigarettes', wear a barely detectable camera which films every altercation they witness and is later used as the primary source of evidence. More often than not – Rory was being particularly grumpy at this point, so we couldn't get any definite figures out of him – but we think at least two thirds of incidents have a decoy dog, to make them less conspicuous. That way, they could be out anywhere, at any time of day or night, without bringing any attention to themselves.'

'That is particularly clever, because really, who would look twice at someone with a dog and a fag?' said Bob, begrudgingly impressed.

'And also, using ordinary people... Folk may recognise their local police officers, or have an idea what a military type might look like, and if you were looking for an off-duty sort who might be out and about, that's what you'd be thinking of. But recruiting a retired postman... of course he's going to fly – or dog-walk – under the radar.'

'It also explains the resurgence in cigarette advertising,' said Magnus. 'Supporting their cover, given what a decline there had been in smoking.'

'But the thing is, what do we do next?' said Womble. 'We've got Rory tied up, and that's bad enough as it is, but we can't hold onto him indefinitely, and as soon as we let him go, of course he's going to tell the police, or whoever else he answers to, exactly what we've done and what we know. What if there are people he's supposed to check in with? There could already be alarms going off that he's not been heard from.'

'We didn't think about that until after the sleeping tablet,' said Helena.

'So we do need to come up with a plan pretty speedily,' said Eve.

'What would you like to do?' Annie asked.

'We want to request a halt in the Purple Scheme, pending further discussions – with police, psychologists, convicted criminals, victims' support organisations, representatives from countries with lower crime rates than our own, whoever might have sensible input to give – about alternatives. We want those already Turned given a fair trial, or in some obvious cases, the charges against them dropped, and for everyone to be Re-Turned to normal. And to discuss this, we would like a meeting with the prime minister.'

'*You* would like a meeting with the prime minister,' said Womble.

'Yes,' Helena agreed. 'This has all been down to you.'

'Not quite,' said Eve. 'It was Bob who made the biggest discovery. And we had help from Magnus and –' she stopped herself before she uttered Carla's name. 'Debs and Frankie helped with the ISON footage. And, weirdly, Simon…'

'Enough, already,' said Helena. 'Just accept some credit. And as to that louse, Theo Fletcher…'

Magnus smiled at this; he and Helena clinked mugs.

'My guess is that he'd rather attempt to negotiate with us, or have some input or control over this, than have the video and my report available for everyone to see,' said Eve. 'We'll give him a twelve-hour deadline, and if we don't have a meeting by then, we release the details.'

'I could help arrange that,' said Annie.

'You can't do that,' said Eve. 'Surely the repercussions for you would be terrible.'

'I could say we'd received a tip, and present it as an opportunity for him to intervene before this is made public.'

'You would do that for us?' Eve asked. 'Why?'

'I may be officially impartial,' said Annie, 'and I really do believe Theo Fletcher is acting in good faith. But the scheme is very divisive, and it's only going to get worse. Plus, even us strait-laced news broads like to be a bit unpredictable on occasion.' She looked at Eve and winked. 'I think Pam would be proud, don't you?'

'I can get Humane involved,' said Magnus, 'and I'm guessing that's why you asked me to be here. I'm sure their lawyers will be eager to help, and it would be savvy to have a legal person coordinating the proceedings.'

Eve nodded.

Magnus paused. 'I'm gobsmacked by what you're doing here, but you shouldn't undertake it lightly. Are you absolutely sure about this? A really bleak, worst case scenario would be that they won't let you foil the scheme and stay anonymous. There are so many people who support the Purpleness, and you could become the figurehead for that being taken from them. You could be blamed for anything that happens – a rise in crime, retaliations by those Turned, all sorts of things – that's seen to be the result of the Purple Scheme being forced to end. And that's all aside from the shifty government bods, like the kind gent who gave you the bruise.'

'You should think about that,' said Duncan. 'I'm not exactly happy with what's happened to me, but I could be considered collateral damage.'

Eve looked at him. 'I don't think that's acceptable,' she said. 'And anyway, Magnus, you're not suggesting we shouldn't go to them at all, are you?'

'I'm not saying you shouldn't do it. I think you have an incredible opportunity here, but just be aware of what the consequences might be.'

'You sound like Theo Fletcher,' Helena teased.

'Ouch,' said Magnus.

'Yes, you do need to be mindful of what might happen, consider all eventualities,' said Annie. 'I'm sure Magnus or some Humane reps can present this for you if you'd rather err on the side of caution.'

'What do you think?' Eve asked, looking around the table.

Duncan said, 'I think you should follow your instincts.'

Eve looked at him. 'I think I should be brave,' she said. 'So let's give it a whirl. What do we do next?'

In the living room, there was the surprisingly restrained sound of a choir singing, as Womble prepared a lesson featuring songs of worship. He studied a record cover featuring young cathedral choristers sporting red robes and bowl haircuts, then held up the LP sleeve and, mimicking the choir boys, pulled a mock innocent expression.

'Look at that face,' said Helena, sweetly prodding his cheek. 'Though I hope your lesson is also going to include some livelier options.'

'It will, my love,' said Womble, reaching behind him to retrieve a pile of records which included country and gospel platters, in addition to some less likely suspects that he'd shoehorned in.

Eve smiled, enjoying their interaction, the increasing lack of tension. There was a way to go, still, but the incident at the vets' had helped, as had Womble's conversation with the mysterious recruiter he'd been due to meet. When the chap had called to find out why Womble had missed their meeting, Womble had excused himself from the scheme, as Helena looked on. The man hadn't been best pleased, in response to Womble's apology, saying, 'And I'm sorry that you've wasted our time'. Womble had, with a sheepish smile to Helena, held up crossed fingers as he assured the caller that he wouldn't breathe a word of their communication to another living soul.

Eve looked at her lap, where her notebook lay with an assortment of papers piled on top – documents hurriedly prepared by the Humane lawyers, some newspaper cuttings, and a copy of her all-revealing piece about the Purpleness.

Her breath had caught in her throat when she'd called Magnus that next day, Rory lying Purpled nearby. She worried that he would think – what? That there was more she hadn't said that she wanted to share? That now she'd seen him again she'd want to maintain this oddly rekindled contact? In fact, the thought of facing him again after all she'd said was more daunting than the prospect of confronting Theo Fletcher. But of course her reason for contacting him couldn't have been more redeeming (if she'd needed it to be), and he'd practically whooped down the phone.

'Eve Baxter, that is *breathtaking*!' he'd said.

Phew, Eve thought. She laughed. 'I thought you might be pleased.'

'That is unbelievable, completely unbelievable. Wow. This sounds like quite a story. How does it feel to have solved the riddle?'

Eve had pictured the final bunch of cherries whirring into place.

'Satisfying. Mostly,' she said.

She didn't feel any less distressed by her inaction, back in the day. The dull ache of regret was just the same when she thought of him, of the trail of disasters since. Short of a time machine, how could she ever put it right? Oh, how she wished… She stared at her younger self. Keep trying, she thought. Better late than never.

Eve entered the kitchen, where Womble and Helena were harmoniously preparing supper.

'What's news?' said Helena.

'The lawyers are waiting to hear, but they're pretty sure we'll get the meeting,' said Eve.

'They were quick,' Helena said.

Eve nodded.

'No time to snooze, what with Rory—' said Womble.

'Yeah, what's happening with him?'

'Still helping Humane with their enquiries.'

'He must be thrilled,' said Helena, adding, 'Magnus is lovely, but I don't think I'd want to be on the wrong side of a grilling by him.'

'Speaking of grilling,' said Womble, serving up plates of hot crumpets.

Sven and Mr Bailey wandered close to the table, tails wagging.

'And if they don't agree?' said Helena.

'Adio will post the video and my whistle-blowing article, as will Humane. And Adio's got copies ready to go to all the news outlets.'

'Did Bob finish editing the video?' Helena asked.

'Yep.'

'It looks great,' said Womble. 'You come across as very professional. An old hat.'

'Um, thanks,' said Eve.

'How are you feeling?' said Helena.

'Terrified,' said Eve.

It had all happened so quickly that she'd barely had time to think, and now she had the time, the cogs in her brain would barely turn, stalled by the glue of petrification.

'Bringing down the most gobsmacking government scheme of our time – what could possibly go wrong?' Womble joked.

Helena rolled her eyes.

Eve tried not to pass out. She bit into a crumpet.

'Who'd have thought it,' said Womble, as he drove up to the Downing Street gates.

He showed his pass, and the guard nodded, letting them through; inside another guard directed them to where they should park.

Eve bit her lip. She turned to Womble. 'I think this will turn out for the best,' she said, 'won't it?' She looked out of the window towards the ominous black door, wondering just what was in store for her on the other side.

Womble nodded. 'I don't mean to be all soppy or anything, but I'm really proud of you – even if you are about to bring down the Purple Scheme.' He smiled. 'You might have made a bit of a detour, and an extended one at that, but you got there in the end. I think you get an Annie Morris-worthy gold star.'

'Thank you. Though you might not want to congratulate me until afterwards. Who knows what could happen? It could go horribly wrong. They could still cart me off to the Tower.'

'If they do, make sure they let you stop in the gift shop. The kids from school went there and they loved it.'

Womble was quiet for a moment.

'Break a leg,' he said, adding with a grin, 'hopefully not on the rack.'

Eve got out of the car. It was such an early morning meeting

Kate Bulpitt

that the sun hadn't long risen. Eve liked that; the serene daybreak hours when anything was possible.

The Humane lawyer, Sonia Aziz, was already waiting for her, smart and crisp-looking, despite the time. As Eve got closer, she noticed Ms Aziz was wearing a small smiley face badge on her lapel. The lawyer looked down at it.

'My daughter insisted I wear it,' she said. 'She was sure that it was good luck.'

'I'll take any help I can get,' said Eve.

'Ready?' asked Ms Aziz.

'As I'll ever be,' said Eve, feeling fairly sick.

Eve's head felt fuzzy as they approached the door. While they stood on the step, Eve noticed Ms Aziz's smiley badge reflected in the shining varnish; hopefully a good omen, she thought. One of the police officers on straight-faced sentry duty glanced towards the door, as though surprised it hadn't yet opened. Eve looked questioningly – was this usual? – at Ms Aziz, just as the mirroring blackness retreated. They stepped across the threshold, where an aide was waiting for them. He wore navy trousers and a surprisingly crumpled shirt.

'Hello, I'm Louis,' said the aide, with a fleeting, efficient smile, and the air of someone who had pressing things to return to. 'Follow me.'

He led them through the entrance hall and down a long corridor. Eve blinked, taking in the deep carpet, the elaborate cornices, and the medley of artwork – mostly grand old oil paintings – hanging on flocked-papered walls in between. She attempted to play guess who? with the portraits, but found her historical-political knowledge was rather lacking.

They turned off into a small, sparsely furnished room with wood-panelled walls. There were two tiny tables, each supporting an ornate lamp, and then a larger, round table, surrounded by a quintet of chairs covered in moss-green velvet. In the centre of this table was a large Chinese bowl, intricately painted. It was empty and, her thoughts rambling nervously, Eve wondered if Theo Fletcher ever had the urge to fill it with fruit, or toffees, for waiting guests. Which then reminded her of a *Say Fantastique!* story about a dog that loved toffees; even the thought of the video clips of him, jaw stretching as he chewed, made Eve laugh. She felt a nervous giggle rise in her throat, and tried to swallow it back down.

Louis gestured that they take a seat.

'Tea, coffee, something herbal?'

As someone whose time was priced by the minute, Sonia Aziz was accustomed to swift actions and gave a quick shake of her head.

'I'm fine, thank you,' said Eve.

'Right. Excellent,' said Louis. 'The prime minister is running late this morning, so you may have to wait, I'm afraid. Unfortunately at the moment I can't confirm an estimated time of arrival. Of course, we can reschedule if that's easier...'

'Obviously, that won't be necessary,' said Ms Aziz, taking a seat at the round table and placing some files neatly in front of her. She gave Eve a reassuring smile.

'We'll wait,' said Eve.

Louis closed the door behind him, though the latch didn't quite catch, leaving it ajar. As it swung very slightly open, Eve heard Louis's footsteps retreat down the hall, the floorboards creaking below him (just think of the significant figures who've also creaked along those, Eve thought).

'Have you been here before?' Eve asked Ms Aziz.

She shook her head. 'No. And it turns out that of all the places I've been to for work, this is the one that has most impressed my mum.'

'Really? The grandeur of Ten Downing Street?'

'Not quite,' said Ms Aziz. 'She really likes Theo Fletcher.' She sighed. 'But then, don't they all?'

Eve kept thinking of the prime minister's impassioned comments about his fiancée, and how he wanted to protect everyone, and she felt guilty. Eve was about to destroy – hopefully – the Purple Scheme. Her feelings still flip-flopped about that. Helena and Magnus were ecstatic, and Duncan was cautiously optimistic. Womble was pleased that Helena was pleased – and he was aware that his agreement beside the operating table had had a significant effect on the future of his marriage. Those tiny moments with huge consequences…

Fifteen minutes later, Louis returned.

'I'm so sorry to keep you waiting,' he said. 'The prime minister has been detained by a call with the American president, and may be a little while. Due to the urgency of the matter they're discussing, I'm afraid I can't guarantee how long they'll be.'

'That's a shame,' said Ms Aziz, with a look that implied there was no wool being pulled over her eyes. She opened one of her folders, and took out a pen: she wasn't going anywhere.

'The American president?' Eve asked.

'That's correct.'

'In America?'

Louis nodded, his face registering surprise that such an apparent simpleton had an important meeting with the prime minister.

'Goodness, you'd hope he'd be in bed with a cup of cocoa at this hour, wouldn't you?' said Eve.

Ms Aziz pursed her lips, hiding a smile.

Louis took a deep breath, his chest puffing out, before he responded. 'I'm sure you can imagine that being a leader of the free world is not a nine to five job. They're not working in Woolworths.'

'I can indeed,' said Eve, politely. She sensed something fishy was afoot, which was confirmed by Ms Aziz.

'Interesting,' she said. 'I was under the impression that the president was in Brazil at a security summit this week.'

'Oh,' said Louis, his eyes narrowing. 'Yes, you're right, of course. That slipped my mind – I look after the prime minister's diary, after all, not the president's. The progress of the talks will be what they're discussing.'

He turned and left the room.

'What time is it in Brazil?' Eve asked.

With a look at her watch, Ms Aziz said, 'Three fifteen am.'

They heard a small shriek, followed by the creaks of quick footsteps somewhere in the corridor outside.

'What on earth do you think is going on?' said Eve.

'I've no idea.'

'Maybe they have mice,' said Eve.

'I knew they would make us wait,' said Ms Aziz. 'Trying to rattle our nerve, underline that they're in charge. Standard tactics.'

Unruffled, Ms Aziz took a flask of coffee from her bag, and returned to her papers.

Forty-five minutes later. Eve's mouth felt dry. She swallowed.

'I think I'm going to take Louis up on that tea after all,' said Eve. 'Can I get you anything?'

Ms Aziz shook her head.

Eve peered out into the corridor to see if there was anyone in view whose attention she could get. Nothing.

'Hello?' she called hesitantly, and not daringly loudly. 'Louis?'

How unusual that there wouldn't be more staff around, Eve thought (though it was still early), if only to be keeping an eye on Ms Aziz and her, particularly given that they were surely considered to be troublemakers. Eve noticed a woman at the far end of the corridor, but she rushed past and almost as soon as she'd appeared was again out of sight.

Eve stepped out carefully into the hallway, listening for the sound of Louis's voice. She heard part of a conversation from within a nearby room, and made her way towards it, as quietly as she could. As she got closer she noticed this next door was also ajar – you'd think they'd be better with locks and latches, Eve thought, thinking of hushed conversations and all the state secrets that must be floating around.

'Yes, sir,' Eve heard someone say, before the sound of a chair scraping. Eve could see a flicker in the increasing light, indicating movement. She knocked. There was no answer. She heard a cough and assumed someone must be in there, so pushed the door and peered inside. There was no one in the room, but then she heard the cough again, the sound seeming to be emanating from a computer on a desk to the left of the room; the screen was facing away from the door.

'Louis?'

The voice also came from the computer, and it sounded distinctly like Theo Fletcher.

Eve took a couple of steps towards the screen, and peered around at it. There was the prime minister alright. And he was Purple.

Chapter Twenty-Two

Eve took a seat in a chair close to the desk, rolling it back and swinging round to face the screen. Theo Fletcher's attention was caught by the sound, and he looked up.

'Hello, Prime Minister,' said Eve. Too surprised to effectively censor herself, she added, 'I have to say, sir, you're looking a bit peaky.'

'You must be Eve.' Theo Fletcher stared out sadly from the screen. 'I suppose this,' he said, 'is what could be described as me being a victim of the scheme's success.' Then – and Eve couldn't detect any irony in his voice – he added, 'Sorry to have kept you waiting.'

It occurred to Eve to comment on the curfew – *not to worry, Prime Minister; after all, you're not allowed out before seven am* – but she held her tongue.

'If I'd realised you'd come looking for me... Always on the trail of something, are you?'

'Not quite,' said Eve, not admitting that the thing she had actually been on the trail of was a cup of tea, and she wouldn't have stumbled across him had she not been parched.

A second door in the room opened and Louis appeared.

'What are you—' he began, at the sight of Eve at his desk. 'You can't be in here. You need to leave.'

'It's too late,' said Theo, looking towards – beyond – the edge of the screen.

Louis scrambled towards the computer. 'Sir, I'm so sorry – I told her to wait—'

'Just leave us now, please, Louis,' said Theo.

'Yes, sir.' Louis hesitated, took a few steps backwards, still looking at the screen, then turned and walked out. When he closed the door, Eve noted that this time it clicked shut.

There was a momentary silence. Theo Fletcher sat, facing forward, a slight hunch to his shoulders, his eyes cast down, as if he was looking at something on the table in front of him, or was just lost in thought (Eve had seen that look often enough recently with Duncan). He was wearing a wrinkled white shirt, was unusually unshaven, and his thick hair was unbrushed. Despite his pallor, there was something strangely appealing about this unkempt prime minister – and Eve wasn't usually so susceptible. Unpolished, subdued, vulnerable; Eve almost felt the odd air of morning-after intimacy, and to see him so quiet was disconcerting – he was never without something certain to say, always had a steady gaze and a sure answer. She wanted to reach through the screen and hold his hand (would he flinch at any touch the way Duncan did?).

'What happened?'

Theo Fletcher looked up. 'I'm sorry?'

'What happened, that you're... Turned?'

He stared at her. Eve couldn't detect anger, or upset, just melancholy contemplation.

'Obviously that's not something I can talk about,' he said, twitchily shifting an object that was out of view, which Eve could hear slide across the desk. A pen, perhaps.

'But you must feel... out of sorts.'

The prime minister shifted in his seat.

'That's somewhat accurate, yes.'

'I can imagine because I've a friend who was Turned recently. He's a good guy, was in the wrong place at the wrong time, trying to help someone else. To see the change in him... the humiliation, the hopelessness. He couldn't leave the house. Could barely go to the shed at the end of his garden.'

Eve expected Theo Fletcher to be pleased, a flickering acknowledgement of success. Instead he just gazed off to one side, his focus somewhere she couldn't see.

'Maybe you can imagine that,' she said.

His head was bobbing gently, but Eve wasn't sure that he was nodding – he was still looking away from her, and she couldn't tell if he was listening to what she had said.

'What do you think of the initiative?' he asked.

'I...'

Theo was now facing her; still, focused.

'Go on.'

'Well, I...'

'You obviously disagree with it or you wouldn't be here. You know how I feel about it, why I created it, even if you've not read or heard anything else – which, from what I'm told about you, I think unlikely. So I've made my case, I'd like to hear yours.'

'I don't need to make a case though, do I? We can prove how the Turning is happening, which will ruin the effectiveness of the scheme.'

'Oh, yes – *we*,' said Theo. 'You, and Magnus Jones, and Humane, and – was Annie involved?'

'No,' said Eve, cautiously. 'But I told her what I knew, afterwards.'

'Maximum exposure for the story?'

'No,' said Eve, taken aback. 'Advice.'

'But this is about furthering your career? Graduating from what you do…'

Eve braced herself for another dig about cats and toasters.

'… To something bigger.'

Eve waited. No mention of felines or frivolousness.

'It's not about that,' she said.

'No?'

'Well…' She was about to acknowledge that there was an element of truth to it – but why make any kind of confession to Theo Fletcher?

'If you're going to try to curtail this scheme,' he said, 'I'd like to know why. I think you can be gracious enough to do that. You know why I'm so passionate that it exists. Let's hear why you are not.'

What kind of trap could this be? Surely she had the upper hand – with the evidence they had, and now a Purple prime minister?

'I was curious, at first. It was one of those stories that just grabs you and you want to know it all. What, where, why – how. It was incredible, and I wanted to be in on it. It seemed–' surely she wasn't going to admit this, and to Theo Fletcher of all people? – 'it seemed made for me. Here was a story – a proper story – but it was loony as well. I don't know – it sounds ridiculous, but it felt like a gift. A challenge. I had to be part of it.'

'So you came back here.'

Eve nodded. 'And then Duncan…'

'Your Turned friend.'

'Yes. When he was Turned, I wanted to help him, get him Re-Turned.'

'But?'

'But what?'

'You haven't said anything to me about how despicable the scheme is, or unjust, or against people's human rights.'

'I suppose that goes without saying.'

'Does it?'

'I'm here to finalise our deal.'

'What if we agree to Re-Turn Duncan, and we delay halting the scheme?'

'I can't do that.'

'Why? Because that's what Humane wants? What about what the British people want?'

'Why are you trying to save the scheme when *you* have been Turned? That's insanity.'

'No, it's not. It proves the initiative works.'

'This is—' Eve searched through her repertoire of words – bonkers, bananas, demented, delirious – before giving up.

'How does it prove it?' she asked.

'As I've already said, I can't tell you that.'

'Oh, come on. You asked me to be honest and I have been. I believe, Prime Minister, you can do the same.'

'It was a mistake.'

'So the scheme is not so infallible after all?'

'Oh, I made a mistake, it wasn't incorrect that I be Turned. The circumstances were unfortunate, but what I did wasn't right.'

'Go on.'

Theo Fletcher shook his Purple head.

'It's not going to be any worse than my knowing you're Purple, is it?' Eve asked. 'Or maybe it is.'

Theo conceded defeat.

'I went to the shop to buy a packet of cigarettes—'

'You smoke?'

'Yes.'

Eve tutted. 'Honestly, you boys. It's so bad for you. And

anyway, don't you have elves to do that for you? Are you allowed out on your own?'

'Even I need some normality, a few minutes to myself, you know. When I can, I like to walk my dog and get some meditative time outside. And there's always a security officer right behind. Besides, I like to be out and interact with people, though it may surprise you to hear that. I am in this job to serve people, to listen to them, despite what some people may think.'

'You were saying.'

'I was leaving the shop. A young man saw me. He came up, started shouting, "Who do you think you are?" and swearing, threatening me. He was leaning right up to my face – so I punched him.'

'You punched him?'

'Yes. Not a wise choice, admittedly. It was the oddest thing. I've never hit anyone – or felt the compunction to hit anyone – in my life, but… it just happened.' Apparently without thinking, Theo had been moving his arm in a gentle re-enactment of this, and he now gazed down at his Purple fist, surprised, as though it had swung into action entirely of its own accord. He frowned. 'Just after it had happened, out of the corner of my eye I saw a woman with a dog turn the corner, and I did wonder…'

'Would she have seen who you were?'

'Well, unlike the young man, she was a little way away, and behind me, and it was dark, and I was wearing a hat, so – it's unlikely.'

'What happened to her?'

'What do you mean?'

'Well, what if she realises it was you? She'll have the footage, won't she?'

'We already have the footage.'

'And the woman?'

'She's being questioned, routinely. But as no one will ever see me Purple, she won't have any reason to believe it could have been me.'

'How long until the antidote kicks in?'

Theo looked at his watch. 'I'm not sure. It can take up to twenty-four hours.'

'That's unfortunate,' said Eve. 'And risky, for you. You're here, somewhere in the building, are you?'

'Possibly.'

'So, back to what happened. A guy is attacking you for Turning people—'

'You're assuming it was about the Purple Scheme. We don't know for sure what he was disgruntled about.'

'But it's most likely about that, isn't it? *Who do you think you are*, playing God? You've been Turned for attacking someone who's attacking the Purpleness.'

'Apparently so.'

'Remarkable,' said Eve.

'But look at it this way: I behaved badly, and I was punished accordingly.'

'Except that you're just waiting for the antidote to take effect. But when you look at yourself right now, does it *feel* wrong?'

'Nothing could dissuade me from believing in this. I want people to behave decently and respectfully, and this works. The statistics prove it.'

'I don't have much faith in statistics. Slippery things. Adjusted to suit whatever it is they're selling.'

'So you really want to interrupt the scheme?'

'That's why I'm here, isn't it? As you know, I have the full set of facts regarding how people are being Turned. The release of this information to the general public will make the scheme

422

unsustainable, and make Turning agents, or anyone who looks as though they could be an agent, vulnerable.'

'You would want to do that to them, would you? You would be willing, through your actions, to put them in danger? People like your friend, Womble.'

'The public has a right to know how this is happening. And once they do, there won't be any point putting any agents in danger. The scheme will be unworkable. As you know, we request that the Purple Initiative be suspended, and that, as stated in the documents you've seen, discussions are held to find fairer options for crime prevention.'

'I haven't agreed to that.'

'Yes, you have. That's why I'm here. You don't have a choice.'

'What if I can convince you otherwise?'

'It's not just me! And anyway, why are you trying to negotiate with me, when you're Purple? That's just more ammunition for our camp.'

'In a matter of hours I'll be back to normal. No one would believe you.'

'I think you'll find that they will.'

Eve held up a tiny plastic device which had been clipped to a bangle on her wrist. Rory's undercover camera.

Theo's response was composed; a picture which in her head, Eve titled 'Chess match: an elegant defeat'.

There was a knock at the door.

'Eve?' It was Ms Aziz. 'Are you in there?'

'Yes! I'm almost done,' Eve called back. To Theo she said, 'So, do we have a deal?'

'For now.'

'You're hardly going to be able to renegotiate later.'

'Today's hardly the best day for me to be making important decisions, given my rather impaired condition.'

'Nice try. Are you going to sign the agreement, right now?'

'Are you going to hand over that camera?'

'When Humane have filed the fully executed copies of the agreement,' said Eve, thinking that should give her time to make a copy of the gadget's footage.

'Very well,' said Theo Fletcher. 'I shall agree to a temporary suspension of the initiative, pending further discussions.'

'Prime Minister,' said Eve, 'I think we have a deal.'

Eve stood on the pavement outside Number 10, taking in the normal, pink and brown tints of the police officers flanking the door. Soon everyone will be back to normal, she thought. Including Duncan.

'I'm glad it went well,' said Ms Aziz. 'How was he?'

'Not his usual self.'

'Had we made him reconsider his stance, do you think?'

'I don't think anything could do that. He was still fighting for the cause.'

'He must be devastated at the initiative being shot down,' said Ms Aziz. 'I almost feel sorry for him.'

'Me too. But I don't think he's giving up on it quite yet.'

'We'll be awaiting official notification from the prime minister's aides – an advance copy of the announcement that it's being stopped,' she said. 'And we'll be monitoring developments, to make sure the agreement is kept on track.'

Eve nodded. 'Good.'

She had put the tiny camera into an envelope, which she handed to Ms Aziz.

'Could you see that Magnus gets this? For him only. There are some instructions in there, too. When he's done he'll have an item to be sent with the final copies of the documents.'

'Of course.'

They made their way through the Downing Street gates. As Ms Aziz walked towards the waiting car, she turned back and said, 'Come in for a celebratory lunch one day this week. The rest of the staff would love to thank you.'

'That'd be lovely, I'll round up our gang,' said Eve, with a wave.

She crossed to Womble's car. He was watching her eagerly out the window, eyes wide in anticipation. Eve opened the door.

'How'd it go?'

She stared ahead, brain whirring, the jackpot machine spinning, a blur of bells, plums and cherries.

'You wouldn't believe it.'

'Try me,' said Womble.

'Just when you'd think this whole scenario couldn't get any madder.'

Womble pulled out into the traffic. 'Well?'

'Honestly, if I told you, I really *would* have to kill you.'

'You can't possibly say that and not tell me.'

'I can't tell you. You'd never be able to tell another living soul.'

'Tell me.'

'Do you *promise*? Never a word?'

Womble nodded.

'He was, you know—'

'What?'

'Purple.'

'No!' Womble looked both horrified and crestfallen. 'So that really is it then?'

'I think so,' said Eve. 'And I would kill for a cup of tea.'

*

In an unexpected u-turn, the government has announced a suspension of the crime-busting Purple Initiative, citing medical concerns regarding the colourant used. All of those Turned will be treated with an antidote. Those Turned for minor offences will be pardoned; for more serious crimes, offenders will be taken into custody and sentenced in accordance with traditional legal procedure. Many supporters of the scheme are upset at its interruption, but human rights campaigners are claiming the development as a victory for justice. It is not yet known whether the scheme will recommence at a later date. The prime minister is said to be 'extremely disappointed' at having to call a halt to the scheme. And the American president was quoted as saying, 'We were sorry to hear about the current discontinuation, as we were about to start trialling a Purple Program of our own.'

After Duncan had been injected with the antidote, they'd returned to his house, and sat beside one another on the sofa, Eve turned towards him, legs curled under her, watching his profile, awaiting the happy draining of damson from his face, his neck, his hands, and all else that was tinted, out of sight.

'It's like Christmas,' she said, addressing his cheek.

'Oh yes, excitement, anticipation, can't sleep for thinking about presents to be unwrapped.'

Unwrapped. Eve looked at Duncan's shirt, thought of the molecules changing colour beneath it, soon to be seen.

Duncan's mouth twitched, suppressing a smile.

'Anything?' he said.

Of course, he knew there wouldn't be, but there *could* be, any minute.

'Um…' Eve leant close to him, gazing at his skin, at the mauve-ness which they'd beaten, which was about to make a defeated retreat. Indigo-a-go-go. She stared at the stubble around his chin, half expecting to see it grow, as they waited.

'No change,' she said. 'Too soon. I'd put the kettle on, but I don't want to miss anything.'

Duncan laughed. 'They did say up to twenty-four hours for complete recovery. We could well be sitting like this 'til tomorrow.'

'Suits me.'

Eve rested her head back against the sofa.

'Thank you for going above and beyond the call of duty.'

'Mm,' she mumbled, puffing her cheeks out. 'I was just, you know, being daft and curious.'

'I see. Well, thank you.' He squeezed her hand.

'Welcome.'

'Imagine what could have—'

'Don't,' said Eve.

They were both quiet. Then Eve manoeuvred herself so she was on his lap, her face leaning towards his. She placed a hand on his cheek, gazed intently at him.

'You do know,' she said, 'how brave and amazing you are? And so kind and loyal that even Simon dotes on you. That would be true whether you'd stayed Purple or not.'

Duncan didn't make a sound. Not even when Eve ran her fingertips gently down his still-tinted arm, or kissed him. His eyes were locked onto hers, and he put his arms around her waist. Limbs entwined, pink and purple, for now.

The discoloration had been so gradual they could hardly be sure it was happening. The purple became paler and paler, parts of Duncan's body changing so subtly that it seemed certain swathes of skin were just affected by the light. By now he was shirtless, and Eve put her hands on his chest, a colour comparison. She gazed at the lilac-less vision before her.

'Look at you,' she said, 'all peachy.'

Duncan beamed. He looked down at his arms, his chest, peered over his shoulders at his back, and, with an elated laugh, pulled forward the waistband of his jeans to check everything covered was back to normal too. Then he held out his hands again, slowly absorbing the lack of lavender in them (and his future). He gave a joyful yelp.

'I'm me again,' he said.

'So it seems,' Eve managed to say, before he kissed her.

Annie backed into the room holding a pair of mugs in one hand, and a bottle in the other.

'Would you believe there wasn't a glass to be found,' she said, 'so I'm afraid it's champagne out of these, rather incongruously.'

'I think that's quite fitting,' said Eve, 'given how unconventional this whole experience has been.'

Annie popped the cork, and Eve held the glasses as she poured.

'To you, Eve. The gal who got the scoop,' Annie toasted, holding up her mug. Printed across it in a faux computer font were the words 'Tinter Electricals – For All Your Outside Broadcast Needs'.

'Thank you, and cheers.' Eve raised her cup, featuring an illustration of a Collie who was the mascot on a children's magazine show, and his name, Pepper, printed in big red letters. She leant against Annie's desk. 'It all seems too incredible.'

'Doesn't it just. How are you celebrating?'

'Oh, you know. Drinks at The Fox with the gang. And my mum's doing a tea at the weekend, which is… weird.' Eve looked into her mug, watched the frothing bubbles. Only half jokingly, she said, 'Family stuff. Well, it makes me want to run back to New York.'

'While you're considering what might come next,' said Annie, 'I've lined up a couple of meetings for you, if you're interested. One with a producer here, who I think might be able to find something for you…'

Eve was agog, and coughed in surprise at that and some champagne bubbles going down the wrong way.

'And Elaine Collins at *The Tribune* said to give her a call. Plus, I picked up some details for a trainee broadcast scheme that I thought might intrigue you. That's for on camera.'

'Crikey,' said Eve. 'I don't know what to say.'

There was a knock at the door and one of Annie's production team appeared.

'Hiya. Can you be ready for your pre-record with the PM in fifteen?'

'Absolutely,' Annie replied. 'Thanks.'

'His first interview since the Purple-ending announcement.'

'Yes. He said you told him I advised you not to release the video until you'd approached the government to try and negotiate a deal,' said Annie.

'I did say that. I think he was relieved.' Eve gulped her champagne. 'I should go and leave you to get ready. Also,' she took a look at her watch, 'Adio and I are due to be mulling over some jolly options later, so I should get back before he calls.'

'Tell him I loved Pam at the hairdressers!'

'Getting her lilac rinse washed out.'

'Yes, that was brilliant.' Annie was taking a jacket out of a dry cleaners' bag. 'How's Duncan? It must be odd for him, being back to normal, mustn't it?'

'Yes – though that kind of odd he can live with.' Eve laughed. 'And he's become rather partial to wearing shorts.'

Annie put the jacket to one side and gave Eve a hug goodbye.

'Keep me posted on everything.'

'Of course!'

Eve put the Pepper mug next to the champagne bottle, and made her way into the corridor.

She was handing her visitor's pass back to the receptionist when Theo Fletcher arrived. He approached the desk, a pair of aides two steps behind him. He stopped when he saw Eve.

'Miss Baxter,' he said.

'Hello, Prime Minister. You're looking very well.'

A pause. 'Thank you. What brings you here?'

'Just hopping about, you know. Places to go, people to see.'

'I can imagine. What's next for you?'

'Goodness knows,' said Eve.

'How's your friend?'

'Friend?' Was he referring to Womble? Was this about to be some kind of threat?

'The one you mentioned, who'd been Turned.'

'Oh. Duncan. Better, thank you. Relieved.'

Theo Fletcher nodded. How peculiar, Eve thought. He was willing to Turn people, and yet he cared?

'What's next for you?' she asked, almost blushing at her own unanticipated cheek.

He wagged a finger at her, with pantomime sternness.

'Doing my job, to the best of my ability, of course.'

The aides had collected their passes from the receptionist, who – obviously a fan – looked towards Theo.

With an enlivened smile, he responded to her attention by saying, 'Good afternoon, young lady. I'm here to see Annie Morris.'

'Young! Aren't you the card, Prime Minister. I haven't been called that for thirty years!' she said. 'I was very sad to hear that

430

you're scrapping the Purpling. I know we all thought it was a bit batty to begin with, but it was going great guns, wasn't it? There was a lad round my way – ooh, he was a devil.'

'Was he Turned?'

'No, but he had a friend who was, and as soon as that happened you could just see him looking over his shoulder. Barely said boo to a goose.'

'I'm glad you shared that story with me, thank you—' Theo Fletcher leaned forward, peering at the receptionist's enamel name pin.

'Betty.'

'I do agree, Betty. It's a terrible shame, especially considering that other countries were about to adopt the scheme too, seeing obvious value in it. But we'll be undertaking some research, and who knows…'

'So you might bring it back? Why don't you put the decision to the public? It's been so popular, and that would be democratic, Prime Minister, wouldn't it? Let people have a think, and make up their own minds.'

Theo Fletcher said, 'I couldn't possibly comment on that.'

'Well, Prime Minister, I'm sure you'll do what's right,' said Betty.

'Of course he will,' said Eve.

'Thank you for your help, Betty,' said Theo, 'it was good to talk to you.'

He took a step away from the desk, turning to address Eve before he disappeared towards the studio.

'It was a pleasure to see you again. Perhaps you'll be staying here in Blighty, observing how things progress while the Purple Scheme is dormant?'

'Maybe.'

'I'd be interested to hear your thoughts if you do. After

all, you've not experienced how lively things are usually, have you? Let me know – we can arrange a meeting.'

Eve opened her mouth to respond, and Theo held his hands up, deflecting her answer.

'Don't say no now, just think about it. It's not too much to ask, is it, under the circumstances?' He smiled.

Then Theo Fletcher gave Betty a wave as he made his way towards the lifts, his aides behind him.

Betty swooned a little. She looked at Eve and said, 'He's a handsome devil, isn't he?'

Eve nodded politely, not sure that those were the best words to describe him.

Helena glanced at the man behind them, smoke from his cigarette wafting towards their table as he selected tunes on the jukebox.

'It's been lovely having you back,' she said to Eve, 'irrespective of you happening to bring down an evil plot against humanity while you were here.'

Womble rolled his eyes. 'My love, you could say that anti-social behaviour is a plot against—'

'Stop it, you two!' said Eve. 'Don't even joke about it. Besides, I might still have some work to do – I can feel Theo Fletcher already trying to butter me up for something.'

'You don't think he's going to wriggle his way out of the agreement?' Helena asked, horrified.

'No... I mean, in theory he can't... But—'

'Cheeky git,' said Helena. 'Magnus and his crew will be on the case, legally, won't they?'

'Yes,' said Eve, 'and they've said multiple times that it's watertight, that it would be foolish for him to try and go back on it.'

'So it must be.'

Eve nodded. Theo Fletcher had something up his sleeve, she was sure, but the folk at Humane, together with some high-flying human rights lawyers and Magnus, had all insisted that they had everything they needed to keep the Purpleness at bay ('Plus,' Magnus had told her, 'that video footage is absolute dynamite').

Womble quietly drank his pint.

'So, what are you going to do now?' Helena asked Eve.

'There's a job going at Helena's,' said Womble.

Helena groaned.

'You know the only animals I can deal with are ones with comedic talent or bus passes,' said Eve.

'Seriously, though,' said Helena, 'people in the know are contacting you. Annie's got you some fancy meetings. Do you think you'll stay?'

Eve looked at the lime slice floating in her whisky glass. She kept thinking about this, considering the possibilities. What to do?

'What do you think?' she asked Duncan. 'I know your work is here, but do you fancy a spell in New York?'

'What do *you* want to do?' Duncan asked, attentively – and tickled pink.

'I don't know,' said Eve, with most certain uncertainty. 'Me and Adio – we're partners in crime. We've rustled up some pretty exciting new prospects at *Say Fantastique!*, but maybe there's room for other things too.'

She glanced towards a television mounted on the wall above the bar, where the ticker sliding across the screen declared the last Purple antidote would be administered by the end of the following week. When she turned back, Duncan was removing a hand from his pocket. He smiled.

'Heads or tails?'

Eve thought of tipping ducks, dipping upside-down in the water.

'Tails.'

Duncan tossed the coin into the air.

Eve had her eye on the half-pence piece about to be uncovered, suitably distracted from the muted television screen in the corner, where a newsreader in a pussy-bow blouse silently announced headlines, her words tip-toeing, typed, as subtitles:

In Westminster there have been reports of a prohibition-style alcohol ban being considered for the UK, for 'health and behavioural reasons'. The rumours are unsubstantiated, however, and ministers have yet to comment. There's no word yet as to whether that's something he'll be addressing, but the prime minister is scheduled to give a press conference in an hour...'

Acknowledgements

It's been quite the journey getting to the point where you're holding this book in your hands, and here are some sort-of chronological thank yous.

Anna Davis and Chris Wakeling at Curtis Brown Creative, thank you for your wisdom, and belief in this daft dystopia.

The CBC gang, aka the novel-writing class of 2011. I know I'm the soppy nit who always says this, but you all are the best. It's been truly life-changing to have a bunch of brilliant writerly souls to share things with – and the group has become so much more than that. I hope when we're ninety we end up in an old folks' home together (Emily and Julia, you'll just have to visit us, with bags of Murray Mints, until you're elderly enough to move in).

Some early readers provided thoughtful, insightful notes on the whole shebang: Kate Hamer, Lisa Berry, Theresa Howes, Annabelle Thorpe, Katie Gordon, Sarah Box and James Burt. Kate Hamer – thank you, too, for being a super champion of the book, and providing an ace endorsement.

I started this book with a question – why do people commit the thoughtless, violent crimes they do? – and as I neared the end of the first draft, I was fretting about not having answered that. Thank you James Box for the sage advice that sometimes what's actually most important is not finding the answers so much as (hopefully) asking the right questions.

Michael Thomas – thank you for taking time to ponder the possibilities of why folk commit criminal acts, and having sought out useful research papers in advance of our meeting. Also for 'purpetrators'! (Thank you, too, to Eric Drass for that introduction.)

To John Mitchinson, Kwaku Osei-Afrifa and Xander Cansell at Unbound for taking a chance on this book, and me (and to Port Eliot Festival for being the magical place where those wheels were set in motion...).

Also at Unbound HQ, thank you Georgia Odd, Sara Magness, Caitlin Harvey and Anna Simpson for support and exceptionally efficient author air traffic control.

Craig Taylor, Andrew Chapman and Mary Chesshyre, you all are excellent, and exceedingly patient, editors – thank you for making this such a better book.

Thank you Mark Ecob, Unbound's alchemy-conjuring Creative Director, for the absolute corker of a cover. I can only hope that folk judge the book by it!

The Unbound Social Club for always-on-tap wisdom and merriment. What a fountain of knowledge! What a pool of talent!

Claude Annels – those Purple People cupcakes were delicious *and* persuasive – thank you! (I still get cravings for them...)

Katch Skinner – thank you so much for the beautiful, quote-rustling, lilac lass eggcups.

I've been extremely lucky in always having been encouraged with my writing. Teachers at infant school (Mrs Ranaboldo), junior school (Mrs Knight) and secondary school (Mrs Mead, Mrs O'Sullivan, Miss Lobban, Mrs Churchward) showed a belief in me that I wouldn't understand or appreciate till much later.

Over the years, writers whose work I love have been incredibly gracious: a handwritten letter from Millie Murray; the cheery welcome and offer of breakfast – when faced with an unexpected interview, no less – from Kathy Lette; long-running kindness from Jonathan Trigell (and thanks for the fortuitous tweet that led me to Curtis Brown Creative); loveliness from Sylvia Patterson; tip top-ness (and what a quote, merci buckets!) from David Quantick; kindly effusiveness from Emma Jane Unsworth (what a brain-fizzing treat to receive!)... I'm very grateful that people I admire would generously give time and encouragement, and receiving it always feels like a fantastical treat. Thank you.

Steve Rosenfield at American Comedy Institute – I structure all my sentences differently since studying comedy with you!

Mary & Michael, William & Suzanne, Mark and Jane at the Northbank Hotel – thank you for looking after me during my many visits, and for being the best place to escape to when there's writing or editing to do (even if the sea view is mesmerically distracting...).

I don't think I could begin to thank the amazing friends that I'm lucky enough to have. I'm often pretty sentimental, but in case I don't tell you – or tell you enough – please know how gobsmackingly grateful I am to have you in my life.

Also, I've had a very topsy turvy, bruising few years – mostly snakes, rare ladders – and am not sure how I would have stayed afloat or retained much faith in humanity without the following: Jo and Matt Hardy, Rowena Price, Jane Bedwell-Mortishire, Abby Hitchcock, Selma Attride, Katie Gordon, Richard Gordon, Lisa Berry, Lorna Woolfson, Jill Kaplan, Mary Ann and Tim Le Lean, Laurie Sitzia, Josh Emerson and Kyle Bean, Mish Maudsley, Kate and Marc Hamer, Julie Nuernberg, Alex Mullen, James Bates, Rifa and Chris Thorpe-Tracey, Roger Horlock, Beth Dodson, Marja Kivisaari, and the Razavi clan. You are spectacular, and have kept me upright on the treacle-covered mountain. I so appreciate it.

(also, to Becs Ewbank and Julie Sharp: thank you for always checking in, even though I can be rubbish with smoke signals).

I wouldn't have been able to take the Curtis Brown Creative course were it not for the typical (if heartbreaking) generosity of the extraordinary Lucy Gordon. Thank you, Lucy (and Richard, when you said you hoped that gift would mean I'd be able to do something I wouldn't otherwise have had the chance to do – this was certainly it).

My family – the Bells, Gateses, Lauristons and Hendersons – thank you for being so super. I definitely hit the jackpot in the family lottery, getting to be related to all of you.

Grandma and Grandad – what a pair! Ever encouraging, very much missed. Hope you're toasting this somewhere with a tea/sherry/Guinness. Grandad, your enthusiasm, optimism and lack of judgement (of anyone) was awe-inspiring. What an utterly exemplary human (also, I'm still using that thesaurus).

Dad – thank you for all the things in recent times, and for providing life-saving support during the edit! It's much appreciated.

And Mum... you are the loveliest, most wondrous human in all the world. Always supportive, cheerleading, wise... always making me laugh, and knowing the best thing to say when I'm stuck on a treacle-covered ledge and not sure how to get up, or down. Thank you providing the best foundation a gal could have, and being a quietly shining example of kindness, empathy and positivity.

Most importantly, to all who pledged. This book being brought into the world with Unbound has been life-affirming in that I've been able to experience the enthusiasm and generosity from all who supported it. It's felt like a crowdfunding version of *This is Your Life* – that lovely folk from such varied times and adventures have helped make this happen. Hopefully even for those of you far away or with whom I haven't crossed paths for many years, I'll get to toast you in person with an appreciative cuppa (or Old Fashioned) before too long...

And finally, to anyone who doesn't know me but took a chance on this wonky story, thank you. It's appreciated more than you know.

Unbound is the world's first crowdfunding publisher, established in 2011.

We believe that wonderful things can happen when you clear a path for people who share a passion. That's why we've built a platform that brings together readers and authors to crowdfund books they believe in – and give fresh ideas that don't fit the traditional mould the chance they deserve.

This book is in your hands because readers made it possible. Everyone who pledged their support is listed at the front of the book and below. Join them by visiting unbound.com and supporting a book today.

Beth Allen
Emily Alpren
Claudine Annels
John Auckland
Emil Björklund
Tracey Booth
Tomas Cronholm
Jane Dallaway
Emma de Polnay
Louise Farrow
Barbara Feinstein
Sylvia ferreira
Matt Gibson
Tim Glencross
Thomas Godber
Geetha Gopalan
Eamonn Griffin
Robert & Shirley Hardy
Jane Hemery
Sheila Howes
Charlotte Jackson
Jo Jackson
Oscar Johnson
Kate Jordan
Jill Kaplan

Dan Kieran
Rosemary Lauriston
James Madson
Sarah Mason Walden
Lucy McCahon
Barbara Joan Meier
John Mitchinson
Jane Mortishire
Tatiana N
Carlo Navato
Molly Norris
Lewis Nyman
Ruhee Padhiar
Mick Perrin
Hugh Platt
Justin Pollard
David Quantick
Craig Reilly
Anne Rupert
Mike Scott Thomson
Julie Sharp
Remy Sharp
Mark Sykes
Amber Wilson